KJELL ERIKSSON is the author of the internationally acclaimed Ann Lindell series, which includes *The Princess of Burundi* and *The Hand that Trembles*. His series debut won Best First Novel from the Swedish Crime Academy, an accomplishment he later followed up by winning Best Swedish Crime Novel for *The Princess of Burundi*. He lives in Sweden.

By Kjell Eriksson

The Hand that Trembles
The Princess of Burundi

THE HAND THAT TREMBLES

KJELL ERIKSSON

Translated from the Swedish by Ebba Segerberg

First published in Great Britain in 2011 by
Allison & Busby Limited
13 Charlotte Mews
London W1T 4EJ
www.allisonandbusby.com

Copyright © 2011 by KJELL ERIKSSON
Translation © 2011 by EBBA SEGERBERG

First published in the US in 2011.
Published by arrangement with St Martin's Press.

The moral right of the author has been asserted.

A CIP catalogue record for this book is available from
the British Library.

10 9 8 7 6 5 4 3 2 1

ISBN 978-0-7490-1231-1

Typeset in 10.5/15 pt Sabon by
Allison & Busby Ltd.

The paper used for this Allison & Busby publication
has been produced from trees that have been legally sourced
from well-managed and credibly certified forests.

Printed and bound by
CPI Group (UK) Ltd, Croydon, CR0 4Y

THE HAND THAT TREMBLES

DECEMBER 1956

He had been sent to get more firewood. His mission was of the utmost importance. It was bitingly cold; the snow in the garden sparkled and smoke rose like a grey-white genie above the cottage tucked in the hollow.

Suddenly a shadow darkened the bark- and sawdust-covered earthen floor. Sven-Arne had just added a split log to the others he carried in his arms. The piece wobbled, then slid out of his grasp along with most of the rest of the load.

'Shall we do it together?'

Sven-Arne dropped the few remaining pieces.

'Did I frighten you?'

He shook his head, too annoyed to say anything. Ante stepped into the shed and looked around at the stacked wood.

'Well, someone's been busy,' he said, and smiled unexpectedly.

He bent down and grasped a couple of logs.

'Hold out your arms,' he said, and Sven-Arne obeyed.

Sven-Arne wiggled his knees back and forth. If he came in with this big of a load he would be praised. He wanted to hurry out of the woodshed and back to the cottage, but his uncle stood in the way.

'I remember the winters during the war. We burnt a lot of wood back in those days.'

'Your war?'

Ante shook his head.

'That one was hotter than hell.'

Sven-Arne was getting cold. He misjudged shifting his weight, and stumbled slightly.

'I'll tell you about it sometime,' Ante said.

He was missing two fingers on his left hand. Emil had once mumbled something about how it was Ante's carelessness that had been the cause, but no one really wanted to talk about Ante's war adventures, not even Ante himself. That was why his comment about how he would tell him about it one day was a little out of the ordinary.

'You seem to have your head screwed on right. Olars doesn't understand anything.'

Ola Persson was Sven-Arne's cousin, older by ten years. He was having a cup of coffee inside the cottage. He was a dynamite expert and smelt funny, even when he changed into his nice clothes. Ante insisted on calling him Olars.

Sven-Arne's arms were aching, but his irritation vanished at the moment that his uncle criticised his cousin.

He couldn't help staring at Ante's left hand as it searched for suitable pieces of wood. He stretched right and left, and after a while his arms were full.

'Head back together when we're done?'

Sven-Arne nodded. He tried to shift the weight of the wood, get it closer to his chest.

'We'll take only birch,' Ante decided, and tightened his right arm around his load.

When they were done, they could hear the tinkling of bells and shortly thereafter the muted thuds of hooves against the deeply rutted gravel road.

'That's Rosberg,' said Ante, who had a curious way of tilting his head as he listened.

They left the woodshed. The sun blinded his eyes. Sven-Arne caught a glimpse of his grandmother's neighbour behind the lilac bushes. Rosberg was sitting on the load of timber with his hat jauntily askew and holding the reins as if he were driving a four-horse hitch.

His horse, an unusually light-coloured Ardennes by the name of Lightning, shook its head as it passed the cottage. Maybe it disliked the smell of smoke, or else it was just anxious, very conscious of its proximity to the barn.

Sven-Arne was still cold, but enjoying it. The cottage stood out more clearly than usual in the afternoon sun. The snow was piled all the way under the windows, the chimney almost as crooked as the house, but the sun made it gleam red-brown. Sven-Arne repressed a laugh.

The tinkling from Rosberg's sled died away. A flock of bullfinches fluttered about the Swedish Whitebeam tree in the middle of the garden. A swing still hung from the lowest branch. Now it was topped with a white cap like a chef's hat. He had to admit that he still loved to swing back and forth with the great Whitebeam tree above him like a protecting giant. No rain could penetrate it. In the wind, it simply turned up its leaves and showed the silver-fuzzy underside. In the spring, it was covered in white flowers, and in the autumn there were clusters of berries, some years so heavy that the colour could be seen from far away. Sometimes his grandmother brought in clusters and laid them in a bowl of water. She maintained that her grandfather had planted the tree, even though most people did not believe it was that old.

'That Lightning, he was also in the war,' Ante said, and Sven-Arne was suddenly unsure which war he was referring to.

'The only ones they get are horses and idiots.'

They walked back to the house, Ante in the lead. It was only three degrees Fahrenheit. Ante spat in the snow, smiled at Sven-Arne, and pushed open the door.

'Damned excruciating,' he said, and stepped into the hall.

Sven-Arne assumed he meant the cold. Or else he meant being in Grandmother's kitchen.

Even though she had built a fire in the parlour, it was too cold in there and so everyone had crowded into the kitchen. Sven-Arne's parents, Erik and Lisbeth, were there, as was Uncle Emil and his sons Ola and Tommy. Their mother was in the hospital, but no one talked about that. She had weak nerves.

Grandmother's brother Edvin and his two unmarried daughters were sitting by the window. Majvor – large as a house, who breathed laboriously and liked to complain about everything and everyone – and Inga-Lisa, always on her way up to assist Grandmother Agnes but who was trapped between Edvin and Majvor so she remained seated. Both sisters were active members of the society 'Friends of Jerusalem' and considered a bit quirky, but tolerated.

A neighbour woman, who kept track of all social engagements in the area and made sure to stop by if there was going to be coffee and cake, was sitting on a stool next to them.

'I'll be damned. We should make sure to send Sven-Arne out to get the firewood from now on,' Emil said.

The cousins gave Sven-Arne a look of indifference.

Ante and Sven-Arne dropped the logs straight into the wood bin.

'Your boys will have to top it up before we leave,' he said.

'Of course they will,' Emil said good-naturedly.

Agnes patted Sven-Arne on the head.

'Make sure you warm up now.'

He sat down at the end of the table with his back to the stove. His grandmother opened the door and pushed in a log. Ante remained standing, a cup of coffee in his hand.

The warmth in the room made the birthday guests drowsy but the conversation gradually picked up again. Clearly the trio of men, Erik, Emil, and Edvin, had been involved in a discussion that had been interrupted by the return of the wood-bearers. Maybe Ante had gone out to the woodshed to escape it, not primarily to help Sven-Arne. When Emil said something, Ante sighed heavily and mumbled something that to Sven-Arne sounded like 'Damned whining.'

Ante was different, not just because he had been in a war and was missing two fingers. He maintained a skeptical attitude to most things. Emil called his brother a 'Snuffy Smith' and they quarrelled often. It was as if they were drawn into a lifelong duel, only interrupted from time to time simply because they could not stand to listen to the other's words.

Later, Sven-Arne would understand Ante's irritation and hopelessness that no words or phrases could persuade or change. When he himself was accused of being one-sided and not flexible enough, then it was Ante's inheritance making itself felt, for it could not be Eric's genes that had moulded

11

his mindset. Sven-Arne's father was 'flexible' in the personal sphere as well as in his work as a printer at A&W. Only in his meetings with his brother did he display a tendency toward obstinance.

In general, Eric did not say very much, did not anger, and those times he spoke up it was in a soft-spoken way and with such a disarming smile that any antagonists let down their guard, perhaps in the belief that they had changed his mind.

Since a couple of years back he had been secretary of the local chapter of the Typographical Society, in the eyes of many the ideal of trustworthiness – taciturn, dutiful, and as precise and predictable as the calendars he produced. Eric most often came with not amazing ideas, but well-reasoned propositions, which he called his suggestions, always timely, delivered in a dry, somewhat formalistic, factual tone that vouched for rationality and continuity. The protocols were miracles of meticulous attention and the arrangement of the paragraphs beyond reproach.

Sven-Arne was drinking coffee with milk. He had no idea where the coffee came from, but the milk came from his neighbour's cows. Rosberg had seven milk-producing cows in a dilapidated barn that threatened imminent collapse. They were discussing whether or not Sven-Arne and his cousins should go over and help clear the snow from the roof. It had been snowing nonstop for two, three days and now warmer weather was coming. This would make the snow heavy as lead and endanger the barn in its frail condition. Ola and Tommy had refused, and Ola added that it was just as well for the barn to collapse. He said this with such assurance and such a grown-up air that no one chastised him. Sven-Arne had realised that adults were allowed to say things without being corrected. If he had said anything to this same effect, he would have been told he was impertinent.

Not even Agnes said anything, even though everyone knew that she and Rosberg were as close as two good neighbours who had lived next to each other their entire lives could be.

That Rosberg himself was missing from the party, and out driving timber, was nothing remarkable. Everyone knew he would come over once the family had gone. After the evening milking he would wash up and take the well-worn path to the cottage. They would have a couple of sandwiches and share a beer. Maybe they would listen to the radio. Not much would be said. At half past nine he would take his leave.

Come spring, Rosberg was planning to get rid of the critters, so this was perhaps the last time that Sven-Arne would drink the neighbour's milk. He had always liked Rosberg. The warmth of the cowshed, the low grinding sound of the animals masticating, and the smell of the farmer's entryway were intimately connected with his childhood.

They would have been able to shovel the snow from the roof with ease, it would be done in half an hour, but they preferred to sit in the warmth and pretend to be city-modern and adult.

'I can do it,' he said.

'What?' his uncle said.

'Go over to Rosberg's.'

Emil did not reply, but flashed a grin. Agnes put a hand on Sven-Arne's shoulder.

'Me and the boy,' Ante said.

'You want the boy to fall to his death?' Erik objected.

'The cows can't get up there,' Ante said. 'Rosberg can't either. The snow has to come down. Someone has to do it, that's all there is to it.'

The view from the barn roof made Sven-Arne pause in his shovelling for long periods at a time. The road to the church curved at the horizon and was swallowed by the forest. From up here the narrow road looked completely different, much more interesting than from the country bus. Ax – the bus driver – would joke with Sven-Arne and call him his 'little pal.' Once he had stopped the bus, climbed out, and urinated on one of the front tyres. He did as he pleased, but was generally well-liked. He made an effort, made sure packages got to the remote cottages, and ran errands for the isolated elderly in the village.

Two other small farms also took on a different perspective from above. The distance ennobled the small outhouses. What looked insignificant from the ground attained grandeur from another perspective. Sven-Arne saw someone moving on a plot of yard several hundreds of metres away.

Rosberg was on the hill leading up to the farm. He had not showed any surprise when Ante and Sven-Arne turned up and offered their services, and had immediately gone out to unhook the ladder from the wall.

'You'll be careful, won't you,' he yelled.

Arne waved reassuringly, turned to Sven-Arne, and smiled. 'You cold?'

Sven-Arne shook his head.

'I'll tie the rope around you so you can slide down to the edge.'

It was around six metres to the ground, but since the

14

barn backed onto a hillside that sloped sharply down, the impression of height appeared great. Sven-Arne slid across the roof tiles, a shovel in his hand, pushing the snow in front of him. He felt the rope around his middle. The thudding sound of the snow masses leaving the roof and hitting the ground made him smile and turn.

'Good job,' Ante said. 'You can do almost anything.'

Bam went the next landing. Ante pulled him up to the ridge and then they kept going. Ante like a conquering general, broad-legged, with bowed legs but a straight back. Sven-Arne like a front-line soldier on the attack, pulled back by the commander only to attack the enemy once more.

'Doesn't matter,' Ante said, when a roof tile clattered with an almost metallic sound. 'The barn's coming down in the spring anyhow.'

Maybe it was the windowpane in the front door, flashing with a reflection from the sun, that caused Sven-Arne to turn his head. He spotted his father and cousins on his grandmother's garden.

'Do you see the bugs?' Ante asked.

Should he wave to them? No, they could stand there and stare. Soon they would get cold and have to go in. Sven-Arne unconsciously slowed his pace, resting a moment with his hand on the handle, and spitting over the edge of the roof. He shot Ante a look.

'What is it with Hungary?' he asked. 'You're always arguing about it.'

'Just shovel,' Ante shot back.

'But what is it about?'

Sven-Arne saw the indecision in his uncle's face. If he hadn't known him so well he would have interpreted it as pain.

15

'Doesn't matter,' he said with nonchalance and picked his shovel back up.

Rosberg had also gone over to the other side and was watching intently. Suddenly Ante sat down on the roof ridge, pulled his gloves off, and laid them beside him.

'Sit down,' he said, and made a gesture of invitation. 'Sit on the gloves!'

Sven-Arne did as he said. His uncle looked off toward the forest.

'Sunset,' he said after a while.

Then he started talking about the war he had been in. Sven-Arne did not understand everything, but did not want to irritate him with questions. His uncle's stubble glowed black. The high cheekbones he had inherited from his mother and the large nose created a sharp profile. He talked slowly, as if he had to look for the words a long way back in the past.

He repeated some of the words, particularly place names. I want to go there too, Sven-Arne thought, each time his uncle mentioned the name of a village or city.

Sven-Arne relived the feeling of grandeur he had felt earlier in his grandmother's garden. It felt as if every individual word his uncle was uttering was important, as if Ante was sending them out into space as a message. He was sending a message from Rosberg's roof. He was addressing the forest, and Sven-Arne. Rosberg heard him but understood nothing. The bugs heard but understood nothing. Only he got the message. Only he was allowed to take part in the knowledge of what really happened.

Suddenly Ante finished, smiled sadly, and looked at Sven-Arne.

'You know, sometimes I don't want to live,' he said. 'It's

as if nothing means anything anymore. I look around me and nothing seems appealing. There is no medicine for the pain I feel. It's in here.' He thumped his chest. 'I knew it would go like this. Do you know what I had in my backpack when I walked ashore in France?'

Sven-Arne shook his head. He wanted to reach out to Ante, hug him.

'Children's drawings. Hundreds of them. Dreams, terror, and all the longing the children felt, all that I carried with me.'

Ante turned his head and stared off toward the church and the community house.

The stillness over Rosberg's farm and the village was monumental. The winter afternoon was resting in silence. Say something else, Sven-Arne pleaded in his head. Tell me about the children. Who were they? Why did you bring children's drawings back with you?

But he felt as if he were walking on the frozen millpond. A single word could shatter it, not only the silence but also the connectedness, just as a careless movement could crack the thinnest ice.

Sven-Arne put his hand on Ante's.

'Are you cold?'

Ante shook his head.

'Only in my missing fingers.'

When they were done, Rosberg insisted that they come in. He poured Ante a shot of aquavit, and a bowl of warm milk for Sven-Arne.

'*Skål*,' he said, and raised his glass.

Sven-Arne noticed that he had only poured half a shot for himself.

17

Ante's face was flushed. He downed his shot in one gulp and put the glass down on the kitchen table with a bang.

There was a smell of stove, barn, and damp clothes.

'That was well done,' Rosberg said. 'Another?'

Ante shook his head. 'So are they going?'

'In the spring,' Rosberg said.

'Thanks for the shot.'

'I'm the one who should be thanking you.'

'A pension from now on?'

'That is unchristian,' Rosberg said.

'Doesn't matter what we do,' Ante said.

Sven-Arne listened to the conversation and was amazed at how little was said and yet gave the impression of a lively conversation.

Rosberg hauled himself up out of his chair.

'There's one more thing,' he said, and went out into the room next to the kitchen.

Ante glanced at Sven-Arne. 'You warm now?'

Sven-Arne nodded and drained the last of the creamy milk.

Rosberg reappeared with a clock in his hands. He stroked his walrus moustache, in which a couple of drops of melted snow gleamed.

'I know you've looked at this before,' he said.

Sven-Arne had admired the old-fashioned alarm clock many times. One of Rosberg's relatives had bought it in America many years before, maybe back in the 1800s. Rosberg did not need an alarm clock, but kept it as a decoration. The outside shone like gold, the hands were black and ornately wrought, just as the numbers on the face; the enormous ringer mechanism was ear-deafening. There were winding keys on the back, both for the alarm and the time, also a lever that could be placed in two positions: 'Long alarm' and 'Rep. alarm.'

Its ticking was as irregular as it was vehement. Sometimes it seemed to be holding its breath and it grew completely silent until it realised it had to keep the time and returned to a vigorous tempo in order to compensate for its momentary lack of industry.

It was a remarkable object, and it radiated dignity. In the parlour, it was the alarm clock that drew one's attention, and not only due to the sound of its ticking. Perhaps it was the otherwise spartan furnishings that accorded the clock its special glow.

'I was thinking . . .' Rosberg said, and held it out to Sven-Arne, who took it with bewilderment.

'If you want it,' Rosberg went on.

'You're giving me this?'

'As sure as it is standing here before you.'

For a few moments, Rosberg grew positively loquacious as he related the clock's history, something he had done many times before.

'Forever?' Sven-Arne asked.

Ante chuckled.

'Nothing is forever.'

NOVEMBER 1993

Åke Sandström was pursuing his point as slowly and painstakingly as ever. Sven-Arne Persson had almost forgotten what it was.

Amazing how many words could be used to say nothing, he thought, and glanced at his watch. A quarter to two.

The meeting had been under way since the early morning, with a break for lunch.

'If we regard all the circumstances, there is still much that indicates that proceeding according to the existing plans will go against the spirit as well as the letter of current county regulations, but on the other hand there are no actual reasons for . . .'

'Åke, if we are to arrive at a—'

'I'm getting there. It is not as simple as some appear to believe.'

Sven-Arne Persson sighed, pointedly closed his folder, and started thinking of other things. There was not much competition for his attention except the 'big question,' as he called the line of thinking that had been claiming more and more of his time the last year.

Is it time? Can Sandström's soulless droning be the signal I have been waiting for? Sven-Arne drew a deep breath, which caused Sandström to pause for a second. But then he continued implacably.

Sven-Arne looked around at the assembled, all familiar to him for many years. Some he would have called his friends, others simply party colleagues. But he knew that fewer and fewer of them were listening to him. He suspected it was more an expression of his own frustration and growing indifference for the burning county issues than the party's view of him as a politician, for surely they considered his views as seriously as before.

They did not like him. He knew that without a doubt. There was an aspect of his personality that few of them could stand. He was generally held to be personable and normally had no problems circulating around the city, getting to know the town's citizens and voters. He was a good listener, allowing others to finish talking, had the knack of looking genuinely interested, and could be either serious or joking, as the situation demanded. As with all elected officials in the public sphere, there was a measure of calculation in his attitude, and adaptability, but his concern for those he had been elected to represent was generally acknowledged. This was also his foremost ability and it made him a party asset. If at times he came across as a pompous ass there were few who regarded him as one.

In his internal work the situation was more complicated. In county administration his flexibility was nowhere to be seen. He was a Dr Jekyll and Mr Hyde of county politics, impatient and often abrupt, and always seemed in a hurry to bring the matter at hand to a close under his hammer.

Toward the latter half of the 1980s, a number of party colleagues – mostly from the women's caucus – had tried to get rid of him. Gerda Lyth, who was his harshest critic, had called him a power-hungry chauvinist pig.

At first he had taken the matter lightly. She had difficulty making inroads since she had no base in the city. She was a political blow-in from the south and therefore also had her dialect against her. Gerda Lyth was employed at the university. Sven-Arne was from the working class and had at least ten years of physical labour behind him, before he had been lifted into the union ombudsman position and later into county assignments, and there was a dearth of his kind of experience in the Labour Party.

In his battle with Gerda Lyth and her followers he made conscious use of this class background, which appeared spectacular in this city so dominated by academics and the bourgeoisie. It was first in hindsight that he fully realised how close they had come to removing him from power in the Labour community and thereby the county board.

When pressed in some way, he could fall back into the naked Uppsala dialect that had dominated his childhood, above all through his uncle Ante. There were those who claimed that Uppsala had no dialect, but nothing could be more wrong, in his view. He could identify a genuine native after only a couple of sentences, someone sprung from the Uppsalian working class, but had to admit that this rare tongue was heard increasingly seldom. Everything was getting mixed, the language was getting smoothed out. Class sensibility and class language were awkward tools for a Labour Party flirting with the middle class. They functioned more as flourishes, markers of a proud past that lent a legitimacy in speaking for the masses.

But they could also be used as weapons in the internal

22

struggles, and Gerda Lyth had had a taste of it. After the first few attempts, which he had mainly waved away in irritation, the attackers had gathered in a renewed and more organised offensive and then Sven-Arne Persson had to show his colours.

He mobilised his old war buddies, calling upon a former county commissioner, and won over the older ones in the city districts; there was intrigue behind the scenes and thundering argumentation at the meetings. He reached out to the media, writing up something called the 'Persson Appeal,' a skillfully constructed document centred on 'caring for the city of Uppsala' and 'moving the centre.' The second expression could be taken literally, as the majority of his power base lay in the old working-class parts of Salabackar, Tunabackar, Almtuna, and Svartbäcken, but it could also be interpreted ideologically.

In the article he talked about 'good work' as an independent, almost magical concept, and used a couple of anecdotes from his days as a plumber, with a metaphorical language that characterised class-bound supremacy and the secretive language of the craft, which he knew presented a temptation for both the knowledgeable and the ignorant.

He spoke of tradition and renewal, worn concepts that in his appeal emerged as genuine since he skillfully connected his and others' experiences of the poor Sweden, tradition with class, the smell of wet wool and dreams of holiday and dental care, with those of new technology within the fields of computer and biomedical research that would put Uppsala on the world map.

An area that he touched on only briefly was that of 'the new Swedes,' which truth be told he did not know, more than the fact that they lived in the outskirts of the city. Even here he successfully employed symbols. He was able to squeeze in Vilhelm Moberg's Karl Oskar, Walloons, and Greek feta cheese in a piece that, viewed superficially, was unassailable, but that did not articulate a single problem and was not beholden to anything.

Sven-Arne Persson received flowers. His office at City Hall smelt of greenery. A multitude of Letters to the Editor streamed in to *Upsala Nya Tidning,* all positive. 'At last someone who dares to talk ideology,' someone wrote. 'This is a Social Democracy we can recognise,' said another.

The opposition was wise enough to hold off. The article was too generally supported and rhetorically so well constructed as to rule out the possibility of a counter-attack. Persson's foremost opponent, the commissioner Herbert Gunnarsson of the Moderate Party, realised this gesture was intended for internal affairs. Privately he detested women in politics, and above all those with socialist leanings, and he was happy that Lyth was struck a blow, even though she was not actually referred to by name.

The only one who offered any criticism was Ante. He called right after the piece was published and laughed abrasively. He was not tricked. He undressed the words, and Sven-Arne silently cursed this person who stood nearest to him. Ante's words would become etched in his body like rusty staples. Each time he employed this method, the rhetoric and the compelling but intentionally vague political language of the political appeal that he had mastered so well, the staples twisted and turned inside him.

Sven-Arne did not engage his uncle in debate. There was no point in gilding the lie. After Ante was done with his sarcastic tirade, Sven-Arne enquired about his hip. This was his uncle's Achilles' heel, since he was no longer able to move about without effort and was dependent on his nephew if he needed to travel any distance.

The result of Sven-Arne's offensive was that Gerda Lyth had to back down. Sven-Arne pitied her for a moment, but immediately put this thought behind him. He was a power player and knew it. There was no room for doubt or regret.

Not a single word in his text was incorrect but he knew the whole was flawed. It was not an ideological manifesto, but an Orwellian betrayal.

After his victory over his internal critics, Sven-Arne sank into a deep depression. It went on for six months. After the refreshing power struggle, only indifference remained.

It was as if his disingenuousness not only revealed his true self but that of his colleagues, the ones who had supported him, cheered, and slapped him on the back. Shouldn't everyone have been able to see through the dishonesty? Was his oration so convincing or was his party colleagues' longing for ideologically coloured argumentation so great that they allowed themselves to be tricked by fanfare, which after it had died away left the same vacuum that they were looking to escape?

After hardly a year, Gerda Lyth left Uppsala for Gothenburg, where she had applied for and received a position within the university administration. When Sven-Arne met Gothenburg's strong man in politics at a conference, he had asked about Gerda Lyth but the politician had never heard her name. Perhaps she had had enough of politics?

* * *

'What do you think, Sven-Arne?'

The county commissioner was jolted out of his reverie and stared blankly at Sandström.

'I have to admit I haven't really followed you.'

'Are you unwell? You look a little pale.'

'A headache,' Sven-Arne Persson said. 'Perhaps I'll take a break, if that's all right with you.'

He did not expect any protest, just stood up and left the room. And in so doing, also his wife, municipal politics, Uppsala, and Sweden.

ONE

It was at the corner of Brigade and Mahatma Ghandi Road that he had the first intuition. Not that he was superstitious, quite the opposite. Over the course of his career, rationality had been his trademark. It rendered him ill-suited to this country, and yet sympathetic to the Indian fatalism that he had grown to appreciate over the years. But he should have heeded the signs.

First this so unexpected thought of 'home': Whenever he thought of this word it was usually in conjunction with the flat in Bangalore or, more rarely, the town house in Uppsala. But this time a vision of his Vaksala Square neighbourhood rose before him. Of course he thought of his childhood street from time to time, but this time the recollection gripped him with unexpected force. He paused, was pushed aside, and came to a halt outside the entrance of a shop that sold Kashmir silk.

There was nothing about MG Road that was reminiscent of Uppsala. Absolutely nothing. The intense, almost insane traffic, the eternal honking, and the cloud of exhaust fumes hovering over the street, all this was unthinkable around Vaksala Square. Almost everything he saw was unimaginable on Salagatan; the holes in the pavement, some so deep they seemed like portals to another world – a darkness into which to descend. The stream of people, who adeptly veered to avoid the stopped man; the vendors of 'genuine' Rolex watches and 'police glasses' who avoided him with equal adeptness; the security guard from Guardwell posted outside the shop that promised excellent deals on shawls and saris but that in reality milked Westerners' credit cards for a couple of thousand rupees extra. No eye-catching sums but enough to ensure that the Mafia from the north made handsome profits. At least that was what Lester said.

He saw the block of flats in which he grew up, the courtyard with the newly raked gravel of Fridays, the neatly edged lawns and plantings of roses and lilacs, the obligatory mock-orange bush and the unpleasant-smelling viburnum by the park down toward the railway tracks. An almost rigid order reigned over the landscaping around the buildings. An impression of immutability that he, at a brief visit many years later, could testify had lingered a surprising number of years. A utility building had been added, poorly placed and completely different in style; the gravel was no longer quite as attractively ridged; the flag post had been removed, perhaps temporarily; but the fundamentals remained, and the substantial lilac trees leant thoughtfully, heavy with age and with twisted trunks as if they writhed in regret at the passing of time.

All this came before him as he stood on the pavement along MG Road. The guard looked more closely at him, perhaps nervous that the old man was about to collapse and thereby force him to engage.

Sven-Arne smiled reassuringly. The guard jerked his head but remained otherwise impassive.

Was it nostalgia? Could it be called that, although before

this moment he could not have been able to imagine returning to Uppsala? But suddenly this dreamlike vision appeared, as when one imagines soaring like a bird or diving into the depths like a fish.

It was most likely the lack of possibility that caused his pain. He even lacked a valid passport. He took a couple of steps, mostly to escape the watchful eyes of the guard, stopped, then walked off in the direction of St Marks Road.

The next warning came shortly thereafter.

After a few hundred metres, he saw a couple walking in his direction. He was immediately convinced that they were Swedes, even though there was nothing in their clothing or behaviour that gave this impression. He walked toward the catastrophe without a thought of slipping into the alley he had just passed. He would have been able to get away, as he had done so many times before when he had had this premonition. But it was as if the learnt defence mechanisms that had functioned so well for over a decade had now collapsed after the odd experience outside the silk shop. He walked toward them, defenceless.

Their gazes met when they were ten or twenty metres from each other. The woman scrutinised him, her eyes going from his face to his strange clothing (in her opinion, most likely) and then she looked away with indifference. As they passed each other he heard her say a few words to her companion, a man around forty years of age. He was sweating in his suit and tie, one pace behind the woman.

She was speaking Swedish. Northwestern Skåne, maybe Helsingborg, he thought, always childishly pleased with his ability to place a person's dialect. 'I think we should ask Nils anyway.' Her tone was decisive, almost aggressive. Sven-Arne had time to catch the man's unease. It was clear that he did not want to place a question to this Nils.

Just as they reached each other, the man glanced at Sven-Arne and for a moment the latter thought he saw a subtle shift in the man's facial expression, as if he recognised him, and Sven-Arne also caught an imperceptible reaction. The man slowed down slightly and lost even more ground to the woman. Was it just an unconscious reaction, an appeal, as if to say, 'Help me get away from this woman, distract her for a moment so that she'll drop the idea of talking to Nils'?

Sven-Arne hurried on his way, without turning around.

The street noise grew louder the closer he got to St Marks Road. A rickshaw had collided with a motorcycle, and two men were involved in a heated dispute. A woman standing next to the motorcyclist was crying. Blood trickled down her forehead. The rickshaw driver was screaming out his fury, saliva was spraying out of his mouth, and he was gesturing wildly to underscore his arguments.

The crash had blocked traffic and caused a serenade of honking, from the bellowing of the lorries to the ridiculous high-pitched signals from all the yellow rickshaws trying to manoeuvre their way through. Sven-Arne slowed down but did not stop. He had his inner crash to sort out.

Afterward, when he had caught his breath at Lester's, he cursed his own stupidity. He should have interpreted the signs better. Despite the evident warnings, he had continued along the street.

His goal had been Koshy's, where he returned to eat dinner once a year, for sentimental reasons. It was the only nostalgic act he allowed himself.

One evening in November 1993, disoriented and hungry after having vomited on the plane from Delhi, he had found himself standing outside the airport and had asked a taxi driver to take him to a good restaurant. That had been Koshy's.

Now he was going there to celebrate the twelfth anniversary of his arrival to the city that had become his home. It was, especially at first, an expression of self-torture, to test his own resolve.

The very first visit had not gone very well. He had burst into tears. Perhaps it was the exhaustion from the painful journey through Europe, the long flights and the extraordinary tribulations that caused him to collapse silently at the table. The waiter became aware of his distress and hurried over, but Sven-Arne waved him away, dried his tears, and opened the menu.

He was a stranger when he staggered out of the airport, and the sense of alienation had grown during the short ride into the city centre. At his table at Koshy's he realised for the first time the enormity of his actions. Until this point he had been acting automatically without any thought of the consequences, from Uppsala to Arlanda airport, at Heathrow, at the terminal in Delhi. He had only one goal: to get away.

The yearly visit to the restaurant was therefore a test. He always sat at the same table. If it was occupied, he waited. Then he recalled in his mind the first experiences of Bangalore, the confusion and indecision, the uncertainty if he had done the right thing. Every year he came to the same conclusion: Yes, it had been the right thing to do. What other conclusion could he come to?

He stepped into Koshy's, relieved to escape the noise of the street and any possible new unsettling events. He went to the right, to the somewhat more exclusive part, pushed open the swinging door, and set his sights on the table, which was obscured both by a pillar and the maître d'. The latter had been the same for all these years, a broad-shouldered wrestling type whose hair was growing thin on top but who still had an imposing handlebar moustache, large hands, and a heavyset, choleric face whose expression could nonetheless lighten at a moment's notice.

It came as a complete shock. Sven-Arne Persson turned on his heels and fled.

TWO

Jan Svensk got halfway to his feet, had automatically stretched out a hand as if to detain the fleeing man, but then realised it was meaningless. The doors swung back and forth a few times; he was gone.

It isn't possible, he thought, frozen for a few moments before he flung himself out of his chair and onto the deafening street. The heat struck him. He stared in all directions and glimpsed a grey head of hair through the filmy plastic window of a rickshaw. The driver set off and the vehicle was swallowed up in the heavy traffic.

He returned inside. The other guests, about a dozen, stared at him with undisguised curiosity. The waiter regarded him quizzically.

'Is anything wrong, sir?'

Jan Svensk shook his head.

'I just thought . . . there was a gentleman . . .'

'Oh, you mean "the Polite One"?'

'You know him?'

The waiter waggled his head, a gesture that Jan Svensk had never really grasped the meaning of. Was it an answer in the affirmative, a 'no,' or did it stand for the more diffuse notion of 'maybe'?

'Does he come here regularly?'

The waiter glanced around. The maître d' approached.

'Who is he?'

'No one knows, sir.'

The waiter started to draw away from the table, but Svensk grabbed hold of his arm.

'Does he come here often?'

'No, not very often.'

They looked at each other. Jan Svensk felt the waiter had the upper hand, perhaps because he was standing. How tall could he be? Five foot four at most, he thought, not without bitterness. He himself was six foot one.

The waiter smiled, straightened his sleeve, and turned his attention to the next table after having delivered another waggle of his head that Jan Svensk interpreted as 'That is all I know' or perhaps more precisely, 'That is all I will tell.'

He resumed his eating, with a lingering feeling of having been unfairly treated. The food was not tasty. It reminded him of excrement, or perhaps it was the other way around. That which he was able to excrete into the hotel toilet retained its original form; a brown, sometimes yellow, stinking mass that dribbled out of him and left a burning sensation. At least it smelt better beforehand, he thought, and swirled his spoon in the bowl of lentils. The consistency was that of a thin porridge.

Could it be Persson? And what was his first name? It was a hyphenated name, something a little nerdy. Sven-Arne, that was it!

Jan Svensk had read about doppelgangers; from time to time one saw published pictures of people who closely resembled each other. Often it was someone from Tierp or Alingsås who looked ridiculously like a film star or other celebrity. Could someone really look that much like Persson? Jan Svensk shook his head.

'No,' he murmured, deciding the matter, and looked around for the waiter, who very likely harboured more information, he was sure of it.

The maître d', impeccably dressed in a suit and tie, glided over to his side.

'Is everything to your satisfaction?'

Or at least this was what Jan Svensk thought he said, and he nodded.

'I was wondering, that gentleman who came in here . . . Is he someone you know?'

The maître d' made a dismissive hand gesture.

'He has dined here a few times, but we do not know him.'

They are protecting him, Jan thought.

'He is . . . an old friend from my homeland.'

'Really?' said the maître d'.

He wants money, Jan thought.

'A friend of the family,' he went on.

'I am sorry you did not have a chance to talk to each other.'

You old bastard! You know who he is. The maître d' disappeared as suddenly as he had appeared. Svensk turned his head and saw him exchange a few words with the waiter.

Svensk waved his arm and the waiter approached.

'The bill, please.'

The waiter returned with it after ten minutes. Jan Svensk gave him around 500 rupees.

The waiter looked at the bills.

'It is too much,' he said, and opened the brown leather folder that held the bill.

The total came to 420 rupees.

'The rest is for you,' Jan Svensk said.

The waiter put one bill back on the table.

'It is enough, thank you.'

Then he smiled. Jan Svensk became bright red in the face.

'I thought . . .'

'I understand, sir,' the waiter said slowly, 'but like our guests, we have our dignity. I do hope the food was to your liking.'

THREE

The rickshaw took him away from Koshy's. He had given the driver his address, but after a couple of minutes he changed his mind and gave him another: South End Circle. To Jayanagar, just south of Lal Bagh, the botanical garden, where Lester lived. He could spend the night there. He had done that before; the first was when his work at Lal Bagh had taken longer than expected. Lester had invited him for a late supper and thereafter offered to let him spend the night on a camp bed in the inner room.

This, like his visit to Koshy's, had become a tradition. Lester invited him over several times a year. Sven-Arne always knew he would be treated to something special.

Now he would arrive uninvited, but was convinced his colleague would find nothing extraordinary in this. And if he did, he would not show a trace of it to Sven-Arne.

Lester was hardly the kind of man to be taken by surprise. He faced every new development, whether unexpected or not, with the same equanimity. He was also the only one who knew enough about his past that Sven-Arne would be able to tell him about what happened at the restaurant. Lester would listen, send one of his sons out for some beer, maybe a small bottle of rum, then dispense some sound advice and an invitation to stay overnight.

Lester's father was British and sometimes Sven-Arne had the impression that Lester had designated him to be a stand-in for his biological father, a man who had come to Bangalore in the mid-fifties and settled in a decent house in the otherwise so rundown streets around Russell Market. No one knew what he lived on, perhaps a pension. He had been injured in the war, in the battles just outside of Rangoon, Burma, and he was missing the lower half of one arm, but had also been psychologically damaged. Lester had told him that as a child he would sometimes be awakened by his father's screams when the nightmares set in.

Lester's father not only hated all Japanese, but all Asians. It was therefore a bit of a puzzle why he had decided to stay in Bangalore and marry a woman from Madras, who had given birth to three children in rapid succession. In the early 1970s, when Lester was eight years old, the one-armed Englishman disappeared for good. Six years later the family was notified that he had died in a hospital in Mombasa. He left the house in Noah Street, and five thousand pounds in an account in a Hong Kong bank.

The money made it possible for Lester and his two brothers to get an education. Lester did a three-year horticultural degree in northern India and returned to Bangalore on his twenty-third birthday. He received a post at Lal Bagh and had stayed. Now he was responsible for the arboretum, care and replanting.

Lester opened the door, quickly scrutinised Sven-Arne's face, but did not reveal by the slightest gesture what may have crossed his mind. He stepped aside and called to his wife that they had a visitor, while he observed Sven-Arne.

'Is everything all right?'

Sven-Arne nodded, took off his sandals, and placed them by the door where they had to fight for a spot next to half a dozen others.

'I come unexpectedly, I know, but something has happened.'

'Nothing serious, I hope,' Lester said, and led his guest into one of the three rooms of the flat. The caterwauling of a television could be heard from the adjoining room.

His wife stuck her head out of the kitchen.

'A little tea,' Lester said.

Sonia disappeared.

'Are you hungry, perhaps?'

'No, thank you,' Sven-Arne said. 'Tea is good.'

Any trace of appetite was gone. He was still shaken and it was an effort to keep his voice steady.

'Is everything well with your family?'

'Everything is fine,' Lester said. 'John took his test the other day. I think it went well. Lilian is full of life. She is with a friend. A school assignment. Joseph bought a moped yesterday.'

Lester had a habit of speaking in abbreviated sentences – he sort of thrust out the information, drawing in air through his thin lips and then forcing out another sentence. Sven-Arne had always thought it must be difficult, but was no longer bothered by his friend's strange way of speaking.

'I am sure the exam went very well,' he said. 'John is a very gifted young man. He is sure to go far.'

Lester waggled his head modestly. John was his favourite, even if he treated the other two with equal love.

Sonia came back with tea, black for Lester and with milk

39

and a lot of sugar for Sven-Arne. Thereafter she withdrew to the kitchen. Normally she might have stayed for a few minutes in order to listen to the men talk, but Sven-Arne could not help noticing Lester's discreet hand gesture.

They drank tea in silence. On the television, a local news program came on.

Lester listened to the listing of the main stories before he repeated his question, whether anything in particular had happened. He knew that the twentieth of November was an important day for Sven-Arne, the day that he went to Koshy's.

'A man from my former life was at Koshy's.'

Sven-Arne was not sure how to proceed. How much should he tell? Lester knew that he had more or less run away from his homeland, that he now lived stateless and without any identifying documents, basically free-floating, but he did not know all the details. Sven-Arne had told him very little, and Lester had never pushed to know more.

'He was a former neighbour of mine,' he went on. 'Back then, a long time ago, he was a young man, perhaps twenty, a little wild perhaps but basically a nice guy. Now he looks like the typical sort who comes to Bangalore on business, but it was definitely him.'

'Did he recognise you?'

'Yes, I'm sure of it.'

'Did you speak to each other?'

Sven-Arne picked up the teacup but his hand was shaking so badly that he decided to put it down again.

'You walked out,' Lester said.

'Ran.'

Lester smiled and Sven-Arne thought he knew why. He

was not known for his rapid pace – quite the contrary – and his friends at Lal Bagh would tease him about his slow gait, and sometimes called him 'the snail.'

'Can this harm you?'

'I am dead,' Sven-Arne said.

'It is not that bad, I hope!'

Lester put his hand on Sven-Arne's.

'I am officially dead in Sweden.'

'You live here.'

'One is not allowed to be dead in Sweden and at the same time living somewhere else. Sweden wants to keep track of its citizens.'

'Have you played a trick on Sweden?'

It was a funny question, and it made Sven-Arne smile. Yes, he supposed he had. He had pulled their leg – his wife's and his old friends' – and not only them. He had even betrayed the official Sweden, with all its record-keeping obligations and responsibilities. Not in a flamboyant way, but by simply slipping away unnoticed and in secrecy dissolving all ties to the homeland, he had placed himself outside of the order upon which Sweden was grounded, a system he himself had supported and helped develop. In many respects he had personified and been a spokesman for that order. Therefore his escape was a double betrayal. He was not a 'nobody', someone who lived on the outskirts of society, who had refused all responsibility.

He had erased his identity, transformed himself into John Mailer, and been swallowed up by the human mass that was India, making himself as anonymous to the kingdom of Sweden as all his newfound Indian friends were. Lester did not exist to Sweden anymore as an Indian, one of at least a billion, so unimportant as to be dispensable, someone one did not have to take into account in the overall social structure.

To this – Lester's level – was where Sven-Arne had taken refuge. Had become one with those in a sense untouchable. Now Sweden, in the guise of a former neighbour, had caught up with him and he realised that he would not be able to escape so easily. Svensk's boy was sharp. His father, Rune Svensk, and Sven-Arne were the same age and had been in primary school together, they had played in the neighbourhood and later, many years later, become neighbours.

Jan – that was his name – would never keep quiet.

'John, my friend.' Lester interrupted his thoughts and placed his hand on Sven-Arne's arm. 'Don't worry too much about this. You former neighbour may not be sure of himself.'

'I must leave,' Sven-Arne said.

'Where will you go?'

'It's better that you don't know. There are a couple of things I must do first.'

'What will happen to your youngsters?'

Sven-Arne shook his head almost imperceptibly. He would abandon them, disappear without a word of parting or explanation. What would they think? Fatigue, hunger, thoughts of the school and the friends in the garden caused him to let out a sob.

Lester leant forward across the table. Sven-Arne smelt his onion-heavy breath. Everything is about to be determined, he thought. Everything depends on what he says next. But Lester remained quiet. The sound of the television dampened suddenly and Sven-Arne realised that Lester's wife must have left the kitchen.

They poured themselves more tea. Sonia supplied a plate of cookies. Only at this sight did Sven-Arne become aware of how ravenous he was. With the intention of dining at Koshy's he had not eaten anything since breakfast. He ate a couple of cookies, glanced at Lester and met his gaze.

Did Lester sense that it would be a long time before they saw each other again, if ever, that the friendship of many years would end here at a table with two cups of tea and a plate of cookies? Sven-Arne had Lester to thank for many things. He was the one who had put in a good word for him, taken him on as a helper in the garden, and this without asking any questions. 'Merciful' was the word that Sven-Arne came to think of. Lester had been merciful. This was a word that had dropped out of common usage and was only used by believers, something he had never been.

He had made a place for Sven-Arne, skillfully bypassing the Indian bureaucracy, and presented it as if Sven-Arne was a middle-aged man who needed a change of scenery for a short while, would only play a visiting role, and then return to his country. But Lester must surely have guessed that day he first saw him that this was a man who would be a lifelong fugitive.

Sven-Arne had never asked why he had been received with such a humble and unquestioning welcome; he knew there could be no rational explanation. This was what Lester was like. He would have been embarrassed to entertain such a question.

It was not a matter of religion. Lester rarely or never participated in ceremonies or services; his empathy was simply there. At first Sven-Arne assumed it was Lester's half-British background that was the source of his genuine kindness toward the stranger who wanted to help dig. Or else he had been taken aback and decided to test the stranger's mettle. Sven-Arne would never know for sure, and had long since stopped wondering about Lester's original motivations. Nowadays he simply warmed himself with the memories of his first stretch of time in Bangalore.

They parted without much ado, shook hands and – after a moment's bashful silence – gave each other a quick embrace. Sven-Arne asked Lester to hug the children for him and forward his best wishes. Sonia stood quietly by the kitchen door. She was holding a plastic bag with naan and a jar of pickles of the kind she knew Sven-Arne liked. She gave these to him without a word. Sven-Arne took the bag before he headed out the door.

FOUR

Each time he stepped into the bathroom he felt as if he were entering a Monty Python sketch. The hotel room was more or less quiet, despite the noise of the traffic, the honking and the recurring high-pitched signal that he always mistook for his mobile phone. But when he opened the door to the bathroom it was like stepping into a roundabout with traffic rushing from every direction. It would not have surprised him if a rickshaw had rushed out between the shower and the toilet in a crazy driving manoeuvre.

Jan Svensk sat in the midst of this tumult, in deep reflection, as he at the same time followed the exertions of an insect ascending the shower curtain. When it tumbled down, rolled over onto its legs, and set its sights on the shower for the third time in a row, he stretched out a foot and crushed it against the floor.

His irritation at the attitude of the waiter, and above all, the maître d', had subsided. In a way he understood them. They did not know him, whereas Sven-Arne Persson was probably a regular. One protects one's habitual guests, that is simply a fact. Why should he let this irritate him?

Maybe it was his general frustration at the Indian reality that had so incensed him. He had left Koshy's in a rage without leaving a single rupee in tip. Now he was ashamed.

45

Against all odds, he was also constipated. Everyone had assumed something else, but the past two days he had spent several sessions on the traffic-exposed toilet. Now, finally, his own gases mingled with the exhaust that penetrated through the always-opened vent at the very top of the wall. He sighed with relief, but also pure exhaustion, tore long strips from the roll, dried himself with care, and washed his hands three separate times. The natives rarely used paper, from what he could understand, and simply rinsed after their bathroom visits. He wanted to try it, but his upbringing was too conventional. He imagined that it was healthier with only water, gentler on delicate skin, but hesitated to try it.

He did not regard himself as a particularly ethnocentric being. In theory he had always extolled the virtues of understanding between persons from widely differing parts of the world. He wanted to see the good, the new and exciting, in other people and cultures but was catching himself getting more and more upset at, in his view, the decidedly irrational India.

Why? Those colleagues who had been in Bangalore for a long time floated naturally in this environment and accepted apparently without friction the most bizarre, almost shamefully idiotic behaviours – to his surprise and dismay.

Couldn't they express their disapproval? He – as a newcomer – couldn't do it. It would appear insensitive and insulting. Maybe there was a resistance to taking on another tradition and culture. Jan Svensk was bewildered enough after his week in the city. He was attracted by the foreign but at the same time wanted things as cozy as back in Uppsala.

He left the bathroom, closing the door behind him, checked the time, and threw himself onto the bed.

'Sven-Arne Persson,' he said out loud, 'what are you doing in Bangalore?'

He knew he ought to hook up to the Internet and send a couple of emails but remained where he was, staring up at the ceiling, while he thought about Persson, the county commissioner who went up in smoke. He remembered the whole thing very well, especially since the Persson family had lived only one town house down from him and because Sven-Arne's wife and Jan's mother were social.

There was some speculation that he had been murdered, but most people were convinced he had killed himself. A goodbye letter had never been found, and his wife was at a complete loss, as he had never shown any signs of depression or anything else that pointed to suicide. The couple's finances were good and his political career was going swimmingly. There had even been talk about a position in parliament, maybe even a cabinet post.

Then, on a normal business day, during a meeting in City Hall, County Commissioner Persson had excused himself and left the room. Everyone assumed he had to use the restroom or perhaps make an important phone call. The meeting was more or less over, there was nothing of importance left to cover, and no one thought it strange that he left the room.

The meeting was called to an end twenty minutes later, without Persson having returned.

One hour later, Councillor Hellmark of the opposition party had a meeting scheduled with Persson. They were to have tried to reach common ground on some issue, maybe one of the intractable ones that the county was known for.

Persson never turned up. His secretary had no idea

where he was. Persson was not known for forgetfulness or nonchalance. The building was searched to no avail, calls were made to his home.

At eight o'clock that evening, the 19th of November, his wife contacted the police. By that point she had called all of his acquaintances, including the Svensk family, as well as the emergency room at the Akademiska Hospital. No one had seen or heard from her husband.

Until now, that is. Exactly twelve years later. Jan Svensk felt a tingle of excitement as he realised the full extent of how unlikely the encounter at the restaurant had been. He did not for one second doubt that it was Sven-Arne Persson. His reaction, the surprise and horror Jan had time to glimpse in his eyes, spoke all too clearly.

What was he doing in India, of all places? How was he supporting himself? Was there a lover in the picture, someone who had convinced him to leave the family, his work, and his country? Had he embezzled funds from the county or the party?

As Jan Svensk lay on the bed and stared at the ceiling fan, and the call to prayer started up its monotone litany, he came to the decision that he was going to get an answer to the Persson riddle. How could he possibly return to Sweden without it? He chuckled to himself. What a sensation it would be. Suddenly he wished he was a journalist. He could see the headline: *County Commissioner, Ruled Dead, Found Alive in India.*

Of course it was one thing to decide on this investigation, but how to proceed? In a city like Bangalore it was like looking for a needle in a haystack. The old proverb here took on a literal significance. It was a dizzying prospect to think of locating Persson among all these people. Granted, he stood out from the crowd, but right now he was most likely keeping as low a profile as he could muster.

Suddenly the light went out. The only thing illuminating his room was the screen on his laptop, which reminded him of his work.

Jan Svensk heaved himself out of bed, sat down at the computer, opened a report and gave it a once-over, adding a couple of comments, connected to the Internet, and sent it off. At that moment the power came back on.

Thereafter he opened the bottle he had bought at the Arlanda airport, got a glass from the bathroom, poured himself a generous whisky, sat down in the only armchair, and started making his plans.

FIVE

If there was anything that frightened him, it was the thought of having to leave Bangalore for good. Where would he go? He had spun himself a delicate net in which to rest. At the least movement the threads would tear and he would fall down into an old age of poverty, perhaps destitution, and even worse, isolation.

Lester and his family were a thread that gave him a feeling of family life he could take part in. Sven-Arne followed Lester's children as if they were his own flesh and blood, he took delight in their successes at school and worried about them when they were sick. They celebrated family events together. He could remember the first one, six days after Lilian's birth. A steady stream of relatives, neighbours, and friends came by the flat, admired the newborn, and presented little gifts.

It was a matter of some notoriety that a foreigner was taking part in the ceremony, and he thought for a while that this was the reason for his presence – that Lester in some way wanted to brag about the fact that he was close to such an exotic personage – but then he realised the invitation was well intended and that Lester genuinely appreciated his attentions for his daughter's *chatthi*.

His work at the botanical garden was the other dominant

thread. At Lal Bagh, he felt useful, he carried out practical work that meant something. He had been there so long that he could point with pride to the trees he had planted. Some had had time to become tall and offered a welcome shade in summer. Others flowered beautifully. His favourite was the temple tree.

The lessons at the school that was very close to his home was a third thread. For the past five, six years, on a volunteer basis, he had been teaching a group of children English, European history, and what one could call social studies. This took place outside of regular scheduling and had nothing to do with the children's official educational program, but the four hours a week were always well attended. Some thirty children in their early teens followed his lectures on the breakthrough of industrialisation in Europe, of technical advances and developments in production methods, but also of terrible conditions, child labour, and the budding struggle for human rights, against drunkenness, and for freedom of religion.

He also lectured in geography and after every lecture would congratulate himself on having imprinted the countries of Europe in the heads of his pupils. Most of them could pick out Germany, Italy, Poland, and about twenty other countries on a blank map. He thought it was more than most Swedish children could manage with regard to Asia.

These were the areas he knew – European geography and history – and these were what he confined himself to.

They always concluded with conversational exercises in English. In his youth, Sven-Arne had only attended community college, but in connection with being drawn into county politics and from time to time receiving international visitors and guest researchers who came to the university, he had studied his way through primary and secondary school English.

Class after class went through his lectures and discussions. Young people who had graduated several years ago could stop him on the street, still with an embarrassing amount of respect, and tell him how much they appreciated his teachings. Sometimes he was moved to tears by their kindness.

Through these young people, he even gained a place in the world of their parents. He became known throughout the area and was received with goodwill in the small shops in his neighbourhood.

He was a volunteer teacher not only for the sake of the children. He did it as much for himself. Something of the skills he had gained in his old life could be drawn upon in the planning of the lessons and in the actual instruction. He always tried to encourage discussion in his classroom, inviting the students to articulate a point and to use their imagination. He was not always successful in this. Even in this sense, he recognised situations from political life in Uppsala.

Perhaps he also taught in order to assuage his bad conscience. He had chosen not to delve deeper into this, just acknowledge that he was privileged. He had chosen a simple life. Planting trees and bushes placed him far down on the social scale. He observed almost daily the surprise of the more well-to-do Indians who came to Lal Bagh. They would stare unabashedly at the white man who was dressed like a Dalit or Untouchable, bare feet in rough sandals, dirty, with calloused hands, engaged in highly unusual behaviour: He was doing the dirty work, the heavy, manual, poorly paid labour. This was somewhat of a shock to the middle-class population. They took him for a fool, a failure, who perhaps had come to India to seek God but had found a spade. They pointed, they laughed at him, and thereby felt themselves somewhat elevated.

Some of them spoke to him and found to their astonishment a well-versed man who spoke good English, frequently even better than themselves, and who explained his position with a smile – how he had freely taken on the work of gardening because he wanted to make a contribution – but who painstakingly avoided mentioning anything about his background. Sometimes it sparked respect; there was something Ghandian about the gaunt man that was appealing to a faithful Hindu. But mostly it brought him ridicule.

These threads, the contact with Lester and his family, his contributions as volunteer teacher, and his work in the botanical garden, constituted the safety net of Sven-Arne Persson, former county commissioner. The net that transformed the officially deceased county commissioner into a living being.

Now all this was threatened. An unlikely encounter had brought two Uppsala citizens together.

Suddenly it occurred to him that this might not be a coincidence at all. Was there a possibility that Jan Svensk had in some way been informed of his whereabouts? Had he been sent out from Sweden for this purpose? What was his profession? Could he actually be a police officer? Sven-Arne had no idea. If he was, he was the right person to send to Bangalore as a spy, old neighbours that they were. If this was the case, then there was every likelihood he was working with the Indian police, and then the situation was even more precarious.

Sven-Arne tapped the driver's shoulder and gave him a different address.

'Yes, sir,' he answered, with a nod of his head, and made a daring U-turn that caused the rickshaw to lurch and the drivers of surrounding vehicles to throw themselves on their horns.

He turned onto Regency Road and drove north, passing Brigade Street and taking a left onto MG Road.

Sven-Arne Persson leant back in the rickshaw but observed everyone who drove up alongside them and he scrutinised the pavements as if he were a newcomer to the city.

Somewhere in the crowd was Jan Svensk.

Hotel Ajantha was located at the end of a side street on MG Road. He had never been to the hotel before but knew that its clientele consisted of Indians from the lower middle class as well as the occasional European on a tight budget. His chances of encountering Jan Svensk here were minimal.

A man was snoozing on a couch in the dingy reception area, but he woke up when Sven-Arne walked in. The man blinked at him but made no attempt to get up. Sven-Arne greeted him in English and asked if there was a room for the night.

The man got up reluctantly and walked over to the front desk, opened the ledger, and pointed at a row without saying a word, then turned and pointed to a posterboard that stated the cost of the room was 990 rupees per night. That was more than he spent on food for a week.

'Okay,' he said, and wrote down a name that he made up that instant: Lester Young.

'Passport number,' the receptionist said, unselfconsciously scratching himself in the crotch.

Sven-Arne wrote down eight numbers without hesitation and said he was Australian.

'One night, pay now.'

Room 101 was spartan: a bed, a chair, a rickety table with a television set. That was all. Sven-Arne lay down on the bed. He stared at the blades of the fan and noticed the grey layer of dust that had sprouted like a fungus over the base attached to the ceiling. Somewhere a telephone rang and someone hollered 'Hello.' Muted voices floated through the open ventilation to the courtyard, steps on the stone patio and a man's hoarse laughter. There was a life out there, a contextual web that had been torn from him in the blink of an eye.

Images of his former native land came and went over the next few hours as he lay on the bed, incapable of getting to his feet, much less undressing and crawling in between the sheets. It was images of his past that he was fishing up out of his inner depths. He rarely or never read about Sweden in the Indian newspapers and was completely cut off from the great, decisive political events. Sometimes he accidentally came across a news item on Sweden, often about sports or amusing writings on climate or other rarities that had to do with the country's exotic placement on the globe. It could be some ice hotel in the north, or now most recently a storm that had struck the southern parts and apparently taken out forests. Of course he had read about the killing of the foreign minister. He had met her during her time in SSU and recalled an enthusiastic young woman, and he remembered thinking she would either be broken or go very far. Now she was dead.

About the small world, about Uppsala county politics, his old friends and acquaintances, who had married, had children, or died during his twelve years abroad, he knew nothing.

From time to time he experienced a burning anxiety, a longing to meet someone from the past who could tell him. This happened especially in the beginning of his stay in Bangalore, but now and then this gnawing desire to get the information that created connections returned.

Out of nowhere he had the thought that Jan Svensk was perhaps the person who had been dispatched by an unseen hand as a messenger from his former life. Perhaps he had messages such as . . . well, what? What kind of information could seriously mean anything? What was there to gladden the expatriate, to add anything to his life? What did he need? Wouldn't the knowledge of births and deaths, about neighbours' and local politicians' lives, simply knock him off-kilter, perhaps risk his entire existence?

He did not need this knowledge! But sometimes he wondered if his wife was still alive, and if so, how she was doing. Had she taken up with someone new?

Sven-Arne suddenly stood up, walked over and turned on the television, found the remote control, and started to cruise through the channels.

He sank down on the bed and stared unseeing at a film. A woman ran up a gentle slope, paused at a tree, melodramatically surveyed a valley, and then started a languishing song. Sven-Arne gathered that she had run away from her husband and was now looking for the man she had loved from early youth. Always the same story, he thought, convinced that she or her beloved would die before the film came to an end.

He pressed the remote and came to the local news channel. There was a picture of the Swedish king in the background, as well as Taj West End hotel, one of the more luxurious in the city.

Sven-Arne chuckled. The events of the afternoon and evening were such an unlikely chain of events that it was almost a parody. First the memories of his childhood streets, then the meeting with the Swedish couple in MG Road, then Jan Svensk at Koshy's, and now the Swedish head of state on the television screen. Maybe Jan Svensk was in town for the Swedish activities that the news anchor was talking about? The Swedish Trade Council was opening an office in Bangalore and had invited King Carl Gustaf for the event.

The streets were probably crawling with Swedes. He had to be careful. It was completely possible that there were others among the accompanying Swedes, beyond Jan Svensk, who would recognise him as the missing politician.

Sven-Arne Persson fell asleep very late. The last conscious thought in his head was centred on the children of St Mary's school. How would they react if he simply disappeared from town, as much as he had always lectured them on the importance of punctuality?

SIX

It was just before two o'clock. The sound from the street had abated in intensity but a car or motorcycle would occasionally drive down the monsoon-ravaged street. It had been one of the rainiest Bangalore Octobers in memory and this had left its mark. The streets were ruined, large potholes created dangerous traps, the water had turned the surface to washing boards, and whole pavements had collapsed, so undermined had they become.

And still it rained. More sporadically in the interior and not as violently as two, three weeks ago, but as recently as the past few days hundreds of people had died. Weddings had been rendered impossible because brides and bridegrooms had not been able to be brought together. School instruction had been suspended and everyone talked of 'the great depression.' Jan Svensk finally understood that this referred to a powerful low pressure weather system out at sea.

In addition, it was unexpectedly cold. The newspaper, which appeared tucked into the door handle every morning, indicated that it was time to get out one's winter clothes, as the temperature the day before had sunk to the record low of fifty-six degrees.

The hospitals had been deluged by those seeking assistance, suffering coughs and fevers, and even Svensk had been stricken by 'the big depression.' He could not sleep, and it was not the rain that was keeping him awake, nor – as in the first few days – the jet lag; it was his thoughts of Sven-Arne Persson, and by extension Uppsala and his own life. Anxiety caused him to writhe on his bed, turn on the reading lamp, open a book for a while only to lay it aside, turn out the light, and try once again to fall asleep.

Now he had given up. He glanced at the telephone. Should he call home to Elise? It was only half past nine in the evening in Uppsala. But he abandoned the thought. They had spoken recently and she would wonder why he was calling so soon after they last talked. A conversation that contained the usual phrases but lacked all warmth. Jan Svensk had replaced the receiver with sadness, well aware that something was missing, and he grew increasingly morose as he recalled how joyless their exchange had been. No words of love, nothing of longing or desire, only the routine talk of everyday, if there had been exciting mail, if someone had called, how the weather had been, how the children were. He had talked about Bangalore in an uninspired way, the weather, the masses of people, his ongoing work.

Everything was fine. No one had called. No, mostly bills and some of his magazines. The children were well. No, they were with friends. It was snowing.

It's raining here, he thought, and looked at the brick tiles that covered the hotel entryway. Many of the tiles were chipped, which he found irritating. Suddenly he caught a motion on the wall above the entrance. A squirrel scampering along a thirty-centimetre-wide ledge running under the windows on the third floor. It was running back and forth in an anxious manner. Clearly it wanted to get down. But how had it ended up there? At one end of the ledge there was only a ninety-degree corner to a smooth concrete wall and the other end looked equally unpromising. But there was also a tree – it looked to be a rubber plant – admittedly a couple of metres out from the wall, but it was also the only thing that could offer a way out of the nervous back and forth. It was clear that the squirrel had also come to this conclusion, because it started pausing for longer and longer stretches at this corner, leaning forward daringly and examining the leaves shiny with rain, before leaving once more for the other end.

And so it went on. Jan Svensk followed it with his gaze, increasingly sympathetic to the miserable creature. No, don't stay there, he thought, as the squirrel calculated the distance to the tree. Jump! You can do it. You're a squirrel.

A final check, a quick shake of his body, stillness and concentration for a couple of seconds, and then came the jump.

The squirrel disappeared into the dark interior of the tree. Jan Svensk remained standing at the window for a little longer. A moped sputtered along on the street. The rain fell.

The distraction offered by the moments when he had been so absorbed by the squirrel's actions had somewhat lightened his mood.

It occurred to him that he could call home and talk about the unlikely chance encounter with Sven-Arne Persson, but put this out of his mind. If he was going to call anyone about this, it would be his parents. They had been acquainted with Persson. He should call them anyway; they always received his calls with genuine warmth and gave expression to an embarrassing mixture of pride and worry. But he decided he would put this off for one more day; he needed to think the whole thing through.

He crawled into bed, turned off the light, and rearranged his pillows in a way that he thought would facilitate sleep.

He woke up at half past four, awakened by the signal from some kind of service phone on the wall of the corridor outside.

The call was over after a brief but loud discussion. Jan Svensk then heard the lift mechanism start up and in his half sleeping and dazed state he associated it with a war film he had seen in his youth. There it was the mechanism to a giant piece of artillery that regulated the sight of a cannon – a contraption that set its sights on the intended target with no apparent human intervention. The machinery was composed of well-oiled cogs and pins that coldly and unhesitatingly brought the deadly things into firing mode.

For a second, there was a cut to the triumphant face of the commander, and thereafter the flames from the fire against the backdrop of the night sky. The mighty thunder and high-pitched whine of the projectiles were amplified by the speakers of the cinema.

Jan Svensk could no longer remember what the target was, but most likely it was a ship making its way through the Atlantic night, whose crew was secure in the belief that they were at a safe distance from the enemy coastline and firepower.

How wrong they were, Jan Svensk thought, and shortly returned to sleep.

SEVEN

He was number sixteen. An inquisitive fellow from Trollhättan had once asked if he could name his fifteen predecessors. No one knows, not even the man asking the question – who was quickly escorted out – what the answer would have been.

Jan Svensk had heard about this incident and came to think of it as he watched the Swedish regent enter the ballroom at Taj West End hotel. All of the other guests turned their heads in unison as if they were watching a tennis match, but without the return volleys. Their heads and eyes were locked on the king.

'How short he is,' someone was heard to remark.

He was relatively casually dressed, no medal-weighted uniform, but he moved jerkily, perhaps because he was not in control of where he was going. An experienced aide-de-camp in a white uniform led him around.

The noise level resumed after a while and the approximately three hundred returned to the gossip and easy chatter so characteristic of an event such as this. Sometimes, however, faces lit up with a genuine joy, old friends reunited.

A handful of photographers circulated in the crowd, but mostly around the king and those who had managed to capture his attention. It was obvious that the goal for many was to be photographed with the famous guest.

'A spectacle,' Jan Svensk commented to a co-worker.

'And we get bread,' the latter said, skillfully snatching a toothpick-pierced morsel from a passing plate.

A number of people from the Swedish Trade Council were gathered in a circle like a flock of schoolboys, one peal of laughter ringing out after another.

It was a relaxed atmosphere. Young and old jostled at the bar, Indians and Swedes, like gnus at the watering hole.

The king was led around, a strained, somewhat uncertain smile on his lips.

'Poor man,' someone said.

'He probably would like nothing better than to have a drink and take it easy,' said a young woman, whom Jan Svensk had noticed already when she arrived.

He approached the group she belonged to, and looked to see if he could spot anyone in her midst that he recognised.

An Indian man, dressed in what appeared to be a down jacket and a long kurta, and his friend, with a narrow face, thin moustache, and kind eyes, were introduced to the king. Jan Svensk drew closer in order to listen in. They turned out to be theatre people from Mysore.

A man with a blond crew cut, wearing a Nehru jacket, was explaining their work to the king.

'Ah, children's theatre,' the regent said finally.

The men nodded and smiled.

'Very good,' the king said, and then that audience was over.

Jan Svensk drew back, mingled, but mostly longed for the buffet. An old acquaintance, whom Svensk had got to know when they worked together at Arcore but had not seen since then, came over and thumped him on the back.

'It wasn't exactly yesterday,' he said.

Svensk examined his former colleague. He was one of the ones who had sold in time. It was rumoured that his profit was close to 70 million kronor. He was the same, the same smile and boyish appearance. But Svensk would never again allow himself to be taken in by such appearances. He had lost some of those kronor.

'Feeding at the trough, I see,' Svensk said.

'Of course,' his former colleague replied. 'What are you up to these days?'

Svensk suddenly felt that he had no desire to discuss what he had done since they last met, not what he was up to, nor what he was doing in Bangalore, not anything actually that had to do with work.

'Various things,' he said.

'Good stuff,' his former colleague said, and sailed off. The message had gone through.

Elise, he thought, you should be here. An unexpected longing for her made him withdraw, back up for a party crossing his path, and set his sights on the buffet that had not yet been opened up. Then he went around and read from the small labels what was hiding under the well-polished lids.

'Hungry?' he heard a woman say behind his back, and he was taken with the thought that it was the young woman he had spied earlier and he turned expectantly.

Before him stood a woman in her sixties. She was wearing a light blue sari folded around her generous body.

'Well, well,' he said.

'I don't recognise you,' she went on.

He pulled out the same old story again, for God knows

which time, who he was and why he had come to Bangalore.

'Gunlög Billström,' she said, introducing herself. 'I belong to the residents. I was "bangalored" long before most of the others.'

'How long have you lived here?'

'In India almost eighteen years, in Bangalore fourteen.'

'Then you know most of the Swedes in the city?'

'It is my area,' she said with a smile. 'I am the one who keeps tabs on the colonials.'

'Sven-Arne Persson?' he said.

The woman shook her head and her large earrings rattled.

'From Uppsala. Around sixty, tall, fairly thin . . .'

A new shake.

'He may have been here ten years.'

'Strange,' she said.

'I thought you kept tabs on everyone,' Svensk teased.

His comment had the desired effect. He saw her make an effort to play out the role she had laid claim to.

'What does he do?'

'I've no idea. He disappeared from Uppsala some ten, twelve years ago. I think it was 1993. Without a trace. And now I saw him here yesterday.'

'That sounds exciting. A man who disappears.'

'He was a county commissioner in Uppsala.'

The woman took a step closer. 'Where did you see him?'

'At Koshy's.'

'Strange,' she repeated.

Then the lids to the food came off and the human wave that welled forth came between them. He saw her grab hold of a plate and be carried off by the race to the dishes that caused the ravenous masses to stream over to Svensk's side of the festively lit ballroom. In the background, the Adolf Fredrik Boys' Choir was singing 'Uti Vår Hage'. The sound of talking in the room had died down. The focus was now on the food. Jan Svensk lingered in the background for a while observing the action, although he was very hungry. He exchanged a glance with the kitchen staff and they smiled at each other.

When the worst of the rush was over, he took a plate and helped himself to the delicacies.

When the time was approaching eleven, the crowd had thinned considerably. The king had retired. A couple of Svensk's colleagues were standing around the bar, but he did not feel like joining them. It was enough with work during the day.

Gunlög Billström had also stayed behind. She was talking with the Swedish ambassador and the general consul of Chennai. Their gazes met and it made Svensk think of something important.

He approached the trio of women.

'Excuse me,' he said, and it was only the wine that allowed him to be so forward.

He introduced himself, told the ambassador and consul that he was looking for a Swedish man, missing for many years, and then turned to Gunlög Billström.

'There was a piece of information I forgot to give you. Sven-Arne Persson is wall-eyed.'

'Wall-eyed?'

'Cross-eyed, only his eyes go in different directions,' Svensk clarified.

'Oh, then I know!' Billström exclaimed. 'I have seen

66

him. It was at Lal Bagh. An extraordinary thing.'

She grabbed his arm, looking from the ambassador to the consul, and nodded enthusiastically, clearly satisfied to be someone who knew what was going on, before she turned her attention back to Svensk.

The ambassador and consul took the opportunity to slip away.

'You see, it was perhaps three years ago. I was walking in Lal Bagh . . .'

'What is Lal Bagh?' Svensk interrupted.

'The botanical gardens. I was there with a couple of girlfriends and then we see a man who is standing in some kind of thicket. Maybe it was bamboo, I don't know. In the middle of that mess, with a big knife in his hand, or perhaps a saw, hacking wildly around him. It looked very funny. Suddenly, just as we were walking past, he called out. In Swedish! As you can guess, I was flabbergasted. A worker at Lal Bagh who speaks Swedish, can you imagine?'

'What did he say?'

Gunlög Billström lowered her voice. 'He said "Fucking hell." He had cut his arm, not anything serious from what I understood, but there was some blood. We stopped and one of my friends asked him if he was all right.'

'In Swedish?'

'No, no, she is Indian. She was speaking English, not fluently of course, but fully comprehensible English. He was very polite, thanked her for her concern, and explained that it was a minor laceration. He actually used the Swedish word "a minor *blessyr*".'

'Did you talk to him?'

'No, I did not want to embarrass him by speaking Swedish.'

Jan Svensk sensed that it was she who had felt embarrassed by a fellow countryman doing simple gardening.

'What did he look like?'

'He was cockeyed. We commented on it afterwards. My friends said they were convinced he must have some kind of special task, perhaps something to do with research.'

'Because he was cockeyed, or because he was a Westerner?'

'Oh, something like that.'

'Can you describe him?'

'Fifty or sixty, quite tall and lanky. He was stuck in all that greenery so it is hard to say. He was barefoot but his sandals were placed next to the bushes. I thought that would have been strange if he was a researcher. Surely they don't work in bare feet?'

'No,' Svensk agreed, 'I wouldn't think that would be usual. You haven't seen him on any other occasions?'

'No, strangely enough. I have been to Lal Bagh many times since, but have never bumped into him again. I have not wanted to ask for him, either. It seemed intrusive.'

Jan Svensk asked where the garden was located.

'It is so pleasant to walk there, in Cubbon Park also for that matter. But especially in the morning. Of course, I don't like all the doves.'

Jan Svensk laughed.

'But,' Gunlög Billström resumed, while she carefully but deliberately placed her arm around Jan Svensk's back and guided him to a calmer part of the room where they sank down into armchairs, 'is there something mysterious about him? I mean, is he a fugitive from justice?'

'Not that I know. He just disappeared.'

'Was it love?'

Gunlög Billström's expression, and the way she leant in toward Svensk, clearly said that this was something she viewed with a benign eye and that he should feel free to tell her everything he knew about the amorous adventures of the former county commissioner without reservation. Her confidential tone, which Jan Svensk sensed was not based only in curiosity but at least as much in a desire for something romantic and deeply human in the mystification around Sven-Arne Persson, caused her to lower her voice so much that he had trouble hearing her.

'You see, we just run after material things,' she said, and let her gaze sweep over the room. 'It would be so liberating if someone gave way to their heart. I can see him there in the garden, going about his trivial tasks, but, in his heart of hearts, so very happy. Wouldn't that be fantastic?'

Her face glowed, and in some obscure way Jan Svensk was moved by her words. She was no longer just a gossipmonger, one who closely followed the goings-on of Bangalore's Swedish colony. Suddenly she appeared beautiful, with her somewhat wilted features.

'Yes, it would be amazing,' he agreed.

She clasped one of his hands in both of hers.

'We can go to Lal Bagh together,' she enthused. 'I can show you around and then we might find your mysterious friend together.'

Jan Svensk carefully retracted his hand.

'I don't think I will lay down more trouble on this. I was mostly curious. Would you like another glass of wine?'

Gunlög Billström shook her head. Jan Svensk sat back.

'He isn't really my friend. I was just curious in general, as I said, but I am not prepared to run my legs off for his sake. If it really was him, then perhaps he wants to be left in peace, what do I know?'

She looked at him. He knew she was trying to discern something in his face that spoke against his apparent indifference. He smiled at her.

'I think I will refill my glass,' he said. 'If you will excuse me . . .'

She made a quick gesture with her hand and almost immediately a waiter with a bottle appeared beside him. He held out his glass and the waiter refilled it.

Gunlög Billström opened her purse and held out her card.

'Do as you like,' she said, and smiled, 'but if you change your mind, give me a call. I just mostly sit around at home, staring at a bloody cricket field, going to pot.'

He took her card, surprised by her choice of words, studied it, and then slipped it into his coat pocket.

'That's kind of you,' he said, and tried to think of a comment that could dampen her outburst.

'The boys are fun to look at but cricket drives me crazy, can you understand that? Cricket gives me a migraine.' She spat out her words. 'They can go at it for days, the newspapers are filled with drivel, and there is national mourning and rioting if they lose. As if what this country needs is cricket!'

Gunlög Billström changed as her bitterness was revealed; a desperation appeared in her eyes and her apparent dissatisfaction which she was unexpectedly sharing with him – a newcomer and temporary visitor and therefore

70

perhaps safe – sullied her features, almost to the point of disfigurement.

Jan Svensk was filled with pity, but also regret that he had turned down her suggestion that she help him find Sven-Arne Persson. He regretted even bringing up the subject to begin with.

'You feel sorry for me, you think I am a pathetic failure,' she said, and quickly waved away his attempts to dispute this. 'And you are right. I am going to pot in this town. Have you seen the filth, the substandard streets, and the decay in old Bangalore? Once this was a beautiful city.'

He nodded and leant forward in order to hear her better.

'Now it has collapsed,' she went on, and made a sweeping gesture with her arm, as if to illustrate the razing of the city.

He followed her gaze. The company of men in dark suits next to them was becoming increasingly boisterous. Among them there was a successful Swedish banker next to another gentleman from Sony Ericsson.

'Is that progress?' Billström asked, rhetorically.

'What do you mean?' he wondered.

'Haven't you seen the industrial complexes? All these call centres and corporate parks. Not to mention all the hideous shopping malls springing up like mushrooms.'

'It creates jobs,' he objected.

Billström snorted.

'Impoverishment,' she said curtly, standing up abruptly and touching his shoulder before she left.

71

EIGHT

Berglund could have left his bed but preferred to remain there. The former athlete – active in bandy and orienteering – had grown lazy. I have a right to lie here a while longer, he thought.

The first snow of the season was falling outside. He felt the nurse, the new one whose name he had not yet learnt, watching him. She was standing at the window. She was talking about the snow, how beautiful it was.

'I know,' he said, straight out into the open, 'I know I can walk.'

'You won't fall anymore,' the nurse said.

'I know,' Berglund said, but at the same time he was irritated by her persistence.

The day after the operation he had lost his balance when they forced him to get up and go to the bathroom. That time he had cursed the staff. The cut above his eyebrow still stung.

'I know,' he repeated, 'but I would like to lie here a bit longer.'

He wanted her to leave the room. Didn't she have any other patients to attend to? He could take care of himself. He wanted to be alone. The nurse smiled at him. He didn't see it, but he felt it.

'I hate snow,' he said.

It was as if the procedure had reshaped his temperament, rearranging his brain in a way that caused him to say things he didn't really recognise.

'I'm not a winter person,' he added.

He had the idea that it might soften his outburst, make her realise that he wasn't really so grouchy and categorical, that it was just the snow that was affecting him.

'It isn't snowing in here.'

He turned his head and looked at her.

'No,' he said, 'but at some point I have to get up and go outside. And then the snow will be there.'

He could see she had an objection ready on her lips but she chose to refrain from arguing further.

'I'll be back at half past nine. We'll get you up then,' she said, and left the room.

He sat up in bed, pulled out the drawer in the bedside table, took out his glasses but replaced them immediately, pushed his covers aside, and swung his legs over the edge.

I survived, he thought suddenly and was filled by a singular feeling of gratitude. He was uncertain to whom he should direct this gratitude, to God or science? Perhaps a combination of the two? God had always held a place in his conceptual world, ever since his first experiences in childhood of something mysterious that connected him to his parents, his little world with the big world, and the incomprehensible universe outside his window, which had given way to the secure knowledge of mature age of a higher order that simply was there. No mystery, no jubilant salvation, no punishing Lord, just a feeling of connectedness, resembling the one he had felt in his younger years with his teammates on the bandy field, in the locker room, and later in life with his colleagues on the job.

It was the relationship with those who stood closest to him that was like God for Berglund. It was a closeness that arose out of the goodness and willingness to cooperate with others. It was the goodness of God. He could not explain it any other way and he did not trouble himself to seek a deeper answer. It was enough as it was, enough for him to become a human being.

He rose carefully, testing his legs to see if they would hold him and if the vertigo would return. He set his sights on the window.

Let it snow, he thought, at peace with winter. Let it come down until the earth is blanketed like the landscapes of my childhood, with snow piled a couple of metres high and the streetlights reflecting in the glittering crystals. He suddenly recalled a wintery taxi ride in the late 1940s. The driver, a good friend of his father, had taken them on a ride through town. Was it a Packard? Large, black, with a scent of leather and tobacco. Berglund was five years old. His first car ride. He was convinced that God had a hand in the matter.

He smiled to himself. Over half a century ago. The same city, the same snow, the same Berglund – amazed he was still alive, that he was still allowed along on the ride through his city.

The door to the room was pushed open with that whispering sound that he had registered even before reaching full consciousness right after his operation.

Convinced that it was the nurse returning, he did not turn around, being slightly shamefaced, as if caught doing something he wasn't supposed to.

'Hello, my friend,' he heard a familiar voice say from the door.

She had never called him 'my friend'. He was known as Berglund, nothing more. It was only Ottosson who on rare occasions called him by his first name. No one had referred to him as 'my friend' for a very long time.

With the thoughts that had dominated his morning, he was as raw as an open wound. It was only his extensive police experience that made it possible for him to control himself.

He turned around. In some strange way it was like seeing her for the first time. He remembered the first time she turned up at the division. He recalled what he had thought that time: How young she is, what is a girl like her going to be able to do around here? Riis said something stupid as usual, while Ottosson laid it on thick like always. He had bought a cake to celebrate the 'new recruit' as if she, like a professional football player, had been recruited to team 'Homicide'.

'Well, hello,' he said, clearing his throat.

Ann Lindell remained standing by the door, observing him for several seconds before walking over and gently giving him a hug. He knew she was as emotional as he was, and that she was also doing everything she could to conceal it.

He pulled away from her, shuffled over to the bed, and sat down.

'How's it going?'

'Moving right along,' he said, but felt the vertigo return at that moment.

He wanted to lie down and close his eyes, but forced himself to look at Lindell.

'Otto said you could have visitors.'

He nodded. She looked at him in silence as if to check if the intrusion was affecting him.

'And how do things look?'

'A foot has washed ashore outside Öregrund,' she replied. 'Apart from that, everything is fine.'

She had misunderstood his question.

'A foot?'

'Yes, just the foot.'

'A foot can float?'

'It was in a boot.'

He chuckled.

'You're just the same,' he said. 'Are you going to—'

'No, not Öregrund,' she said quickly.

He sensed why not, and left the subject.

'But tell me,' she said, 'how does it feel? You should know that we have been . . . worried.'

'I feel fine,' he said, smiling. 'A bit boring to lie in bed flat as a pancake.'

'Are you tired?'

He nodded. 'Tired and a bit dizzy, but that will go away, they say.'

'Will you have . . . I mean . . .'

'Any permanent damage?' he helped her along. 'No, not really. It may be difficult at first, according to the doctor, but I don't know. They don't tell you everything. But I'm counting on getting back to normal.'

Berglund was not being quite honest. Ever since he woke up from his operation he had toyed with the idea of taking early retirement. No one would blame him. He had served on the Uppsala police force for forty years.

Again, he was overcome with an unexpected wave of sentimentality. He had to make an effort to appear, if not carefree, then at least somewhat relaxed and content with his situation. The feeling of ingratitude, as he now arose from his sickbed after an illness that had caused many others the loss of well-being or even life, was also irritatingly strong. His childhood faith – be humble and thankful for the time you have received – was not strong enough to battle the thought that life had treated him unfairly. What had he done to deserve this? Berglund knew it was a ridiculous thought, but the passive waiting in his sickbed had transformed him into a teary and disobliging old man.

The insight struck him with full force; he was afraid. Afraid to grow old, afraid to die. Afraid not to be counted among the active and living, those who meant something.

The sight of Ann Lindell only strengthened this feeling. She was still young. She even smelt of life. A faint but unmistakable scent of snow, fresh air, and soap had been brought into the room.

'We received a call,' Lindell said, 'that I think may interest you, if you aren't too tired, that is.'

He gestured for her to continue.

'An old acquaintance to you called. Rune Svensk. He had been called by his son, who is in India on some kind of business. He had observed something.'

Berglund grinned. 'If you travel to India you can bet you're going to make some observations.'

Lindell looked surprised but also relieved. It was as if his comment confirmed that he was the old Berglund, who for the moment was dressed in some loose-fitting hospital-issue trousers and shirt, but was definitely back and, in a way, on duty.

'Whatever,' she said with feigned irritation. 'The son saw a man who had disappeared from Uppsala. A former county commissioner whom everyone believes is dead. He went missing many years ago.'

'Sven-Arne Gotthard Edvin Persson. 1993.'

'You remember?'

'Of course. I worked on the disappearance for several months. There were those who spoke of murder.'

'What did you think?'

'Suicide,' Berglund replied without hesitation. 'There was nothing to support homicide. Absolutely nothing.'

'Was he depressed?'

'No, not that we could find. He was . . . how can I put this?'

Berglund hesitated. When he went up in smoke, Sven-Arne Persson had been a typical middle-aged man, socially well adapted and successful, but what did one know about his inner thoughts? Berglund had tried to map every inch of the county commissioner's life but had not found any blights on his, to all appearances, blameless existence. Nonetheless he had drawn the conclusion of suicide.

'There were not motives for murder, no irregularities and no threats. He simply disappeared.'

'No body?'

'No, no body. Not a trace. It was actually completely incomprehensible. No one saw him leave City Hall, no one saw him on the street or at his home. I mean, he was a public person, someone that people recognised.'

'But he could have fled overseas?'

'We checked up on everything. His passport was in his desk drawer at home. No money was drawn from his account. You can appreciate that the conclusion was suicide, even though everyone had trouble believing it.'

'And now he turns up in Bangalore,' Lindell said.

'If it's really him.'

'The witness is completely sure of himself. And they are former neighbours.'

'I know,' Berglund said. 'I have met Jan Svensk.'

'What is he like?'

'Oh, what should I say. A normal guy. Had a somewhat rocky period in his youth but has been fine ever since, at least according to his parents.'

'How do you know them?'

'From church,' Berglund said. 'And they are Uppsala old-timers. Like Sven-Arne Persson. I remember him from my youth. We were the same age.'

'Was he sporty?'

'No. Tall, but not exactly an athlete. He may have been able to handle chess.'

'Married?'

'Yes, with Elsa. No kids.'

'Is Elsa still alive?'

Berglund's gaze flickered. Through the window he could see that the snowfall had grown heavier.

'She's barely sixty, I would guess,' he said. 'A teacher.'

'Remarried?'

'No, but I have heard rumours of a relationship.'

'What do you think?'

Berglund looked out the window again. What should he think? Jan Svensk was no hysteric but the story sounded fanciful.

'I don't know,' he said finally. 'It sounds strange to say the least. Why India?'

'We'll have to keep sniffing around. Svensk returns in

79

about a week or ten days, according to his father.'

Suddenly Berglund made a face, closed his eyes, and put his hands over his face.

'What's wrong?'

Lindell got up from her chair and started to reach a hand out to him.

'Nothing,' Berglund said. 'I . . .'

He slowly turned his head. The look he gave her was one she had never seen before.

'I'm raw,' he said finally. 'I'm just so damned raw inside.'

Lindell could not recall ever hearing Berglund use such emphatic language before.

Is he going to die, she wondered, terrified at the prospect. Was it sadness she saw in his gaze? Berglund was a smart man. Did he sense something that could not be said? Was he being less than honest when he claimed the operation had been a success?

'Are you anxious?'

That was not really a question she was allowed to ask, Lindell thought.

'I don't know what it is,' Berglund said.

He got to his feet slowly and walked over to the window. Outside the specks of snow were whirling more than ever. Without turning his head he started to talk about the melancholy that had come over him. The feeling had come creeping even before the operation but now it was threatening to take the upper hand.

'Maybe they have taken something from me, I mean . . .'

Lindell knew what he was talking about. She wanted to say something comforting, but refrained.

'Do you want to be left alone?'

'Maybe we should have a cup of coffee. Like the old days.

Do you remember when you started in the Crime division?'

Lindell nodded, glad at the turn in the conversation. When she had been new in the division, she had quickly appointed Berglund her mentor and confidant. They would withdraw over a cup of coffee, sometimes in his office, sometimes at the café, sometimes at the Savoy, the bakery that he had started patronising already in the sixties and that had come to be Lindell's retreat when she wanted to be alone to think.

'Let's do that,' she said.

She walked over to him, standing quite close, and leant her head on his shoulder. Suddenly it was as if he was the stronger of the two.

'Maybe he did the right thing in taking off to India,' Berglund said. 'Do you know how much I've come to hate snow and cold? I used to love winter, we would go cross-country skating, long before it became popular. We would pack our backpacks and set out, to Tämnaren or Funbo Lake, or to the coast during frigid winters. We would park the car on Blid Island or Yxlan and then we could skate all the way to Rödlöga, once even all the way to Fredlarna. We could just make out the Swedish Högar. It feels so long ago. Now I hate winter.'

'You've never told me. I thought you were a snow man.'

Berglund put his arm around her. They stood quietly, watching the snow.

'At this time of year in Ödeshög there's just a lot of wind,' Lindell went on. 'I don't remember any good snow winters. My father never ventured out to do more than brush off the front steps.'

'Was he sick?'

'No, superfluous maybe. He drove a beverage lorry and

81

became superfluous. He missed the boxes, the clatter of glass, and talking with the shop owners and the kiosk keepers.'

'Superfluous,' Berglund said.

'That's how he felt. My mother was the one who suffered. Dad got more quiet over the years. And now he is getting senile and you know . . .'

Lindell felt Berglund stiffen. He let go of her and leant his head against the windowpane.

'I used to believe in God,' he blurted out with such sharpness in his voice that Lindell jumped.

'And you don't anymore?'

Berglund shook his head. It looked like he was rubbing his head against the glass.

'What do you believe in?'

'I don't know,' Berglund said. 'Maybe I just need some fresh air. Yesterday a fellow from my congregation stopped by. We've been friends since childhood. He is a good man, a good person, but listening to him I felt wrapped in a haze of indifference. I felt nothing, no joy, you know that sweet feeling of friendship.'

'And then I barge in.'

Berglund turned his head and looked at her.

'I didn't mean it like that. I am happy you're the one who's here. I wouldn't be able to take Ottosson. He would just get chipper. Allan would look sad, Sammy nervous, and Haver even shakier.'

'Do you want to be left in peace?'

'I guess death is breathing down my neck.'

'Did these thoughts start with your health problems?'

'You're an investigator,' Berglund said, but did not answer the question.

Lindell started to sense that his misgivings had their root

farther back and that the discovery of the brain tumour had forced everything to the surface.

'Do you want to take a peek at the file?'

'Which file?'

'The one on the county commissioner who disappeared?'

'You want to put me to work? Yes, maybe it would . . .'

'Can I do anything?'

Berglund left the window and sat down on the bed. His cheeks were sunken and the dark circles under his eyes made him look somewhat demonic.

'You could talk to the widow, well, if there is a widow.'

'Want to go get a cup now?'

'Another time,' Berglund said. 'I'm a little . . .'

'You should rest. I'll talk to Elsa and then I'll make sure the file is sent to you.'

He nodded absently. Lindell hesitated for a moment before she went over to her colleague and stroked his cheek.

Lindell paused in the hallway. She felt uncomfortable, as if she had done something she was going to regret in the future, as if she had intruded on a private area. She had expected a tired and haggard Berglund, but not this, a man questioning the faith he had followed his entire life.

He reminded her too much of her father, bent before his time, his life juice dried up, casting a frightened glance at death.

In a way she did not accept Berglund's sadness and doubt. He had made it through brain surgery and should be praising the God he had worshipped. Instead he was drawing the completely opposite conclusion: His God no longer existed. Lindell was not a believer, had never been, but found it sloppy and unfair to treat one's faith in this way. If it could not stand up to an illness, it was not worth much.

It occurred to her that she should perhaps contact the hospital minister and ask him to pay a visit to Berglund. Clearly he needed someone to talk to. But maybe the best medicine would be to dig into an investigation.

She could not claim that the missing politician intrigued her. The naked foot in the boot was far more compelling, but Ola Haver was leading that investigation and that was fine by her. Driving the ninety to one hundred kilometres out to Öregrund was difficult for Lindell, since she had to drop off and pick up Erik at day care. The town was so small that it would have been a high-risk project. She could bump into Edvard on any corner. It still hurt to think of him even though she had learnt to handle the feelings and thoughts that could so suddenly flare up. Just a couple of years ago the ground trembled at the very mention of his name or when her memories took a stranglehold. All too often it was wine that would deaden her unease, but since a couple of months back she had decided not to drink a single drop for a while. She convinced herself she was living a good life. She had finally produced order out of all the threads that went this way and that.

In the parking lot she had trouble remembering where she had parked, and at the same moment she spotted the car the mobile phone rang. She saw from the display that it was Ottosson, head of Violent Crimes. She considered ignoring the call but finally answered.

'How is the old man?'

'Fine,' Lindell said. 'He's a little dazed but up and about.'

Ottosson talked on but Lindell picked up something in his tone of voice that put her on edge. Finally he reached the real reason for his call.

'Ola isn't feeling well.'

Ann Lindell realised immediately what this meant.

'I won't take it.'

'He's throwing up like a pig.'

'Fredriksson will have to go to Öregrund.'

'That's not a good solution and you know it. It'll be quick. Our colleagues out there just need a little attention and encouragement, and then you can go back home.'

Lindell sighed. She knew exactly how it would be. She would not be able to turn him down; her working relationship with Ottosson depended on cooperation. Even though he was a fantastic boss who had always supported her, she could not say no to him. Both of them knew how things looked in the division. Everyone was weighed down with work. Fredriksson had his battery cases, Riis was on disability, Sammy Nilsson was attending a course, and Beatrice Andersson was investigating a rape in Tunabackar.

She also knew that this was not simply a matter of driving out to Öregrund, chatting a little, and heading back home.

'It's a woman's foot,' Ottosson said.

She cast out her last card.

'Erik has been a little under the weather this week.'

'You know my wife likes to look after him,' he said.

Asta Ottosson had jumped in as babysitter many times before, and even picked up Erik from day care. Ottosson's statement was the nail in the coffin to her objections.

Ottosson may have realised the unfairness of his dealings, as he hurried to add that Sammy Nilsson would immediately take over once he returned from his course.

NINE

Once upon a time, Uncle Ante had been part of a mission to blow up a bridge over a river. Sven-Arne Persson could not remember what the river was called, but he could remember his excitement as Ante narrated – slowly at first, and then with increasing engagement – how they crawled between the boulders, how they approached the start of the bridge. Sven-Arne could feel the sharp stones cutting through his trousers, his breathing grew quick and yet controlled, and he scrutinised his uncle's face in order not to miss a single detail.

It was cold and it was night-time. The decimated troop took advantage of the fact that there was a new moon. Above them there was an outpost, an old stone house with a tile roof. It was most likely just Moroccans, and they stayed inside. The smoke from the chimney blew down over Ante and his three comrades. They had been forced to leave the fifth man, a German, when he sprained his ankle and could not continue up and down the steep slopes.

'We never saw him again,' Ante said. 'His name was Ernst.'

His uncle went silent for a while, and Sven-Arne knew he was thinking about the German. A thing like that, to have to leave someone behind, a trifling matter in a war that had cost hundreds of thousands of lives, brought Ante to silence, sometimes for days and weeks. He would refuse to continue his story, became grumpy and got something in his eyes that made Sven-Arne avoid him. The war inside Ante was thundering, a battle noise that seldom quietened. 'The Africans were the worst,' he said finally, 'they fought like animals. They terrified us, as if they did not know what death was.'

The bridge operation, the in part failed mission to cut the supply chain to the Fascist armies gathered just outside Teruel, was something that returned again and again in Sven-Arne's mind. It symbolised something more than the targeting of a poorly constructed wooden bridge.

'The timber was popping in the cold, kind of whiny. It was around minus fifteen degrees Celsius. One of my companions, who was from southern Italy, was also whining. He kept talking about Sicily and the heat. He was a farmhand and used to hard labour. But he hated the cold.'

Sven-Arne never figured out what the bridge stood for. It was just one of the stories he had grown up with.

He rolled over onto his back. It was almost ten o'clock. The voices in the corridor had died down. The hotel had suddenly grown unbelievably quiet.

Sven-Arne stared up at the ceiling where Ante crawled on toward the bridge. The Italian was right after him, thereafter the two Bulgarians. One of them was a miner, he was the one who was going to set the explosives. He was big, almost too big, well over six feet tall and 'wide as a barn door' and Communist like most Bulgarians. He had been a body guard for Dimitrov and spoke both Russian and German fluently.

'I felt safe when "the Brush" was around,' Ante said. 'That was what we called him; the hair stuck straight out of his ears like a brush. He did everything right. He was a good buddy.'

That was the highest praise one could get. Once he had called Sven-Arne 'my little pal.'

But did the Bulgarian actually do what was right?

'It was war,' Ante said. 'Not everything goes like you think it will. You die. No one thought they were going to die. At least not when we landed or came hiking through the Pyrenees; there we were invincible. The Brush did what he could, and more. He was a piece of fly shit, like the rest of us. A speck of dust.'

A good buddy was suddenly a piece of fly shit who didn't mean anything. Sven-Arne wanted everyone to be a hero. Surely the Bulgarian miner did not blow himself up for nothing.

'No, maybe not,' Ante said, and Sven-Arne noticed that his uncle was close to the big silence.

It was as if there was always a fight going on inside him, a battle flowing back and forth. All of the battles had a place inside his head, nothing was forgotten. Not a single speck of dust.

That afternoon on Rosberg's rooftop, when Ante stood up and screamed something in Spanish, was the only time Sven-Arne had seen him really worked up, off-kilter in a way he had never seen him either before or after, but he calmed down almost immediately. Rosberg waved. Perhaps he thought Ante was yelling something to him?

'War is so damned dirty,' he said, before he climbed down.

On their way home, Sven-Arne walked as close to his uncle as was possible.

'Aren't your hands freezing?'

Ante had left his gloves on the roof.
'You can borrow mine. They're big.'
Ante shook his head.

He stood up reluctantly and studied the filthy floor. Then he let his gaze travel over the sparsely furnished room, before he got himself together and walked to the bathroom. The cracked glass of the wall mirror reflected a divided image where the two sides of his face did not quite connect, as if the picture had been cut in two and someone had tried to paste it back together again.

In his reflection, a wide black line ran down his forehead, nose, and mouth like a monstrous column. He turned his head, made a face, monkeyed around, creating new images, fully conscious of the fact that it was a game, a way of postponing the inevitable decisions that had to be made. Soon he would have to decide where to go. The filthy hotel room was a bus stop, the starting point for his new life. His journey to death started here. What was it he had dreamt during the night, a nightmare that had bathed him in cold sweat? In his reflection, he saw himself as an old man with tired features and a muddied gaze that begged for mercy. The nightmare had ridden him like a young woman. She had laughed at his impotence. Weeping, he had tried to hold her fast, but she shrugged off his limp arms.

He looked away and turned on the tap but out came only a few drops and a hissing sound that caused the pipes to vibrate and sing.

'I don't feel so good,' he said out loud but somewhat haltingly, mostly in order to calm himself with the sound of a voice, prove that he could still talk, that he was alive. A dream was a dream.

The shocking encounter with Jan Svensk had shattered much of the defences he had built up over the better part of a decade. He looked straight into himself and it was not an encouraging sight. The repressed feelings of alienation and emptiness, despite the friendship with Lester, his work in the garden and teaching at St Mary's, lay bared, woven together with the lies of his flight.

He realised that the complicated dreams of the night were the answer from his unconscious. They had not let go yet and at night he could not escape. His thin legs trembled, his chest rose in ragged breaths, his hands unconsciously found their way to his genitals, shaped like the faucet and as dry, and he felt a shiver of the impotent lust he had experienced during the night. Staring into the cracked mirror he tried in vain to satisfy his lust while his inner vision of the mocking woman – more and more coming to resemble a young Indian woman in his neighbourhood – became increasingly difficult to catch hold of, blurred at the edges, only to disappear completely.

Not even this, not even his desire remained. He had not made love to a woman for many years. The last time was with a young Indian woman, too young, whom he had been with for a short time. Every time she fumbled for his wrinkled member, he became depressed. Finally he had been unable to achieve an erection. His self-disgust conquered his self-pity and his need for another's hands on his body. He cut himself off, did not want to be some old white lech for whom gratification and artificial warmth were bought for a few simple rupees.

Before this brief adventure, he had had a relationship with a co-worker, a widow barely forty years old, originally from Chennai, who had moved to Bangalore and her brother's family. When her brother died in a head-on collision on the road to Mysore, she was thrown out. She got a job at the botanical garden, living very simply and not speaking much, and she lived near Sven-Arne. Sometimes he accompanied her on the way home; from time to time they had had a meal at some street café.

The whole thing had started with an accident. Sven-Arne was clearing the area around the Japanese garden, picking up fallen branches, sweeping up leaves and paper. It was trivial work, but gave him a great sense of satisfaction. He liked the little oasis, even if the division was painfully neglected and did not have many similarities with a Japanese garden.

When he completed his work, he sat down on the slope to the drained pond. It was early in the morning, still cool in the air, at least in the shade of the trees surrounding the pond. He remembered that he felt happy, not simply because his morning work was done – new sticks, leaves, and papers waited – but because of the stillness of the entire garden. Before the school groups and other visitors arrived, he was shielded from their curious gazes and could think in peace. He used to plan his lectures at St Mary's during this time. These did not take a great deal of preparation but it gave him pleasure to think through some subject or theme.

He stood up in order to make his way down the slope and toward the nursery. Perhaps he had been sitting too long, he had been training himself to sit in a crouch, so that his muscles had become stiff and his joints immobile, for after only a couple of steps he tripped and pitched forward headlong. He automatically threw his hands up to break his fall. When he landed, a root poking out of the ground cut into his right arm, into the flesh from his wrist to his elbow. He remained prone for a while, in shock, shaken by his flight, experiencing a burning pain. Shortly thereafter he felt blood running down his arm. At first he did not even want to look at his injury, as he knew it was serious. His thoughts went – strangely enough – to Ante, and how his uncle with his all-seeing gaze, like a worshipped but also feared god, pointed his finger as if to say that sin punishes itself.

Finally he lifted his head and looked at his arm. The blood was flowing and had already formed a neat pool at the bottom of the pond. He managed to crawl to his feet and felt at that point that one knee had been banged up and that blood was also flowing from his forehead. He fumbled with his shirt, pulled it off, and wrapped it around his forearm.

On his way over to the nursery, he started to think of the consequences. He was not insured, but that was less important as he – in contrast to his co-workers – had enough money to pay for healthcare. What was much worse was the fact that he would be unable to work. He would have to take it easy and recuperate for a while. The routine of going to the garden every day gave his life meaning. A long convalescence, with a lack of assigned tasks and the anxiety-infused thoughts that he knew would come, would throw him off balance just at the time when he after many years had managed to find a kind of equilibrium and peace of mind.

But as it turned out, it was just the opposite. The period that followed the unfortunate accident was the best of his time to date in Bangalore.

After bandaging Sven-Arne with materials from the paltry first-aid kit at the nursery, Jyoti took him to a hospital in Vasanth Nagar that she claimed was good.

The long laceration needed nineteen stitches, his head was cleaned and bandaged, and he received a support bandage for his leg. He was treated quickly and well. Jyoti pointed out that he went before many others. When she saw his expression she smiled and said something he did not understand, but it sounded like a saying.

Jyoti hailed a rickshaw and they went home to Sven-Arne's place, where she took charge and made him lie down while she made tea. His head throbbed and his limbs ached, but he took pleasure in listening to the rattle from the little kitchen alcove.

The next day she returned, changed the bandage on his head, massaged his leg, and made tea.

He was close to tearful gratitude for her attentions. He gave her money so that she could buy some food. Perhaps he exaggerated his pain, made faces when he tried to cross the room, and took his head in his hand as he rested on the bed.

Sven-Arne started to long for the sound of her footsteps on the stairs. Misfortune turned to joy.

After only a week, they embarked on an intimate relationship. He decided that they should celebrate the removal of his stitches and on the way back he bought delicacies, beer, and a bottle of Old Monk. He had imagined that it would be difficult to get Jyoti to indulge, but she ate with a wonderful appetite. They became somewhat intoxicated, she spoke about Chennai and described the life of a single, childless woman. He lied as usual about his life, now without hesitation. The friction he felt in the early days when he narrated his fictitious tale had evaporated.

He looked at her from across the table, wanted her, and

when she got up to clear the table he made some clumsy advances. To his great surprise she did not reject them.

They undressed in the dark, lying close to each other all night, and when she left early in the morning Sven-Arne was possessed with happiness, a feeling from a very long time ago.

She returned the next evening and thereby confirmed their budding relationship. He knew it was not easy for her. The rumour that she was associating with 'the Englishman' and spending the nights there would soon spread. He could only imagine how it would affect her life, but when he asked her, he only received an embarrassed reply.

Their bliss lasted only half a year. Then Jyoti wanted them to get married. She gave him an ultimatum. The rumour of their relationship had reached Chennai. He had to explain he could not get married, but was obliged to lie as usual. He could not give her the real reason. He was already formally married, but above all he lacked an identity. He would never be able to register for anything in India, definitely not a marriage. His invented alias was all too transparent, he was convinced the Indian authorities wanted documents to prove who he was, perhaps a birth certificate.

She went without a word, gave up her post at the garden and left. To Chennai, Sven-Arne supposed, where else would she go?

He asked himself if he would have married, if he were free? He did not think so.

He wanted love, but no longer believed himself capable of receiving it, and definitely not giving it. This insight came to him one day in the alley outside his home. He sat, as he often did in the early evening, on a stool leaning against the wall.

There he could follow life on the street, catch his breath after work, and exchange a few words with his neighbours. A cat, or rather, a kitten, rubbed against his legs and unexpectedly jumped into his lap.

The emaciated body immediately started to purr. It stretched its paws, showed its puny claws, found a comfortable position, and purred loudly. A feeling of well-being arose in Sven-Arne, perhaps it was even love, that such a vulnerable creature found a haven in his skinny lap. He was also slightly ashamed. Would the street's 'Englishman' play a host to a miserable, bony kitten?

But it was as if he grew a little more human with his temporary visitor, because he cherished no illusions that it would ever return. To be a cat in Bangalore was to be jilted, cast aside. Passers-by did not ridicule him, quite the opposite. They paused, stroked the cat, and smiled. And Sven-Arne felt he got a drop or two, he felt they were patting him.

It struck him that he loved the cat and that animals were perhaps the only thing he was capable of loving. Mute creatures who came and went as they pleased, who exchanged warmth, stole a few minutes of rest and security, perhaps a morsel of food, and showed a form of trust in return.

While he slowly ran his hand along the cat's back he thought of Elsa, how much he had taken for granted, and how little he had given in return.

He had not loved. He had simply not been capable. He had loved the cause, the task, the movement. There was his source, the tenacity, after the initial passion had died away, which is necessary in order to have a long life together.

He realised this in a narrow alley in India, miles and years from Uppsala, with a flea-bitten cat in his lap. At that point it was too late. Nothing could be made undone. He mumbled something. A woman passing on the pavement stopped questioningly but Sven-Arne waved her on. At the same time he hoped that she, in some unconscious way, could accept his tardy apology, make it universal, and in this way reconcile him with Elsa. At that moment he wished for nothing else.

'Is it my fault?' he asked of the cracked mirror, well aware of how the answer would sound, raised as he was on Ante's doctrines.

All of a sudden he perceived the smell of cut grass. He stared down at his body but realised his unconscious was playing a trick on him. He was back in his grandmother's cottage, back in Rosberg's fields. Lightning, so strong in his calmness, made his way across the meadow with the harvester as a laughable burden. Rosberg smiled at him. The cap that he always wore from the spring planting to harvest had that jaunty proletarian style that Sven-Arne had never seen after, that reminded him of the figures in Ante's photographs from the 1930s.

TEN

'Maybe it's a Blackfoot Indian,' Bosse Marksson said.

'What are you talking about? Is it a black foot?'

'Well, I don't know about black, but it's a bit charred.'

Ann Lindell tried to picture her colleague from the Östhammar police who was on the other end of the line. She had a vague recollection of having met him, his name sounded so familiar. But she could not conjure up a face to match the gravely voice.

'Do you have a cold?'

'No, I always sound like this. It's hereditary.'

'Okay, and you found this foot in a boot that was bobbing around in the sea.'

'Three mistakes in one sentence; you need someone from Crimes for that. First, we weren't the ones who found it, that was Örjan Bäck; second, it was a sandal; third, it was washed up on the beach.'

'Who is Örjan Bäck?'

'An old friend from school who lives out there. Right now he's home on furlough.'

'A sailor?'

'Right you are, this time.'

'Was he out taking a walk on the beach, or—'

'Örjan doesn't walk, he rushes. Yes, he was on his way to

97

check on his dad's boat. The old man is starting to fail. And he has a prosthesis.'

'I get it. And then he called you?'

'Yes, we're old friends, as I said. He has my mobile phone number.'

Bosse Marksson snuffled. I'll bet he's got a cold after all, Lindell thought.

'And what then?'

She was getting tired, mining her co-worker for information. Bosse Marksson was not one to rush anything, that much was clear.

'I went out there.'

'Of course you did. But can't you just tell me what has been done so far, if you have secured any—'

'Hold your horses, partner. Why don't you come out here so we can chat. I've heard that you're crazy about murders and island life. I'll send some info by email.'

Lindell was taken aback. Was 'island life' a reference to her relationship with Edvard on Gräsö Island? Did all of Roslagen know about this?

'I'll be there at ten a.m. tomorrow,' Lindell said, in a much meeker voice than she had intended. 'Will that work?'

'Bring your boots,' Bosse Marksson said, ending the conversation.

Lindell turned on her computer, but did not log on. She thought about the foot by the sea. Had forgotten to ask if it had belonged to a man or a woman. She guessed the latter. Who wore sandals in November? Perhaps it was a slipper.

Her visit with Berglund and his melancholy had slowed her down, as if he had transferred some of his sadness to her.

She opened the telephone book and immediately found Elsa Persson. She dialled the number but no one answered, and she hung up with a tired gesture. Perhaps Elsa was at the school. Berglund had said she was a teacher.

A faint knock on the door made her jump. Ottosson poked his head in.

'I'm driving out to the coast tomorrow,' Lindell said as a way of anticipating his question. 'And I'm supposed to tell you Berglund says hello. He is a bit tired and I don't think he wants people to come visit, but he does want to get the files from an old case from the nineties. The county commissioner who disappeared, Sven-Arne Gotthard Edvin Persson, has surfaced in India.'

Ottosson stepped into the office, closed the door behind him, and sat down.

'I know,' Ottosson said, 'but Berglund has changed his mind. He doesn't want to look at that case anymore. He called and told me he didn't want it.'

'He wanted another case?'

Ottosson nodded.

'An old homicide where Berglund was the investigative lead. It was at least ten years ago. He didn't manage to crack it. It was an old guy who was killed at Kungsgärdet. You know, in one of those little houses, the sugar cubes, as people called them when I was growing up. Despite prints and a couple of witnesses we drew a blank.'

'He's never talked about it.'

'I think he might feel some shame,' Ottosson said. 'Maybe not shame exactly, but you know . . .'

'Yes,' Lindell said. 'I'll go check out the foot tomorrow. We'll see.'

'That Marksson they have out there is a good sort, but his voice takes some getting used to. His dad sounded just like him. He was also a police officer. He was an extra in *Bathing Devils*, if you remember that film. I'm an Ernst Günther fan.'

Lindell had a little smile on her face long after Ottosson had shut the door behind him. He knew how to handle her.

She logged in and discovered to her surprise that the 'good sort' had already sent her a report on the foot. She printed the document and started to read.

'A foot, female,' she muttered.

ELEVEN

Jan Svensk knew he was paying too much, but nonetheless gave the rickshaw driver a smile, which the driver replied to with a vague shake of the head.

Bangalore's botanical garden was impressive, at least the main entrance. The ticket seller explained that he had no change for the twenty-rupee note that the Swede handed over, which was a blatant lie since the next visitor received a ten-rupee note. But Jan Svensk took it in stride. Normally he would have stood his ground but today he felt generous. Why argue about a couple of pennies, he thought, and walked into the garden. It was easy to be magnanimous in India.

He immediately encountered a man in a wheelchair who offered to take his picture, a memory for life, and then, when Jan Svensk declined the offer, declared he was the best guide in the garden, even authorised. He held up a wrinkled piece of paper.

'No, thank you,' Svensk said, and continued farther into the park before changing his mind and walking back.

'Could you tell me where the staff area is?'

'Do you mean the office?'

'Yes, that is . . .'

He did not quite know how to express himself.

'Do you know if there is a foreigner working here, a European?'

The man came closer, so close that a wheel touched Svensk's pant leg, looked swiftly around, bent to the side and spit, before he answered.

'Englishmen,' he said, and made a sweeping gesture with one hand toward the garden. 'Without the English we would not have had a garden.'

The man smelt of sweat and onion, the bushy eyebrows partly concealed his eyes, and his hands were large with swollen bluish purple veins. Even though he was confined to the wheelchair he emanated strength.

'Guide?'

Jan Svensk chuckled but shook his head.

'No, I am looking for a Swede. I am not interested in flowers.'

He considered offering some money for information, but the man beat him to it by telling him that there was a white man who had worked in the horticulture division for many years.

Jan Svensk took out his wallet and fished out several notes.

'I don't know his name,' the man said.

He took no notice of the money.

'But I do,' Svensk said.

'Are you a relative?'

'No, not at all.'

He put the money in his hand.

'Where can I find him?'

'Go to the little nursery.' He pointed in the right direction.

'It is strange,' the guide said. 'I greeted that man when he came here the first time. I remember it so well, he did not look happy.'

'When was this?'

'Many years ago.'

'Is he happier now?'

'Are you going to make him unhappy?'

Jan Svensk smiled and assured the man he did not wish him ill.

'His name is John.'

'John?'

The guide grabbed at Svensk. 'Don't tell him that I . . .'

Jan Svensk was suddenly infuriated by the man in the wheelchair. He wanted to get away from his stinking breath, the overly intimate hands, and the professional greed that could not be concealed. He was prepared to betray a man for a couple of hundred rupees.

'Goodbye,' said Jan Svensk, and set off at a pace that he did not think the guide could match.

He found the nursery immediately and walked in after a moment of hesitation. Masses of potted plants were placed around both sides of a wide gravel path, shaded by large trees. Even though Svensk was not the least bit interested in plants he found it a convivial sight. There was something peaceful in the arrangements. People moved more calmly. Here there was nothing of the noise and stress of the street, quite the opposite. There was something static about it.

Perhaps it was the collection of everything green that was so refreshing, that caused everyone to move so slowly. A couple of men helped to load earthenware pots on a large cart. Between loads they paused and talked with each other, joking. A woman in a green sari spoke with a man who

Svensk believed to be a staff member. He walked closer. They glanced briefly at him. The woman in green smiled.

He walked around for a couple of minutes, following the paths in the various areas, reading the signs, and to his astonishment he recognised many of the plants from his childhood home. No one addressed him or wanted to sell him anything. To him it was a moment of freedom and he temporarily forgot why he had come to the garden.

Sven-Arne Persson worked here, in this oasis in the middle of a clamouring metropolis? Well, why not, Jan Svensk thought. If one is interested in plants this must be a paradise. No rush and a calm, green colour that was soothing for the eyes, for the entire body.

After a couple of circles he walked over to a woman and asked for 'John.'

'You mean John Mailer? I thought I just saw him. Check with Lester,' she said, and pointed to one of the men who was loading pots.

'I mean the Swede.'

'There is only one European here, and that is John. I did not know he was from Sweden. I thought he was English.'

The man with the pots – Lester – took on a stressed expression as Jan Svensk approached. He said something to his companion, who immediately left them alone. Svensk had the impression that Lester was preparing himself. He turned and looked back at the shop that lay at one end of the nursery. Svensk followed his gaze.

'May I help you?'

'I am looking for a mutual acquaintance: John.'

'He is not here.'

Lester bent down and grabbed hold of a box, but it

was a job for two – the boxes were too heavy – and so he immediately let go.

'But you know him, this Swede?'

Lester's pained smile when he realised the uselessness in trying to appear otherwise occupied, and the fact that his eyes flitted to a spot somewhere next to Svensk, spoke clearly that Lester was a man who had a hard time telling lies.

He scratched himself in the crotch and did not reply.

'His real name isn't John, you know that, don't you? It is Sven-Arne.'

Lester looked up, surprised.

'He's talked about me, hasn't he? That a man would turn up and ask for him, say he was hiding out in Bangalore.'

Svensk felt energised, enjoying the Indian man's confusion and unease, and he knew that his offensive had had the intended effect.

'He has asked you to be quiet, hasn't he? You may be protecting a criminal. What do you really know of this Swede who goes by an assumed name?'

'Are you a policeman?'

'It doesn't really matter who I am.'

They stood quietly across from each other. Lester pretended to study a couple of small birds who were jumping around on the ground, and he was markedly disturbed. Jan Svensk also felt anxiety rise in his body – why was he putting pressure on this man? What did he have to do with Sven-Arne Persson? As far as he knew, he had not made himself guilty to anything criminal. Why then burst in like someone from the Gestapo and beset peaceful civilians?

'He was my neighbour,' Svensk said finally.

Lester nodded absently but Svensk took it as encouragement.

'I don't wish to hurt him, but you have to understand that you get curious if you see a man who has been missing for twelve years. What do you know of his background?'

'Nothing,' Lester said softly.

'Can we sit down somewhere?'

Lester waved toward some recessed areas of the garden. Svensk started walking toward them without a word, came around a shrubby area, and sat down on a log. Lester followed and crouched down, two or three metres away. Svensk thought he glimpsed a smile before he resumed his expressionless face.

'Why don't you tell me where he is?'

Lester stood up and walked over to a shed, the door of which was hanging from one hinge, reached in behind the door, turned his head and gave Svensk a look before he held out an axe.

Svensk stood up. 'What are you doing?'

'I have a job to do,' Lester said, and again sat down in a crouch. The axe rested against the ground, the handle against one knee.

Svensk was struck by the scene. An image, a stereotype, and at the same time a vivid illustration of a worker of the third world, the axe an expression of underdevelopment but also of power. All at once, he became afraid.

Lester's inscrutable expression as he gazed at the Swede did not reveal anything directly threatening but nonetheless a feeling of danger hovered over the little clearing in front of the shed. Perhaps it was Lester's blankness that was most alarming. It could conceal anything.

Svensk looked around. A faint murmur of traffic could be heard, muted by a thin hedge and a high fence.

'I could kill you,' Lester said.

'Why would you do that?'

'You don't know why.'

'Will you let me guess?'

Jan Svensk felt the sweat run down his back and under his arms. I should sit down again, he thought. The Indian nodded and it struck Svensk that he – as opposed to all other Indians – used the nod as an affirmative.

'Our mutual friend is hiding something, and you may be guilty by association.'

'That may be,' Lester said, with an indifference in his voice that increasingly irritated Svensk.

Lester picked up the axe and tested the sharpness of the blade against his thumb.

'I know that John is an honest man, but are you? What do you want with him? What has he done to you?'

'Nothing, as I said. But he is a friend of the family and it is understandable that I am curious.'

He proceeded to tell him about Sven-Arne, that he had been a public figure and that his disappearance had attracted a great deal of attention.

The Indian man did not appear to be listening. He stood up in one swift motion. The axe lay at his feet.

'You may leave now. There is nothing for you here.'

'I can speak with the office.'

Lester shook his head. Suddenly Jan Svensk realised the entire conversation had simply been an evasive manoeuvre.

'He's given me the slip, hasn't he?'

'I am sorry,' Lester said, 'but John does not wish to meet with you. I don't know why, and I don't want to know.'

'Are you involved?'

'In what?'

Jan Svensk did not reply. He turned on his heel but a sudden fury brought him to a halt. Lester jerked back. Jan registered the axe on the ground, had an impulse to pick it up and swing it toward the Indian, but controlled himself at the last moment.

'Fucking hell,' was the only thing he managed to get out.

He ached with a feeling of having been deceived. Sven-Arne Persson had probably been nearby but was now gone and probably in a rickshaw on his way somewhere where he would never be found again.

'I am staying at Hotel Harsha. Please let him know I do not want to hurt him,' he said finally, and left the nursery at a rapid clip, without looking back, without bothering to find out how everyone was reacting to his exit. He was certain they were laughing at him behind his back.

'Damned Indian scum,' he muttered, and kicked a pot so that it rolled off, struck a fence post by the entrance, and cracked.

A lizard crossed his path and Jan Svensk was gripped by an irrational hatred of the land to which he had been dispatched. He found a deep unfairness in the fact that he was forced to put up with this chaos of exhaust fumes, lizards, and fugitives.

Sure, he could leave Sven-Arne Persson to his fate and round off his last days in Bangalore in the same routine that he had worked up, like that last time when he had put up with Singapore for three whole months. For three months he had perspired on the streets on the way to work only to freeze in the air-conditioned offices.

But the feeling of having had the wool pulled over his eyes constituted a bigger defeat than having been taunted. His search for the county commissioner had unconsciously been what he had used to repress the ever-intensifying discomfort at his stay in India. The creeping feeling that everything was partly a chimera, all this chaos that his work and the work of other people was creating.

For his overall impression of Bangalore was chaos. The new technology that was to revolutionise and improve life, speed up communications between people and continents, had a back side that appeared in a clearer light. He had sensed this before, all puffed-up successes in the IT industry, all castles in the sky that had been built up and collapsed, and then the short memories of people as new bubbles were blown up.

They said the future was being built in Bangalore. Was this what it was supposed to look like? Was this the price we were supposed to pay? Or 'we,' he thought as he walked quickly through the avenue of mango trees, it is all of these stressed Indians with their exhaust-induced coughs who will pay the highest price. Was it progress that more and more could ride motorcycles in a country where hundreds and millions had to struggle for their day-to-day survival?

Most of all, he wanted to pull out of the entire mess. But not to return home. During his last conversation with Elise the resentment had bubbled up in both of them, the growing aversion to a marriage and life that was running on autopilot. He sensed a connection but could not grasp it clearly.

His humiliating exit from the nursery was now added to the string of failures. He stopped and watched a group of schoolchildren that had sat down on a large lawn. The children's clothing was identical: The girls had blue dresses and the boys were in blue shorts and white, short-sleeved shirts. Their backpacks were neatly stacked against each other. One of the teachers was trying to attract the children's attention and managed to do so surprisingly quickly given that there were at least fifty children.

The teacher spoke in a stern voice, reprimanding, a little nagging. He looked displeased, not to say outright mean. Jan Svensk sat down on a bench and studied the children. They whispered to each other, moving around almost imperceptibly, teasing, in appearance unconcerned about their teacher, accepting a blow on the back or head without a change of expression or desisting from their civil disobedience. The mass of children was admittedly obedient, but in such a way that their freedom appeared limitless. They led a life out of reach of the tired and increasingly irritated teacher. He was large, he had a stick, but he was powerless.

All of a sudden a flock of children broke away from the rest in order to fill up their water bottles from a tap. The teacher lunged in order to herd them back, but at the same moment a minor tumult erupted on the other side of the group. The teacher hesitated for a moment before he ran forward to the tap where several of the children had already managed to get their fill. While the teacher reproached them, the other children continued to fill their bottles. Some received a rap on the arm, another one had her hair pulled, but most of them escaped the teacher's assault.

Svensk looked on with amusement. The teacher glared at him. Svensk smiled back. The unfettered joy of the children and their anarchic behaviour made him forget about the county commissioner until a park labourer walked by pulling a cart loaded with leaves and sticks.

Jan Svensk rose hastily from his seat on the bench and walked down the rest of the avenue leading to the exit.

TWELVE

Good God, how she had cleaned house: first the anguish and the fury, thereafter the physical memories, all these objects and papers, folders and photographs, and finally, thoughts. And then the call from Rune Svensk. She was still sitting as if turned to stone, one hand on the receiver and with her gaze fixed on the spot where the hedge gave way to a poorly painted fence, the border to the Svensks' house. Twelve years of effort to build an independent life came tumbling down in an instant. At first she did not believe her neighbour, then she was angry that he had called rather than come in person, and finally there was just paralysis.

She knew that Jan Svensk had not been mistaken. Sven-Arne lived.

The past few years the memory of him had only come back to her from time to time. It could be a smell or a phrase that made her think about Sven-Arne, but then it was never as heavy and piercing as in the beginning.

If only he had died of a heart attack she would have been able to grieve and talk about him as a widow, receive condolences and pretty talk, put on a suitable face and then slowly but surely resume her own life.

But he had been swallowed up by the earth. So typical of Sven-Arne: always the big words about solidarity, but when it came to the small details he was a worm who, egotistically enough, simply disappeared. And in this way, as always, he had the last word. She could never be done with Sven-Arne, shut the book and go on. The uncertainty and the speculations that surfaced from time to time – most recently around the ten-year anniversary of his disappearance – meant that she could not end the chapter.

She had never believed that he had committed suicide. He was too much of a coward for that. Most likely it was a woman – she did not want to use the word 'mistress' – who had led him to leave everything: his family, career, and politics.

During the first few months she wanted to stand on the main square, at the county labour meetings, or at City Hall, and just scream out her rage. But it was only Anna-Stina, who had been her best friend since adolescence, with whom she shared her feelings.

When a year had gone by her anger started to fade. She became reconciled with her husband's disappearance. Or rather, the fact that he was missing made her more conciliatory.

Her financial situation had become more strained, but that wasn't something she took hard. She had never lived extravagantly and could easily adjust to a more meagre budget. The feeling of having been abandoned gave way to a sense of freedom. She took care of everything herself, she did not have to put up with his monologues at the breakfast table and all of his papers, 'documents,' that lay spread out around the house. After only a couple of days she had burnt them in the fireplace.

Now she could not even think the thought that he would float up again, she did not want to imagine him alive. If he were to return to Uppsala against all expectations, she would immediately demand a divorce.

But it would make one person happy: Uncle Ante. Elsa had never understood the love-hate relationship that had existed between him and Sven-Arne. They had almost always fought; it could be about trivial matters, but above all about politics. Nonetheless, Ante was the relative that Sven-Arne had maintained the closest contact with over the years.

For a while she had suspected that Ante conspired with Sven-Arne, that the uncle was in on why and how her husband had disappeared. He denied it, but Elsa was never really sure. If there was anyone to whom Sven-Arne would confide, it would be Ante.

Now he was in an assisted living facility, as good as immobile, one leg amputated below the knee.

His life had consisted of hard labour on the farm and in the forest, thereafter many years as a plumber, and the last few years doing facilities maintenance at a school. That had been easier physically, but with Ante's temperament it was stressful enough. He was always irritated by the students, seeing them all as hooligans. In 1980 he finally reached retirement age.

Despite his handicap he was unbroken mentally. He seldom to never complained about his aching joints or the vertigo that he suffered – this, Elsa had to admit, was his greatness – but instead he had started to express himself about society with more frequency and intensity, high finance and the 'overlords.' He had been a Communist for seventy-five years and he was still the same: incorruptibly loyal to the ideology. Elsa knew that it was this that had both appealed to and irritated Sven-Arne.

She got up from the chair, walked out into the kitchen, but only to sit down once more. She stayed there, staring unseeing into the garden and her thoughts on her husband, whom she had once loved so much. Back then, forty years ago, when he was a plumber – which in hindsight seemed like the most honourable of all professions – he would return all filthy to their little flat in Petterslund, imbued with many smells. There was sweat, welding smoke, a rough smell of iron, and something organic that she could never figure out what it was. It was simply Sven-Arne.

He used to sit down in the kitchen, his hands resting on the table, always with raw knuckles and soiled wrists, and he would smoke a cigarette, every Friday downing a Pilsner, and talk about the events of the day. There was rarely anything out of the ordinary.

Sven-Arne was not a forceful man, but there was a strength in the stories he told and in the lazy tiredness that characterised him an hour or so after his work was done. He did not brag, but Elsa could discern a sprouting self-confidence surrounding him.

She, who had just started her studies, daughter to two teachers, let herself become intoxicated by his scent. There was something exciting, if not forbidden, then veiled in his world, concealed from her. But she could taste it by way of him, his experiences at work, and she felt it so strongly that first year that she would always remember the smell of the young, optimistic plumber, captured by the marked physicality of his being at the kitchen table. You are my man, she often thought, and she laid so much love in those words, which gave way to an increasing distance when the smells disappeared and his wrists were no longer soiled but clad in shirt cuffs.

114

Sven-Arne started to talk labour unions and politics at the kitchen table, at first casually and with nonchalance, but later – as he became schooled in his profession and the professional community and became more secure in his role – with increasing self-confidence and precision.

He did not appear to realise how this affected her. That was at least what she believed then, forty years ago. But a long time later, when, as a politician, he started to use his experiences from the workplace and his class background, she was struck by the thought that he had always been aware of his position in society, and their relationship. A sort of self-sufficient class pride that he may have sensed attracted her. But at the same time he excluded her – the teachers' daughter – from his world. He was a man whose justification lay in his story, in the trade he plied and in the language that he spoke. She believed that her education and her future role as university instructor both attracted and frightened him. None of his co-workers was married to an academic.

For many years, Elsa had longed to get back to that feeling in the kitchen, the peaceful chatter and the smell of sweat and welding, even though she understood that it belonged to a time gone by. Now and again, when he had been drinking, the old words and phrases could come back. Then he laughed, for a moment freed of the politician's mask that he had so carefully adopted. He grabbed her, heavily, drawing her to him, clumsily but with determination. She liked it, but was also embarrassed, because of his lust, his own weakness. Finally she pushed him away, disgusted with her two-faced husband.

* * *

Elsa thought about calling the assisted living facility to tell Ante that Sven-Arne had been spotted in India, but she decided to wait and go to see him instead. Maybe she could surprise the old man and get him to reveal something? If he really had been in league with Sven-Arne.

THIRTEEN

He cursed himself. How could he have been so stupid as to return to the garden? He should have left town. He knew that Jan Svensk came from an unusually stubborn family. He was probably like his father.

It was only sheer luck that Svensk had not caught him. Sven-Arne had observed him entering the nursery and taken refuge in the little shop at the back of the garden, and there he had hidden himself away while Lester had detained Svensk.

He had watched him leave after a while, and in the Swede's movements he read anger and frustration. It gave him no satisfaction. Instead, he just felt guilty. Jan Svensk was probably not a bad man, he was simply curious.

Lester immediately came into the shop. He was amused, that much was clear, but made an effort not to show it.

'He has gone now.'

'I saw that,' Sven-Arne Persson said, with curiosity but at the same time unwilling to listen to what Svensk had said.

'Do you know where Harsha hotel is?'

'Of course,' Sven-Arne said, 'in Shivajinagar, not far from Russell Market.'

'If you want to, you can find him there.'

Lester smiled, and Sven-Arne did not understand what was so funny.

'Sven-Arne, is that your name?'

Lester had such a peculiar pronunciation of his name that at first Sven-Arne did not catch it.

'No, my name is John Mailer. I am John Mailer. And what would I want with him?'

'I don't know,' Lester said, 'but he said that you had been a powerful man in your country. That you were a politician and in charge of many, like a governor. It confused me.'

'A powerful man!' Sven-Arne stared at his co-worker. For the first time in twelve years, Sven-Arne mistrusted his motives. What was he trying to say?

'I am not powerful,' he said. 'I am just a human being like anyone else.'

'You are an unusual person,' Lester said slowly. 'You may have a terrible past.'

Never before had he censured the Swede, never snooped in his background or his reasons for coming to India, never questioned his work as a day labourer in a botanical garden, and had never pressed him in this way. For that was what it was. In his words there was a criticism, Sven-Arne understood this.

'You may be a murderer,' Lester went on, unconcerned.

Sven-Arne stared at him, even more perplexed.

'It is of no consequence to me.'

'What do you mean? Do you think I—'

'It does not matter who you were!'

A couple of shop clerks looked up.

'Here in India we are equal,' Lester said, now much more softly, 'at least those of us who dig in the earth. Even if you had been the governor it doesn't matter. You have no servants here. Here we are equals.'

Sven-Arne relaxed. He smiled at his friend and took hold of his left upper arm, squeezed it and felt the sinewy muscles under his shirt.

'I won't leave Bangalore immediately,' Sven-Arne said abruptly. 'I don't think the Swede will come back. And it may be a while before he returns to Sweden and talks. He may go to the police, I don't know, perhaps my . . . It doesn't matter. I will stay here a few days, then we will see.'

'Can't you talk with this old neighbour? Perhaps convince him to keep quiet?' Sven-Arne knew that Lester was testing him. If he had made himself guilty of 'something horrible' in his homeland, then chances were minimal that Jan Svensk would be willing to forget the whole thing.

'I think he will tell his family and they will not be able to keep quiet.'

'And if you ask him to?'

Sven-Arne smiled.

'Shall we get back to work?' he said, and felt a sudden surge of joy. He needed the exertion of digging, weeding, watering, and carrying pots in order to keep his thoughts from Sweden and his former life, from the threat of being exposed. This last day had been discombobulating. He had not been able to think clearly, but it was as if his talk with Lester made everything fall into place again. Perhaps he didn't need to worry? If Jan Svensk was going to announce his 'find' in Bangalore when he returned home, who would believe him – the county commissioner as day labourer in an Indian garden? Would anyone take the trouble to travel all the way here in order to check it out?

Sven-Arne Persson decided not to let Svensk trouble him any longer. The humiliation he experienced when he left Lal Bagh need not awaken any need for revenge; instead Jan Svensk might prefer to forget the whole thing. Sven-Arne convinced himself that the Svensk affair was over.

FOURTEEN

Two days later Jan Svensk stood once more at the entrance to the nursery. He was one of the first that morning to have bought a ticket to Lal Bagh. This time he had demanded to get the change. He had nodded at the man in the wheelchair and quickly walked past him without a word.

He walked down the main path with a determined stride, so different from the hesitant steps he took last time, scanning the side paths with radar alertness, rounding a thicket, and there, by the shed out of which Lester had taken an axe, was Sven-Arne Persson sitting on a low, three-legged stool. He was setting the teeth of a saw. He moved the file back and forth across the teeth, paused and tested the sharpness with a finger, then continued with his work.

His long, bony back was bent over, the hair on his neck sparse, a little grey, and sticking out in different directions. Through a tear in the dingy tank top that Sven-Arne Persson was wearing one could see his spine.

It had been a long time since Jan Svensk had seen someone sharpening a saw, in his childhood maybe, at his uncle's, whose cleverly stacked woodpiles were known all over Järlåsa. For a moment he felt uncomfortable at the idea of interrupting his work, but nonetheless took a couple of steps closer. The sound from the file was mechanical and regular.

'Hello there, Sven-Arne.'

The filing stopped, the county commissioner stiffened but did not turn.

'I come with greetings for you.'

Sven-Arne turned his head. The look he gave Jan Svensk was filled with disgust, not fear; pure unfettered loathing, as if his visitor had brought with him a stinking load of something intended for the heap in front of the shed.

'You recognise me, don't you? We were neighbours. I have . . .' He fell silent, unsure how to proceed.

Sven-Arne put down the file. 'You should leave,' he said. 'It's not good for you to be here.'

Jan Svensk looked around. 'What do you mean?'

'Go. My friends are here. You have no place here, unless you are looking for work. Do you want to dig? Can you dig? Eight hours a day in ninety-degree weather. Not much pay. Can you even begin to—'

Sven-Arne's fury caused him to fling the saw aside.

'Don't you come here with your questions and your shit!'

'There's no point in threatening me. I don't want to hurt you, and you should know that. I've got a message for you.'

'I don't want a message! I want to be left in peace, and *you* should understand that!'

Sven-Arne had risen to his feet and stretched out his right hand, pointing at his visitor. Jan Svensk noticed a scar that stretched from his hand far up his arm.

'From your wife, Elsa.'

Sven-Arne dropped his arm and stared at the intruder.

'Elsa,' he managed to get out.

Jan-Svensk nodded, vengefully pleased at the shock he

had managed to cause, but the message he had to deliver was no joyful greeting.

'She has been run over by a lorry and is currently unconscious.'

'Then how can she send me a message?' Sven-Arne spat.

'They operated on her and she has not woken up. But before then she was able to speak.'

'Speak?'

The former county commissioner had trouble envisioning his wife 'speaking' as if she were standing at a podium, orating.

'Your parents must have squealed.'

Svensk nodded. His mother had bumped into Elsa Persson on the street outside the row of town houses where they lived. She was barely recognisable. The normally so well groomed and balanced woman had looked 'terrible', with her hair in disarray and her features twisted in a combination of confusion and anger. Margareta Svensk had asked her if she was all right. At first Elsa Persson had simply stared at her neighbour, as if she did not understand the question or even recognise who she was. Then she had burst into tears.

Margareta Svensk had pushed open the gate and firmly guided Elsa into the house, taken off her coat, and prevailed upon her to sit down at the kitchen table. And there she had sat with a catatonic gaze, muttering, crying, and cursing.

'And what did she want to tell me?'

'According to my mother she had been to see your uncle Ante,' Svensk said placidly, unaffected by Sven-Arne's aggressive tone.

Sven-Arne stared at him in bewilderment.

'He must be one hundred years,' Svensk continued. 'I

remember him from when I was a child, he was old even then.'

'Get to the point, you bastard.'

Sven-Arne Persson tasted his own words. It was the first time in twelve years that he was speaking Swedish with someone eye-to-eye.

'She was extremely upset by the visit. When she came home she was like a zombie. Mother had all the trouble in the world getting even so much as a single word out of her. When she had calmed down a little, she went home. One hour later, my mother saw her leave again. Then came the police. According to witnesses she had gone straight out into the traffic on Luthagsleden Expressway. The light was red, but she walked straight out. A lorry ran over her.'

Sven-Arne sank down on the stool.

'Why did she get so upset? The day before my mother had told her that I had seen you here in Bangalore and she took it in stride. She actually did not react at all. "I see," was all she said. No questions, nothing, but then after visiting your uncle it was as if her whole world came crashing down. Ante told her he was working on his memoirs and that all would be revealed. What did he mean by that? My mother didn't get it. Do you?'

Sven-Arne did not reply. After a long period of silence Svensk sat down in front of him.

'What are you doing here? Why did you leave?'

Sven-Arne looked up.

'Because I am a traitor,' he said finally.

'What or whom did you betray? Your wife?'

The one-time county commissioner snorted. He saw an image of Uncle Ante. The old man was still affecting his life.

124

'Almost one hundred.' Yes, in ten years. He would probably live another ten years. What had he said to Elsa?

'How did you get out of the country?'

'By air, of course.'

'But you had left your passport at home.'

'There are other ways,' Sven-Arne said. 'I was a parole mentor. I did that for about twenty years. Small-time guys whose life had taken a wrong turn. I got to know a bunch of them real well, some of them became my friends. They taught me a lot.'

He let the words sink in, proud in an indeterminate sort of way over the fact that he had managed to trick everyone and go up in smoke without leaving a trace. He had often wondered if he had left some clue behind, but realised now that everyone was still puzzled by his disappearance.

'I was a court-appointed guardian as well,' he went on. 'John Lundberg recruited me. There are no politicians like him anymore. Talk about betrayal.'

'What do you mean?'

Sven-Arne shook his head. He didn't really want to talk politics, especially not about the movement he had served for almost four decades, ever since he had become a member of SSU Club in Svartbäcken as a fourteen-year-old, but for some reason he was pulled into the discussion. Maybe because for the first time in twelve years he had an audience, the old rhetoric floated up like a greeting from an age gone by.

'If you look at the party, the one I belonged to, as a body – a living organism – then it was poisoned in small doses. Gradually there were changes for the worse, so that with each new generation it developed a new handicap, a new defect.'

125

'But you were part of that body,' Svensk objected. 'You were Mr Socialist around town.'

'I know. But I left.'

'And ended up here?'

The politician turned day labourer nodded and smiled tightly.

'Here,' he repeated, and waved his hand, 'in the centre of the world. Right here, in this insignificant little garden, is the centre of the world. For Lester and for everyone else who works here. We see the world from here and it looks very different compared to the perspective from Uppsala City Hall.'

'Why Bangalore?'

'There are worse places. I do good here. The garden I help to plant will survive both you and me.'

'Was coming here a way to make amends? For your sins in the rich-man country of Sweden?'

Sven-Arne chuckled.

'Have you seen anything of India, other than your air-conditioned office?'

'Not much,' Jan Svensk admitted. 'But you gave up on the ones who believed in you. You were popular, people liked you. I know Dad talked about it all the time: If they hadn't had Sven-Arne then . . .'

'That's a load of shit,' Sven-Arne said, and stood up. 'You don't understand anything. You must be one of these IT idiots who comes over and destroys this country. What do you know about suffering?'

'Then tell me! I'm not as stupid as you think. And if you think that computer technology and the Internet is destroying India then you haven't understood one iota of the world.

You go around planting trees and that's fine, but there is also another world. People want to meet each other, not just in a garden but online. Last time I was here I saw a school class playing in the park. Do you think they want to be labourers when they grow up?'

Sven-Arne turned on his heel and left, with steps at first as if he wasn't sure he wanted to leave his countryman and their exchange, but the closer he came to the exit the more he hurried his pace, so that finally he was half running out of the garden.

Lester and a handful of his other co-workers observed him but did nothing to stop him.

They did not know it was the last time they would see the man they had got to know as John Mailer.

FIFTEEN

They walked through the forest. Bosse Marksson had told her that the original owners of the land – an older couple with no children – had subdivided the property bit by bit to make way for half a dozen holiday home lots, and sold the remaining acres to a retired executive director ten years ago.

'They had a small farm, which is common around these parts. A free life, but a slog, you could summarise it,' he went on once they had reached the beach.

They looked around. The sun reflected in the water and created a play of sparkles when the occasional breeze ruffled the surface.

'Can you see the sheep fence?'

Lindell nodded.

'The new owner, the General as he was called, got himself four sheep and fenced off the whole lot, stopped people from using the docking places they had used for a couple of generations, and put up signs saying it was private property. He even pulled the fence right through a lilac bower. It hadn't mattered before, if a couple of lilac bushes had ended up in the wrong spot by a couple of metres, but the General corrected all that. It was like the Berlin Wall through a coffee table.'

'What had he been the executive director of?'

'Oh, I don't know.'

They walked a while before Marksson suddenly stopped.

'Here it was,' he said, pointing. 'You've seen the photos.'

They remained standing at the spot. Nothing about the little stretch of beach was out of the ordinary: some exposed rock face, stretches of nothing but round stones sanded by the water, occasional juniper bushes and unruly mops of brown-yellow grasses. A few metres from the shoreline there was a tall pine tree, at least seventy centimetres in diameter at the base, which supported a rough trunk and a sprawling crown in which half of the branches were dried up.

'You searched . . .'

'Yes, all of the forest up to the gravel road, about a kilometre in each direction, but probably more carefully to the south. We found nothing. At least no matching right foot.'

'Why more carefully to the south?'

'As I wrote in the report, we thought a fox had dragged the foot here, and it couldn't have got through the fence to the north. We had snow a couple of days ago and I saw fox tracks myself not far from here.'

'So you think it came from the south? If it was a fox.'

Marksson nodded.

'You wrote that there are thirty-eight properties in a radius of a thousand metres. You have of course visited all of them?'

'Yes, we've gone door-to-door in a much bigger area than that. All the way to Näsviken and along the road to Almbäck.'

The place-names did not mean anything to Lindell, but she was convinced her colleagues had put in a considerable amount of work. She looked out over the bay, which was more like a gulf carved into the land. On the other side of the water, about eight hundred metres away, there was a low wooded ridge, connected with the mainland by a thin strip of land. The open sea lay to the south. Smoke from what she guessed were chimneys rose up from the point. She glimpsed a couple of houses but the shoreline was completely undeveloped. It had surprised her earlier that such large areas were untouched, although development on the coast had been significant, with the construction of holiday homes for residents of both Uppsala and Stockholm. The legal protection of the coastline had worked more or less as intended.

'It's sheltered in here,' she said, indicating the bay.

'Yes, Bultudden Point acts as a wave breaker towards the north and east,' Marksson replied, after a long silence.

She had grown used to his voice. The fact was that he was indeed a 'good sort,' as Ottosson had claimed, not particularly chatty but communicative and open. Lindell guessed that it had mainly been her prejudices coming into play – assuming that a policeman from the most remote part of the county would be dismissive and patronising toward a female colleague from the big city.

'What do you think? You have far greater experience,' he said, as if to confirm his unusually enlightened attitude.

'I don't know. You've done a good job so far, but I see nothing in this material that gets me to think—'

'We have one observation that seems more exciting,' Marksson interrupted. 'About a week ago a car came down into this area, past the General's place, and it returned after half an hour. The General's wife keeps an eye on everyone who comes by.'

'And she didn't recognise it?'

130

'No, nor could she say what kind it was, other than it was small and red.'

'Then we have a couple of kinds to choose from,' Lindell said.

'At this time of year most of the summer cottages are closed up. People may come out on the weekends, but other than that it's quiet.'

'But there are full-time residents farther down the road?'

'Four of them, but none of them have or have had visits from any red cars, as far as they say, at least.'

'Too late for mushroom pickers,' Lindell said, mainly to herself. 'Is there any hunting at the moment?'

'No.' Marksson chuckled. 'Not legal, anyways.'

'You think the foot belongs to a foreigner.'

'I don't know about foreign.'

Lindell smiled to herself. 'Blackfoot Indian' and 'charred' was what Marksson had said on the phone.

'Size five,' she went on. 'Can it be from a child, or a teenager?'

'I don't think so. It looks well used, as it were. We have combed through all the missing-persons reports from a couple of years back and there is no one who matches this foot.'

'Can it have washed ashore?'

'It's possible, but the doctor didn't think so. No, I believe in the fox. There were also marks of what I think are teeth. They can run quite a ways with a tasty foot in their mouth.'

The conversation came to a halt there. The offshore wind had increased somewhat but they could still cling to the illusion that they were on the beach on a summer's day as long as they kept their gazes fixed on the sea and disregarded the patches of snow that remained in the shadowy areas below the thickets of alder behind them.

Lindell closed her eyes and let the sun warm her face. She felt Marksson stealing glances at her but did not care. She felt a stillness that was the first she had in a long while. The surge of the waves and the occasional cry of a gull only underscored the compact silence that reigned.

God only knows how long she would have stood cemented in this way if her colleague had not coughed discreetly.

'The kind of place that's hard to forget,' Marksson said.

She smiled at him and nodded, grateful that he did not mention Edvard in so many words. Edvard, who was possibly as little as twenty or so kilometres away as the crow flies. Nonetheless his words let her understand that he sensed what might be stirring in her mind.

They walked back to his car. The path they followed was trampled by animals, and snaked through the sparse deciduous forest. Marksson went before her and Lindell followed him with her eyes, his back and shoulders. Along the way she grabbed some alder cones, smelt them, and let them rest in her hand before she forcefully tossed them back into the thickets, unexpectedly near to tears. Not on account of the woman who had so violently lost her left foot but because she felt she had walked along this kind of path so many times before.

Back in Östhammar they had coffee at the police station. Marksson was more than willing to admit that they had hit a wall. This had been evident to Lindell the day before when she had read his report. She had the feeling that he did not want to proceed, that he had simply given up all attempts to find the owner of the foot. He never said as much and would never have admitted it. After having stated that all avenues, all reasonable and unreasonable hypotheses, had been aired and examined, it was easy to lose focus and unconsciously grow comfortable with the idea that the investigation had come to an end. This gave way to a period of doubt in one's own abilities, mixed with anger over the fact that no one else appeared to have come up with something conclusive. Finally it gave way to a creeping feeling that one was wasting all one's time, while at the same time other, newer cases made claims on one's attention.

She recognised this from her own investigations. Her role was to breathe life into this ice-cold thing.

They were on to their second cup. Until now there had only been small talk.

'I have to head back to Uppsala now, but I think it's good I got to see the place,' Lindell said. 'I'm going to think about it. As I said, you seem to have done everything—'

'Not well enough,' Marksson interrupted, 'or the whole thing would be wrapped up by now.'

'It's a bit hard with only one foot,' Lindell said, and he smiled.

'I heard you have a little one,' he said.

Lindell nodded and pushed the coffee cup across the table.

'It's hard to drive back and forth,' she said. 'It may be a colleague of mine who takes over. Then you'll have to take that walk all over again.'

Marksson shrugged.

'A little legwork never killed anyone,' he said.

Lindell raised her eyebrows at his word play. Typical male pig of a policeman, she thought, but couldn't help smiling when she saw his mischievous look.

SIXTEEN

The label read ERIK AND ANN LINDELL. Next to it was a sticker with the wholesome message *No advertisements, public notices ok*.

She had asked the building manager to put up both names. Maybe in order to give the impression that a couple lived in the slightly cramped two-bedroom flat, and for this reason the man – even though he was preschool age – had come first.

The bone-white letters had ended up slightly askew. The last *L* had a phallic look, pointing up at an angle, or else it was a leg about to march off, out of the sign.

A female neighbour had once asked her if she was from Jönköping. Lindell had explained she was from Eastern Götaland.

'I was thinking of the scales,' the neighbour said. 'You know, the scales.'

Ann did not know what she was talking about, but the woman was a bit peculiar, as Sund – another neighbour – liked to point out. She received an explanation much later. It was in an antique shop, into which she had been tempted by an assortment of glasses in the window. On a sideboard there were some scales, manufactured by Lindell's in Jönköping.

She flicked the glass in front of the names. The *L* toppled forward and onto its back. *A* jumped and ended up somewhat inclined to the left.

'Why are you doing that?' Erik asked.

He asked many questions, almost all the time.

'I don't know,' she answered.

He was satisfied with the answer, but took the opportunity to flick the sign himself. The second *L* followed its friend and fell forward, while the *A* jumped back up.

Ann chuckled. Encouraged by having made her laugh, he knocked it again. Now the *E* fell down completely.

'—rik,' Erik read.

He could read well even though he had not started school. He knew all his letters and could sound out the most difficult words, so 'rik' or 'rich' presented no problems.

'Are we rich?'

Ann shook her head, took out her keys, and unlocked.

'No,' she said. 'But we aren't poor either.'

She decided she would talk to the property manager. Even if the flat looked a bit messy, the sign on the door didn't have to.

Erik went into his room. The floor in there was right now covered in small plastic men that he arranged in long rows according to an intricate system that she – despite Erik's long explanations – could not manage to make head nor tail of.

Ann unpacked the bags from the grocery shop, but it was the foot that occupied her thoughts. It had been sawed off, that much was clear. 'A big-toothed saw, perhaps a power saw, or possibly a bandsaw,' the pathologist had written in his report. There were traces of vegetable oil on the foot.

She realised that up to this point she had spent much too much time thinking about whom the foot belonged to and not about the perpetrator. Who saws off a foot, and why? A psychotic killer? Someone who has been wronged?

She fetched the map of Östhammar, its archipelago, and found the bay, Bultudden Point, and the places that Marksson had mentioned. She now saw that the Östhammar police had covered a considerable area in their door-to-door investigation.

Assume approximately one thousand people lived in the area – excepting Östhammar city – as well as summer residents. One of these was crazy enough to take out a big-toothed saw and sever the limbs of a woman with a shoe size of five. She was convinced the body had been cut up in order for the perpetrator to have an easier time getting rid of it. Or else it was a result of the fact that the killer, even in death, wanted to humiliate his victim, a ritualistic completion, as if the murder itself was not enough.

Lindell pushed the grocery items aside, sat down at the kitchen table, and let her gaze sweep over the map. The remarkable thing was that no one who could be a match had been reported missing during this time, now almost two weeks since the foot had been found.

She searched with a finger across the map, tracing the roads curling through the landscape, turning in to farms and groups of holiday houses, stopping at road crossings, taking turns, turning around and going another way; trying to imagine a crazed driver, perhaps desperate and careless – a foot had been misplaced, after all – maybe cold and calculating, pieces of a woman's body in the trunk. Maybe a red car.

Had the foot been put on the beach deliberately? No, she reasoned, no one was crazy enough to leave such traces after himself. But if there was something really twisted behind the deed, then perhaps the foot should be seen as a kind of message? Would more feet turn up, haphazardly strewn around the area?

'Mama, I'm hungry.'

Erik had snuck up behind her back without her noticing.

'Of course,' she said, putting the map away. 'I'm just putting dinner on. We're having lentil stew.'

'I want sausages and mashed potatoes,' Erik grumbled.

She had made the stew the night before so all she had to do was heat it up. She stood up and put away the remaining grocery items left on the table, setting the table while the stew simmered on the stove, and prepared a pitcher of lingonberry cordial, Erik's favourite.

Erik plunged into 'twenty questions' while they ate. He had started to take a serious interest in her work. Having a mother who was a police officer afforded a little bit of status at day care. In part it made up for the unfortunate fact that he did not have a father to brag about.

'If a thief gets nice again, is he let out of prison?'

'Sure,' Lindell said, who did not add the fact that most thieves never ended up in prison.

'Can you tell if a guy is a thief by the way he looks?'

'No, they can look like anyone.'

'Johannes says that all thieves have a screwdriver in their pocket.'

'Maybe some, but not all of them.'

'It's for breaking in,' Erik explained.

If only it were that easy, she thought. That everyone with a screwdriver was a bandit.

'Have you ever caught a thief?'

137

'Once or twice, but most of the time I work on people who have done other dumb stuff they shouldn't have.'

Erik looked at her.

'Eat a little salad,' she said.

'Murderers,' he said abruptly. 'The guys who shoot people.'

'Eat,' Lindell said, even though she knew very well he wouldn't drop the topic.

'I know you catch murderers,' he said. 'That's what my teacher says.'

'What teacher?'

Erik heard from her voice that he was out in unchartered waters, skillfully dropped the question, and started on another line of inquiry.

'If all the nice people had police cars, then that would scare the bad guys,' he said.

'Yes, maybe that would be a good idea,' Ann said, and scraped the last bit of food from the plate. 'Did you eat any salad?'

Erik sighed and took a piece of cucumber from the bowl.

After dinner, Erik turned on the television, inserted a video, and sat down. Ann had made a cup of coffee and stood in the doorway to the living room. She observed her son, who was engrossed in *Monsters, Inc.*

He would start school next autumn. He was looking forward to it, often bringing up the exciting subject of starting school. Maybe he was hoping to find the answers to all of his questions there. His mother unfortunately did not know everything.

Where do you get all of your energy and unflagging curiosity, she wondered. Maybe your father was a little rascal too. 'The Engineer,' as Ann secretly referred to Erik's father. She had no name and barely any memory of how he looked. Erik was the result of a couple too many glasses of wine, a desire for skin and a sweaty night.

Ann Lindell had been a shy and quiet child. She only came to life in her teens, as far as that was possible in a place like Ödeshög.

She returned to the kitchen, worried that she did not know what she should do with Östhammar. If she became engaged in it, the trips back and forth would pose a complication. Not that Erik would suffer, she would drop him off and pick him up at day care the same time as she had been doing all autumn.

But long drives were tiring, as was a murder – as she and everyone else assumed – investigation. It devoured energy, she had noticed that after only one day. She could say no, she knew Ottosson would give in. But how fair was it to dump the foot on someone else? Haver had his hands full, on the job and at home. Sammy Nilsson was overladen with work and the bandy season was in full swing. He trained kids and youths two nights a week. Fredriksson had grown too tired. Lindell could not imagine him driving back and forth to the coast, and he would not get along so well with Marksson. They would not function well together. Berglund was laid up for a while and Beatrice, no, that wouldn't work.

She got out the pad of paper that she kept on her bedside table, flipped to a clean sheet, and started to write down questions.

SEVENTEEN

After leaving his workplace, Sven-Arne Persson immediately went home. He had a mist before his eyes that only let up once he was lying on his bed. He did not speak, he did not think. All his energy was focused on staying in motion.

Slowly but surely the impact of what Jan Svensk had told him started to seep into his consciousness. He accepted the fact that Elsa had been run over, without much surprise. He tried to imagine her under a thundering lorry but could hardly recollect her face anymore.

The fact that Uncle Ante was writing his memoirs, however, and that in these he would 'tell everything,' terrified him, since he knew what Ante was capable of. When his uncle decided on something he was almost impossible to divert from his cause. The fighter from the Teruel front took no orders.

Sven-Arne tossed and turned on the bed, thumping his fist into the wall and cursing all damned Swedes and above all the one with the very name of the Swedes, Svensk. He went through the events of the past few days, and above all he returned to the visit to Koshy's. Why had he gone there when he had received so many signs along the way that something was up? He should have better interpreted the signals. Instead, he had walked straight into the establishment in a foolhardy manner, to his doom.

What had Ante told Elsa that had made her so upset? What was there to tell, except one thing? Elsa had heard, seen, and understood everything that had to do with him, perhaps even better than Ante. She was the one who had seen through him both in public life as well as in the bedroom. He was for her the impotent rhetorician, the personification of hypocrisy. When he had claimed that it was her coldness and clumsy manner that had made him impotent, she was not hurt – as he had intended – she laughed. She had laughed straight in his face, and in order to humiliate him further, had taken out the dildo she had bought many years ago.

'This is my county commissioner.' She had grinned and moved the mechanical member up and down.

She, who had shown no genuine happiness for years, had laughed.

Now she had become bewildered to the point that she had stepped out in front of a lorry. Not intentionally – Sven-Arne was convinced of that. Elsa would never willingly take her own life, that much he knew. Not the Elsa he knew, not with her calculating logic.

And yet now she had been thrown off her stride. Unconscious. He came upon himself wishing she would die. No, he recalled those thoughts. It was too low. The one whose turn it was to die was Ante. He was old. Why should he start to blabber? The last time they talked, half a year ago, he had seemed spry, at least not confused and demented. Quite the opposite: He had analysed the Swedish political situation of the day more clear-sightedly than in a long while. He had taunted the prime minister, who, like a nobleman, was renovating a manor house in his castle-rich home district.

'He probably also has tenant farmers,' Ante had declared cheerily, as he always did when he wanted to take aim at some elevated social democrat.

No, it was not very likely that he was confused. He would probably die with a cutting phrase ready on his lips.

Sven-Arne decided that Ante must have upset Elsa by saying that it came as no surprise to him to hear that Sven-Arne was in India. It must have hit hard, the discovery that his uncle – a man that Elsa had always disliked – had known these past twelve years what had happened to her husband. It must have been a blow to her pride. She had been doubly betrayed. Thus her bewilderment, and the anger that had come after the initial shock.

He decided that this was what had transpired. Everything else was unthinkable. The mention of memoirs was just idle talk. But on the other hand, if they were published posthumously he would be victorious even in death. For who would seriously be able to criticise the old man, and what would be the point? It was Sven-Arne who would become the target, he would be publicly flogged, hung out to dry. His sentence would be another matter altogether.

He stood up from the bed so quickly that he grew dizzy.

'What's the point?' he screamed.

He already knew the answer. He would have been able to live with the consternation and the general hullabaloo, the critique, the outrage, yes all this he would have been able to take, but he would never again find peace. Not one second of peace. He would be pursued wherever he steered his course. Public interest would never wane, everyone would want to know. To know! All of these damned Swede-bastards who devoured all the shit, hair and all, wallowing in the mass

142

media's rubbish. They consumed the rotting headlines with a ravenous appetite, as if they were delicacies, and slurped up the offerings of retarded hoaxers as if they came from the king himself.

Ante's triumphant voice would ring in his ears, whether or not the old man was dead. He had nourished himself with bitter fruit ever since he had returned from Spain, now some seventy years ago. The old man had become broken down, but his ideology had turned to stone and remained unchanged by the tooth of time. He was going to rub his poisonous balms into Sven-Arne's open wounds.

As a fourteen-year-old on the roof of Rosberg's barn he had sensed something of Ante's dream, it was as if he could touch it, and since then he had never been able to cut that feeling out of his chest. When Ante said 'someone has to do it, it's just that simple,' Sven-Arne had interpreted it literally. That time it had been about Rosberg's roof. Twenty years before it had been about the Spanish Republic.

But Sven-Arne had also seen something deeply tragic in his uncle. The adults had quarrelled about Budapest in Grandmother Agnes's kitchen. The fact was that the people of Hungary were being trampled.

Sven-Arne chose a different path. He joined SSU, which pleased his father but gave rise to a lifelong conflict with Ante.

Now he just wanted some peace and quiet, to work in the garden, to teach the children at St Mary's, get his shave at Ismael's once a week, chitchat with his neighbours on the street, have a beer and drinks with Lester. Nothing else. He had no passions left.

Lies! He could touch the lie, it lay like a swollen cadaver before him, stinking, but as a politician he could close his nostrils. He had done that so many times before. At the budget preparations, in pre-election discussions, at county and judicial meetings, in Poland on the fuck-and-drink trip underwritten by the Skansa company in return for which they were allowed to buy land at bargain prices, on the way to New Zealand when Lisbet Manner vomited on the plane, started to cry and became emotional. Conservative bitch, he had thought then, but pushed it away. Once they arrived, more sobbing and tears, but he had held his tongue rather than reveal the whole spectacle.

He should have dragged everything into the light, but shadowed it instead, playing along like the power politician that he was. How often had he not kept silent with the truth in order to protect his own position and due to his loyalty to the party? And perhaps also out of consideration for a political system that appeared to be the only one possible.

But deep inside – this was a conclusion he had arrived at after many years of pondering in India – he had not wanted to grant Ante that he was right when he thundered about corrupt politicians bought by the capitalists, even if he agreed with much of what his uncle had to say. It would have been too painful. The decision he made as a fourteen-year-old to get involved would have been a gigantic mistake. The fact was also that Ante's dream society did not seem so tempting. The constant, hardened defence of eastern socialism undermined Ante's legitimacy. He disqualified himself, even if Sven-Arne understood that Ante in his heart and soul did not approve of either Stalin or Gomulka. What Ante was defending was something else, the right of the worker and the dream of revenge.

You made it so damn easy for yourself, Ante! You placed yourself outside, leant on a Bulgarian miner who ended up blowing himself up, you sang your old songs and you shovelled snow. You did actually shovel snow. You put your gloves down on the ridge of the roof so that I would have a warm place to sit.

But you couldn't save the republic. You blamed the governments of Western Europe while your Communists were advocating the same superpower politics. How many times hadn't they gone over this subject?

1956. How old you were already – forty-one years – used up in a way that not even Grandmother or Rosberg were. Your movements were often impulsive but in a reflexive way, as if nerves and muscles allowed themselves to be steered by old, accustomed signals but did not reflect an inner life. The spark you showed was habitual, sadly antiquated.

You were strong – no one in our family could measure up to you – but at the same time inexplicably weak. Back then there was an oomph in your movements, it was reminiscent of a time when physical labour gave a man the legitimacy to speak for many.

I understood all this – others saw only your impetuousness, your anger and dogmatism. You became a clown.

The years after the Spanish War were hard. No one wanted you. You were a skilled plumber but got no work. You were – like the others who joined up – blacklisted. Anders Diös laughed right in your face, as did Lindgren and Quiet Kalle. As Europe was choking under the Fascism that you had tried to fight, you were being mocked.

You became a farmhand and felled trees in the forest in the winter. It was not a good fit for you. You wanted noise and masses of people around you. A farmer in Rasbo – even if he was decent enough – was nothing for you. You were widely known as 'the Bolshevik.'

The royal family and nobles gathered at the county manor house. There were hunting parties and dinners. You knew what they were toasting to, the table servants reported it back to you.

You refused to work as a beater at the great elk hunt.

You lived in a tumbledown cottage among other tumbledown cottages. The old woman Björk and her daughter in Sandbacken gave you cheese, eggs, and rugs. There was never enough of anything, your large body begged for more, and the floors were cold. You held Björk in high regard. In her there was nothing of the blood-red that you were fighting for, only humility, but also a warmth that must have saved you from the deep despair you must have felt.

Then it turned. In 1943 the forest was a terrible place to work but you were warmed by the news from the eastern front. The manor house dinners did not decrease in frequency but the intoxication of victory was transformed into a fear of the red hordes that threatened to roll back the German war machine. How far it would reach was the question they anxiously posed.

You triumphed in 1944, agitating in Film, where the party received twenty-six percent of the vote, you got a job with a smaller construction manager firm, you were put on foundation-laying jobs in Almtuna and Svartbäcken, moved into town. The tide had turned.

You fell in love unexpectedly. Ann-Marie, who lasted eight years, even managed to get you to learn to dance.

Is this what you are going to cover in your memoirs? If so, they could be good. If you could start in the poor cottage kitchen of the forties, when desperation overcame you, to the sound of a weaving loom and the rattle from the neighbour's kitchen in Sandbacken, among the only confidantes you had, and then look back, to Spain, to the hovel on Dragarbrunn where Emil, Erik, and you grew up, then it could be really good. But I know you, Ante, you want to get even.

You neither can nor want to write some sugary working-class epos, because how would the Bulgarian miner fit in? There would be no place for your never-ceasing fury, it would fight itself free and destroy the inveterately sentimental. No, it would be overwhelmingly sentimental, because in actuality Ante was a romantic, something that Sven-Arne had pointed out on many occasions but that Ante had always dismissed with an angry snort.

Sven-Arne Persson was in agony as never before. His entire life – a mirror image of his uncle's – was mercilessly exposed, and it was hardly an encouraging sight.

'That bastard,' he said out loud.

For a long time, Sven-Arne had wanted to become like Ante, but also not. He wanted to be, if not loved, then at least liked, and Ante was neither. Sven-Arne wanted to win but Ante had always bet on the wrong horse, and what irritated Sven-Arne the most was that his uncle appeared to favour the losers.

He sat down on the bed and tried to think clearly. He laid out the problems as if in a numbered list: First, he had been recognised. Rumours that the former county commissioner was alive – and how he lived! – had probably already started to circulate in Uppsala. Second, Elsa had discovered Ante's duplicity. Third, Elsa was badly injured, lying unconscious in a hospital. Fourth, his situation in Bangalore would become untenable – journalists would soon appear. Fifth, Sven-Arne Persson was dead. He was John Mailer. He had no passport and could not leave India.

These were the known facts. Then came some hypotheses: Elsa knew of Ante's plans to write his memoirs but did not know what they might uncover. Or did she? Was that why she had become so upset? Lastly, if Ante felt that it would benefit him and his survivors then he would tell all.

He lay down, stared up at the ceiling, and went through the seven items. After half an hour of deliberation, he got up and went out to make two calls, the first to Delhi and the second to a former colleague in Sweden. A man who did not hesitate to make himself guilty of manipulation if it were to the benefit of the party or himself, a man who Sven-Arne Persson did not believe had ever planted a tree his whole life, a man who had had enough of scandal and would probably do everything to avoid yet another.

After the calls he felt ashamed. He thought of Lester and the others at Lal Bagh.

EIGHTEEN

Berglund thought so much about his old murder case that his head started to hurt. An old headache becomes like new, he thought, and recalled all the days, evenings, and nights he had turned Nils Gottfrid Dufva's life – and above all, death – inside out.

Nils Dufva's death was due to blunt trauma to the head. A single blow would probably have sufficed, Kalle Modin observed. He was still in service then, before he was fired for ongoing alcohol abuse. That was actually the last service he performed in the name of law enforcement.

The strike had caught on the left side of the head, pushed in the skull bone, and caused a massive haemorrhage. Modin thought that Dufva had not died immediately, but later during the night.

When he was found – about twenty-four hours after the murder – he was lying prone on the floor, in front of his wheelchair. The remote control was in his hand. The TV was on.

The murder received a great deal of attention: The brutal slaying of a wheelchair-bound eighty-five-year-old was especially disturbing. The Letters to the Editor section of *Upsala Nya Tidning* was filled with agitated voices and the newspaper took the unusual step of interviewing a notorious thug, Runar Karlsson, who had been apprehended for assault a thirteenth time. 'I only beat people who have a chance of defending themselves,' he communicated proudly from the Norrtälje prison.

If Dufva had been sitting at his desk, and not in front of the television in the living room, he might have had a better chance of defending himself. In the uppermost, unlocked drawer of the desk there was a loaded army revolver, a Luger. No weapon license could be found, but Dufva could no longer be consulted.

A burglary was immediately suspected, but nothing appeared to have been touched or removed from the house. This did not rule out that the intruder may have originally been intent on robbing the old man, but ended up overcome by panic and fleeing the scene.

The front door was closed but not locked when the man's niece – actually his first cousin twice removed – came by to visit him. She did so almost daily, although not on the day of the murder. The woman, who was in her twenties, was his closest relative in Uppsala. He had a cousin in Malmö and another who lived in southern Germany. The cousin in Skåne was seventy and had not met Nils Dufva for over twenty years. They had no contact whatsoever. It was the cousin who lived in Pforzheim who had arranged for his granddaughter, Jenny Holgersson, to look in on Nils.

There were a couple of clear prints on the glass pane of the outer door. The same fingers had left prints on an old-fashioned oak sideboard in the living room. It appeared that someone had pressed hard with the palm of their hand on the polished door of the sideboard. Berglund had always suspected that the owner of the hand had stumbled, or lost their balance, and steadied himself with his hand. In addition, the rug under the sideboard was noticeably wrinkled.

In the hall they secured the very unclear print from a men's shoe, right foot, size ten.

That was all.

The motive was unknown. The most likely explanation was still a failed robbery attempt. There was around two thousand kronor in a kitchen drawer. There were few items of any value, a gold watch for long and faithful service, some antique sables, a set of tin plates from the seventeenth century, and three gold rings in a case in one of the desk drawers. There were also five medals, of which one originated from Finland and two from Germany.

In a small room off the living room there remained that which the intruder had probably been searching for: one of the most distinguished coin collections. The value was appraised at over three million kronor.

The entire collection was to go to the Uppland museum, according to Dufva's will. Everything else – the house, furnishings, close to two million in a savings account in SEB, a stock portfolio worth almost as much – was to be shared equally between Jenny Holgersson and a scholarship fund that Dufva had written up the statutes for a couple of years earlier. It was an annual scholarship of at least 30,000 kronor for the 'person or organisation who best serves to further the independence of the nation.'

For three months Berglund had basically spent all of his time on the case. Thereafter, it became more sporadic. Most of the murders that the Uppsala police had investigated in recent times had been solved, even if in one case, 'the man from Dakar,' they could not track down the perpetrator.

But Dufva's killer was still on the loose. And it was Berglund's case.

He sat at the window with a couple of folders in front of him. This was not really in accordance with regulations. The material was not supposed to leave police headquarters, but when Berglund pointed out that perhaps it was not completely kosher to peruse internal documents in a hospital room, Ottosson had lightly waved it away.

He had read everything, the forensic report, the interview transcripts, and everything else, several times.

There were three witnesses whom Berglund found trustworthy. Dufva's neighbour on the other side of the street had seen a car stop and park outside Dufva's house sometime between eight o'clock and half past eight on the night of the crime. She had only glanced out the kitchen window since she was preoccupied with preparations for a birthday celebration, and she had not seen more of the driver other than that he was a man. Later, when she went out with the dog at around nine, the car was gone.

Berglund had browsed through car models with the woman and finally she had picked out a Saab 9000, a 'dark blue shiny car.'

Shortly before eight, a younger couple who were walking from their home on Tegelgatan and turned down toward Arosgatan had seen a dark car come driving up Norbyvägen. 'Much too fast, there are so many children biking on these streets,' the young woman had said.

They were almost certain it was a dark Saab, but neither of them had seen the driver nor been able to tell if he was alone in the car.

Early on in the case Berglund had decided that this was the car of the killer. It also fit the time frame. The pathologist had determined Dufva's time of death to be between seven and nine in the evening.

This was where the case stood at the end of 1993, when Berglund reluctantly de-prioritised it. Nothing new had emerged since then. Everyone at the station was convinced it would never be solved, unless something extraordinary occurred.

What Berglund had been hoping for all these years was the fingers on the sideboard. Perhaps the perpetrator would be brought in on other charges, burglary for example, and then be tied to the old man's murder.

Or was the crime a one-time act that would not be followed by others? There were those who said it was the work of an amateur. To drive over and park in full view indicated terrible planning. Moreover, it was perplexing that nothing had been stolen. Dufva had immediately been as good as dead, no one had heard any noise, so why not continue and search the house?

Panic, Berglund thought. Perhaps the intention had been to temporarily silence the old man, to muzzle him and take time in picking out the valuables. And then he died. One blow on the head had been enough. The unwilling murderer had fled the scene in a panic.

Five years after the murder, Sammy Nilsson had come into Berglund's office. He held a book in his hand.

'Turn to page 233,' he said.

Berglund looked at the title, then turned to the page. The name 'Nils Dufva' was highlighted in yellow.

'An unusual name,' said Sammy Nilsson. 'I read it last night and jumped. Is that our friend from Kungsgärdet with the crushed skull?'

'What is it about?'

Sammy Nilsson explained that Nils Dufva was listed as one of the Swedes who had tried to rebuild the Nazi movement in Sweden after the Second World War. He had played a prominent role.

'If he was a Nazi after the war, then he was probably one before and after as well,' Sammy Nilsson said.

'There are more Uppsala residents in here,' Berglund exclaimed.

'Yes, a furniture dealer, a builder, and a lieutenant at the regiment.'

'That was the one, I've shopped there,' Berglund went on. 'We bought a dining table there in the sixties. If I had known . . .'

'That was nothing they advertised,' Sammy said. '"Buy the Himmler sofa" is not exactly a catchy slogan.'

'He's listed in here as "employed in defence". What does that mean? Did he work in the warehouses of S1, or what?'

'It's mysterious. I think I remember him as having worked in an office before retirement,' Sammy Nilsson said.

'But we didn't find anything at his home . . .'

Berglund broke off. He recalled the medals from Germany.

After that he put down a great deal of effort in trying to chart out Nils Dufva's earlier life. He even contacted the author of the book that Sammy Nilsson had stuck in his hand.

The author, a historian from Göteborg, had no further

information about Dufva other than that during the fifties and sixties he had probably been employed by some organisation within the defence department, maybe the military information service.

When Berglund wanted to keep researching this he came to a dead stop. Dufva was not listed in the defence registers. No one wanted to or could give him more meat on the bone. One theory was that Dufva had been subcontracted by the defence department through the private company who employed him.

The company was called Bohlin's Agency and was dissolved in 1989. When Berglund started to delve into what Bohlin's Agency had worked with and who had managed it, he found an August Bohlin, deceased that same year.

His son, Jerker Bohlin, who worked in Florida, had told him over the phone that his father had worked with tax declarations, accounting, and wills. He had not been a lawyer or accountant, but had always kept busy. If the company had been hired by the defence department he did not know, but found it hard to believe.

According to the son, his father's clients were mostly elderly women. One summer he worked at his father's company and said it might as well have been a nursing home. He visited old people in Luthagen who had to sign documents. Company papers were probably no longer in existence.

Jerker Bohlin had a faint memory of the fact that he, after his father's death, had stored a couple of boxes with folders in a storage unit in Boländerna where he kept a few things he wanted to save but not ship across the Atlantic. He still retained a storage unit.

He had naturally met Nils Dufva many times over the

years but had no idea what tasks he had undertaken or how he had been as a person. Dufva was not a talkative sort. Bohlin remembered, however, that Dufva collected old coins.

Berglund had the feeling that no one wanted to dig in all of this, at least no one who had any information, but he still received permission to look through the remaining documents in the storage unit.

These turned out to be an unholy blend of copies of agreements, contracts, and estate inventories, spanning a period of twenty years. Berglund looked through the papers without encountering anything out of the ordinary. August Bohlin had clearly maintained his papers in an exemplary order; everything was sorted and numbered. On many of the documents, in his beautiful and delicate handwriting, he had made comments of an exceedingly personal character. In an estate inventory he might have said 'a most honourable person who unfortunately passed away at too young an age', whereas another one received the appraisal 'a scrooge who never made anyone really happy except on aforementioned date'.

Berglund had still taken the trouble to write down all the names that appeared in the documents, without nursing any real hope about its usefulness, and attached the list of names to the case files. Then he had returned the five boxes to the storage unit, contacted Jerker Bohlin, and asked him to keep the documents from his father's agency.

Now here he was, seven years later, at the Akademiska Hospital, looking through the materials. The leads were colder than ever. The ones who could talk were either old or gone for good, or simply unwilling to cast any light on Nils Dufva's career.

Whether Dufva's past had anything to do with his murder was as unclear as before. If the intention had actually been to take out the old man then the deed was almost macabrely amateurish. A natural preventive measure would have been to try to conceal such a motive by stealing such items as could have been carried off, in order to make the whole thing appear as a straightforward robbery-killing.

'Saab 9000,' he muttered. 'It pulls up, parks, drives away.'

He could picture the whole scene: the curious neighbour, her hands in the dough, peeks out but turns away to take a tray of cinnamon buns out of the oven. The man gets out of the car and walks up to Dufva's door. The concrete walkway is five, six metres long, the stairs have three steps.

Does he walk straight in, does he ring the doorbell, or does he even have keys? Whichever it is, he gets inside. Dufva is in a wheelchair and defenceless against his attacker, who rushes toward him and hits him in the head. The power of the blow sends him tumbling to the floor with enough force to kill him instantly.

Did the murderer bring the weapon or simply pick an object at the scene? Jenny Holgersson, the cousin twice removed, did not believe that anything had gone missing, but admitted that she did not have an exact inventory of all the items in the house. The murder weapon had never been located.

The film played in Berglund's head in meaningless reprise, but the sequences rolled of their own accord.

His headache intensified. The effect of the tablets he had been given in the morning had worn off. He was still worried, although less so with each passing hour, that the operation

157

would cause permanent damage, that he would lose his sense of balance, speech, or memory, or anything else that would happen to make a normal life impossible.

He had attempted to walk in a straight line from the door to the window following a seam in the flooring. That he could manage. He had recited the names of all the towns in Skåne, Blekinge, and Halland, the capital cities of Europe, and the English football teams in the highest league. He had managed that too. He understood all the words in the Dufva files and when he read aloud to himself his tongue did not slip once. His handwriting was as even and legible as before.

He would make a complete recovery. What was a little headache compared to when they carved in his head?

He was going to struggle through the Dufva files one more time and find the despicable individual who had clubbed a defenceless eighty-five-year-old to death.

Berglund got up and went back over to the window. He stood there for a long time looking down at the people in the street below and the small parking lot for which there was so much competition. Now they could come, the rascals from Violent Crimes.

He glanced at the stack of papers on the night table and smiled to himself.

NINETEEN

Nilsson, Ottosson, Fredriksson, Haver, and Beatrice Andersson were all listening to Lindell's lecture, but as if through a silent pact none of them revealed how comical her enthusiasm sounded. On the table she had spread out about a dozen photographs of the site and the surrounding area.

She was talking about the archipelago.

'It's chilly out there now,' Sammy Nilsson said.

'Not really,' Lindell said, 'the sun was shining, it was idyllic.'

'If it weren't for that foot,' Beatrice said roughly.

Lindell shot her a look.

'Can you describe the shoe?' Haver asked.

'One of those Chinese shoes made of cloth, with a strap across the foot, size five.'

'It sounds more like a slipper this time of year.'

Lindell smiled at Haver. He wanted to start bouncing off ideas.

'Exactly,' she said, and remembered at the same time that she had decided not to use that word so much.

'So, you're going to look into it?'

Ottosson's question was more of a formality. He knew now that it was Östhammar and not Öregrund, it was no longer an issue.

Lindell nodded.

'I started reading up on it last night.'

She told them about Bosse Marksson observing fox tracks in the snow and getting the idea that an animal had dragged the foot to the spot. In fact he could not imagine another scenario. You just don't go running around with a severed foot, as he put it.

Ottosson smiled sweetly.

'All right,' he said. 'If we look after things around here then you can head out to the coast. Or will you wait until tomorrow?'

'I have some things to get done today,' Lindell said, and stood up as she gave Beatrice a long look, but it was only now that she realised why Beatrice had had that expression and the ironic tone of voice.

Her colleague had never made any bones about the fact that she found Lindell's attachment to Edvard on Gräsö Island bordering on the unhealthy. During one party Ann Lindell had explained to Beatrice that she had left that episode behind her, but Beatrice – emboldened by wine – had told her to stop lying to herself and others. Why hadn't she taken up with anyone new if Edvard was a closed chapter? Lindell had left the party.

And now Beatrice had the stomach to joke at her expense at a case meeting. Lindell decided to ignore her.

The night before, Lindell had called Elsa Persson's home telephone repeatedly but no one answered.

Even though Berglund had chosen another case, she had promised to contact the county commissioner's wife, and therefore she decided to go out to see her. To be honest she was curious about what she looked like and above all how she had reacted to the news from India.

160

Lindell fetched her car from behind the police building and drove out toward Luthagsleden Expressway. After a quarter of an hour she turned onto the street where Elsa Persson lived.

Number 17 did not stand out noticeably from the row of houses that looked like a set of attached boxes. She parked, observed that the newspaper was still sticking out of the mailbox, got out of the car, and walked up the few steps to the front door. Not a sound could be heard on the cul-de-sac.

The doorbell was discreet; a faint buzz sounded. After a second try and a minute's pause she gave up.

'Are you looking for Elsa?'

Lindell turned. A woman had appeared in the door of the next house over.

'Yes, actually. My name is Ann Lindell, from the Uppsala police.'

'I see,' the neighbour said doubtfully. 'Are you investigating the accident? But then you would know . . .'

'What accident?'

'You haven't heard?'

Lindell walked closer to the low fence that separated the properties. She saw that the woman had been crying.

'Maybe you could tell me what happened,' Lindell said.

She was invited into number 19 instead of 17 and got to hear the whole story at the kitchen table.

'Did you know her husband?' she asked when she had a clear understanding of the facts.

'Of course,' the woman said. 'We lived right next door. And I know he has been seen in India recently. It must have been a shock for Elsa. Poor woman!'

Lindell saw that the neighbour was close to tears again.

'I know this is upsetting, but could you tell me a little more about Elsa?'

The woman gave her a quick look.

'What do we know about other people's thoughts,' she said finally.

'But she must have said something.'

'You say one thing, but maybe . . .'

She fell silent.

'Tell me what you're thinking.'

'Honestly speaking, I think she was just happy that Sven-Arne disappeared. But Elsa is so controlled, so measured when it comes to emotions. She was brought up that way. She is a teacher,' she added after a short pause, as if this could further explain Elsa Persson's reserve.

'But then for some reason her world fell apart?'

The neighbour nodded.

'Could it be something financial?'

'I don't think so. Elsa managed well, and I don't understand how a dead man's unexpected return could disrupt her life in terms of money. But there was something that threw her completely off balance. She is not an absentminded person, she would never walk out in front of a car like that.'

'Do you have any ideas?'

'She talked about Sven-Arne's uncle, Ante Persson. I have met him as well. He used to write letters to the editor. A real troublemaker, even in older days. He was against everything. Elsa has never liked him. I think – and now I am speculating – that the uncle said something when Elsa visited him right after she had been informed that Sven-Arne was still alive. He lives in a home – Ramund, I think it is – you know, the assisted living place in Eriksdal.'

'What could he possibly have told her?'

'Elsa said she had been betrayed. That uncle and Sven-Arne were close, maybe they had been in cahoots.'

In cahoots, Lindell thought, and visualised two figures gathered around a pot of stew, nursing secrets.

After a couple more minutes of conversation, Ann Lindell felt she had a clear picture of the situation. This restrained woman, Elsa Persson, had been completely thrown for a loop, that much was clear. It was enough to awaken Lindell's curiosity, but she decided to drop the matter. Now at least there was something to report back to Berglund. Maybe he wouldn't care, now that he had dusted off his old murder case, but she had done what was expected.

TWENTY

'There's something I've been thinking about,' Allan Fredriksson said.

'I see,' Lindell said flatly. She had hardly woken up. She looked at the time: a quarter past seven. Why is he calling so inhumanly early, she wondered, and immediately received her answer.

'I'm going in for a procedure, so I thought I would catch you before you head out to the coast.'

Lindell had not heard anything about a procedure.

'I was looking at those photographs yesterday,' Fredriksson continued. 'Where they found the foot. There was a tree there, wasn't there?'

'Yes,' Lindell said doubtfully, 'there was . . .'

'A pine,' he determined. 'At first I thought it was snow, but then I didn't see snow in the other pictures.'

'There was snow out there,' Lindell said, completely baffled by what Fredriksson wanted. And what kind of examination was he undergoing?

'But not at the scene?'

'No, that area was in full sun, but where are you going with this? It's a little hectic around here, Erik is eating breakfast.'

'An eagle,' Fredriksson said, his tone suddenly crisp. 'The

164

streaks on the tree are eagle droppings. It is an eagle tree.'

Now Lindell sensed what he was getting at. She smiled to herself. Fredriksson was the division's forest and bird fanatic.

'It's not a fox, it's an eagle.'

'You mean . . .'

'Exactly, an eagle was sitting with the foot in the tree when something startled it, it lost its hold of the foot, and flew away. Eagles have favourite trees, a tall pine is excellent, it has a good lookout from there. Maybe it's even a nesting tree.'

Lindell had no problem imagining the eagle. She had seen many sea eagles at Gräsö Island. One winter's day when she had been ice fishing with Edvard, five had been circling above the bay below Edvard's house. She knew that they could get big, with two-and-a-half-metre wingspans, and that they could carry large prey. Viola, Edvard's landlady, claimed once to have seen an eagle with a pig in its claws.

'I don't know if it means anything,' Fredriksson said modestly, but had trouble concealing his satisfaction.

'It could mean a great deal,' Lindell said. 'It could mean—'

'—that the foot came from a long way away,' Fredriksson inserted. Lindell was silent for a few moments. She visualised the bay with Bultudden Point on the other side.

'What kind of procedure are you having?'

'Routine examination,' Fredriksson said.

Lindell was tempted to ask more but ended the conversation by thanking him for the tip.

'It's nothing,' Fredriksson said, and hung up.

Meanwhile Erik had been trying to pour more yogurt

into his bowl all by himself, but with mixed results, and had thereafter managed to tip the box of muesli on its side.

'Good work,' Lindell said. 'We don't need bowls anymore, we can eat straight off the table.'

A couple of hours later she was back at the bay. 'Bultudden,' she murmured quietly to herself, and let her gaze sweep over the terrain and come to rest on the tall pine. The crown of the tree looked strange, the branches like fingers outstretched to the sky. It was probably the result of a lightning strike.

Fredriksson's theory that it could have been a nesting tree was not implausible. There were a number of old sticks in the palm that was created, but not enough for a whole nest. Perhaps the work had been interrupted.

The remains of droppings on the trunk, dirty white streaks, had been left over a long period of time, that much she understood.

The foot had been found next to the tree on a bed of pine needles. She decided to adopt the theory as her own, and dialled Bosse Marksson, who was in Forsmark checking on a series of summer cottage break-ins.

He explained the way to Bultudden Point. There was no direct route from where Lindell was located, so she would have to retrace her steps to the main road, take a right turn north and drive a couple of kilometres, then turn south again.

Lindell did not tell him why she wanted to go out to the point and Marksson did not appear the least curious. He also did not ask her why she wanted the mobile phone number of his friend who had discovered the foot.

* * *

She parked outside the first house half an hour later. Marksson had told her that there were seven properties on the point, but strangely enough none of them were holiday homes.

Lindell stepped out of the car and looked the two-storeyed house up and down. She estimated it dated from the forties, now in terrible condition. The red siding was faded and flaking and the metal roof was corroded. Some twenty metres to the right there was an older barn and a few other smaller structures.

Lindell thought she glimpsed movement in one of the windows and sensed that she was being observed. The gate was hanging on its post and the gravel path was thick with weeds. Beds planted with perennials lined either side of the path, the withered remains of which breathed neglect.

When she was halfway to the house, the front door swung open and a man appeared. He was dressed in blue work clothes, and was about sixty and almost completely bald. He stared at Lindell for a couple of seconds before he launched into a string of invectives.

'Go to hell! I said no, got it? The fact that he sent a woman doesn't change anything.'

Lindell stared back at him with astonishment. The outburst came completely unexpectedly and was so forceful it took her aback. He lifted one arm frenetically in a gesture that indicated she should leave, and his almost distorted facial features intensified with a next salvo.

'Can't you hear me? Go to hell!'

He slammed the door hard. A flowerpot on the porch railing fell down and broke in two.

Lindell walked over to the window where she had thought

she had caught a glimpse of the man, took out her police identification, and held it up against the windowpane.

After half a minute the door swung open again.

'Who the hell are you, anyway?'

'Are you always this hospitable?' Lindell said with a smile.

'Are you from the police?'

She nodded. The man backed up into the hall and gestured something that Lindell interpreted as an invitation.

Torsten Andersson – Lindell had noticed the name on the mailbox – pulled out a chair at the kitchen table. Lindell sat down. She saw that he was still agitated but there was also curiosity in his eyes.

'Are you putting on a pot of coffee? It's been a while since I had a cup.'

He looked at her for a moment, shook his head, then turned, opened a kitchen cabinet, and took out a jar. His hands shook.

'New coffee maker?'

'The old one went bad,' he said, his back turned.

As he supplied the machine with water and coffee and set out two cups on the counter, he snuck glances at the table, but never met her gaze.

He is not used to company, Lindell thought. His movements were awkward and he executed everything very slowly, as if he had to think about each step.

The cups came to the table, as did a sugar bowl and a creamer filled with milk.

'You must be wondering what I'm doing here.'

'Is it about the hens?'

'No, it's about a foot.'

She explained why she had come to Bultudden, but said nothing of the eagle theory.

168

'A severed foot,' he said with disbelief. 'Who cuts off a foot?'

'Is it you?'

He twisted around, a plate in his hand.

'Just joking,' Lindell added hurriedly.

He muttered something, took a couple of cinnamon buns that he had thawed in the microwave and slid them onto the plate, then planted himself to wait in front of the coffee maker.

Everything in this kitchen seemed to take time. Lindell looked around. The forties atmosphere was reinforced by the cabinets.

'You don't have the wood stove going.'

'Only morning and night,' he answered gruffly, pouring out the coffee and sitting down across from her.

They drank in silence. The man made a gesture with his hand as if to say 'help yourself' and she picked up a cinnamon bun. It was still warm. She smiled and chewed, the man peered out the window, but she noted that he was furtively observing all of her moves.

'And I do have a wood-burning furnace in the basement,' he said.

Lindell nodded.

'Wonderful cinnamon bun.'

'They're from Margit.'

'Does she also live out here?'

'Next place over,' he replied, and nodded his head to indicate a southerly direction.

She took out the map that Marksson had given her, and laid it on the table. Torsten Andersson leant over it inquisitively, almost eagerly, as if he had never before seen a map of the area. Suddenly his hand shot out.

'This is where we are,' he said, 'Margit and Kalle live over there.'

The nail on his index finger was cracked.

'This is where we found the foot,' Lindell said, and pointed.

He lifted his head and looked at her, but said nothing.

'Tell me a little about the point,' she said, as she helped herself to another cinnamon bun.

'There's not much to tell,' he said.

Lindell sensed that indeed there was a great deal to tell, and was pleased that Torsten Andersson was the first she had encountered. There was a secure feeling in his kitchen, despite his initial show of anger. She let her gaze wander once more around the room, discovering details, noticing the antique toaster tucked in behind an almost equally old radio, a wall decoration with an embroidered text where 'though we may roam' was rhymed with 'humble home,' the socks that were hung to dry next to the stove hook, and an old cupboard that was topped by a one-litre Höganäs ceramic jar on a moth-eaten doily.

'You've made it look nice in here,' she said, and caught a swift glint of amusement in his eyes.

'I do all right,' he said.

'Can't you light a fire in the stove, even though it's neither morning or night? I like the sound of it crackling.'

He got to his feet, pulled out the wood bin with practised movements, opened the door to the wood stove, popped in a little bark shavings, some kindling and thin pieces of wood, put a match to it, shut the door almost all the way, remained crouched in front of it and watched the fire light before he closed it completely. Then he sat back down at the table and started to tell her about Bultudden.

* * *

170

Margit who had baked the cinnamon buns turned out to be his cousin.

'One of twenty-six,' he said with a crooked smile.

She was born in Bultudden and had been married to Kalle for over forty years. They were retired now. They had three children, all grown.

'Kalle doesn't saw anything other than wood, but he's good at that. We thin the woods together.'

Torsten Andersson stood up again and added more fuel to the fire.

'It's pine,' he said. 'So that should be to your liking.'

Lindell nodded. The heat rose in the kitchen and she removed her jumper and straightened her T-shirt. Torsten Andersson glanced at her breasts but when their gazes met he immediately looked embarrassed.

'I never married,' he said. 'Want some more coffee? But I have been lucky to have Margit,' he added, after Lindell declined a third cup. 'She's very considerate.'

He looked out the window. A couple of raindrops spattered against the glass.

'She sewed the curtains,' he said, and waved his hand.

Unexpectedly, Lindell felt a wave of tenderness toward the man on the other side of the table.

'When I arrived, you became quite angry. Why is that?'

'I thought you were a real estate bitch. They're always running around out here, wanting to buy.'

'You own a lot of land?'

'Margit and I own most of the point, but we are equally stubborn,' he said with a smile.

When he smiled, his whole face pulled together in an intricate pattern of wrinkles.

'We inherited it, and so that's how it should be. Margit and Kalle's boys will take over. I'm leaving it to them as well, and the boys are made of the same stuff as us.'

A new smile.

'The chickens. What was that all about?'

The smile disappeared.

'I had some before, but then there were new rules. They've been after me. I wrung all their necks in the spring.'

Lindell thought about Viola on Gräsö Island. Had the authorities been after her too?

'Did you have many?'

'About three hundred. An infernal cackling.'

Lindell was certain Torsten had taken good care of his hens.

'Tell me more about Bultudden,' she asked, well aware that she should not allow herself to be seduced by his quiet talking.

She had a task at hand. Marksson wanted a report, and not one on wood and chickens. She took out her notebook, writing a one and then 'Torsten Andersson.'

'Two,' he said, and Lindell wrote a two and then 'Margit and Kalle.'

He watched her, straightened his back, and pushed his coffee cup away.

'Five hundred metres past Margit and Kalle there's Thomas B. Sunesson. The *B* is important. He was a repair technician at Vattenfall – an electrician, in other words – and he has lived here for at least fifteen years. Unmarried, but not exactly a hermit. He often goes out dancing, mostly at Norrskedika.'

A list of names followed, residents from north to south on Bultudden. Number four and five were married couples, six and seven unmarried males.

'And then there is Lisen, but maybe she doesn't count. She lives all the way down toward the bay. A strange woman, seems to have problems. Sometimes she drops by. She doesn't live here permanently, she rents an old fishing cottage from me. Comes and goes, a restless spirit. She's here this week. Otherwise she is in Uppsala.'

After concluding this review of residents – which included brief elaborations and biographical details – Lindell thanked him for his help. She had a final question for him when they stood in the hall.

'I saw a large bird on my way over. Could it have been a sea eagle?'

'Sure. We have a couple that hang around here.'

Torsten Andersson looked almost proud.

'Any that nest on the point?'

'Absolutely. Two sets of mating couples, actually.'

She was hungry but decided to skip lunch in order to get in a few more houses. Cousin Margit was probably home, and maybe some of the married couples.

She realised that the single men would be difficult to question during the day as all three worked: Sunesson at Vattenfall, Lasse Malm at Forsmark, and the third bachelor, Tobias Frisk, at a bakery in Östhammar.

It was most likely among the latter that she would find something of interest. She had trouble imagining that the three couples would be intent on butchering bodies. But could she rule out Torsten Andersson?

Why did Bultudden strike her as the most interesting area to work through? One reason was of course that Marksson and his colleagues had diligently visited all of the homes on the other side of the bay and carefully scrutinised its inhabitants. But she was actually enticed by the eagle theory, sending Fredriksson a thought of gratitude. It would be sensational if it turned out to be true. She wished it was – an eagle rising, a murderer who saw part of the body he had butchered disappear into the sky, the eagle that soared above the pine trees, beating its wings with powerful if not elegant strokes, and disappeared.

The likelihood that an eagle could be involved also appeared more plausible after the conversation with Örjan Bäck. He had in fact observed an eagle flying away only a couple of seconds before he caught sight of the foot. It had been flapping low to the water in the direction of Bultudden.

Or am I wasting my time, Lindell asked herself as she slowly, almost reluctantly walked back to the car, Andersson's gaze on her back and the smoke of sap-rich pine in her nostrils.

Dreamy before this landscape, barren and yet so rich, that had been the backdrop against which she had loved and been loved, lost in a dialect that had seemed at first laughably childlike, but that she after her time with Edvard on Gräsö Island soaked up as greedily as a thirsty person reaches for a sponge filled with water, seduced by the sea.

She understood very well that by exposing herself to Roslagen she was tempting herself, toying with herself. A pathetic show dressed up as an investigation with only one actor and only herself as the audience. For with whom could she share this ridiculous passion, this grief, and this truncated love?

But – there was always a but in this play – she could

transform her attachment to the landscape and people to a painstaking and exhaustive investigation. She came from the outside, with respect and a keen ear, not bound by old ties. She would transform her weakness to strength.

Back in the car, bouncing down the road, she stumbled upon yet another reason she liked this assignment so much. She could be alone. No co-worker to take into consideration and measure herself against. Normally it should have been two, but Ottosson was wise enough to pick up on her unspoken preference, and luckily it coincided with their current staffing situation. No co-worker was available, and for his part Marksson was too harried to tag along.

Her need to be alone was growing stronger. She did not know if it improved the quality of her work but that didn't matter. It was a compulsion.

'Misanthrope,' Sammy Nilsson had called her one time. Unsure what it meant she had not commented on it, and looked it up later, finding the synonyms 'hater of the world' and 'hater of mankind.'

She smiled to herself. She was what she was. Sammy Nilsson and the others had contributed. She was a woman without imagination, her emotional landscape a morass, like most a good-enough mother, but she was a good – sometimes very good – cop. She liked the word 'cop,' it sounded ballsy, and testified to courage and effectiveness.

The road took a strong turn along a stone wall. A house could be seen about fifty metres away.

'Bultudden,' she murmured, and slowed down.

This she liked: the sight of a house, a gate to open, and new faces to acquaint herself with.

TWENTY-ONE

What should he leave behind? The question bordered on the ridiculous. He surveyed the small flat. He had not accumulated much. If he were to fill two smallish suitcases, all his clothes and personal belongings would fit. And this after twelve years.

Sven-Arne Persson listlessly picked through the worn things, some trousers, a handful of shirts, and some underwear. He could wear nothing of this in Sweden. Possibly the underpants. He set those aside.

The three pairs of sandals he rotated between – at work, in his neighbourhood, and at St Mary's – were lined up right inside the door. They looked ashamed, or else they were simply fearful at the prospect of being moved to such a remote land.

The light blue shirt had a hole by the collar. He held it up to his face and drew in the scent of detergent. He put it in the pile that he was going to give to his downstairs neighbour.

Two white shirts he kept, hesitated on a third, but let it stay behind.

He walked around aimlessly in the flat for an hour, picking, sorting. The vase from Lester he packed in the handkerchiefs that Jyoti gave him before returning to Chennai for good. A beautiful stone that he found during an outing to Nandi

Hills he slipped into a bag of toiletries. The English pruning shears – Wilkinsons that he had bought for a small fortune – he wrapped in a cotton cloth.

He had given notice on the flat. The landlord had shaken both his hands with a look of concern and assured him that he had been his best tenant ever, and urged him to return as soon as possible. But what did one know about the future? Was it a woman? An inheritance in England that needed to be guarded? The landlord, who had actually searched Sven-Arne's flat several times in secret in order to establish who he was, looked genuinely downcast. You will come again, will you not?

Did he want to return? Was his time in Bangalore, in India, at an end for good? Was he returning home to die? In a way it felt as though he were going toward death, that Svensk had been a messenger who had come with a dire message: It is time to total things up and turn in the final reckoning.

He felt no terror, no anguish before the black hole about to suck him in. Sweden was death for him. There was only one thing he wanted: to speak with Ante. One matter to get to the bottom of. Then he was finished with both India and Sweden.

Elsa he did not want to see, even if she lay on her deathbed, even if she . . . He did not complete the thought.

He couldn't give a damn about politics.

One more thing: He wanted to see his grandmother's cottage and Rosberg's farm, if they were still there.

That's enough of want and not want, he thought. Travel as unnoticed as you arrived. Walk off the plane – it will be December, he thought with something akin to terror, as he surveyed his clothes piles – and walk as through a tunnel toward your goals. Do not state or lay claim to anything. Finish. Write in a final period.

He sat down at the table. Some books lay before him: a flower lexicon, a few thin publications on herbal medicine and traditional folk healing methods, and a biography of Gandhi. He came to think of all the trees he had planted in Lal Bagh. It brought a smile to his face. Lester would remember. He also believed the trees would remember their youth, when the tall but very thin gardener took hold of the trunk and gently placed the plant in the ground, sprinkled the roots with damp earth, shook and lightly tapped the ground, added more earth in a circle around the trunk, added water, let it sink in, and repeated the procedure until the area was well hydrated.

Trees remember. They sighed contentedly once in place, Sven-Arne Persson was convinced of that. It was the memory that allowed them to grow.

He had always been careful, thorough. There were few things that infuriated him as much as when someone was careless with earth and plants. This he had shared with Lester, indeed had it been the very basis of their friendship?

Would he miss Lal Bagh? Maybe, maybe not. The trees would remember, that was a comforting thought as he now collected the considerably fewer items than initially planned. He filled a suitcase and a small shoulder bag, looked around one last time, let the door remain open, and left the building. He stepped out into the cool morning air and waved to Ismael, whom he had bade goodbye the night before. He walked slowly down the street. A rickshaw pulled up alongside but he gestured it away. He wanted to proceed on foot for a while.

178

After about one hundred metres his pace slackened, as if he had remembered something, before he came to a complete stop, put his suitcase down, and turned around. Ismael was still outside his shop, staring after him. It appeared to Sven-Arne that he smiled. But he did most of the time.

The day before he had painstakingly shaved Sven-Arne and cut his hair and talked about the events of the street from the past several days: an older woman who had died – 'she was almost too old' – the couple above the barber shop had had another fight – 'he is not a good man' – and the police had been looking for a gang of boys that often loitered in the copy shop – 'Tamils!' Before they had parted, Ismael had – clearly self-conscious but also childishly excited – fumblingly brought out a small box. 'From all of us,' he had said, and made an indeterminate gesture with his hands as if he were including the entire street. Sven-Arne had accepted the gift but had not yet opened it. The last thing he wanted was to break down in tears with Ismael.

He had let his gaze wander over the worn interior, the cursorily cleaned combs in a glass jar, the bottles of aftershave and tinctures, the mirror with its blemishes, the little table where there was always a vase of plastic flowers, the curtain that concealed the area where Ismael could wash up for Friday prayers. Ismael followed his gaze. Sven-Arne wanted to say something pleasant, something for Ismael to remember, but could not think of anything.

In the street outside there was the usual group of boys. He recognised all of them. Some of them had attended his lessons.

What did the barber say about Sven-Arne? What would he say in five or ten years? How long would he live on in the collective memory of the neighbourhood? What would the boys say?

Sven-Arne knew he was liked. He did not hurt a fly, was attentive and polite, but perhaps he was also not someone they would miss. By way of his careful silence he received respect but an Indian also wanted to see a little drama, and of this Sven-Arne had nothing to add.

Should he have become more involved? He had followed the debate about the development of Indian agriculture, seen how the multinational companies had taken over more and more with their genetically modified seeds and their custom-designed pesticides. The past few years the conflict about water and water resources had raged in the media as well as on the ground. Dams had been constructed that laid waste to half districts and forced people to flee, factories had continued to destroy both surface and groundwater, and along the coast the mangrove swamps were decimated. All of this was clearly evident and deeply unjust, painful for all those who worked with plants, earth, and water. They had often spoken of this at Lal Bagh.

He knew that Bangalore, and all of modern India, was partly built on the sweat and meagre existence of poor farmers.

Even locally there were reasons for activism. There was rubbish collection, the appalling street maintenance, or the renovations of homes by the canal.

He should perhaps have got involved, but he also knew his hands were tied. The police would have been happy to single out the foreigner who was making his voice heard, make a sensation of him residing illegally in the country and deport him, perhaps even throw him in prison first.

In Sweden he did not want to be a public figure and in India he couldn't.

Sven-Arne stroked his smooth cheeks, waved one last time to Ismael, picked up his bag that felt as if it had grown heavier, and continued his march to the bus stop.

TWENTY-TWO

Bultudden Point lay by the sea like its own nation, connected to the mainland by only a narrow strip of land, an electric cable, and a telephone line. Beyond the point there was an archipelago with windswept skerries and rocks and thereafter the Sea of Åland.

Ann Lindell stood at the outermost tip of the point, facing south, and summed up what she had gleaned from her two days. Not that it was much.

The wind was bearing down from the east and whipped the water into waves that crashed against the cliffs. There was snow in the air. She scanned the horizon, eager to perhaps catch sight of an eagle, a sign of life in the wilderness. It would serve as a confirmation that she was not here for nothing. But there was nothing in the sky. Not even a seagull.

She had spoken with Torsten Andersson's cousin and her husband. Margit Paulsson was short and scrawny, Kalle some thirty centimetres taller and broad chested. She was born on the point, he came from the mainland from a village that 'I have forgotten the name of.' She was a talkative woman, full of ideas and activities, did not stay in one place for more than a couple seconds, while Kalle sat securely moored at the kitchen table – a place that he had likely staked out forty-five years ago – smiling quietly, sometimes chiming in with a soft hum, sometimes shaking his head at his wife's harangues.

They were the same age to the day, both born on the morning of Christmas Eve sixty-seven years ago, a fact that they held up as a strong point.

He had worked in agriculture, in the forest, and as a carpenter. Like Edvard, Lindell had thought, and examined the giant at the table a little more closely. Margit had 'stayed home.' They had three sons. Kalle had nodded and a benign expression had come over him as Margit told her about Rustan, Kurt, and Torbjörn.

'Who severs a foot?' Margit had asked, and thereby echoed her cousin.

Lindell had come no closer to the answer other than eliminating Margit and Kalle as suspects. She had also eliminated the two other couples on the point: Ulla and Magnus Olsson in house number four, and Doris Utman and her husband Oskar – who had suffered a stroke and was bedridden – in house number five.

All four were in the same age bracket as Margit and Kalle and no likely candidates as axe murderers.

And then there was Lisen Morell, of course, who Lindell did not believe could lift as much as a screwdriver, even less a saw. She literally swayed on her feet, trying to regain order in her life.

At first Lindell had thought she was intoxicated but found that she was merely befuddled – perhaps from prescription medicine – and had trouble with her balance, to the point of finding it hard to stay upright. She had difficulties with everything. She slurred her speech and substantial portions of her speech were incoherent. Her mouth appeared to have dried out.

'I have no appetite anymore,' she complained, and displayed her bony arms.

She was also cold. Light a fire or put on a jumper, Lindell thought uncharitably, disturbed by the sight of this woman who was her own age.

She offered to light the fire for her and make her some food. The woman stared at her, terrified.

Lindell left, convinced that Lisen Morell would soon die if she did not receive treatment.

The first specks of snow blew in from the sea, diabolically hard and almost painful as they struck her face.

Three houses remained. Three bachelors. Lindell had picked up some information from their neighbours but of course she had to meet them in person. It was as if Bultudden had to be gone through thoroughly in order for her to be able to rest. Maybe it was the absence of other ideas and tasks that she lingered on, maybe there were other reasons. She both did and didn't want the riddle of the foot to find its solution on the point.

All three of the men were employed and could not be questioned during the day. She had no desire or really any realistic intention of calling them down to the police station in Östhammar. They would have to take time off work, and since they were only to be questioned for possible information in connection with the case it seemed beyond the call of duty.

She had instead left notes in their mailboxes urging them to contact her. Malm and Frisk had already called her mobile phone and they had agreed she would stop by to see them on Saturday. She had already arranged a babysitter for Erik. It was Thursday today. That suited her fine. She would get one day in Uppsala.

It was getting dark and the snowfall grew heavier, but she was finding it hard to leave her spot on the point. At last, when her feet were frozen solid and her jacket was completely wet, she walked through the woods to the turnaround where her car was parked.

'Sweden, Sweden, my motherland,' she said softly.

She faced four months of winter. Before her there would be at least four serious violent crimes, perhaps murders, before spring decided to return. She did not complain, not anymore; there was no point. She simply accepted it as fact. That was a victory.

She drove north on the by-now familiar route, waving to the Olssons, Utmans, and Paulssons, convinced they were watching her pass by. She got out at Torsten Andersson's gate and before she had reached the house he had opened the door. He had a little bag in his hand. He had promised her a bit of fish.

'Caught any criminals yet?'

He smiled and Lindell smiled back, shaking her head. She peeked into the bag. There were about a dozen small perch inside.

'We should have the death penalty,' Torsten Andersson said.

'What do you mean?'

'If I have a dog that's mean and bites people then I should get rid of it, shouldn't I?'

Lindell nodded, distressed at hearing this familiar rant, and especially because it came from a man she had taken an immediate liking to.

185

'But a murderer just ends up in prison or hospital.'

'You think we should lead murderers out into the woods and shoot them?'

Her voice curdled in the frigid easterly wind. The snow whirled in front of the cottage. He must be freezing, she thought. Torsten Andersson was in short sleeves.

He didn't reply, simply shaking his head.

'Something is wrong,' he said after a pause.

'Thanks for the fish,' Lindell said, turning and walking back to the car.

'It's bullshit!' he yelled after her.

As she drove through Hökhuvud and saw the houses along the road it struck her that she – if she had had the talent – would have been able to write the story of Sweden. Most of the people she encountered in her work were actually innocent, and even the guilty ones, the murderers and rapists, the manslaughterers, the thieves and dealers, were all a part of the story.

The sniper's story is no worse than the hunting master's.

In Gimo she pulled over at a petrol station, took the bag of fish out of the trunk and stuffed it into a litter bin, then went inside to buy the evening paper.

TWENTY-THREE

'You've got some colour,' Sammy Nilsson declared.

Ottosson was sorting through papers, but glanced up quickly. Ola Haver was filling a cup with coffee from the thermos.

'I'm one of those nostalgic country police officers,' Lindell said with a smile, and took the cup Haver held out to her.

'Thanks, Ola, that's sweet of you,' she said with a warmth in her voice that must have surprised him.

She had had trouble falling asleep, tossed and turned, and woken up with period pain.

'Hey there, Eagle,' Sammy Nilsson said by way of greeting when Fredriksson sauntered in. 'Lindell has just been telling us her ornithological adventures in the outer coastal area.'

'It should have been a flamingo,' she said.

Ottosson looked up, surprised. Sometimes it struck Lindell what an absence of imagination he had.

'But then I would have had to go to west Africa,' she added. Ottosson still looked nonplussed.

Lindell sighed and sat down at the table.

'Today I have some old shit to tackle,' she said, mainly to get a word in before anyone else. Beatrice Andersson and Riis – who was back from his last sick leave – were the last to get there.

'A shooting in Vattholma,' Ottosson said. 'Someone firing away in the forest, unclear why. Most excitement is from yesterday evening and night, otherwise fairly calm. A couple of domestic disputes and a new case of car torching in Stenhagen.'

'Not the right weather for chasing hooligans,' Haver said.

'If only they would torch my car,' Sammy Nilsson said.

'Well, then, how did things go in Östhammar?'

'One more day. I'm going back tomorrow morning for three more interviews.'

'What about Erik?' Ottosson asked.

'I've worked it out,' Lindell said. 'Then I'll wrap it up.'

'Can't the real country policemen take care of it?'

'No, they have enough going on, and I want to finish my work on Bultudden.'

'Something up?'

'It's just a feeling,' Lindell answered unassumingly, and smiled at Fredriksson.

She knew what it would mean for him if a breakthrough came as a result of his eagle theory.

Admittedly she did have a great deal of 'old shit' occupying her desk, but she had been planning to take it easy. In part because the ache in her back was hellish at times, and in part because she wanted time to visit Berglund again.

Listlessly, she checked her email and luckily there was nothing there that couldn't wait.

She gulped down the rest of her coffee and stopped by Ottosson's office.

'Anything new from Berglund?'

'Haver was up there yesterday. Everything seemed fine.

188

Berglund has started taking walks on the hospital grounds. And he's reading through the old case materials.'

'I was thinking of looking in on him today.'

'That will make him happy,' Ottosson said kindly, rifling through his piles of paper, pulling one page out but tossing it aside and giving her a bewildered smile.

'I don't understand,' he mumbled.

Lindell smiled. She knew that Ottosson was stressed, and nonetheless he managed to carry it off. Once again she was able to maintain that she had a good boss. He did not often complain about his work situation, despite often having just cause. He was rarely surly or arrogant, but did become distracted when there was too much on the go, and this morning was coloured by just such an air of distraction.

'Was there anything else?'

'No,' Lindell said, although she would have liked to linger a while, maybe chat, but she decided to leave him in peace.

When she returned, there was a note on her desk with a hastily scrawled name. It was her own handwriting but at first she could not remember where, how, and why she had written down the name, before she realised that it was the name of the missing county commissioner's relative, which she had been given by Elsa Persson's neighbour.

Ante Persson – the one who had most likely made Elsa Persson so upset and distraught that she had walked out right in front of a lorry. Where was it the neighbour said that he lived? Wasn't it Ramund? Elsa Persson had been run over at the corner of Sysslomansgatan and Luthagsleden. That could fit. If she had been coming from Ramund and was on her way downtown she would naturally cross Luthagsleden at that point.

But hadn't she already been there and visited the old man

at the time when she bumped into her neighbour? Perhaps she had been on her way back there, or was trying to leave?

Whichever it was, Lindell's curiosity was piqued. If she went to see this Ante Persson – the name appealed to her somehow – then perhaps she would get her answer. And in addition it would give her something to tell Berglund.

The first thing she noticed was a bookcase, or rather, books in great quantities, many of them shoved on top of ones that were standing on the shelf. Thereafter she noticed a hand resting on a bed rail. The hand was missing two fingers.

'What the hell is this?'

The clerk behind her back let out a giggle.

'What did I tell you?' she whispered to Lindell, who turned her head and stared at the woman. The latter was about to say something else but stopped, her mouth half open.

'Thank you,' Lindell said, turning her back. She heard the door glide shut.

The hand fascinated her. It was powerful. The part of the arm that could be seen was covered in hair. Grey, curly hairs. The muscles in the hand and arm tensed and Ante Persson got out of bed. She caught sight of one shoulder and his back.

She knocked against the doorjamb again, trying to raise her voice above the radio that was on. The voice on the radio was speaking about Iraq.

'I could have sworn,' she heard him mutter.

She took a couple of steps into the flat through the narrow hallway and stopped in the doorway. It was as if he sensed more than heard her, because he turned his upper body abruptly. His face contorted, perhaps from pain. He did not look shocked or frightened, just angry.

'What is this?'

'Hello, Ante Persson,' she said loudly.

'I'm not deaf!'

Lindell nodded.

'Could we turn the radio down a notch?'

'It's the news.'

She took another step, not sure if she should hold her hand out. His left hand hung alongside his body and now it looked surprisingly powerless, while the right hand rested on the handle of a sort of walking aid. If he lets go he will lose his balance, she thought.

'You're not a staff member,' he observed.

Lindell shook her head.

'I'm from the police,' she answered, and couldn't help but smile as a crack momentarily appeared in his dismissive expression, a flicker of insecurity in his eyes.

'What are you grinning about?' he growled.

What an old codger, she thought, and her smile widened.

'My, you're a grumpy bastard,' she said, and unexpectedly his snort turned into a smile. He shuffled over to the radio and turned off the reporter's voice in the middle of a sentence that Lindell thought had started promisingly: 'It will be a mild winter according—'

'All they do is lie anyway,' he said. 'It's going to be a hellishly cold winter. Sit down.'

She sat down at the kitchen table that was pushed up against the bookshelf. A somewhat peculiar arrangement, but she realised immediately that the table was not used for its intended purpose. It was actually a desk with a contemporary desk lamp, a pile of books, a notepad, a portable tape recorder, a magnifying glass, and a jar of pens.

A stack of photocopies and a highlighter were laid out on the desk.

She sat down on the side she thought he did not usually sit at. She examined the room during the time it took for him to take his seat. The furnishings were spartan, if not downright bare. The bed was made. There was an embroidered pillow at one end. On the wall, between the two windows, there was something that she took to be a diploma, behind glass and in a silver-coloured frame. It was embellished with stamps and a flourish in gold and red that resembled a weapon. Ante Persson's name was written in an ornate script.

The stack of books on the table was dominated by English-language works with titles such as *Another Hill* and *Beyond Exile and Death*. There was a large book toward the bottom that she thought was in Spanish.

'You read a lot,' she said, and her gaze wandered along the bookshelves.

'What do you want?'

She decided to get right to the point. Ante Persson was not the kind to be warmed up with a gentle introduction.

'Elsa Persson is in the hospital,' she said, and made an effort to catch his eye.

'What's happened?' he asked, with no discernible reaction.

'She was run over.'

He nodded. No question as to how it had happened or how serious it was. How is this man put together, she wondered to herself.

'She walked out in front of a lorry after paying you a visit last week.'

'I'm sorry to hear that,' he said.

If Lindell were to describe his voice, she would use only one word: harsh.

'Are you? From what I understand the two of you were not particularly close.'

'That's not surprising if you never meet. The last time was two years ago and that visit lasted all of five minutes.'

He looked at her with watery eyes. The irises were of an undefinable colour and the whites were bloodshot. There was, however, an intensity in his old man's eyes that she sensed had either attracted or frightened women, and perhaps also men, when Ante Persson had been in his prime.

She found herself mostly curious. His apparently unbroken intellect, the books and other items on the table, and his still forceful voice did not speak of any debility. It was only his body that did not seem to have kept up.

'What was it that time?'

'She explained that her husband, my nephew, had been declared dead officially. She wanted me to know before it was published in the paper.'

'And this time she came to tell you that he had risen from the dead?' Ante Persson nodded and smiled a faint, possibly ironic, smile.

'You can read both English and Spanish?'

He nodded again. He had resumed the completely expressionless – not to say icy – face. She could tell he was on his guard. His right hand rested over his left.

'And German and a little Russian,' he said after a couple of seconds. 'So I knew that you would come,' he added after an additional pause.

'But you knew he was alive?'

The thought came to her as a sudden inspiration. If you

193

were going to divulge a secret to anyone it would be Ante Persson, that she was convinced of.

'Did you speak to Elsa?'

'No, she is apparently unconscious.'

'I see,' he said. 'You figured it out on your own.'

'Right here and now,' she replied.

Ante Persson gave an unexpected roar, a belly laugh, hearty and contagious.

'You are the nicest fucking cop I've ever met.'

'You've dealt with the police before?'

'More than sixty years ago, but back then it was pretty frequent. Well, and then they came by when Sven-Arne disappeared, but that doesn't really count.'

Lindell wanted to know more but knew the man on the other side of the table was not one to let himself be rushed. He talked about what he wanted to talk about. The rest you had to guess or wait for.

'Tell me about Sven-Arne,' she urged.

'He was a plumber,' he grinned, 'who rose up like a hot-air balloon.'

'And then the air went out?'

'Exactly.'

He leant across the table and the look in his eyes changed for a fraction of a second, as if he was preparing to add something. But he sank back instead.

'The two of you were close?'

Ante Persson did not answer. Lindell glanced at the books on the shelf. She noticed that they were arranged thematically. As far as she could tell they were all about politics; there was no fiction.

'I'm working on my memoirs,' he said abruptly. 'You can read it all in there.'

'Can I get a look?' Lindell asked.

'If Sven-Arne is alive or not doesn't matter. He is a piece of fly shit in the universe, just like you and I, for that matter. He became a politician and that might have been all right but he didn't believe in it, and that's bad. I mean, here, on the inside,' he said, and thumped above his heart. 'In here. There has to be a red thread one follows in life.'

'Like you have done?'

Ante Persson sighed deeply.

'I've tried,' he said.

He massaged the stumps that were all that remained of the little and ring finger on his left hand.

'Even though it's been hard, damned hard, many times.'

Sad men, Lindell thought. Sad old men. How many haven't I met? She thought of her father, Berglund, Torsten Andersson on Bultudden, and of Edvard, who in thirty years would probably sit much like Ante Persson, sighing and grumbling.

She quickly felt very tired. Why am I sitting here listening to this whining? I'm a criminal investigator, not a case worker or psychologist. But she knew that a police officer was every bit as much a social worker. In this mess of human frailties there were lies, squashed hopes, betrayal – and sometimes violence. The question was if she would get any wiser – a better cop – by talking to Ante at the Ramund nursing home. Or did it just serve to make her depressed? She had no answers to Ante's pained questions, she was convinced of that. He, who from a human perspective was now living on borrowed time, had most likely ransacked himself for decades and was clearly still as searching and lost. Am I doing the right thing? Am I? She found herself circling these same questions herself, both professionally and in private, excruciatingly aware that she would never arrive at a definitive answer.

Lindell lifted the head that she had unconsciously lowered, as if in prayer. The old man was watching her. Before his gaze – serious and without a trace of the mockery she had observed earlier – she felt completely cold inside.

'Why did he run off to India?' she asked, mostly in order to get away.

Ante Persson did not answer. She knew the audience was over.

Ann Lindell ended up standing outside the nursing home for a while. It was only a couple of minutes' walk to the Café Savoy but she decided to put it off for another time. She walked along Sysslomansgatan, following it south and crossing Ringgatan, when she suddenly recalled that an arsonist had lived in these parts. Three people, a mother, father, and small child, illegal refugees from Bangladesh, had died in Svartbäcken. Hate and intolerance had characterised that time.

It was quite by chance that she had read in the newspaper recently that the arsonist, together with three others, had escaped from the Tidaholms prison. They were still at large. It made her think of Torsten Andersson's words about getting rid of the murderers.

Children were playing outside the Sverker school. She stopped at the fence and watched the quick bolts across the concrete, listened to the shouts and laughter. A group of boys were bouncing a ball back and forth. Next autumn it would be Erik's turn.

A bus pulled over, the door opened, and the driver gave her an inquiring look. She realised she was standing at a bus stop and got on, mainly so she wouldn't infuriate the driver.

'I was lost in thought,' she said.

The driver smiled but said nothing. She sat down. Take me far away from here, she thought, and closed her eyes. The ache in her back came in waves.

When she opened her eyes and looked out of the window she saw a Christmas display at the Salvation Army. Through the dirty pane she could see a gigantic Santa Claus, smiling a confused smile, as if he were terrified. A heap of red packages lay at his feet.

The bus continued on its way to the centre of town. There were stars and glittering decorations all over. Should she head back to Ödeshög for Christmas? Her mother had called and more or less pleaded for it. 'It may be the last time,' she had added when she perceived Ann's hesitation.

The last time? What did she mean? Was she thinking of Ann's increasingly befuddled father or was it simply a tearful attempt to coax her daughter back to Ödeshög?

Ann Lindell got off the bus at Dragarbrunnsgatan and walked quickly down to the Fyris River, crossed the Nybro Bridge and continued down Västra Ågatan. Her menstrual pain had died down. She slowed down. This was where Marcus Ålander had fought with Sebastian Holmberg, who had later been found dead in the children's bookshop on Drottninggatan.

This was her city. Her memories. Ödeshög was no longer 'home.' She decided to stay in town over the holidays. Take it easy and give all her time to Erik, maybe take him for a spin in a patrol car, which he had been begging her to do for a long time. She would talk to Torstensson. He was good, maybe a little interested in her. That didn't matter, as long as he didn't get any ideas.

How long since she had gone to bed with a man? She did not want to count the months, or rather, years. She was drying up. Her desire came and went, her dreams of intimacy likewise. Sometimes a great longing came over her but her mechanisms to keep loneliness at bay were so entrenched and refined that she rarely felt the bottomless despair that used to plague her.

But deep inside, in the dark crannies, slumbered a bereft little creature, these days without fangs and claws, but with very mournful eyes. Sometimes he – for it was a he – still made his presence known. Like now, on Västra Ågatan, with her body in the midst of its periodic sparring, with Christmas on the doorstep, with people around her, neighbours, colleagues, and friends, all determinedly subjugating life.

She picked up the pace again and tried to think about something else, preferring to let her work mechanism take over. Her thoughts returned to Bultudden. Torsten Andersson's words, or perhaps above all his unexpected display of aggression, still bothered her.

'Damned old man,' she muttered, aware of the fact that her negative feelings resulted almost entirely from having been had. She had felt cozy in his kitchen, become lulled into comfortable repose, listened to the crackle in his stove, registered the everyday objects, seen how well he had arranged his home, liked his thoughtful words pronounced in a dialect that strangely enough sounded like home. He had offered her freshly caught fish, as if she had been an old friend.

She should have known better, she should have learnt the lesson: People are two-sided. She had let herself be taken in.

Maybe he was a killer? Maybe he was the one who had sawed off that foot? The talk of getting rid of the murderers was only a front, or perhaps an internal defence; for he was no murderer, it had been his right to 'get rid of' someone.

She had seen this before, how perpetrators rationalised their actions and justified their crimes: an abused woman had 'been asking for it,' a murder victim had 'deserved' his fate, or a rape victim 'had herself to blame.'

A couple with a small child somewhat younger than Erik were standing at a low fence of the swan pond feeding the birds. The wild ducks were nattering and the gulls were shrieking. A swan slowly floated past.

Lindell observed the three of them, how the man snuck a hand around the woman's waist, and how she laughed at the young boy's excitement. Her high peals of laughter rang out and could be heard above the sound of the traffic for an instant.

Berglund was sitting at the window. He had shunned his hospital clothes and was dressed in jeans, a shirt with a pattern of large squares, and brown slippers edged in fur. Lindell thought he looked ten years younger than at her last visit.

'Here you are enjoying yourself,' she said.

Berglund smiled and gestured to the table in front of him, where papers were stacked up.

'Any strokes of genius?'

He shook his head.

'No, I've gone through this material countless times, always in the hopes I'll find something, but nothing doing.'

The gaze he shot her was his old one. He had not only changed his clothes.

'You look rosy.'

'I was out walking,' Lindell said.

'I see,' Berglund said.

Lindell did not know exactly what he was getting at, but sensed that he realised she was trying to alleviate her cramps while walking. She had done this before, it usually worked, and maybe Berglund had put two and two together.

'I was coming from a conversation with Sven-Arne Persson's uncle,' she said, and sat down right across from him.

He gathered his papers together on the table while she described her visit to Elsa Persson's neighbour, how Elsa was now admitted to this same hospital, maybe even in this same building.

'Yes, it's a strange story, this Sven-Arne,' Berglund said, but Lindell could tell his thoughts were still caught up in the old case.

'What was he like as a politician?' she said, trying anyway. 'His uncle said something about how Sven-Arne never really believed in his cause. What's up with that? Was he just a fake?'

'No, I think people regarded him as honest. He was a champion orator. But it must have dried up. He probably got tired of the nonsense. Or else he just snapped.'

'Was he really a plumber?'

'Something in the construction field. Then he became an ombudsman.' Berglund paused, then continued almost immediately.

'I remember a meeting in town, shortly before some election. It was when New Democracy was in full swing. I was there overseeing Forum Square. There was some kind of threat, some letter that Persson had received. There was a hellish wind but people stayed and listened. I remember thinking he talked like my old man.'

200

'And that felt good?'

Berglund smiled. 'Yes, actually. I actually voted for the Social Democrats that year.'

'Because of Persson's speech?'

'Maybe not only because of that, but there was something there that . . . well, you know how it is . . .'

'Nostalgia?'

He chuckled.

'Did he receive a lot of threats?'

'Not that I know of. It must have been some dingdong who sent that letter.'

'I was thinking maybe he ran off because he felt pursued or threatened for his life,' Lindell said.

'We looked into that, but I don't think that was the case. We found nothing to suggest it, at least. All politicians get fan mail so I'm sure Persson could handle it.'

'But maybe there was a threat you weren't aware of?'

Berglund looked at her.

'Persson's got under your skin,' he said with a smile.

'I don't know, unexpected turns of events are always exciting and that uncle made me more curious. He is writing his memoirs. The whole room was full of books, like a research institute. He speaks several languages. And then Persson's wife, who walks straight out onto Luthagsleden Expressway.'

'Yes, Elsa.'

'You mentioned something about her possibly seeing someone.'

'It's only a rumour,' Berglund said.

'Could it have been the reason that Persson went to India? That there was already a man in Elsa's life?'

'It's doubtful. From what I remember we checked into

their lives pretty thoroughly and found no signs of infidelity or marriage problems.'

'What do you think will happen now? I mean, if it is him – and that's how it seems – his uncle admitted he knew about Persson's India stint. How are we going to handle it?'

'It's not a matter for the police. Persson is a free man and can go as he wishes. He is not suspected of any crime.'

'Isn't it a crime to . . .'

'Disappearing is not a crime,' Berglund said.

'I know, but . . .'

'Forget Persson,' Berglund said. 'Tell me how things are going with the foot.'

'I'm going door-to-door like a salesman. It's kind of exciting in a way, but hasn't turned up much. I'm doing the last three houses tomorrow. I've talked to them and everyone will be home. Then I'll wrap up.'

'How are things with you otherwise?'

'Fine,' Lindell said, unwilling to return to the chain of thoughts she had on her way to the hospital.

She got up, stretched out her hand, and laid it on her colleague's shoulder. There was a new kind of closeness between them. She liked it, even if she was uncertain what effect it would have on their future working relationship.

He put his hand on hers.

'I'm glad you came up to talk for a while. I'll be going home on Monday.'

She spent the rest of the day writing up her notes from Bultudden. Marksson must surely be expecting some kind of report. She didn't have much to show for herself, and took her time.

Sammy Nilsson looked in but Lindell pretended to be extremely busy and only gave clipped answers to his questions, and after a couple of minutes he slunk off.

She was done at half past three. She turned off the computer, got herself a cup of coffee, and returned to her office. The activity at the unit appeared to have dropped off. Everything was calm. Friday. Fredriksson and Beatrice were taking the night shift. Ottosson had already gone home. She heard Riis clomp by. Then there was simply silence outside her door.

She thought about Ante Persson and his memoirs. What would they be about? The red thread of his life?

She recalled his gaze, how it changed in the flash of an instant. A dangerous man, it struck her, without being able to offer a satisfactory account as to what this dangerous quality might consist of. Was it his age that had made him in a way unreachable? She had always had respect for older people.

Or was it simply the case that his evident integrity – perhaps an expression of a heightened self-sufficiency – made her feel uncomfortable? She had felt this same feeling of unease many times when she listened to older people. As if she were inferior in experience and knowledge.

But most of the time the relationship was reversed: Most of them felt inferior and pressed in their contact with the police, and this was something every interrogator could take advantage of. She wasn't the most skillful in this respect. Both Beatrice and Sammy Nilsson were considerably better. Lindell preferred the give and take of open conversation. She didn't like unspoken threats or traps.

Someone like Ante Persson was a challenge. He was

not one to be tempted out onto thin ice. He only shared information that he had picked out and at the pace that he had set.

Riis went stomping in the opposite direction down the corridor and Lindell was startled out of her thoughts. She looked at her watch and decided that the working day was done.

TWENTY-FOUR

Lindell did not wave to Torsten Andersson as she passed his house. It was a ridiculous protest but she knew he would register it.

As she drove by Margit and Kalle Paulsson she swore quietly under her breath. She had forgotten to talk to Marksson about Lisen Morell. That woman needed immediate intervention. Otherwise she would go under. For a moment she considered stopping by her house before she took on the three loners (as she had dubbed the bachelors on the point) but instead decided to end her tour with a visit to the fishing cottage.

Her first 'loner' lived a couple of hundred metres up. She drove into the yard. A line ran from a shed to the main house. She guessed it was a dog run. She couldn't see a dog but still parked her car at a safe distance.

Thomas B. Sunesson walked out onto his front step the moment she opened her car door.

'There's no dog,' was the first thing he said. 'I saw you wondering where to put the car.'

'You never know,' Lindell said, holding out her hand. His grin was in no way unfriendly.

'Before we go on, there's something I have to know: What does the B stand for?'

The grin grew wider.

'Bertram. Like Dad and his dad and his dad before him, all the way back.'

She returned his smile. Thomas B. Sunesson spoke with the broadest Roslagen dialect one could imagine. Yet another Edvard, she thought; and the fact was that Sunesson reminded her of him. The same open face, the at some moments almost childlike features, an impression reduced somewhat by its angular masculinity. This fateful combination that Lindell had found so attractive.

'His name was Bronco. The dog, I mean,' Sunesson added when he saw Lindell's bewilderment. 'A greyhound. An angry bugger.'

So you were forced to get rid of it, Lindell thought.

'He became fourteen years old.'

The man looked over to the shed. Lindell followed his gaze and discovered the dog house.

'But he was my friend, the bastard.'

The melancholy tendency also underscored the resemblance to Edvard.

'Shall we go inside?'

He nodded and walked to the door without further ado, kicking off his clogs in the vestibule and disappearing inside.

They sat down in the kitchen. She got the impression that he had cleaned for her visit. A pile of newspapers were neatly stacked on the table, the countertop was wiped down, no dirty dishes were out, and a clean dishtowel was hanging from a hook.

He offered Lindell coffee but she said no, having already drunk two cups that morning.

'You're involved in a manhunt,' he said.

News about the foot had spread, even if the macabre find on the other side of the bay had surprisingly not been made much of in the media.

She launched into her usual spiel about questioning any people in the area who may have observed something. As she talked he watched her intently, as if he did not want to miss a single word. She assessed his age as around forty. There was a small but marked scar above one eyebrow. He was noticeably tanned, or rather, weather-beaten.

'No, I haven't seen anything out of the ordinary,' he said when she stopped. 'There's not much that happens around here, and if against all odds someone did turn up we would notice. Especially if it was a woman,' he added, and smiled imperceptibly.

'No unknown cars have driven by?'

He shook his head.

'Well, maybe last summer; there are always confused Stockholmers who come by. They're either looking for summer houses, or else they are just lost. Sometimes they stop and ask if you know anything that's for sale.'

'Anyone in particular that you remember?'

'No, they all look the same. There was one,' Sunesson said, and chuckled, 'who wanted to buy this old dump. He offered me a million on the spot. When I said no, he raised it by half a million. Bronco was barking like crazy. He doesn't like city slickers.'

'How much do you want for it?'

His smile widened. 'Interested?'

'Not really.'

'I'm not selling,' he said, suddenly serious.

'Any red cars drive by here lately?'

'Frisk has a red car. He lives at the end of the street, as we say. And of course then we have the magpie in the fishing cabin.'

'You mean Lisen Morell?'

'Not the sharpest tack, if you ask me.'

'What do you mean?'

'She calls herself an artist, but she can't paint, that's for sure.'

'You call her the Magpie.'

'She's always dressed in black and white.'

Lindell dropped Morell. 'So Tobias Frisk has a red car?'

He nodded. 'Are you looking for a red car?'

'We have a witness who saw a red, unfamiliar car on the other side of the bay. That's all.'

'But Frisk isn't unfamiliar.'

'Maybe on the other side.'

Sunesson snorted. 'In other words, you don't have much.'

Lindell acknowledged as much.

'Do you have a saw?'

He looked taken aback. 'Of course I do.'

'A chainsaw?'

He nodded.

'Can I see it?'

'I'm not following any of this.'

'Maybe you even have a bandsaw?'

'That too. And a wood cutter, and a skidsteer, and a trailer and a—'

'Thanks, that's enough,' Lindell interrupted.

The chainsaw was a Stihl.

'No, don't touch it!'

Sunesson quickly pulled his hand back.

'I'm afraid I'll have to take that with me,' Lindell said, and fished a pair of gloves out of her coat pocket. She donned the right-hand glove and lifted the power tool down from the workbench.

'Now I get it, you think I severed that foot.'

He stared at her with suspicion and disapproval, as if she had revealed she was the bearer of an infectious disease.

'We have to check it out,' she said, 'I'm sorry. I don't believe anything. It is simply a routine check. Where is your cordwood saw?'

She got him to remove the blade and treated it as carefully as the chainsaw, wrapping it in a rubbish bag she had in the car.

Sunesson observed the whole process in silence. There was no trace of innocence left in his face when she left the house.

The next loner on the point, Lasse Malm, was perhaps two or three years younger than his neighbour. He was already out in the garden when Lindell found her way to his place. She parked behind Malm's ancient pickup. There was a boat engine in the back of it.

No one, not even the most enthusiastic Stockholmer, would offer one and a half million for his house. Lindell had the feeling one bad autumn storm could blow it on its side.

The panelling was faded, the window frames spotted black with mould, the roof – where the tiles were in uproar – dipped alarmingly around a badly beaten-up chimney, and the front steps had settled at least ten centimetres, more on the right side.

If the house was in terrible condition, its owner was just the opposite. Lindell estimated that he was close to six feet four inches in height, and his broad shoulders bore witness to strength. His handshake reinforced this impression of power. The almost sinister small eyes – the only thing diminutive about him – peered at her with curiosity and scrutiny. She pulled up the zipper on her jacket.

He showed no inclination to ask her inside. Instead, he stood in front of the steps with his arms folded. Lindell thought of a bouncer at a nightclub.

She plunged into her usual routine, as she had done half an hour earlier for Sunesson. He listened in silence and then gave basically the same – if not word for word – answers as his neighbour. No observations, no unfamiliar cars, nor had he seen a woman who could fit a foot with a shoe size of five.

He told her that the only red car on the point belonged to Tobias Frisk.

'Is he under suspicion?'

'No, not at all,' Lindell said.

Malm replied with something that Lindell didn't catch.

'Do you own a chainsaw?'

In contrast to his neighbour, Malm immediately picked up on the implications of that question.

'So that's how it happened?'

'We don't know,' Lindell said truthfully.

She was struck by the thought that they should have collected all the saws and blades in the entire neighbourhood. She would suggest as much to Marksson.

They walked together to the back of the house to a shed, which displayed the same measure of dilapidation and decay as the main house.

This time it was a Jonsered, considerably more powerful than Sunesson's. She wrapped it in a plastic bag, returned to the car, opened the trunk, and placed it next to the Stihl.

'You have quite a collection,' Lasse Malm observed with surprising joviality. 'Do I get a receipt for it?'

'Certainly,' Lindell said, taking out her notepad and hastily writing out a couple of lines. Then she tore off the page and handed it to him.

'Will that do?'

He examined the paper. 'You write better than my doctor, but only by a little.'

He had no cordwood saw.

'I'm not supposed to use the fireplace,' he explained. 'The chimney sweep said so.'

Lindell understood this very well.

'I do it anyway. There are so many regulations.'

'One regulation is that your taxes on the car have to be paid. If you have one, paste a registration sticker on the Toyota. The one currently on it is about three years old.'

He smiled at her.

'It must be here somewhere.'

He waved to her as she backed her car up onto the road.

Men living alone, she thought as she continued along the road the natives apparently referred to as the 'avenue.' They tried to maintain a life but their entire beings cried out for a bit of warmth and care. Malm, this gigantic teddy bear, who really didn't look half bad and seemed to have some basic sense, had a steady job as far as she could tell and should have no trouble finding a partner. If he ever dared invite a woman into the house, or if someone dared to go inside.

211

Same thing with Sunesson, even if he on the other hand appeared overly pedantic, he should also not be an impossible card. But perhaps he was afraid that a woman would mess up his Handi Wipes.

There remained Tobias Frisk, bakery assistant, and owner of a red car. Lindell couldn't help but feel some anticipation. She tried to imagine what he looked like but realised the futility of the exercise. He had willingly called her and confirmed that he would be home, but had sounded noticeably shaken and asked if it was really necessary since he had no information to share.

'I just do my thing,' he said.

As do I, she had been tempted to reply, but reassured him by saying it was only routine and that they had been speaking to hundreds of households around the bay.

'At least I have plenty of treats on hand,' he said, and now she was looking forward to a cup of coffee and slice of sticky Danish pastry.

The house was situated on a small rise and she thought he probably had a sea view, at least from the upper story. The house was surprisingly large for one person, at least one hundred and fifty square metres, probably built for a large family. It reminded her of a house she had seen on Gräsö Island and fallen in love with; red, with many ornately carved details and a glass veranda in which the woodwork of the windows gleamed white. Edvard and she had even stopped for a little while. Both had surely been thinking 'That's the kind of house we could live in.' It was in this period when they both – at the same time for once – envisioned a future together, maybe even on the island.

Lindell parked her car in front of the veranda. There was no sign of life. No dog that barked, no smoke billowing out of the chimney or a quick movement behind a curtain.

He left, she thought, and felt a streak of the fear that came over her sometimes ever since the time she was locked in the cellar and almost lost her life due to her own stupidity. She had been out investigating on her own that time, just like now.

For a split second she considered calling in her location to headquarters, but decided to hold off.

Out of the blue, she recalled a play on words from her childhood: 'two rights and one left,' and couldn't help smiling to herself.

She walked up the steps and onto the veranda. It was noticeably warmer there than outside. A row of pots had been placed along the wall. Geraniums, she guessed; one actually had a solitary flowering stalk. There was no doorbell so she knocked, but no figure appeared behind the translucent glass of the front door. She banged on it with some force. No response.

She counted to ten and then pushed the door handle down. It did not surprise her that the door wasn't locked. This was the country. Her repeated 'hello' echoed with a note of desolation.

As she stepped into the hall she picked up a strange smell. The rug in the hall was dishevelled and lay like an accordion across the wooden floor. She had the impulse to straighten it, but stopped herself at the last minute. The kitchen was to the right. It was dominated by a handsome whitewashed fireplace. The kitchen was empty. But it would not have shocked her to see Tobias Frisk sitting at the kitchen table. She had seen stranger things.

A sparsely furnished room lay straight ahead. There really was only one piece of furniture, an old-fashioned sofa that at one time had probably served as a bed for two or three people. She walked on and all at once realised what the smell was. She halted in the middle of the floor and drew a deep breath. The smell of gunpowder was unmistakable.

Someone had fired a weapon in the house, that much was certain. Not recently, because there was only a trace of gunpowder in the air.

There were two doors in this room with almost no furniture. She chose the one on the right. It was a large room, the drawing room, it might have been called. Not a soul. She walked back and opened the door on the left.

Tobias Frisk was sitting on the couch. A shotgun had slid down on his left side, the barrel aimed almost directly at Lindell.

She picked up the phone. It was time to call headquarters. I'll get no coffee and no cake, it struck her, as she heard Erlandsson's familiar voice.

She told him what had happened and asked him to contact Marksson.

'It's not a pretty sight,' she added.

After hanging up she left the room and searched the rest of the house. It was, as she had expected, empty.

TWENTY-FIVE

Bo Marksson appeared after half an hour, the medical examiner only a few minutes later. He was Lindell's age and they had met in a context that Lindell could not quite recall, though it was clear that he could.

'Good to see you again,' was his opening line. 'That was a nice time, wasn't it?'

Lindell nodded. She had the impression that he was eager to keep talking about their for the moment unidentified shared experience but she sought Marksson's gaze and quickly summed up the situation for him. They were still in the garden. A sudden gust came out of the woods to the south of the house and brought with it the scent of sea and pine.

Her colleague from Östhammar looked uncharacteristically unfocused, was pacing around in the gravel, and kept pulling a hand through his hair.

'Damn,' he said, for the second time.

'Did you know Tobias Frisk?' Lindell asked.

Marksson nodded.

'We played football together,' he said, and his trepidation was so strong she could almost smell it. Lindell sensed he wanted to be miles from Bultudden.

'I know his mother, too.'

So that's it, she thought. He dreads that inevitable call.

'Does she live in Östhammar?'

A new nod. Marksson was staring off toward the trees. Lindell followed his gaze. She glimpsed something white at the edge of the forest.

'What the hell,' Marksson said. 'What was that?'

'It's Lisen Morell,' Lindell said, as a figure emerged from the vegetation. She identified her by her unsteady gait. She walked as if she were intoxicated. 'She lives in a fishing cottage at the end of the point,' Lindell added. 'I should have talked to you about her. She needs help.'

'That's pretty clear,' Marksson said. His pained expression lifted somewhat as they walked toward the woman.

'I . . . the car didn't want to go, I mean . . .'

'You can't start the car,' Marksson said.

Lisen Morell nodded. That was lucky, Lindell thought. Lisen Morell was dressed in black jeans and a white knitted jumper that was at least three sizes too big. She was wearing sandals on her feet.

'What's the doctor's name?' Lindell whispered.

'Bergquist,' Marksson said.

'First name?'

'Janne.'

Lindell turned around. The physician was still standing outside.

'Hey, Janne, over here!' she yelled, before turning to Morell again. 'He's a doctor and can take you home. You need to get warm. I'll be over later. Okay?'

'It'll be a while until the forensic team arrives,' she said to Marksson, 'so Bergquist can't do anything anyway.'

Bergquist steadied Morell by holding her under the arm,

and they walked away. Lindell saw him lean toward her and ask something. She pointed toward a small opening between the trees, through which they left.

'What do you think?' Lindell asked. 'Is this where the foot came from?'

'Unfortunately it looks that way,' Marksson said.

I've got used to his voice, Lindell thought.

'What was he like when you talked on the phone?'

'Nothing out of the ordinary,' Lindell said. 'Maybe a little nervous. He just said that I was welcome to stop in. He called me back on his own.'

'No ifs and buts?'

'No, it was a completely normal conversation, it was over in a couple of minutes.'

'And then he shoots his head off,' Marksson said. 'Frisk was a pretty happy guy. I remember him from the football league. He was a midfielder. Pretty quick on his feet. Up here too.'

'A loner?'

'You mean, living out here in the wilderness?'

Lindell nodded.

'He had a girlfriend, I know that. I think she was from Valö Island. They were together for at least five, six years. A very pretty woman. She works a pub in Öregrund now, waitressing. But he wasn't asocial, quite the opposite. He was always upbeat when we bumped into each other. Bakers – is it even possible for them to be unhappy?'

'Don't know one,' Lindell said. 'How should we do this? Soon the Forensics will be here. If that foot has been walking around here we'll find out. Should we find out if there is a saw?' She pointed to a long storage shed some ten metres behind the house.

The shed was divided into three different sections, each with its own door. None of them was locked; they were closed with a metal clasp. Lindell picked up a stick from the ground and unlatched the clasp on the double doors in the middle of the shed. There was a tractor with a digger mounted on the front.

'A Grålle,' Marksson said. 'He must use it to shovel snow. Maybe transport lumber back from the forest.'

Lindell walked around the tractor and studied the workbench that ran the length of the wall. A bench that was characterised by order – there were small and big jars filled with various nails, screws, and bolts. Several bottles of thinners, an oil can, and a number of small items of the kind that find their way into a work area. The wall was covered in a panel with small holes for holding up hooks from which to hang tools. A monkey wrench was missing in a row of six.

Nothing caught her eye. Marksson stood on the other side of the tractor.

'A chainsaw,' he said suddenly.

'Is it a Stihl or a Jonsered?' Lindell asked.

'Listen to you.'

He shot her a look of amusement. Lindell told him what she had in the trunk of her car. She had to step into the digger in order to get over to his side.

'A Stihl,' she muttered, and bent over the tool. It was resting on a small pan, most likely filled with oil. There were bits of sawdust on the blade and chain, the teeth of which gleamed with oil. She tried to imagine Tobias Frisk holding the saw against an ankle.

'What do you think?' she asked.

'About what?'

218

'The foot was severed with a chainsaw.'

'Everyone here owns one,' he said.

'I think it was this one,' she said, and straightened her back.

She walked out into the area in front of the shed, the smell of oil and petrol in her nostrils, took out her mobile phone, and called Tina, the babysitter.

'I think I'm going to be late,' she said. 'Are you surprised?'

She heard Erik's voice in the background.

TWENTY-SIX

He remembered the sea, of course he remembered the sea, and could still, after almost seventy years, feel its scent in his nostrils. It was remarkable that this smell had imprinted on him so strongly, because the overwhelming emotion that day when he first got back on his legs and was allowed to totter out into the sunshine and onto the boardwalk was rage. He was furious, and tried to articulate this to the woman by his side, a Serbian, who was steadying him. But she only smiled, focused on preventing the enormous Scandinavian from tripping. She would never have been able to hold him. There was a difference of at least twenty centimetres and thirty kilos between them.

He was furious because he was comparing the magnificent villas along the promenade with the houses in the area he had inhabited the past three months. It was nothing new that a few lived royally while the majority of the population were crowded into ramshackle cottages, but his experiences in the mountains and then the contrast to Benacasim was too much.

He was also afraid, or rather terrified, that he would never be able to have intercourse again. This he was unable to acknowledge to anyone else and hardly even to himself, so his fury was unleashed over the disparity of the caves in the mountains and the palaces by the sea.

He was limp. The sliver of a grenade had entered his sack. The pain that first day at the temporary first-aid station had been indescribable. The medics had been able to quell the bleeding but not the pain. He was given some pills, but they hardly made any difference.

In addition to the wound in his groin, his thigh and lower back were perforated with tiny, infernally stinging pieces of metal.

For three days he lay on his side on the stretcher, with a testicular sack that was becoming increasingly infected, before he was transported to the coast. Which in itself was quite a feat.

He was operated on by a Canadian doctor, Norman Bethune, who was assisted by a Swedish nurse from Karlstad. The Canadian, in actuality a lung specialist, was renowned at the front. It was viewed as an honour to be operated on by him. He later died in China, according to the newspaper *Ny Dag*.

'I am only a human being,' the nurse had laughed when he asked her in his feverish state if she belonged to the party.

Pus oozed from his body, a foul-smelling yellow paste, as they cut into the bulges that had formed.

He was still weak but getting better. Slowly but surely, his young and strong body had fought off the infection.

But would he ever again be able to lie with a woman? He was not sure how everything down there was connected, and did not dare ask, but he was afraid he had become ineffectual. A damned, tiny little sliver.

He had glanced down at the woman at his side. She had smiled back, nodding encouragingly. Nothing, he felt nothing.

* * *

Something about that young policewoman reminded him of Irina. That was her name, the Serbian. Sometimes he forgot names. Was it her smile? Or her straightforward manner, which he was to encounter in due course. Irina was sharp enough behind that smile. She was the one who had brought his desire back to life. She must have sensed his fears.

Later she was to sit in the Yugoslavian parliament. In the early fifties, he received a letter from her. He had not replied; Tito was not in such good standing with the party at that point. He had followed the party line even when it came to Irina.

What was it that police girl had said? 'My, you're a grumpy bastard.' He liked that. Her visit had made him think of Sven-Arne. He had suspected his nephew was sweating it out in India. Now he had finally been outed. What would he do? Ante guessed he would try to make his way somewhere else. There was no way back.

Ante Persson had understood his decision, had secretly admired it, perhaps also been envious. He himself would never have been able to up and leave in that way.

'Everyone is dead,' he muttered.

Unease was lodged in his body like the sliver of a grenade. He knew he was unable to work on days like this. The texts rushed at him, images in his interior became too insistent, his buddies – above all those who had remained in Spain – appeared like phantoms and leered at him with their death-distorted faces.

The feeling of failure was never as clear to him as in these days of meaningless revisiting of the past. He knew his time was running out and that the finale was rapidly approaching. He was now as old as his mother Agnes when she slipped into her final slumber.

She had never understood his passion but had also never hesitated to support him, often without words. Perhaps she was afraid of using the wrong word.

Agnes had seen his suffering, understood that every person needed a little pride, a smidgeon of hope. In that way she was like the most persistent fighter, although she never reflected in political terms.

Teruel had made him into a 'grumpy bastard,' but also into a failure. He and his buddies had not only lost the battle, but the entire war. As the brigade pulled back, they lost life and hope. No one admitted it, other than perhaps a few, the ones who slunk away to Valencia to find a boat out, but they were few in number. Otherwise they simply kept their spirits up, or rather, appearances.

He flipped through his papers, stared listlessly at the spines of the books, dragged himself over to the window, and saw that the rain would go on all day.

How long can one live in a dream? One's whole life. If one is a 'grumpy bastard.' A failure never gives up, adding defeat to defeat.

He missed Sven-Arne. He wanted to tell him how it had all really happened. He could have done so immediately, or as the years went by, but Ante Persson had wanted to win so badly, for once in his life, one single time he wanted to deal Fascism a fatal blow.

TWENTY-SEVEN

The forensic investigation of Tobias Frisk's house was exhaustive, and only completed late Sunday afternoon.

When Ann Lindell read the preliminary report on Monday morning she was convinced that the eagle theory had turned out to be true, or at least led them to the unknown woman's killer.

They had found a photograph of the woman who presumably was the victim, the owner of the foot. It had been slipped in between two books in the minimal bookcase in Frisk's TV room, the room in which he had died. The picture showed a woman with Asian ancestry, between twenty and thirty years old. She smiled into the camera, a somewhat hesitant smile. She had long, dark hair tied back with what appeared to be a white bow. Her evident shyness made her seem almost seductive, though surely unconsciously so – Lindell was convinced of this. There was no pretence about her. Sammy Nilsson had studied the picture closely and declared that 'confident women are rarely beautiful.'

They had samples of strands of hair and skin fragments recovered from Frisk's house as well as – perhaps the most spectacular find – traces of blood on the chainsaw in the back shed.

There was much that suggested that the DNA they would

uncover – according to Morgensson in Forensics it would take a couple of days – would match that of the foot. Lindell thought so, too.

She called Marksson on his mobile phone and told him what Forensics had come up with. He did not sound surprised, just tired. During Saturday and part of Sunday he had been struggling to accept the image of Tobias Frisk as a hatchet killer, but had capitulated under the increasing quantity of forensic evidence.

'But we still can't be one hundred per cent sure,' he said with his familiar hoarseness. 'I mean, until we have all the answers.'

'Not completely sure, but confident,' Lindell said, well aware that her colleague wanted to leave the door to an alternative explanation open as long as possible.

Perhaps it was in part because on Saturday afternoon he had gone to see Frisk's mother, a woman in her seventies, in order to tell her in person that her son had died by his own hand. She had received the news silently and thereafter collapsed. Marksson had managed to catch her as she fell. Now she was hospitalised, dumb and sedated in a half-daze. Not a word had passed over her lips.

They decided that Marksson and a colleague would continue the rounds of questioning with the remaining inhabitants on the point. It was clear that the woman had lived with Frisk for a considerable time, shared his bed, and moved freely around the house. There were many traces. Someone must surely have heard or seen something. Bultudden was a relatively isolated outpost by the sea where the inhabitants knew each other's ways and habitual movements very well. A new, unfamiliar element would surely have been noticed.

There was no reason for Lindell to remain engaged, at least not on site. She promised to forward all forensic information.

'She's unknown,' Marksson said. 'I think that's shit.'

It was true. They had hair, blood, and skin, even a photograph, but no identity. They had a foot but no name.

She read through Morgansson's report on the saw one more time. It was in good condition, purchased at Såma in Uppsala, as evidenced by a small sticker. The blade and chain were basically new, the teeth only slightly worn. The oil on the chain was of vegetable origin, probably originating in a twenty-litre container in the tractor garage. Analysis would show if it matched the traces of oil recovered from the foot. There had not been any traces of blood on the blade, but some under the hood where the chain wound around a cog. Lindell had no idea what the interior mechanism of a chainsaw looked like but tried to imagine it.

There was also sawdust inside the hood, most likely from a pine tree. Lindell had immediately been struck by the macabre fact that Frisk had presumably continued to use the saw after he had finished chopping up his girlfriend. Wouldn't a natural reaction have been to want to get rid of the tool? Morgansson believed that after the deed Frisk had at least changed out the blade and chain. She would check if Frisk had been a customer at Såma recently.

In the southern end of the shed there were large quantities of firewood – some fifteen or twenty cubic metres, Marksson estimated. Frisk had needed his chainsaw.

In the northern end of the shed there was a cordwood saw with a hydrolic piston. Marksson had explained how it worked. Lindell had shiveringly imagined Frisk first cutting the woman in two before he completed his work with the chainsaw.

Tobias Frisk had cleared away all of her belongings. There was not a single feminine item of clothing, no make-up or forgotten tampon in the bathroom, no extra toothbrush, no notes, not even doodles in the pads of paper they found in the bookshelf, no newspapers or books that looked out of place. There were several old scorecards in a Yahtzee box but only two sets of initials: TF and LM. Frisk's neighbour confirmed that they had had a habit of playing a game of Yahtzee from time to time, most recently a couple of years ago.

There was no computer in the house. Lasse Malm claimed there had never been one. Tobias Frisk hardly even watched television. The only program he tried to catch was the evening news at seven-thirty.

What did the man do all evening, Lindell wondered. He hardly watched any TV, he didn't surf the Web, his entire book collection consisted of some twenty books, there were no magazines testifying to any special interest, and he did not appear to have had much of a social life. According to one source he visited his mother once a week, always on a Sunday. He had no siblings.

According to the neighbours along the Avenue, he seldom or rarely received any visitors. Lindell's impression of an exceptionally isolated existence, dominated by routine, was growing ever more vivid.

'He liked to fish' and 'Fishing was his thing' were the two comments from his neighbours that indicated any interest. They had also uncovered a sizeable collection of fishing tools. Marksson had deemed the collection 'above average for an amateur'.

They had a photograph. Either he had overlooked it in his sorting or kept it as a memento. One fact that Morgansson had noted in his report was that there was no camera in the house. Had the woman brought the photograph with her?

Frisk's passport lay in a kitchen drawer along with some insurance documents, old bills, and the latest statement about how much in retirement funds he had managed to accumulate. The passport, which had been issued in April 2002, had two stamps. Frisk had entered Turkey on June 12th of the same year, and left a week later.

On the wall above the telephone in the kitchen, there was a list of telephone numbers. It consisted of thirteen names, of which five were work-related. All six neighbours were represented, as well as 'Mum' and 'Mum's property manager'. They called the latter. He was a property manager in the area where Frisk's mother lived and he explained that Frisk had called him a couple of times to do small jobs in Frisk's mother's flat.

Thirteen names. Thirteen numbers. Nothing that so much as whispered a way to proceed. Lindell had never seen anything like it.

The wage stubs from Ahlén's Bakery were neatly filed in a folder, where the past five tax returns appeared in order. He did not make a particularly good salary – barely 250,000 in 2004 – but on the other hand the house was his and very likely paid off. He did not appear to have lived a particularly extravagant life and could probably put away a couple of kronor every month.

Marksson had already called Frisk's employer on Saturday and told him what happened to Frisk, but had not said anything about him being a suspected killer. Conny Ahlén was quite naturally shocked. The news was completely unexpected. According to Ahlén there was nothing in Frisk's behaviour to account for suicide. Quite the opposite; Frisk had been in good spirits all autumn. He had not been sick a single day since his holiday in July. He had been given a raise in September, 'for everyone who works five years.' Ahlén and Frisk had gone out for a bite to eat together in connection with this event. Everything had been hunky-dory, at least on the surface.

When asked if Frisk had had any girlfriends, Conny Ahlén had at first given a vague answer that there may have been some lady friends in his life a couple of years ago, but then changed his mind and said that he could not recall Frisk ever mentioning women. 'To be perfectly honest, we actually used to joke about Tobias. We called him "the island hermit".'

All of the bakery employees had bank accounts at the Föreningssparbanken in Östhammar, and Marksson would check the dead man's balance and potential debts as soon as the bank opened in the morning.

Lindell and Marksson were naturally focused on the unknown woman. All signs pointed to the fact that Frisk had blown his own brains out. Now what remained was trying to establish if he had also taken another person's life. They would never be able to charge him, and Lindell felt almost relieved. He had meted out his own punishment and in this he had made the same assessment as Torsten Andersson: the ultimate punishment.

They had blood, hair, and skin, and a Stihl. That was all, and it would probably last them a long time.

Lindell took out a fresh composition book and wrote 'Bultudden' in large letters on the front.

At the top of the first page she wrote a question. It read: 'How did they meet?' The answer was not self-evident. Frisk had most likely not visited the area – south-east Asia – which they believed the woman was from. All neighbours shook their heads, all equally certain and not a little astonished at the question of whether Frisk had ever travelled to Thailand, Malaysia, or Bali. 'When he was in Turkey, he was homesick every minute,' Thomas B. Sunesson told Marksson.

Lindell tossed a couple of sentences onto the page, paused for a few seconds, staring unseeing at the wall before her where she had a map of Uppland, smiled to herself, and then wrote intensively, turning the page and continuing.

The telephone rang. She glanced at the display and ignored the signals.

After filling two entire sides with what many would regard as hieroglyphics, Lindell put her pen down and read through what she had written. Her conclusion was that if Tobias Frisk had not travelled abroad and met the woman there, the situation must have been reversed: She was already in Sweden when they met.

Two scenarios struck her as most plausible. Either she had come to this country in the company of another Swedish man or else she had worked in Sweden and thus encountered her future slayer.

For a murderer was what he was, she was convinced of it. No one parted willingly with a foot. She chose to disregard the fact that he would perhaps never have been found guilty in a court of law, that his defence could always have claimed she had left the house as well as Frisk and that someone had thereafter murdered and butchered her.

'WORK' was written in her notebook in all caps. The

first thing she thought of was restaurants. She was familiar with a handful of Asian establishments in Uppsala alone – Japanese, Thai and Chinese. There were probably others. She fixed on Thai, reached for the telephone book and looked in the Yellow Pages under the heading 'Restaurants'. Her eye immediately fell on the name 'Sukothai'. She had eaten there once, with a journalist from TV4. A quick lunch, a couple of months ago.

At that moment it occurred to her that she had two chainsaws in her trunk. Instead of calling the restaurant, she called Marksson.

He picked up right away and Lindell told him about the power tools and that she would try to make time to drive out to Bultudden the following day.

Bosse Marksson was out on the point and he promised to leave a note for Sunesson and Malm to this effect in their respective mailboxes.

'How is it going?'

'No one has seen or heard a thing,' Marksson answered. 'And I don't get it. How can a person live in a place like this without anyone finding out?'

'She may have been locked away,' Lindell said. 'It's happened before.'

'But where?'

'Maybe she was scared and stayed inside of her own accord.'

'But when anyone visited Frisk?'

'There is the upstairs,' Lindell said.

Marksson pondered this.

'Perhaps, but what a life.'

'What a life,' Lindell agreed.

She took out the snapshot of the woman one more time. It had been taken outside, in daylight. She was smiling at the photographer. Her dark hair was combed back and the bow peeped out like a white butterfly. She was wearing a short-sleeved yellow T-shirt and something was printed on the left side of it, at the bottom of the picture. They had discussed what this might be, perhaps a logo. The forensic photographer had made an enlargement of the area, but it told them nothing.

She took the photo, slid it into a plastic folder, and decided to drive around to the eateries she knew about.

First she headed to an Indian restaurant in Bäverns Gränd. It was lunchtime and the dining room was full. None of the staff members recognised the woman. Next stop was at Amazing Thai on Bredgränd. Same depressing result. Every staff member shook their heads. She was greeted with smiles at the two Chinese places on Kungsgatan, but no one who worked there could identify the face in the photo.

At Sukothai the lunch rush was over. A woman was gathering up plates and glasses in the dining area. She came over to Lindell with her tray piled high with dishes, smiling as if in recognition, but Lindell interpreted this more as an old habit and not because she truly recognised her.

'Hungry?' she asked.

Lindell explained that she was from the police.

'Anything wrong?'

'No, not at all,' Lindell assured her, 'I just need you to look at this picture.'

She held it up. The woman put down her tray, walked over to a table, and held the photo under the lamp.

'From Thailand,' she said at once.

'So you've seen her before?'

'No, but her blouse. It is yellow. This was taken on a Monday,' the woman said, nodding firmly. 'A Monday.'

'How can you tell?'

'The colour of the king, yellow. Everyone has a yellow top then. Because they like the king. Always on Monday. All Mondays. The king is good. Yellow is the colour of the king.'

The woman's face broke into a huge smile and Lindell found herself smiling almost as widely. They studied the photograph together in silence. The woman grew serious.

'Not a good thing,' she said.

At first Lindell did not understand what she meant. 'No, not a good thing,' she said, and took the picture back. 'What is this?' She pointed to the logo on the shirt.

'The mark of the king,' the woman said quickly.

'Do you have any idea where this picture was taken?'

The woman shook her head.

'She maybe works at a restaurant. You see,' she said, and pointed to something in the background, a detail partly concealed behind some trees, that Lindell had looked at closely but not understood what it was. It looked like the roof of an old-fashioned well.

'For fish,' the woman said. 'The guests are looking at fish.'

Lindell took another look and understood. Restaurant, she thought. That sounded reasonable. A Swedish man comes in, eats, sees this woman and they start to talk, maybe see each other. He is there for a couple of weeks. Once he has left, she follows. Maybe he sends her money for the trip. He buys himself a girl, maybe with promises about work and riches, maybe love and family. Then the whole thing ends out on a windy point.

'Thank you, you've been a pearl,' she said, and spontaneously placed her hand on the woman's arm.

She fired off another smile, showing gleaming white teeth.

'Coffee?'

There was something in the woman's face that made it impossible for Lindell to decline, even though she had already had her daily ration.

She sat down at a table with the photo in front of her. This was no gigantic breakthrough in trying to establish the butchered woman's identity, but at least it was a step in the right direction. Now it seemed even more important to find out who she was.

Edvard had been in Thailand, it occurred to her. Had he bought himself love there? She did not think so, but the very thought of it was enough to make her dejected. All these charter-flying men who took liberties, they were nothing but slave traders. Ola Haver had visited Thailand and said how revolted he was by the fat, middle-aged tourists going around with trim Thai women young enough to be their daughters or granddaughters.

The proprietor came over to her table again, sat down, pulled the picture over and studied it thoroughly, as if imitating Lindell.

She looked up.

'Advertise in the papers,' she said. 'On the coast, that is enough. Everyone can see the picture and they will say if they know her.'

234

She rattled off a number of place names. Lindell recognised at least two of the names: Phuket and Hua Hin. These she had heard of; she thought Haver had been in Phuket. She asked the woman to write down the names of the main tourist towns. It amounted to a good handful.

She left Sukothai with mixed feelings. The dimly lit interior had served as an escape for a few minutes, where she could reflect on the ongoing investigation in peace. In the stairs out to the alley, where her car was parked, it struck her that her role was not set in stone. She ought to drop Bultudden. With Fredriksson's lucky guess of the eagle, she had played her part. Marksson and the other colleagues in Östhammar could take it from here. But something in the young woman's gaze drove her on. Or else was it as simple as the fact that now, when Lindell could place her in a country, the need to know everything appeared even more necessary? No one wants to be anonymous, she thought, and no one wants to die anonymous.

She drove back to the police station. If she had not had coffee at the restaurant she would have gone past Savoy Café, in an attempt to stretch her time of solitary reflection.

At headquarters a whole group was drinking coffee together. It was almost like a morning meeting. Riis was holding forth. Ottosson held up a cup but Lindell shook her head.

'Thailand,' Haver said, as Riis finished.

Lindell wondered how in the world he knew, but tried not to show her surprise.

'And you tell us this now?'

'I didn't think of it at first, but then I thought of it with that T-shirt.'

'Because it's yellow.'

Haver nodded.

'Everybody was wearing one on a particular day, I don't know why, but it looked like a chicken farm.'

'Mondays,' Lindell said. 'Yellow is the colour of their king.'

Even Riis looked impressed.

'Inner and outer investigating,' said Sammy Nilsson, 'and for once with the same result.'

Lindell started to tell them about her visit to Sukothai. Ottosson's smile widened.

'Good work,' he said, and Lindell sensed that he enjoyed Haver's somewhat sulky look. The two of them had not been getting along lately. Lindell did not know why, and did not really care.

'I think we should put an ad in the Thai newspapers,' she said. 'We can get in touch with our colleagues there and they can place the photograph. It should be enough with five locations, places where many Swedes go.'

'What the hell?' Riis exclaimed.

Lindell turned to him.

'Isn't that a bit much?' he went on. 'She is dead.'

'But who was she?'

'What does that matter?' Riis said. 'Her killer is also dead. Nothing can be made undone. We have the motive and how it happened, we have the forensic evidence.'

'What is the motive?'

'Well, that she might have wanted to go home—'

'Maybe,' Lindell interrupted. 'Maybe she wanted to return to Thailand, maybe she . . . No, Riis, that's not good enough. And besides, her relatives must want to know what happened to her.'

'For them she is most likely dead already,' Riis said. 'And as for the ad. She is probably from the north of Thailand. That's where most of the whores—'

'You've been there and checked it out?'

Ottosson coughed, his usual signal when he felt a discussion was going awry. Lindell shot him a quick glance but continued.

'If it had been a Swedish girl we would have left no stone unturned in order to secure an identity, would we?'

She let her gaze wander over the assembled group in order to get their assent. No one said anything.

'And think of the tsunami. We sure as hell made sure every scrap of bone could be connected to the right person. We sent people over there from Federal Homicide and many others besides. You remember that, don't you? That time it was Swedes. I don't think we told their relatives back in Sweden that we already knew they were dead and so it didn't really matter. No, we DNA-tested every single scrap of tissue. So shape up, Riis!'

'That was quite a salvo,' Sammy Nilsson said.

'You want us to send a foot to Thailand?' Riis said sardonically.

'And you remember the Thais? How they helped the tourists?'

When she finished the whole group was completely quiet. Without thinking about it she poured herself a cup of coffee, but remained standing. Her hand was trembling.

'Maybe you're right,' Ottosson said, and broke the silence, 'but the question is, will it help to place the ad?'

'Oh, you too!' Lindell exclaimed, but regretted it immediately.

'And we don't actually know if she's the woman in the picture. It could be anyone.'

Beatrice's comment made Lindell slam her cup onto the table.

'And?' she said, and her growing animosity toward Beatrice almost made her kick her in the shins, but she controlled herself enough to just stare at her.

'What do you mean, "and"?' Beatrice answered calmly.

'The photograph is the only thing we have, isn't it? The only thing we have, and that's what we're going to work with, as long as it holds up.'

Ottosson took out a napkin, reached over, and wiped up the spilt liquid around Lindell's cup.

Lindell and Ottosson had only clashed once before. That had been in the context of an investigation of a young Peruvian's death. That had been eight years ago and Lindell was not proud of her reaction. She sensed that Ottosson agreed with Riis and Beatrice, otherwise he would immediately have jumped to her defence, and that made her almost more chagrined. She felt betrayed but knew that there had to be limits and that they had now reached that point. A continued exchange could only end badly. She was not afraid of the battle, nor of Riis, whom she regarded as a genuine pile of shit, or even to quarrel with Ottosson as she knew she could make amends, but in a strange kind of way she was afraid of Beatrice. To become even more angry and throw out accusations would only play to the advantage of her colleague who had the ability to always keep her cool.

'Okay,' she said, taking a sip of coffee and giving Ottosson a look of thanks for wiping up the spill. 'I'll suggest that Marksson in Östhammar takes the initiative.'

She felt Ottosson's immediate relief.

'Yes, then it will be up to him,' he said in a tranquil tone.

Lindell turned, coffee cup in hand, and walked off. She felt the gazes of her colleagues burn in her back.

Back in her office she sank down in the visitor's chair. She had not exactly expected a standing ovation for her discovery that the woman was from Thailand, but this general absence of interest was shocking to her. She could not understand their reaction. Riis – that was one thing. He was uninterested in most things, and Beatrice now had a habit of taking the opposite viewpoint – either quietly or with a tone of mild superiority – of anything Lindell suggested, but Haver and Ottosson? And Sammy Nilsson, the one who was closest to her when it came to a question of values? Incomprehensible. She re-examined the arguments she had used and found that they held up.

The reason for their indifference must stem from the fact that they viewed their prospects of success as minimal. They probably thought that she would get bogged down in the Thai woman's fate and forget everything else. It had happened before – according to her colleagues – that she had lost her sense of perspective and ended up out of synch with the others in the unit.

She was aware of this undeniable weakness but in this particular case it was a no-brainer. All they had to do was get in touch with a police authority on the other side of the world and let them do the work.

She called Bosse Marksson again and told him she would drive out again the next day. They agreed to meet outside Torsten Andersson's house at half past nine.

TWENTY-EIGHT

Of course he had recognised the rifle, but he hadn't wanted to say anything. Marksson had come by and showed him the antique piece, and asked if he had seen it before. It had to be at least sixty, seventy years old. Why should he say anything? What was done was done. Who could believe that Frisk was man enough to pull the trigger? What he didn't understand was how Frisk had got hold of the weapon.

Now he was out there again, Marksson. Was he whistling? Looked like it. Cops must get cheered up when there is some devilment under way. They come to life. Whistling.

He recognised his dad too. Birger Marksson. That was not a voice you easily forgot. He was still called 'the health enthusiast,' dashing around in tights long before it became fashionable among idiot joggers. Now it seemed almost taunting. Birger Marksson had to use twin walking sticks to get around. Birger's woman, on the other hand, had never gone for a run her whole life. She was from Snesslinge and there one didn't exert oneself. These days she dashed around to every sporting event like a mountain goat, took bus tours, and was active in every organisation in Östhammar.

What was he waiting for? He had been standing there for at least ten minutes. Torsten Andersson had heard Marksson pulling up next to the mailboxes and how he, after a couple of minutes, had stepped out of the car, and then like a restless spirit started walking up and down the street, whistling, like some puffed-up small-town policeman. Now he was taking out his phone and making a call. How much did all these mobile phone calls cost? Everything worked just fine before all those things.

Another car came driving around the bend. Torsten Andersson recognised it immediately. It was her, the Uppsala cop, the one who liked the crackle of a fire. The anxiety he had felt started to dissolve. It wasn't him they were after.

'Sorry,' Lindell said. 'I got hung up at the day care.'

'Doesn't matter. I've been working a little,' Marksson said generously. 'I just called the postman who does this route. His name is Bengtsson, I know him from before.'

Do you all know each other out here, Lindell wondered.

'I asked him if Frisk ever got international mail but he said no. Bengtsson would remember something like that. I was thinking . . .'

'Good thinking,' Lindell said, realising she was starting to appreciate Marksson more and more.

'. . . the woman might have received mail from home.'

'From Thailand,' Lindell said, and told him of her discovery.

'Then we should call Sune Stolt,' Marksson said immediately. 'He lives in Thailand and can investigate on location.'

'Who is Sune Stolt?' Lindell said, laughing.

'A colleague of mine who works with prostitution, paedophiles, and the like. There are probably two, three

Swedish police officers down there. His brother is also on the force, at the Tierp station, but they were both from here originally. Sune was a speedway driver for Roslagen when he was young. Really promising but then he developed a problem with his sense of balance. Something with his ear. But for a police officer that's fine, we're off balance most of the time anyway.'

'You're impossible,' Lindell said.

Marksson smiled, and hissed something imperceptible. Lindell wanted to hug him. The contrast between Beatrice's superior little smile the day before and Marksson's delighted grin brought her an immediate and sudden joy at finding herself on this deserted gravel road, together with a colleague from the periphery, a man who did not make things more complicated than they were.

'I'll call Tierp right away,' he said.

They took Lindell's car. She drove slowly. Marksson was talking with Yngve Stolt and scribbling a mailing address on the back of one of Erik's drawings.

They passed by Margit and Kalle Paulsson's house. Lindell recalled Margit's initial spontaneous outburst when she heard that Tobias Frisk had taken his own life.

'Never,' she had said, 'I can't believe it! Not him.'

Her husband had not shown the same surprise.

'He had always been a little peculiar,' was his quiet reflection.

'How did Lasse Malm take it?' Margit asked next.

'Why do you ask?'

'You don't know?'

Margit glanced at Kalle.

242

'His father committed suicide. That was many years ago now.'

'Twenty-two,' Kalle concurred. 'He put a bullet to his head on the second floor.'

'Did you know that Lasse Malm's father shot himself? '

Strangely enough, Marksson shook his head. He had actually never heard it.

'We should perhaps bring it up gently with Malm and ask him about it.'

'I doubt there's any connection. Was it recent?'

'Twenty-two years ago.'

'You see,' Marksson said. 'If it is an epidemic then the incubation time is long. What kind of weapon did he use?'

'According to Kalle Paulsson it was an old army revolver.'

Lindell slowed down and turned into Sunesson's yard for the third time and was taken aback when he emerged on the steps.

'So you're home,' Lindell said.

'I got called out last night. It was blowing like hell and down in Långalma we had to trim a bunch of trees along a central power corridor.'

'And you managed without a chainsaw?'

'Vattenfall supplies us with the tools.'

'Tired?'

'No, not too bad. I'm used to it. They call me in a lot because I don't have a family to take into consideration. I recover on the weekend, sleep like a log.'

'You're getting the chainsaw back. I was planning to leave it behind the house.'

She opened the trunk. Sunesson looked in.

'Whose is that?' he asked, and pointed to the Jonsered.

'That's Lasse Malm's.'

'Okay, I get it. You've collected every chainsaw.'

'There weren't that many,' Lindell said.

She took out the blade, which was still wrapped in a plastic bag.

'Sorry for the inconvenience,' she said. 'You can put this back on again.'

Sunesson smiled, but it was forced. He had got a remote look on his face. He must be completely spent after all, Lindell thought.

'Go in and catch up on some sleep,' she said.

'Maybe I'll do that.'

He remained standing with the chainsaw in one hand and the blade in the other as Lindell and Marksson left the property.

They stopped at Lasse Malm's cottage. Lindell took out his chainsaw, went around the back of the house, and left it in the same place where she had picked it up the Saturday before. She looked around in the dim interior of the shed where a whole heap of items were arranged, or tossed, rather, into a heap. Island folk, she thought. On Gräsö she had been amazed many times at the attitude of the locals toward their possessions. Farming machinery – new as well as old – could stay out all year round, exposed to snow and rain. Private rubbish dumps with decades of waste could litter the forest edge and slopes, often quite close to the house.

In Malm's shed a rusted barbecue jostled alongside oars; wooden boxes of nets and buoys; a rubbish bag that had fallen over and displayed a mess of old clothes and rags; rusty and relatively new tools; a box of nails, bolts, and screws; a one-bladed plough; and much else.

Time for a garage sale, she thought as Marksson appeared behind her.

'Bargain basement,' he said, and tugged on one of the rags in the black rubbish bag.

'Malm is no neat freak, that much is clear. How can he stand to live like this?'

'The power of habit. Bachelor. Doesn't care. Goes out to fish. Watches sports on TV. Eats, drinks, works, and sleeps.'

'But still,' Lindell said.

She found herself attracted by the multitude of objects, wanted to start digging through the piles of unsorted junk. Maybe there was a find in there somewhere. She loved flea markets, and Saturday mornings she and Erik often went down to Vaksala Square to stroll past the stands. Sometimes she bought something, a glass, a vase, or something else that they did not really have a burning need for. Once she had found a whole box of Legos for one hundred kronor. After a round in the dishwasher they were as good as new. After that time Erik always accompanied her willingly.

It was one of the few pleasures she allowed herself. She liked the atmosphere there, which was almost continental, and she could convince herself they were many miles away, somewhere in southern Europe.

Erik had never been abroad and she had planned that they should go on holiday before he started school, perhaps to Portugal or Spain, but they never got away. She could afford to; she saved and did not live extravagantly. The flat was paid off and she had no debts.

But to travel as a single mother held no appeal. She felt as if she was unconsciously postponing the trip in the hopes of finding someone to holiday with. Someone who . . .

'Should we go down to Frisk's again?' Marksson interrupted her train of thought.

He tossed the rag aside.

'No, I'd rather go to Lisen Morell's,' Lindell said. 'I want to see how she is doing.'

'Then drop me off at Frisk's first. You can talk to her for a bit and then pick me up.'

'You have an idea?'

'I just want to think a bit,' Marksson said.

'Anything in particular?'

Marksson shook his head and headed to the car. Lindell watched him, his lumpy gait and ox-like neck under the short, reddish hair. If it had been Haver, she thought, we could have bounced the ideas back and forth. Marksson has another style, and why not? They worked well together and he appeared effective.

She shot the mess in the shed a last look, then picked up the rag that Marksson had thrown on the ground and deposited it back in the rubbish bag before she pushed the door shut and put the lock back on.

TWENTY-NINE

Lisen Morell sat with her back to the old fishing cottage. Her feet rested on a stool. Her clasped hands rested on her emaciated thighs. She was dressed in the same clothes she had been wearing when she had emerged from the forest by Frisk's house: black jeans and a white jumper, but instead of sandals she was wearing a pair of rubber boots.

She stared out across the sea, which lay almost completely still. When Lindell came closer Morell turned her head and looked at her without showing any surprise or any of the confusion that she had demonstrated earlier. Her gaze was also different. Lindell could establish this when she sat down next to Morell. The wobbly wooden bench let out a groan and dipped.

'It'll hold,' Morell said.

'How are you?' Lindell asked. 'You were a little freaked out when we saw each other last.'

'I'm still freaked out.'

'By what?'

Morell smiled and posed a counter-question without lifting her gaze from the sea.

'What are you afraid of?'

'Getting sick,' Lindell said. 'Seriously sick.'

'You think I'm a wreck, yes, I know.' She raised a hand to

silence Lindell's protests. 'Everyone does, not least out here on the point. They call me the Magpie, do you know that? Is there anything else that you're afraid of?'

Lindell shifted a little. The bench underneath her moaned.

'Getting sick,' Morell said slowly and thoughtfully, as if testing the meaning of the words. 'I am healthy, at least I think so. But to live in this paradise wears on my strength. You see me as a wreck,' she repeated, 'and in a way you and everyone out here are right. I am a ship that started to sink out here on the Sea of Åland, drifted into the bay, and was washed up as a wreck. And here I sit.'

Lindell studied her profile. A beautiful face, perhaps a little too thin. Lisen Morell would benefit from putting on a couple of kilos. A few crow's feet at her eyes and around her mouth indicated that she was not completely young, but otherwise her skin was youthfully smooth. Her hair was gathered in a ponytail. She wet her thin lips with her tongue before she continued.

'My hand doesn't obey me any longer,' she said, and held up her right hand. Long, slender fingers, well-groomed cuticles, and faintly cherry-coloured nails, no ring.

'It shakes from time to time, just a little, but the most insignificant tremble is enough to crush me. I am an artist. It started a year ago, the trembling. I felt it in my heart first and then the movement spread outward to the tips of my fingers.'

'What happened a year ago?'

'Nothing. I came home from New York and was happy, very happy. I had met Watanabe again and I had sold well, was prepared to start saving for a new collection. But I felt

248

at the same time that something was wrong. Not physically – I have always been fit and healthy – but that there was something else that caused my heart to tremble. An arrhythmia of the soul. I practise a method called mezzotint. There are not many of us. It demands years of training, patience, and above all a sure hand. The worst of it is that I don't know what it can be.'

'Maybe you have some idea?'

'I reproduce nature, create small representations of buds, flowers, and animals. I don't dare try humans. There I can't measure myself against Watanabe. I do it with love, become drunk with the minute. A pine cone can make me smile.'

Then being out here should have you rolling on the floor, Lindell thought, but said nothing.

'Yes, I know what you're thinking, a pine cone, rough against your hand and a little unfriendly, but with thousands of seeds, of future life, a pine cone is far more sensual than most of what we humans produce. That may be the source of my downfall. I creep down beside nature's miniatures, breathe on them, breathe them in. I don't touch them, but they touch me. When I stand up and look out over the world – that is when it happens. That's when I feel the arrhythmia. The trembling. It is hard to explain and I don't ask that anyone understand what I mean. Watanabe, perhaps.'

'Who is this Watanabe?'

'A Japanese artist I met for the first time in France. He is so exquisite. We have also met in New York when he had an exhibition at a gallery in Soho.'

'What do you see when you look out over the world?'

Lindell sensed what the answer would be. She rarely or never looked at pine cones herself, much less breathed on

249

them. But in a way she could understand the feeling that Morell described. She had Erik, he was her pine cone. To breathe him in was her greatest possible happiness.

'War,' Lisen Morell said finally. 'War against all that is living. If we took as our starting point these pine cones or buds or the sea,' her hand made an unexpectedly quick sweeping motion, 'or the desert or glaciers, then we would be in better health. Simply put, if we did that we would feel better.'

Or Erik, if we took Erik as a point of departure, Lindell thought, unexpectedly moved by Morell's words, which she in another context in another environment would perhaps have labelled the rantings of a confused person.

'I will show you what Watanabe is capable of,' Lisen Morell said, and stood up.

Lindell followed her into the cottage, which in contrast to the last time she was here was now clean and tidy. Lisen Morell walked over to the wall they had sat leant up against on the outside of the house and pointed to what Lindell at first took to be a photograph. The picture represented a lizard, so exact and detailed in its representation that it seemed alive.

On the opposite wall there was a painting that showed a woman's body in motion, perhaps in water; the movement by the woman's breast suggested rippling water.

'I have many others,' Lisen Morell said, 'I change them out from time to time.'

Lindell looked around. She saw no other art.

'What about your things?'

Perhaps it was the word 'things' that caused Lisen Morell to smile.

'Nothing out here,' she said. 'It's all back in town. Oh, one thing! But it isn't a mezzotint.'

She walked over to a chest of drawers, pulled out the uppermost drawer, and took out a folder. She opened it and revealed a watercolour painting of a flowering branch.

'Cherry,' she said. 'I love cherries.'

Lindell saw a delicate branch with a dozen flowers, some in full bloom, others still buds. The petals were white with a faint pink tone toward the centre. The insides of the flowers were – as far as Lindell could judge – reproduced to the most minute and exact detail.

'This is fantastic,' she said, and meant it. She wanted to touch the flowers, smell them. 'What are these bits called?'

'Stamens and pistils,' said Lisen Morell, and smiled.

She closed the folder and put it back in the chest. Everything was done very quickly, as if she did not want to expose the cherry flowers to either light or eyes.

'Have you shown your art to your neighbours out here?'

'No. They think I'm completely batty.'

'But if they could see . . .'

'I don't talk so much with them. They judged me from the start. Without knowing who I am, what I have done or could do. If you only knew how limited they are.'

'Did you ever talk to Tobias Frisk?'

'Sure, he sometimes helped me with the car. It's as moody as I am. You see, I have to have a car to get here and back, I have to fill up on petrol and blow out a lot of pollution into the air.'

'Was Frisk as judgmental?'

'Maybe not. He sometimes dropped by with cinnamon buns. Sometimes I got the impression he was interested.'

'In you?'

Lisen Morell nodded. 'But he was shy.'

'Were you interested?'

'No, I didn't encourage it at all. And it got better. At first he looked at me as if I . . . well, you know.'

'When did it get better?'

'Last autumn. It seemed like he relaxed. I thought he realised I wasn't interested.'

'Maybe he met someone else?'

'No, but he smelt differently.'

Lindell laughed. 'What do you mean?'

'Haven't you noticed? When they are like males in rut they stink, but when they are satisfied the smell is not as sharp.'

'Is that because they put more effort into their hygiene when they meet a woman? Wash themselves, put on a little deodorant, and splash on a little of this and that?'

Lisen Morell smiled. Lindell liked her smile, especially since it contrasted so completely with the woman she had met earlier.

'Okay, when did his smell change?'

'About a year ago.'

'And then?'

'Until early this autumn. Then he went back to his old self, if you can say that. Clumsy in a way I had never noticed before. I almost felt sorry for him, though he stared at my breasts. He also drove into the ditch, I think he was drunk. Not that that is unusual out here. Regular laws don't apply in Bultudden.'

'When was that?'

'Perhaps a month ago.'

252

'Was he hurt?'

'No, I met him shuffling along the road. He was probably on his way to get Lasse Malm or someone else to get help to tow the car. It was stuck in the ditch. But he didn't want any help from me.'

'Did you hear the shot?'

'Probably everyone out here did.'

The fact was that only Lasse Malm and Sunesson had reported that they had heard anything. The others denied hearing the double salvo just before eight o'clock in the evening – that was the time both Malm and Sunesson had given.

'What did you think?'

'That someone was shooting a wolf.'

'Are there wolves here?'

'There was one a year ago. That was also a lone male.'

'But hunting a wolf at night,' Lindell said. 'Is that sensible?'

'No, but there's so much activity around here that is not sensible, day or night.'

Lindell dropped the theme of the wolf and tracked back to the change in Tobias Frisk after the summer.

'But you never saw a woman arrive or leave?'

'No.'

'And the change happened in late summer?'

'Yes. I remember that he came over the first week of September. I was going to have the car inspected on the tenth and he was going to help me with some small things. And then he smelt like that again, somehow raw. I'm sensitive to smells. You wash with Dove, don't you?'

Lindell nodded.

'And there's jasmine, too.'

'You're right,' Lindell said, and felt a blush spread over her cheeks.

'So for three months he has smelt of lone male,' she summed up, as she bent over to fish out a pen and pad from her bag, not wanting Lisen Morell to notice her embarrassment.

'Like a prowling wolf,' Lisen Morell said.

'And it wasn't the case that a man came into your life last autumn and disappeared in summer? I mean, that Frisk . . .'

'I understand what you're getting at. No, it wasn't like that. I wasn't seeing anyone, then or now.'

Morell looked at the floor and drew a breath as if she was bracing herself.

'I've had men,' she said. 'Many men. I mean, not like that, that makes it sound worse than it is, but I am not exactly a virgin. But now, the past two, three years – nothing. I can't bring myself. Even though I love pine cones, which are a result of reproduction, I can't bring myself to reproduce myself. Even though I love flowers, stamens and pistils, the delicate and beautiful in their construction and whole function, despite this I myself am wilted. Isn't that ironic? Or sad, perhaps? I don't know. Perhaps I am a sterile bloom, like the white outer blooms of the Snowball tree. Or a hybrid, a false flower, beautiful and long-flowering but not fertile. A flower for looks but not for seed. Sometimes I long for a child, but I don't want to bring one into the world. I don't trust the men who are in power. My stigma will never swell up.'

She finished and stared into the floor again, before she gathered herself and anticipated Lindell.

'Yes, I know what you want to say, but if you live with a

man the question of children always comes up in the end. To deny a man children is to deny him, isn't it? A man can't take that. It upsets him. The male wants to reproduce himself, sire offspring. It is the proof of his virility.'

Lindell sensed that she was speaking from her own experiences. There was much to say, but she chose to nod and mumble something about how she understood. Continuing the discussion might cause Lisen Morell to go off-kilter, to revert to the state of mind she had been in the other day, and Lindell wanted to prevent this at all costs.

They said goodbye outside the cottage. Once she reached the car, she opened the door and tossed her bag onto the passenger seat and looked back. Lisen Morell was still standing outside. She was moving her right hand in what looked like a wave.

Lindell hesitated for a second before she quickly walked back over.

'What do I smell of other than soap and jasmine?'

'Loneliness,' Lisen Morell immediately answered.

THIRTY

'It took you a while,' commented Bosse Marksson, who was sitting at Frisk's kitchen table, a stainless steel thermos in front of him.

'She wanted to talk,' Lindell said, 'and I didn't have the heart to leave.'

She told him what Lisen Morell had said about her neighbour, but mentioned nothing of the rest of the conversation, nothing of Watanabe, pistils, and loneliness.

'Want some coffee?'

He poured a cup without waiting for an answer.

'Complicated,' Marksson said. 'I can't get my head around Frisk. I thought I knew him.'

Lindell drank the coffee, which was strong and good.

'There are cinnamon buns,' he said, but Lindell thought they might be from the bakery where Frisk had worked and declined the offer.

'I'll bet a lot of people have had the wrong idea. Remember what Ahlén said: He's never had a better person on his staff.'

'He probably meant as a baker,' Lindell said.

'No, the way he said it, it included the whole personality.'

'People have been wrong before. The fact is that Tobias Frisk had a woman living with him, a woman of foreign extraction that no one says they had any knowledge of, a woman that he most likely murdered and hacked into pieces. And then when you are going to drop in, decides to shoot himself in the head in his best TV couch.'

'But—' they both said, and broke into laughter.

'You start,' Marksson said with a gesture of invitation.

'Morell's story,' Lindell said. 'The woman's foot appears at the end of November while – if we are to believe Morell – Frisk changed back into his old ways and started to smell like a drooling male already at the start of September.'

'Maybe she stopped putting out, like that woman from ancient history. Finally Frisk got tired of it and cut her to pieces.'

'It's possible,' Lindell said.

'Three things,' Marksson said. 'First: Why does he take his own life? Fear of being discovered, that he can't stand the shame of being accused of murder. But he must have realised that we didn't have anything on him with regard to the killing and mutilation?'

'But the chainsaw?' Lindell interjected.

'Yes, that's the second thing. If he had got rid of it, he would have been scot-free, even if we would have been able to place the woman in his house. All he would have to do would be to claim that she up and left. He didn't even know you were collecting chainsaws, did he? If we can assume he was so stupid he didn't think of the saw, that there were remains of the woman on it, then he wouldn't need to get so nervous that he would have to kill himself, at least not because of your visit. And if he was a smart guy, well, he would have dumped the saw into the Baltic and everything would have been roses. Then he would have been able to offer you cake and take it easy.'

'What is the third thing?'

'The gun,' Marksson said. 'No one out here claims to recognise it, which is fucking unbelievable. Out here you know what kind of microwave oven your neighbour has, what kind of fishing rod, lawnmower, and definitely the contents of the gun rack. You hunt together, get to talking about hunting and fishing, you discuss guns, you brag.'

'The gun was unregistered,' Lindell said. 'Is that normal "out here", as you put it?'

'There are probably old rifles tucked away, but not more out here than in other places. Lasse Malm's father killed himself with an unregistered weapon, an army gun that no one knew the origins of. Or so they said.'

'I thought you didn't know he had committed suicide?'

'No, but Dad did. I called him. As usual he had a bunch of good advice for me.'

'I don't think I got a single piece of good advice from my dad,' Lindell said. 'The ones he gave me I didn't take, thank God. He wanted me to become a hairdresser. When I was around nineteen or twenty they closed up three hair salons in Ödeshög, so he saw potential.'

'Smart guy,' Marksson said with a smile. 'He was thinking of your future.'

'I know, but what a future, to stay out there. I would have died of boredom.'

'Like on this point. How long would you last out here?'

Lindell hesitated. Her colleague was born in this area, had his friends here, this was where he hunted and fished, and she didn't want to put down his home. She also thought, for a single brief moment, of Edvard and Gräsö Island.

'It would depend on the context,' she said.

258

'Everything depends on the context,' he said, smiling.

'Once upon a time I was planning to move out here. We would have been colleagues.'

'To Gräsö,' Marksson said.

Lindell nodded.

'You know,' she said.

'Dad,' Marksson said.

Lindell looked quizzically at him.

'He saw you on the Gräsö ferry with a man.'

'He recognised me?'

'You've been in the papers a couple of times and Dad is the kind of guy who keeps track of things, colleagues above all. I think he's a good man,' Marksson said, and Lindell guessed who he was referring to but had to ask, perhaps in order to hear someone say his name.

'Edvard.'

'It didn't work out,' Lindell said.

'The context,' Marksson said.

She wanted to hear him tell her a little about Edvard, but Marksson appeared to have dropped the subject. Was it out of consideration for her? Was Edvard living with another woman? She swallowed hard, audibly. She wanted to tell, she wanted Marksson to understand what even she herself didn't understand. She wanted to talk about things she had never before mentioned to anyone.

Where did this sudden desire for openness come from? And why now in the presence of a man whom she had known all of a week, and who to top it off had a central communications centre of a father. Was it Lisen Morell's words about how she smelt of jasmine but also 'loneliness'?

She was sitting in the killer and suicide victim's kitchen

259

waiting for something, a word, an insight, or perhaps intimacy. She didn't know which and did not dare to take a risk.

'Maybe it's not too late,' Marksson said suddenly, and stood up in the same breath. The chair was sent backward but he stopped it from tipping over with a swift hand. 'Shouldn't we get going? There'll be no babies made this way. Time to show a little nerve.'

He rattled off encouraging stock phrases one after the other as he screwed on the thermos stopper and replaced the cap that also functioned as a mug.

'I'm headed to the big village to pick up some stuff for the wife. She must have sent away for something new.'

Lindell got up from the table. Edvard doesn't have another, she thought jubilantly. As if it made any difference. She would never see him again, she knew that. Maybe *see* him by chance, but never touch.

When she had dropped off Marksson at his car she ended up sitting for a while. She counted the mailboxes at the side of the road. Seven in all, arranged in order from north to south. Andersson came first, Frisk was the last in the row. Lisen Morell had none. She must get her mail in Uppsala.

Why do I expose myself to this, this masochism? Why air this old story, over and over again? There were no obvious answers. She had accepted the job on the coast even though she was aware that the old thoughts would come up.

She sighed heavily, longing for her flat, Erik's chatter, the sofa, a glass of wine. This isn't normal, she said to herself. You aren't normal. Something went wrong.

260

THIRTY-ONE

On the day of the Virgin, the eighth of December, Sven-Arne Persson returned to his homeland. That was the word he mouthed as he looked out of the aeroplane window, the first time in almost exactly twelve years that he had seen Sweden. Homeland. What a sick word, he thought, and recalled one of Uncle Ante's timeworn phrases from his usual rant: internationalism.

The working class doesn't have a homeland, has never had one, Ante Persson would preach. Sven-Arne smiled to himself. Apart from this, the trip had given him little to smile about. His temporary passport – issued in Delhi – had created problems at the Bangalore airport as well as in Paris. Prior to his departure three phone calls had been required: one to the Swedish ambassador himself, one to the consular section of the embassy, and finally a call with a roaring voice at the other end of the line, likely a local official, before he was allowed to leave the country. He did not know what had been said in these calls, but he guessed that the embassy had assured the Indian immigration serviceman that Sven-Arne was not a criminal, just a depressed Swede who – perhaps with religious searching as his source – had confusedly made his way to India and lived there under great privation. A non-threatening man who now had to be sent back home,

261

perhaps in order to receive care. That was how he himself had strategized.

In Paris it had been only marginally smoother. That Sven-Arne's French was non-existent had not made it easier.

It was with ambivalence that he spun his way from India to Sweden. He hated himself for having gone the political way to get his passport, knowing it was the only possibility to get around the Indian bureaucracy. At the same time he was relieved that the whole process had been so relatively painless. He would not have had the energy to do real battle with some overzealous and self-important Indian clerks. He would rather have backed down.

But now, a thousand metres above Uppland, on his way down to Arlanda, he felt only exhaustion. His joints ached. Strangely enough even his arm hurt, the one he injured in the Japanese section, which it had never done before. He saw it as a reprimand from Lal Bagh: 'You are betraying us.' He also saw Jyoti's face before him: 'You betrayed me.' Where was she now? Perhaps in Chennai, a place that now seemed as foreign as it had done twelve years ago. And then Lester, who with a tone of amazement but also irony made his voice heard: 'You were a powerful man in your country, a kind of governor.'

Even Ismael in his salon fluttered past. The Dalit women in the neighbourhood who swept the street and kept the worst of the filth at bay, who carried bricks when the city razed the old weaving factory and built a police station, who sold bananas in the corner toward the market – all of them looked at him with an unfathomable gaze, not repudiatingly, but with a painful distance that no words or assurances, no decency, could surmount. He had been a decent fellow. No one could say anything else. He convinced himself that he had been respected and regarded as a relatively honourable man given the circumstances. His clothing, his rough hands and feet – the emblematic mark of class – and his entire being on the street bore witness to a man who did not think of himself as above others. But still, he had never been able to overcome the distance, and it had pained him. The temporary passport burning like fire in his shirt pocket, and the fact that he was sitting in an aeroplane, were evidence enough to this.

The landing gear was unfurled with a muffled thud and Sven-Arne was shaken out of his reflections.

After having collected his bag and passing through the passport check without significant problems – were they alerted to his arrival? – he sat down in the arrival hall and bought himself a cup of coffee for the astounding price of three dollars.

Passengers and relatives, taxi drivers with signs in their hands with names such as 'Lundgren' and 'Ullberg,' airport staff – everyone arrived and disappeared just as fast, without giving him more than a distracted glance. He was a man on a bench, so far as anonymous as in the crowd in Bangalore.

His hand shook as it brought the cup to his lips. He slurped up the coffee, drinking it without milk for the first time in a long time. I'm going to be stuck here, he thought, suddenly desperate over hearing all the voices around him, Swedish voices. The coffee was drunk up and he placed the cup gently on the floor.

He ought to get up and go, but couldn't make himself. He saw through the windows how it began to snow.

Most of all he wanted to lie down, curl up and feel some merciful person spread a blanket over him. He would live under that blanket.

Sven-Arne Persson sat as if turned to stone, for over an hour. He could have been an installation. *Lone Man at Airport*. He had turned off all systems, his breathing was barely noticeable, not a movement betrayed that he belonged to the world of the living. It was his eyes that betrayed him as they scanned the arrival hall. If he shut them he would collapse, he was convinced of it.

When he finally got up, the ground swayed and he took a side step. The coffee cup on the ground clattered.

'What am I doing here?'

After a couple of seconds everything became still and the floor stopped swaying. He reached for his bag, took a couple of tentative steps toward the exit, and stepped out into the cold December air.

He was dressed in a pair of brown, baggy trousers of unknown origin, a blue and white nylon jacket, and his best sandals.

In his wallet – the same one he had started out with twelve years ago – he had twelve hundred American dollars, which constituted the extent of his earthly possessions.

Subconsciously he had assumed that he would be met by a delegation at the airport, perhaps police officers, and that they would be in charge of the program. But no one cared about the suntanned and somewhat stooped man in the out-of-place clothing. He wasn't sure where he should go. Arlanda he knew well. He had travelled from here many times during his political career. Back then he would take a taxi or be picked up.

264

He was cold and had to make some kind of decision. He looked around. A taxi marked UPPSALA TAXI was pulled up to the curb. The fact that the company still had the same phone number, which was written in large numbers on the side of the car, set him in motion.

'Uppsala,' he said, once he had sat down in the backseat.

The driver turned around and examined his passenger. The snowflakes in his thin hair started to melt in the warm interior.

'What address?'

'I don't know,' Sven-Arne Persson said truthfully. 'What do you suggest?'

He received a chuckle in reply.

'Home, perhaps?'

Sven-Arne Persson tried to visualise the town house. He felt a need to explain himself to the still smiling driver, suddenly convinced that he would make time to listen to him, understand his situation, and after some additional questions produce a sensible solution.

'Where do you come from?'

'Iran,' the driver replied. His smile had disappeared.

'What did you do when you came to Sweden? Where did you live?'

'I was at a refugee centre in Alvesta for eight months.'

'I am like a refugee, but the opposite, do you understand? I am a refugee in my own country.'

'You don't have a home?'

Sven-Arne shook his head.

'No family?'

'No.'

The Iranian had an almost pained look on his face.

265

'No family? You must have a cousin or something.'

'I have an uncle.'

'Where does he live?'

The suburb of Eriksdal had basically been levelled in the mid-seventies. Only a few houses had been spared. Sven-Arne Persson had been party to the decision. The construction company Anders Diös had won the contract – he still remembered the negotiations. It took place within a kind of brotherly understanding between representatives of the county and the builder. Everyone breathed good intentions and mutual understanding.

He recalled the protests and the demolition. The renters in some buildings had refused to move out. The diggers had begun their work, taking out roofs and walls, breaking up concrete, demolishing one-hundred-year-old sheds as if they were houses of cards. Once upon a time they had been used as outhouses, then were transformed into storage areas for the surplus objects of the renters, finally to fall together into an unsorted pile of rubble.

An flat had been revealed when an outer wall disappeared in a cloud of dust. Sven-Arne had been standing on the street and had studied the scene. A guitar had been hanging on the wall. There was a bed below it. The whole thing looked like a stage set. No one would have been surprised to see a person get out of the bed, take down the guitar, and play a song.

The digger had stopped its enormous shovel. A photographer from the newspaper *Upsala Nya Tidning* had rushed forward. Sven-Arne Persson had hurriedly left the area.

Thirty years later he was back on the same street. The area was no longer called Eriksdal except by some older Uppsala residents who still found some value in the old names. Now rows of town houses dominated. Sven-Arne thought they looked like barracks in an internment centre with small exercise yards surrounded by high fences.

A number of day care children in troop formation marched by on the pavement. A rubbish lorry was driving along on Wallingatan. The sour smell lingered in the air, reminiscent of the canal behind Russell Market in Bangalore. The children screamed and held their noses.

On the way here, he had stepped out of the taxi at the Central Station, gone in and located the storage lockers that were still in the same place, pushed in his bag, and quickly returned to the taxi, which proceeded to take him to Ringgatan as far up as the Sverker school. For the past hour he had been wandering aimlessly through the neighbourhoods, and now he approached the nursing home with great dread.

THIRTY-TWO

The night was long. Sweaty. At half past two he got up and walked over to the window. The sky was clear and starry. Once upon a time, a long time ago, he had loved the silence of the night. Now there was only terror and emptiness in the vaulted heavens, an endless longing.

On the way to the kitchen he tripped on the vacuum cleaner and fell headlong against the doorpost. A pain seared above his temple and in his shoulder as he landed on the floor. The pain was almost pleasurable.

'I need to vacuum,' he muttered, and chuckled.

He rolled over onto his back on the cold floor and stared up at the ceiling. He remembered the dream now. The Magpie had come to him. Her breath was bad but her body warm. She spoke with intensity, almost frenzied, in a foreign language. He knew it was the language of women and did not attempt to understand any of her prattling. Instead he studied her features and noticed for the first time that she was beautiful. She lay on him, her body light as a feather. Had they made love?

He fumbled across his body and stuck his hand into his underpants, stiffening immediately.

The chill under his back made him twist his body and roll onto his side. The old rag runner stank of filth. He loosened his cramp-like grip on his genitals and felt about with his hand on the wood floor as if he was trying to find something, then turned his head and stared out the kitchen window. The stars winked at him.

'I could have been happy,' he said out loud.

In all honesty he did not understand why his life had taken such a strange turn. He was just a regular guy. Life flashed by so quickly, and he who had existed in the periphery was on the verge of being flung out into space like a powerless package of blood, flesh, and bone. Once he had been in the centre, warmed by people, hearing laughter and voices, but slowly and imperceptibly he had been forced out until one day he found himself alone.

He had been out drinking the night before. Now he had to pay the price; the ache was like a vice on his forehead. Even though suffering was at his side right now he would soon get up, he knew he would. And again. And again.

THIRTY-THREE

The old man was sitting on the side of his bed when Sven-Arne entered the room. He had managed to make his way through the building and up to the third floor without bumping into anyone.

Ante had heard him coming, Sven-Arne was convinced of it. His door out to the corridor had been open and the old one must have identified him by his footsteps. He had heard his nephew come and go for fifty-one years. That it had been twelve years since last time made no difference.

He was staring straight ahead, his eagle profile the same as always. His left hand lay on his thigh, veined and lined, the tops of two fingers missing. The wrinkled trousers – were they the same gaberdine trousers he had helped him buy shortly before India? – were stained. Egg, Sven-Arne thought, the old man must still eat an astounding number of soft-boiled eggs.

Ante fought hard not to show how emotional he was, but the tense jaw muscles gave him away.

Sven-Arne rubbed a hand over his own face. The muscles above his right eyebrow twitched spasmodically. They had not done so during all his twelve years in India.

Ante slowly turned his head and looked at his nephew.

'You're older,' he said.

Sven-Arne nodded.

'Twelve years older,' he said in a rough voice. 'And that goes for you too.'

'Should think so.'

Sven-Arne took a couple of steps closer to the bed. He stretched out his hand. Ante grabbed it, pulled him toward him. There was still strength in his arm.

'It was good that you came.'

Sven-Arne suddenly remembered that December day half a century ago at Rosberg's, how he had laid his hand on Ante's as they sat on the roof, Sven-Arne on his uncle's mittens, which they inadvertently left behind. How Ante for the first time told him about Spain with seriousness. Sven-Arne thought he could remember every word that was said, the bridge they were going to blow up, the Bulgarian miner 'the Brush', Ante's Spanish words shouted across the roofs and woods that must have been a kind of greeting or an urging to fight, for resistance. And thereafter the shots that Rosberg and Ante took, their almost wordless conversation, his own warm milk with the line of cream in the glass and the American alarm clock he received with 'Rep. alarm' and 'Long alarm' and the seemingly unbreakable mechanism.

It was as if all of the memories streamed through their fingers. Sven-Arne saw Ante's hand in his own. Two Persson hands, snow-shovelling hands, plumber's hands – like a design on a table runner in a Folkets Hus community centre.

Then he remembered something altogether different and immediately let go.

He looked around the room. The sight of the crutches, leaning against one end of the bookcase, increased his sense of confusion.

'You still have the crutches?'

Ante followed his gaze, as if to check that they were still there, and nodded.

'They're hanging in there,' he said, and Sven-Arne caught a flash of his ironic smile of old for a second.

If Sven-Arne in that moment would have been able to turn the clock back a couple of days, he would have set his sights on Ismael's barbershop and walked back.

He understood that nothing had changed in twelve years. The old man was the same, as was his sickly pride and Sven-Arne's disapproval. No, disapproval was too weak, more like revulsion.

'I've brought you a present,' he said, and bent down.

He wanted to get it over with, hand over his package in order to, yes, in order to do what exactly? Talk about old memories?

'I see,' Ante said, and tried to look indifferent, but his curiosity made him follow Sven-Arne's movements intently as he searched in his bag.

'It's a small thing.'

'It's the thought that counts,' his uncle replied, and Sven-Arne gave him a quick glance. He couldn't tell if he meant it ironically or not.

Ante stretched out his hand and took the gift. Appropriately enough, the wrapping paper was red. Now Sven-Arne saw that his uncle was moved. How long has it been since someone has given him anything, he thought.

With clumsy movements and his lips moving soundlessly, Ante finally managed to peel off the wrapping. The cardboard box was of poor quality and the top almost fell apart as he removed it.

'A sickle,' he said, and got a somewhat uncertain expression on his face.

Ante sat quietly for a long time and studied the tool, the hand-made blade, and the handle of wood.

'There's a hammer here already,' Sven-Arne said.

'What? Oh yes, of course,' Ante said, bewildered.

'You can hang it up.'

His uncle nodded. Sven-Arne's gaze swept along the walls. He recognised everything that Ante had put up: the recognition from the Spanish state, the poster with the message that Barcelona did not give up, the group photo of a party conference at the end of the forties, and the little photograph of Agnes's cottage.

'It was a nice present,' Ante said finally, then put the sickle back in the box and scrupulously packed it all up again. Sven-Arne even had the impression that Ante was going to rewrap the box in the red paper, but the latter put the box on the ground and pushed it off to the side with his foot.

'It was a nice present,' he repeated.

All at once Sven-Arne felt extremely tired. It was as if the long trip and the anticipation of meeting his uncle now hit him with full force. He pulled up a chair and sat down. He wanted to say something, tell him something, but most of all he wanted to lie down.

He looked at the old man, who seemed equally exhausted.

'You still read,' Sven-Arne said finally.

Ante looked up.

'Elsa came by,' he said.

Sven-Arne did not want to know anything about his wife's visit or how she was, but forced himself to ask anyway.

'She is in the hospital,' Ante said. 'Unconscious.'

Sven-Arne nodded. Strange, he thought, that's as far as my interest reaches for this woman I lived with for so many years.

'You are writing your memoirs, I hear.'

The old man nodded.

'About Spain?'

'Among other things.'

'And more?'

'Everything,' Ante said. 'Do you remember Anders Bergström?'

Sven-Arne did not, but saw from his uncle's expression that it had to do with Spain.

'I've told you about him, I know I have, but you probably don't remember, probably don't want to remember. The one from the Workers' Syndical Union who taught me—'

'How to handle a machine gun,' Sven-Arne filled in. 'Now I remember. You've talked about so many.'

'It was an old Russian piece that was in the school in Albacete, heavy as all get out. It was a Maxim from World War One. I'm writing about Bergström right now. He went on to meet a strange fate.'

'Wasn't that true of all of you?'

He did not want to hear the story over again.

'Bergström was a good shot. He belonged to the Reserve Unit at Teruel and there he froze to death. It was probably twenty-five below zero at New Year's. I didn't know anything about it until I was stationed in Morella. It was before I came back to the hospital at the coast, but of course I heard what had happened. There were oranges there. Bergström would have wanted one. He often talked about food, not least oranges. You understand, we missed fruit. We didn't talk politics as much as one would think, mostly it was about food and how things were back home, what we wanted to do later on.'

He shot Sven-Arne a quick look.

'There's only two of us left,' he said after a moment's silence.

Did he mean Spanish veterans or was he referring to the two of them? Sven-Arne decided he was talking about the International Brigades. He knew that the society with the old volunteer republicans had been slumbering for a number of years. The members had fallen away or become too old to manage the organisation. Was it true that only Ante and one other was still alive?

He had accompanied Ante to a number of meetings over the years. It had always been a remarkable feeling to meet Ante's old comrades, tremulous old men who once had been battle-ready youths and who for so long had nursed memories of their fight against the Falange.

'Are you still living in Spain?'

'Are you afraid that the truth will come out? Is that why you have returned?'

Sven-Arne lowered his head, tried to think, tried to get himself to understand Ante, and thereby perhaps himself, but his thoughts went round in circles.

But Arne appeared to have gathered himself and continued to talk about Bergström and his machine gun. Sven-Arne's apathy grew. His uncle's words became a murmur.

'You aren't listening,' Ante declared.

Sven-Arne opened his eyes.

'I'm a little tired,' he said. 'I have had a long trip.'

'You're as mixed up as you were twelve years ago. Don't you understand that there is no alternative?'

'There are always alternatives!'

'It was justice,' Ante said. 'And you know it.'

'Your justice.'

'Our justice.'

Now he's going to start talking about class, Sven-Arne thought. The suffering, the burden. As if we aren't reminded enough about it.

'No, I'm not going to talk about class,' Ante said, and smiled when he saw the perplexed look on Sven-Arne's face.

The old bastard isn't normal, Sven-Arne thought. Now he's reading my thoughts.

'I have left the party,' Ante went on. 'Oh, come on, don't look so baffled. I've thrown in the towel after seventy years. Not even Hungary got me to go, I didn't quit with Seth Persson, even though I thought he was reasonable, or with the Holmbergs, even though I knew him so well, and not after Czechoslovakia either. I stayed on when that bitch became chairman and everything was just women's blather. But then it was time.'

All at once Sven-Arne's head cleared. Not in his wildest fantasy would he have imagined that his uncle would leave the party he had been so faithful to for so many years. Granted, it was a party that had changed appearance, from an almost purely working-class membership to a party for all manner of types from the middle class, now with a minister's son presiding at the helm. But it had been a party that was Ante. The organisation had been his whole life and being.

'Why?'

'I realised that it was easier to act as a socialist from without than within a Socialist Party.'

How much longer does he think he is going to live, Sven-Arne wondered. Is he going to 'act' as a socialist here at the nursing home?

'You're bluffing.'

'Not at all, why would I do that? You drew the same conclusion, didn't you? Ran off to India to dig in the dirt and that schoolteaching you talked about. Wasn't it easier to be a Social Democrat there, in the garden and in the school, than in the party? No circulars and briefs that laid out how you should think and act. No high-and-mighty chairman getting applause for every smelly fart he lets out.'

Sven-Arne could not believe his ears. Had Ante ever had difficulties adjusting to the party's directives and violent swings?

'You if anyone should know why I left.'

Fatigue came creeping again, now accompanied by a headache.

'That was just a pretext. You also thought this whole thing smelt like shit.'

'Maybe,' Sven-Arne said weakly.

He did not want to go on digging through the past. Maybe he should tell something from his time in India. A small episode, some vignettes from the street or Lal Bagh, or about Lester's family, anything that could get him to think about something other than his time as an Uppsala politician.

'Doesn't matter,' Ante said, and heaved himself to his feet with the help of the walker. A tremor shot through his upper body before he found his balance.

'You are here now, and that makes me happy.'

Sven-Arne stared at him, dumbfounded.

'Yes, happy,' his uncle went on. 'I haven't had a debate in twelve years.'

'Someone to debate, you mean?'

'We are the same kind, you and I. You are thirty years younger, but you've sort of caught up with me. Now you can also start to sum things up. And I don't have to explain so goddamn much, you know from your own experience what life is like. I don't want to debate anymore. I want to conclude. Don't you think I realise what my life must have seemed to those around me?'

He sank back down on his bed.

'Are you depressed?'

'You are the only thing I have,' Ante said.

Sven-Arne looked at him. If the news that Ante had left the party was sensational to say the least, then this was no less earth-shattering.

'The only thing or the only one?'

Ante looked uncertainly at him, then his face broke into a smile.

'Both,' he said. 'Olars comes up once a year. For Christmas! As if Christmas was anything special. He has a box of chocolates with him every time. I give it to the girls. Olars, he is starting to get old and decrepit. . . . Do you remember Rosberg's roof? I remember everything, that is my biggest problem. Most people go on, but I'm still thrashing around in the same muck.'

Sven-Arne looked at Ante in amazement. During the approximately twenty telephone conversations they had had during the past twelve years – Sven-Arne had called every spring and autumn – his uncle had not said a word that could imply a change of heart. Not even his letters had contained any of this.

'I thought that was your strength.'

'Maybe it is,' Ante said. 'You see,' he went on, and waved his hand in the direction of the books on the shelf, 'all the words, all the visions, it is as if I can reach out and touch the dreams, I see them before me.'

'Maybe the dreams were unrealistic?'

Ante shook his head slowly.

'No,' he said, 'our dreams were too small. In Spain we dreamt of the defeat of Fascism, violent defeats, we were so young, we wanted to see blood, I admit that. But we also dreamt of culture. We were envious of the knowledge of the bourgeoisie, their sureness, fine words, and carriage. We knew there was something behind it, something that we never reached. Do you understand what I mean? We were proud, of course, but inside us there was the gnawing feeling that we were still poor, as if we were not worth as much. And then we dreamt of women, of course, comrade women, beautiful women in battle.'

Ante smiled unexpectedly as if he remembered something. Sven-Arne knew he had fallen in love with a woman during his time in Spain, but he had never talked about her other than telling him her name was Irina.

Sven-Arne wanted to say something beautiful and inspiring, but as in so many other cases his uncle pre-empted him.

'Don't say anything. I know what you can do. Words, words, and more words. I'm sure you still have that ability. I am glad that you came, but maybe you should have stayed where you were. There is nothing here. In India, yes . . . there is . . . what is there there, anyway?'

'But you haven't exactly given up and laid yourself flat on the ground.'

'I have tried to fight back,' Ante said. 'But now everything is about defeat. Yes, we won a little, I am the first to admit that, but the final conclusion will not be affirming reading. And now everyone is talking about the fact that the world may be coming to an end, the ice caps are melting and we will drown like cats. That may be just as well. Everything will be ocean.'

He stopped and Sven-Arne thought for a moment that he was about to burst into tears. His upper lip trembled and his watery old-man eyes twitched.

'I often think about a little village by the name of Forcall. There was a whole gang of us there – a Pole, some Germans, and then me. Blom was off on some errand, maybe a woman, he was always after them. You must remember Blom.'

Sven-Arne nodded. Ante's talk was calming him down.

'Everything was fine. Sometimes an Italian surveillance plane would go past, but everything on the ground was still. The Polack was a little hurt and one of the Germans was helping him with the bandage. We sat and talked about life. One of those times when you really get close to each other. It must have been our proximity to the Fascist positions. We had nothing to lose except our lives. I talked about Irina, the Serbian. You know, the one who made it into parliament and later became one of Tito's trusted circle. I believed I would never see her again. It was fated that I should die in the mountains. I had been given a warning, been perforated by a grenade, but returned. I was in love with those villages.'

'But also with Irina,' Sven-Arne said. He had shifted his chair a little closer to Ante, who for once was speaking quietly, almost mutteringly.

'Also with Irina,' he echoed.

'But you chose the villages and the conflict,' Sven-Arne said.

Ante nodded. 'I thought I would meet her again when I was injured the second time, but she had been transferred.'

'You lost both the villages and her.'

Ante lifted his head and looked at his nephew.

'Did you have a woman in India?'

'For a while,' Sven-Arne said. 'But she moved on.'

'Do you miss her?'

'Sometimes.'

Ante nodded again. 'Then I was captured.'

'Where did Irina go?'

'When the republic fell she fled to France with everyone else and ended up in a camp, Barcarès. There she met a Spaniard from Lerida, an anarchist who had fought alongside Durutti. He ended up in the Resistance movement in France, but the Germans got him and he died in Mauthausen. Irina was able to get back to Serbia.'

'You've never talked about how you got yourself out.'

'Nothing extraordinary. Bribes. I was being held with a Yankee from the Lincoln brigade, a lift technician from New York. A Jew. There were a lot of them in the republic. We managed to bribe a guard, that's all it took. We parted ways north of Valencia, then I headed north. I had some things hidden away in a village.'

'The children's drawings?'

'Among other things. You remember them?'

'You told me about the drawings when I was a kid. What was that all about?'

'You'll have to read about it,' Ante said. 'It was a nurse

281

from Karlstad who . . . but I don't think I can go through it right now. I was just going to talk a little longer about that moment in Forcall. The Polack groaned a little. He was in pain, but it was nothing compared to what he was to experience the following day. Then he died, just like the Germans. Blom hung on for another week, then he went. He was from Hälsingland. I was the only one in the group who pulled through.'

Ante looked at Sven-Arne with moist eyes.

'Things like that prey on your mind, you know.'

Sven-Arne had known this for fifty years, ever since that winter's day on the roof.

'I think about all the hopes they had. We were simple fellows, no big players. We just wanted justice. Then, when they started going on about Stalin and the camps in Siberia, what were we to think?'

Sven-Arne stretched out his hand in order to put it on Ante's stained trouser leg but pulled it back.

They sat quietly for several minutes. The clatter of footsteps and the rattle of a passing cart could be heard from the corridor.

Sven-Arne thought about what Ante had said, that he had only been fighting for justice. It could have been used for his own part, but he felt that the words were too big, words that no longer had any grounding. Now it was too late to back up the tape and start wreaking havoc, agitating. That time was over and the fault was partly his. He had let go of his dreams and become a prisoner of his situation, and what credibility would he – a fugitive county commissioner – have? In the best-case scenario, people would laugh at him. Wouldn't they? He hadn't embezzled any funds and made off with the coffers, had not been bought by the money men or left on a well-paying international assignment. He had spent his time planting trees, weeding, and picking up litter. Would he be able to speak as he had used to? And perhaps some things really had changed. Perhaps people were more receptive to talk about the things that lay beyond the most immediate matters of everyday life. He knew so little about what had happened in Sweden the last decade.

Sven-Arne realised his uncle was studying him. He is reading me, he thought. To break it up he again stretched out his hand. Ante grabbed it.

'We're sitting on the edge of a piss-pot,' he said. 'We're in a hell of a hole, aren't we?'

His hand was bony and cold.

'We're in a hell of a hole,' Sven-Arne agreed.

'There are a couple of thousand in every generation, the five thousand worst bastards, and I am glad I've belonged to that bunch. That will be on my tombstone. I am an odd duck, but . . .'

'In India . . .'

'What about India?'

Ante sounded almost eager, but Sven-Arne shook his head and withdrew his hand.

'Another time,' he said, but sensed there would not be many more of those.

In the same moment that he stood up and straightened his journey-stiffened body he made his decision. Suddenly it appeared as a simple alternative, the only one really. To once again become an honourable citizen in Sweden and Uppsala was not possible and to return to India was just as unthinkable.

'I'll see you later,' he said, and picked his bag up off the floor, but then he hesitated. He wanted to put his arms around the old man, who now observed in bewilderment that Sven-Arne was gripped by a sudden fervour. But he couldn't do it. This was not because hugs had never been part of the Persson family repertoire but rather that he was convinced it would cause him to fall into an unconsolable fit of weeping. He had to stay upright and make his own decisions.

'You're leaving?'

Sven-Arne nodded.

'Will you be back?'

Sven-Arne hated lying to Ante, and to top it off he was bad at it. Ante had almost always seen right through his hemmings and hawings, but this time he looked pleased when Sven-Arne explained that they would soon see each other again.

'I just have some things to sort out again,' Sven-Arne said from the door, and left the nursing home as unnoticed as when he arrived.

THIRTY-FOUR

One of the advantages of police work, Ann Lindell thought, was that no environment was inconceivable. For the first time in her life she stood leaning over a snowblower.

'You have to prepare yourself,' she heard a voice say, and turned.

'How does it work, anyway? No, forget it. What I really want is to discuss chainsaws. I see that you carry both Stihl and Jonsered.'

The young salesman nodded. I started wrong, Lindell thought, as she saw his watchful, possibly defensive stance.

'I'm from the police,' she continued, 'and I am certain that you can help me. I think you can tell me about almost anything in this shop.'

She smiled and was rewarded with a self-conscious grin.

'What is your name?'

'Daniel Andersson.'

'Daniel, I would like you to look at a photograph,' she said, and took a folder out of her bag.

She held up the photograph. The picture of Tobias Frisk was one year old, enlarged from a group photo taken at a party in Östhammar. It was Frisk's employer who had produced it. Conny Ahlén had claimed it was very like Frisk.

'No, it's no one I know. But maybe Martin would, he has worked here a little longer.'

They walked inside the counter and arrived almost immediately at a small office. A middle-aged man was sitting at a desk, leant over a folder.

Lindell presented herself and her reason for being there. He took the photo without a word and examined it for a couple of seconds.

'He's one of our customers,' he said, and then returned the picture.

'Are you sure?'

Daniel grinned again.

'Okay,' Lindell said, and smiled. 'You are sure. You're often sure, right?'

Martin closed his folder, rubbed his hand over his face, and looked at Lindell.

'I've sold chainsaws and all manner of other things to half of Uppsala's inhabitants. I remember the faces of eighty per cent of them.'

'What about the other twenty per cent?'

'They only come one time, so I don't need to remember them.'

'That's a good ratio: eight of ten return.'

He nodded.

'Good ratio,' he said. 'Not that it helps.'

'Do you know what his name is?'

'No, we're not the KGB, but I think he is from Roslagen.'

'Why do you say that?'

'His dialect.'

'He bought his Stihl here.'

'I see . . . if you say so. We carry Stihl, so that sounds plausible.'

'Why would a person change the blade? Aren't they expensive?'

'The blade can be damaged. Amateurs aren't careful. They get the saw caught and bang it and bend it so it ends up crooked.'

'Was he an amateur?'

'What's happened? You said "was".'

Lindell tucked the folder into her bag. 'That's true, he doesn't use his saw anymore. But was he an amateur?'

'I don't know,' Martin said. 'What happened?'

'An accident,' Lindell said. 'Thanks for your help.'

'What help?'

Yes, what help, Lindell thought when she was standing outside the shop. The third salesman, Thomas, had a faint recollection of Tobias Frisk, but could not recall if he had seen him in the shop recently.

The visit to Såma had been a shot in the dark, and was probably a waste of time. They had the saw, and that was the most important thing. Where it had been purchased was of less significance. It would have been reassuring to establish that Tobias Frisk had bought a new blade and chain during the autumn. On the other hand there were probably a number of other places where he would have been able to pick up replacement parts.

Lindell hated the very idea that a chainsaw had been used to butcher a young woman. Through the shop window, she saw the rows of chainsaws hanging on the wall. Saws were tools and not to be used as weapons other than in horror films, and definitely not by a bakery employee in the outer coastal area.

'Not that it helps for shit,' she muttered, and hunted around until she found Conny Ahlén's number.

287

The bakery owner only picked up on the fifth signal. He sounded stressed, so Lindell skipped over the polite phrases.

'Hi! Lindell, Uppsala police, a quick question. What was Tobias Frisk doing last autumn, in August and September?'

'Working, of course.'

'Was there any change in his routine, no new employee who started at the bakery, or anything else that you can remember? Was his mood different during this period?'

Conny Ahlén was silent for a couple of seconds. Music and clattering sounds could be heard in the background.

'Now that you bring it up,' he said finally. 'He went to Norrland for a bit of fishing. He used to go up for a week or so every year.'

'When was that?'

'I can't really remember, but I can check if I go into the office.'

Lindell heard Ahlén's steps and he talked to someone else. She caught the word 'dinner rolls.' When he returned to the receiver he was out of breath.

'It is amazing. Sometimes everything gets messed up.'

'I know how it is,' Lindell said. 'But I won't keep you long.'

'Don't worry about it,' Ahlén assured her. 'Now let's see . . . That was at the end of August 2004. He was away from work for eight days and returned at the beginning of September.'

'How was he then?'

'He was always pleased after his fishing trips.'

'Do you know where in Norrland?'

'If there's a place called Sorsele then he was there somewhere. I think he mentioned something like that, but it

288

may have been the year before. The fact is, I didn't listen so closely to his fishing stories.'

'He didn't tell you anything else, that he had met anyone or experienced anything unusual?'

'No, not that I remember, but he was pleased, as I said.'

Lindell was about to ask if Frisk's scent had changed after his fishing trip but she changed her mind, thanked him for the information, and brought the conversation to a close.

Back at work she went straight to her office and turned on the computer. She had no idea where Sorsele was but she thought the name sounded good somehow. The fact was that this fishing trip was the only thing she had encountered so far that made Tobias Frisk into a human being. His home and for all appearances non-existent social life gave no clues and made him appear strangely anonymous.

But now she had something to go on: Frisk's interest in fishing, coupled with a trip that had changed him, if Lisen Morell's judgment and sense of smell were anything to go on.

After fifteen minutes' worth of surfing on the Net she had located Sorsele on the map and familiarised herself with rivers and fishing camps in the area, and even turned up the name of a fishing consultant.

She called Torsten Stenberg and explained what she was after.

'I see,' the consultant replied hesitantly, 'there are many who come to Sorsele to fish. And it is over a year ago. Was it trout or something else?'

'I don't know,' Lindell replied. 'I only know he went up to fish.'

'Is he a fly fisherman?'

Lindell didn't have an answer.

'If it was trout or charr then it had to be before the middle of September.'

'Why?'

'Because the season ends,' Torsten Stenberg said. 'But it was probably grayling.' He sounded surer now, as if simply the names of the various species of fish had given him a shot in the arm, or as if Lindell's lack of fishing knowledge made him chatty.

'It's a nice fish,' he continued, 'but it needs immediate consumption because it loses its taste almost immediately. Do you know it tastes a little of thyme?'

He told her about the various offerings that a visiting fisherman had to choose between. Lindell made a written note of the Laisa and the Vindel rivers, as well as a number of different options for guest accommodations. There were fishing campsites, hotels, private cottages, and youth hostels. She had her hands full making the notes as he spoke and realised that it would probably take a while to establish where Tobias Frisk had stayed.

'Maybe at the campsite,' Stenberg said calmly. 'I would call them first. Who did you say you worked for?'

'I'm with the police,' Lindell said, astonished.

'I got that, but what kind? You're probably not solving bicycle thefts.'

'I work at the unit for violent crimes.'

'That's what I thought, that it would be something big. What has he done, your fisherman?'

'We don't know,' Lindell said, and could not repress a deep sigh. 'We are only the beginning of the investigation.

I think I'll come up to you for a while and fish. It sounds relaxing.'

Stenberg chuckled. 'You should be happy that you . . .'

He stopped himself and Lindell waited a few seconds for a continuation.

'I mean about the work,' he said. 'It's worse up here. I would welcome a little stress sometimes. And we need the police. Now there are only two of them and soon they'll be down to one.'

'In Sorsele?'

'Yes. Do you know how large the county is? At least two hundred kilometres long and fifty or sixty kilometres wide. And we have two policemen, Hallin and Lindgren, and neither of them is young anymore. It's probably fifty years since we had a murder and soon there will be no one around to kill. But go on and call the campsite. And if you want to fish, all you have to do is come on up.'

Lindell ended up sitting for a while after the phone call. She studied her scrawls in the notepad and thought about what the fishing consultant had said. She tried to imagine him, a telephone voice, an unfamiliar person in the same country, speaking the same language – even if he did so with another dialect. Nonetheless Sorsele seemed foreign. She tried out the word 'charr' and smiled to herself. The unfamiliar word echoed in the room. She said it again, louder this time. It sounded like a promise.

He had told her about his county, where the police had seventy kilometres to the nearest colleague – was that Arjeplog? – and two hundred and sixty kilometres to backup, the day such was needed. I will never again complain about

291

distance, she thought. Östhammar and Bultudden are right around the corner.

The conversation with Torsten Stenberg had affected her mood in two ways. The feeling that there was another life, in a foreign landscape, with a different sound, but still so recognisable and near. If she stretched out her hand, her life with charr would be there.

'Damn Bultudden,' she mumbled, but it was the bay at Gräsö she saw before her.

At the same time this initial contact with Sorsele meant a small break. Something that was immediately confirmed with her next call. Sorsele Campsite was first on the list of likely accommodations for a visiting sport fisherman. Ten or so signals rang out. Lindell was about to hang up when someone picked up.

Lindell said what she was looking for.

'That's easy enough to take care of,' said the man who had answered the phone, and introduced himself as Gösta Ohlman. 'I'll look him up in the book. What was it you said he was called?'

'I didn't mention it yet, but the name is Tobias Frisk.'

'Has he gone missing?'

'Not really,' Lindell said. 'I just wanted to check if he—'

'Fishermen are good people,' Ohlman said.

Lindell heard the receiver put down and thereafter the sound of footsteps. Several voices in the background, perhaps a radio. How did a campsite in Västerbotten in northern Sweden look at the end of December? She had never been so far north.

'They don't cause any trouble.'

His voice reappeared quite unexpectedly in her ear and it

292

took a second for her to realise that he was continuing his argumentation about fishermen.

'He was definitely here,' Gösta Ohlman went on. 'He arrived at the end of August and left a week later. I think I remember him. He's from the coast, isn't he?'

'Yes, from Roslagen. Why do you remember him?'

'He caught a grayling that was almost three kilos.'

'And is that a lot?'

'I should think so.'

'Do you remember anything else?'

The silence at the other end spoke vividly and Lindell could almost see how Ohlman hesitated.

'You don't have to feel that you . . .'

'He met a girl up here,' he said abruptly. 'We weren't too excited about that.'

'A girl from Sorsele?'

'Not exactly,' he said. 'Quite the opposite, in fact.'

THIRTY-FIVE

A pigeon was sitting on the left fence post and when Sven-Arne Persson approached it slowly turned its head. The perfectly round eyes regarded him without any apparent anxiety.

He took this as a good sign but then became uncertain. Perhaps it was injured and unable to lift into the air?

The street was completely empty and Sven-Arne had not seen a single person on the short walk from Norbyvägen where he had asked the taxi driver to let him out, except for a couple of schoolchildren in the distance. He had asked himself where this reluctance to be driven all the way up came from but had not found a good reason. Perhaps he had wanted space between himself and the destination in case he changed his mind at the last minute?

He stopped a couple of metres from the gate. The pigeon was motionless. Sven-Arne pulled his coat tighter around his body.

'What do you want?' he muttered.

The pigeon took some careful steps along the rail. Sven-Arne looked around. The small houses in a row with low fences or hedges toward the street looked like they had always done. The street had looked like this for approximately fifty years.

Most of the original owners were likely gone by this

point but maybe a few of them had hung on past their time. Sven-Arne believed the area was inhabited by younger families, the houses a typical starter home – in the career as house owner – before the children came.

His father had had several acquaintances who had built homes in the area in the forties. These construction projects could take several years to complete at a time when decent industry and construction workers with fairly secure positions could take advantage of each other's skills and helpfulness. One year basements could be dug out and the foundation laid. Thereafter they raised the frame, walls, and roof, and during the third season the house would be ready for occupancy.

The work was done on evenings and weekends. There was a great deal of barter – the only possibility for workers and tradesmen to scrape together the material. It was possible to buy refabricated framing and lumber cheaply, or even get it free in return for hauling; it could be stripped of nails and scraped clean, to be reused again and again. Bricks could take the most remarkable journey through town, to finally end up in a self-built house. Wood from sugar crates was painstakingly freed from brackets and nails and lined walls in storage areas.

It took years but finally these projects turned into homes that then represented the highest attainment of happiness for a factory worker at Ekeby or a heavy construction worker at Diös. A feeling of harmony characterised the neighbourhood, a sense of proportion between house and lot, something missing from the terraced houses in Eriksdal that Sven-Arne had just left behind.

The pigeon broke into a sudden flapping and, alarmed,

Sven-Arne backed up a step. The bird took flight in a wide arc over the tops of the apple trees, who with their abundance of thin upward-turned shoots mostly resembled clumps of reeds. Sven-Arne followed the bird's flight with his gaze and saw it disappear between the houses.

He was awakened out of these thoughts by a passing car. It slowed down a couple of houses away and turned in to the gravel area in front of the very small garage. A man got out of the car and as he took out a couple of grocery bags he subjected Sven-Arne to curious examination. Sven-Arne smiled and nodded at him. The man closed the car door with a bang and went into the house.

The streetlamps flickered and turned on. Yet another car drove past. Sven-Arne walked in through the fence posts and walked up the path, just like twelve years ago, and set his sights on the front door. Everything was going much easier than he had thought.

NIKLAS ÖHMAN – JENNY HOLGERSSON said the enamelled nameplate. He chose to use the clapper instead of the doorbell and in a way he wished that no one would open.

The door was opened with a quick movement and a man stared at Sven-Arne with astonishment.

'What do you want?'

The directness of the question surprised Sven-Arne.

'I . . . it's a little hard to explain . . . but I am acquainted with the man who lived here before.'

The man looked closely at him.

'With Dufva?'

Sven-Arne nodded.

'That's the most ridiculous thing I ever heard. He didn't have any friends.'

'I didn't say friend. And to be precise he was not really my acquaintance.'

'Are you a policeman?'

'No, I just wanted to—'

'Come on inside, there's too much cold air blowing in.'

Sven-Arne hesitated. He could still extricate himself, but he was more or less physically dragged inside the house.

'There's something wrong with the furnace, that's why it's so cold. Let's sit down in the kitchen. It's warmer there.'

The man disappeared into the kitchen and sat down at the table. Sven-Arne followed him but ended up standing in the doorway, looking around. He could smell fish. Fresh vegetables were spread out on a countertop.

'Sit down.'

Sven-Arne obeyed. The man, who looked to be between thirty-five and forty, grimaced, pressing his lips together as if experiencing a sudden pain.

'I must be intruding, I see you are in the middle of preparing dinner,' Sven-Arne said. But the man waved this away. 'I don't know how to express this, but Nils Dufva meant a great deal to my family. What do you know about him?'

'Not much,' the man said. 'But who are you?'

'I am Sven-Arne, but the past couple of years I have gone by the name of John for the sake of expediency. I have been away for many years and now I am trying to get some order in my life again.'

The man nodded and appeared genuinely interested. Sven-Arne was slowly starting to warm to him, considering how he had let him into his kitchen without reservations.

'Nils Dufva was in Spain during the thirties.'

'That's nothing new,' Niklas Öhman said. 'He was always going on about Spain.'

'So you met him?'

'Of course. Jenny and I have been together almost twenty years. We met in school and she cleaned for the old man, bought his groceries, that kind of thing. Sometimes I helped around the house, things that Dufva couldn't manage. Two or three times a year he would invite us to dinner, either here or at the pub. They were crazy events. The old man went on about all kinds of historical shit.'

'What did he tell you about Spain?'

'That he was down there fighting in the war, but it mostly came out in episodes. I'm not so sure about the facts other than that they had a civil war, and to be totally honest I didn't listen particularly carefully.'

'You didn't think that there was anything out of the ordinary about the fact that he was there and—'

'Nothing could be out of the ordinary with that old man,' Niklas Öhman interrupted. 'He was odd, to say the least. You know that he was in Germany later during the war?'

Sven-Arne nodded.

'A real Hitler lover. He hated Russians and Communists. That was his thing.'

'My uncle Ante was also in Spain.'

'Damn. Did Dufva and your uncle know each other?'

'Ante was a Communist.'

Niklas Öhman stared quizzically at Sven-Arne.

'They fought on opposite sides?'

'You're quick on the uptake,' Sven-Arne said. 'Maybe they bumped into each other down there, I don't know, but Nils Dufva was important in some way for my uncle. I came here to possibly get some clues. I knew that Jenny had moved in here after her relation died, and I thought that she might have had some information—'

'Has your uncle died?'

'No, he is still alive, I have just come from him at any rate, but he doesn't tell me anything, not about Dufva at least.'

Niklas Öhman got up and walked over to the kitchen counter, took up a knife, and started to cut up what Sven-Arne believed was fennel, while he went on to talk about how they had renovated the whole house. Jenny Holgersson had developed an almost fanatical obsession with obliterating all the old traces of her relative.

'Jenny doesn't want to talk about him either.'

'But she wanted to live here?'

'The price was right. When he died Jenny had lived in rental flats for many years. To get a house was . . . you understand, I'm sure.'

'So she inherited the old man? Did she get a lot?'

Niklas Öhman stopped his knife.

'Quite a bit,' he said, and then halved some carrots with a couple of swift slices. 'He was richer than you would have thought. He never talked about money or . . .'

'So they weren't close?'

'Jenny and Dufva? No, not at all, but she felt a duty to step in, with housecleaning and the like.'

'But she stood to inherit,' Sven-Arne observed.

Niklas Öhman glanced at him over his shoulder.

'What do you want, anyway – I thought you wanted to find something out about Dufva?'

'I don't really know what I want. Perhaps get some order to the story, or to understand my uncle. The fact is that you

299

are the first person I've really talked to since returning to Sweden. Besides Ante, of course.'

Up until this point in the conversation, Niklas Öhman had turned his head from time to time and looked at Sven-Arne over his shoulder, but now he put down the knife, turned, and leant up against the counter.

'Why was Nils Dufva so important?'

'He died,' Sven-Arne Persson said.

'As we all do at some point. You should ask me, I associate with human remains a great deal.'

'Are you—'

'Archeologist,' Öhman said. 'And now Dufva is a heap of bones in the earth. And that is nothing that concerns me. He is history. And that's fine by me.'

'Would you mind if I took a quick look around the house?' Sven-Arne asked suddenly.

'Why would you want to do that?'

'I don't know how to explain it, but it would help me understand my uncle's argumentations.'

He felt his cheeks heat up. Perhaps the lie was too weakly constructed for Niklas Öhman to swallow.

'I definitely don't want to go nosing around, I don't want you to think that. But I would like to see the room where Dufva died. I believe—'

'What do you know about his murder?'

'Nothing,' Sven-Arne replied. 'I just know that Dufva and Ante were up to something.'

Some of his confidence returned and he now launched into a wordy explanation that he deliberately left somewhat unclear. He sensed that if he presented himself as somewhat confused it might help his cause. Öhman might think he may

300

as well authorise a short tour of the house, and then try to convince his visitor to leave.

'I want you to be gone when Jenny gets back. She has put all that behind her. Most of all she wants to forget about the old man. It was hard enough to find him dead. He was lying in the living room with his head bashed in. She had to have therapy for a couple of years in order to try to forget and move on, and still, I can sometimes see on her face how hard it is for her and sometimes she can't even walk into the room. She'll never be free.'

'Could I possibly have a carrot? I haven't had much to eat for a while.'

Niklas Öhman stared at Sven-Arne Persson, shook his head, and gave him a peeled carrot.

'I don't want Jenny to become upset, that's all.'

'It's okay,' Sven-Arne said, without thinking of the fact that he was speaking English, and took a bite of his carrot.

'Just a minute, then maybe Ante's talk will make more sense to me.'

'It's okay,' Öhman echoed. 'I'll show you.'

He left the kitchen and led the way into the hallway before Sven-Arne had time to get to his feet. They walked out into the living room that was directly connected to the entry hall.

'Well, this is it. This was where he died,' Niklas Öhman said. 'He was lying face down. We have redone everything, painted and hung wallpaper.'

The furnishings were relatively contemporary and Sven-Arne realised it would have looked completely different in Dufva's time.

'So they met here?'

301

'I don't know,' Sven-Arne said. 'He rambles on about so many strange things.'

He felt Öhman's eyes on him.

'Does Jenny grieve for him?'

'What do you mean?'

'I mean, is that why she doesn't want to go into this room?'

'I don't think you understand. She found him, and it was not a pleasant sight.'

Sven-Arne nodded.

'Thanks for the carrot,' he said. 'It tasted good.'

He walked back into the hall, slipped his feet into his sandals, and unhooked his jacket from the peg. Niklas Öhman was watching him from the doorway to the living room.

'You need new shoes,' he said.

'Not where I'm headed,' Sven-Arne said, and put his hand on the front door handle.

At that moment the door opened and he stood eye-to-eye with a woman. He understood at once it was Jenny Holgersson. She was flushed red and panting. Her cheeks bore vivid acne scars.

'Hi, Jenny,' he said.

Niklas forced his way past, put a hand on Sven-Arne's shoulder, and pushed him out so that he almost tripped in front of Jenny.

'Go!' he rasped in Sven-Arne's ear.

Jenny Holgersson managed to slink in between the doorpost and Sven-Arne, but he had time to catch sight of the fear in her eyes.

'What's going on?'

'He invited himself in,' Niklas Öhman said.

'Not at all,' Sven-Arne said. 'We've had a nice conversation. And I got a carrot.'

He felt strangely elated. He was glad that he at least got a look at Jenny Holgersson, even though he was not likely ever to get to talk to her, but to get a face meant he had an easier time imagining Dufva's life and death.

'Go away!'

Niklas Öhman slammed the door shut with a strong bang.

'I want to talk to a homicide detective,' Sven-Arne Persson said, and at the same time presented his number slip. He was customer number sixty-eight.

The receptionist took the slip and inspected it before she tossed it into a basket on the counter.

'What does this concern?'

Sven-Arne shivered and felt his face grow warm and probably flush a flaming red.

'That's not important,' he said.

The woman studied him and he realised he must present a remarkable and foreign sight: bearded, with hands marked with labour, his skin weathered by wind and sun, and clothes as out of place as when he stepped off the plane at Arlanda. In addition he probably smelt strange, of curry most likely.

'Are you reporting a crime?'

Sven-Arne nodded. She thinks I am an alcoholic, he thought. But the idea of how he was judged did not affect him at all.

'A crime,' he said. 'A serious crime. My name is Sven-Arne Persson,' he added after a couple of seconds, as if that would explain something.

Suddenly there came the sound of shouting from the entrance and he turned around. There was a man there dressed in a gigantic ankle-length overcoat, and a fur hat of the kind that older men wore in the sixties. He was gesticulating wildly.

A younger man, probably a relative, Sven-Arne determined by their resemblance, was trying to calm the older one.

The woman behind the counter sighed. Sven-Arne smiled at her.

'Nice to have a little life around here,' he said, but realised as soon as the words came out that it was the wrong thing to say.

'You want to meet with a homicide detective and report a serious crime? It can take a while for—'

Sven-Arne nodded again and could not repress a second smile when he had the impulse to pull a couple of notes out of his pocket to hurry along the process.

'One moment,' the receptionist said, and picked up the receiver.

Sven-Arne turned and watched the quarrelling pair. It was like a scene out of a play. Now it was the younger one who seemed most upset.

'Please have a seat,' he heard the woman say, and without looking at her he walked off toward an armchair, sat down, and prepared for a long wait. But he had only just settled in comfortably when a police officer in civilian clothes appeared by his side.

'That's quicker than in Bangalore,' he said, and rose, not without some difficulty. It struck him that he had not eaten much more than a carrot all day.

'What was that?'

'Fast work, I mean.'

'Sammy Nilsson,' the police officer said, introducing himself and stretching out his hand.

Sven-Arne answered his gesture, but hesitantly, as if he was suddenly uncertain he had made the right decision. He mumbled something incomprehensible.

The policeman seemed to wait him out, as if he sensed his unease and wanted to give him a moment to pull himself together.

'Are you ready?'

'I'm not entirely sure of that,' Sven-Arne replied truthfully. He knew that if he now followed the inspector into the interior of the building he would change his life more drastically in one blow than even his flight from India had done.

'But I think we need to talk,' he said. 'I don't see another way.'

Sammy Nilsson nodded and could not conceal his satisfaction. Sven-Arne realised the police officer's curiosity had been aroused and all at once he felt well disposed toward him. He did not want to disappoint Nilsson, and he decided to make his story a good one.

THIRTY-SIX

It was thirty-two degrees Celsius in the shade. How hot it was in the sun, Sune Stolt did not dare to guess. He walked as close to the building wall as possible in order to maximise his shade. Business was in full swing, the shops had been open for a couple of hours. From time to time he heard people speaking Swedish.

He liked Krabi in spite of the tourists, because the city had not been as ruined as many of the others. Here there was still a somewhat intact Thai atmosphere. He hated Phuket. Phuket City might be all right but the beaches to the north were dreadful. Perhaps it was because Stolt mostly got to see the dark side of the tourist business: prostitution and drugs.

He was on his way to the police station in the centre of town. He had been there several times before and then always met with Mr No, as he was called. Stolt had forgotten his real name. Everyone knew who Mr No was – a legend in the corps – unusually tall for a Thai and known for his hard hands. Perhaps he was corrupt – there were rumours that he was involved in real estate transactions on the islands south of Krabi and that his methods were not always above board – but he had always been friendly to Stolt.

Mr No had called in the morning. Stolt could not help but smile as he thought of how pleased he had sounded as he told him that the missing-person report had gone out in Krabi the same day and that a woman had come to the station the following morning. She had brought her brother. That was all Stolt knew. Now he would find out more.

He had just completed a visit to Bangkok and was standing at the airport preparing to fly to Phuket, where he was stationed, when Mr No called. Stolt had managed to rebook his ticket, and a couple of hours later he had landed in Krabi.

It could be nothing more than a false alarm, but something in Mr No's voice told him it was a bull's eye. Mr No liked appearing capable and here was an opportunity to display his Thai efficiency.

Stolt was relieved to enter the station's air-conditioned and almost arctic climate. Mr No was waiting for him in front of the reception desk. They greeted each other as warmly as usual. Sune Stolt asked him how his wife and children were doing. Mr No was clearly flattered by the fact that Stolt remembered the names of his twins. Stolt had checked the names in his notebook just before walking in.

After a couple of minutes of conversation, Mr No took him by the arm – a gesture he only bestowed upon Westerners – and showed him into a corridor, stopping at a door and opening it.

The room was bare and empty, with the exception of a wooden table and a couple of chairs. A man and a woman were sitting at the table. They immediately rose to their feet. The first thing Stolt noticed was the fear in their eyes. Thereafter he felt astonishment. The woman before him was identical to the woman in the photograph.

Mr No introduced him. Stolt nodded, smiled, and greeted

the woman. She immediately began speaking in an intense torrent of words, and Mr No waited for her to finish. When she was done she stared at Sune Stolt as Mr No translated.

The photograph was of herself. It had been taken two years ago outside the restaurant where she still worked. The person who had snapped the picture was her sister, who shortly thereafter travelled to Sweden.

'Why did she go to Sweden?'

Mr No shot him a look that expressed as much irritation as sorrow. The woman answered with another long explanation. Again Mr No waited patiently for her to finish.

'She was going to pick berries in the big forests,' he summarised. 'She was going to make a lot of money. You have big forests, isn't that right?'

'Yes, we do,' Stolt said. 'What is her sister's name?'

He used the present tense as the woman did not know her sister's fate.

'Pranee Kaew Patima,' said Mr No.

It was an hour later, when Sune Stolt had checked in to the hotel, that the grief washed over him. As long as he was at the police station he could retain his composure, but outstretched on the bed in his room, prey to the vertigo no physician could find a reason for, he gave way to the bottomless black void that had recently grown deeper and wider. He felt ashamed, both as a Swede and as a man. Bosse Marksson had given him enough information so that he gathered how it had gone. The same old story, this time with a deadly outcome.

Thailand let its young women go to humiliation and death. Sune Stolt hated the Scandinavians, British, and Germans, the old men, the gangs of rowdy twenty-year-old men, the pudgy pale middle-aged men, and the well-established ones with gold clubs in their luggage. All came for the sake of flesh.

Most of them were content to screw their way around massage parlours and in dim rooms behind bars, others moved down for a few winter months in order to live like kings, and still others imported the reed-thin girls to a cold and loveless life in Europe. Of course there were exceptions, of course there were instances of real love and concern, but most of the time it was purely a matter of commerce with bodies.

Now yet another name could be laid alongside the earlier ones, Pranee Kaew Patima.

How long would he be able to stand looking up close at this misery? He knew this hatred threatened to make him a poor policeman. He glanced at the clock. He knew he ought to get up from the bed, turn on the computer, and email Marksson what he had discovered.

THIRTY-SEVEN

Ann Lindell could not help feeling a smidgeon of triumph as she thought of Beatrice's haughty face and the rest of her colleagues' resistance to her suggestion about advertising in Thailand.

'Fucking brilliant!' she exclaimed.

Bosse Marksson, who had read Sune Stolt's entire email, was more restrained.

'It's a relief to have a name,' he said. 'But how is it pronounced?'

'Let's just call her Patima,' Lindell said. 'The identification of the woman in the photograph is one hundred per cent? No doubt?'

'No, Sune is completely convinced that the picture is of the woman he met in Krabi. He even went to the restaurant where she worked. And the police there were going to get a photo of sister Patima and send back that—'

'—we can test at the campsite,' Lindell completed.

Marksson grunted.

'The timing fits,' he said. 'She left Thailand at the beginning of August last year.'

'Okay, then we are a step closer.'

But Lindell also realised that the investigation had ground to a halt. They had a name for the woman and a connection to Tobias Frisk, they had a DNA match between the hair they had found in Frisk's house and the foot, they had the chainsaw, but there it ended. They could conclude that there was a great probability that Frisk had murdered and thereafter dismembered Patima. How, why, and when they would never know. Most likely they would also never recover a body to go with the foot they had found. She had probably been buried or dumped into the sea.

The case was solved but left a bitter taste. The usual sense of satisfaction wasn't there, something Marksson also commented on.

'I wish the bastard hadn't been such a bastard and blown his head off.'

'Should we keep going?'

'Can we keep going?' Marksson countered. 'We have questioned everyone we can think of, neighbours, his former girlfriend, and co-workers.'

'And what do their contributions have in common?'

'That Tobias Frisk was an unusual fellow but no one who would have taken his own life or that of another person.'

'What do you make of that?'

'That life is full of surprises,' Marksson said.

'Okay,' Lindell said. 'We'll drop the whole thing. I can check with the campsite. It would be good to get a positive ID on the woman, but then we'll close the file.'

'What should we do with the foot?'

'Save it for now,' Lindell said, after a moment's reflection. 'I don't think we'll send it to Thailand. That would feel rotten.'

'A foot may be better than nothing. What do we know,

perhaps there may be some kind of religious point to it, I mean in Thailand.'

After having called Sorsele Campsite and agreeing with Gösta Ohlman that she would shortly be emailing a picture of the woman, Lindell left the police building. She needed to walk, to get a little air, even if the weather wasn't the best. The whole city was wreathed in a damp fog.

She walked west along the Luthagsled. Her goal was the Café Savoy. During the quick walk she came to think of the old man, the county commissioner's uncle, who lived only a couple of blocks away, and from there her thoughts wandered to Berglund. He would be discharged from the hospital soon and after that there would be some weeks of convalescing. She wondered how it would be. Her image of her colleague was altered in its very foundation and Lindell didn't like it. She wanted her old, secure colleague back, not some shaky, troubled, and pessimistic old man.

The tables at Savoy were filled. That was more and more the case. Lindell looked over half a dozen mothers who occupied two tables with their offspring in high chairs and on their laps. They looked to have been there quite a while. All of the coffee cups were empty and the tables covered in rubbish. Lindell thought it was out of line to occupy a café for their mum gatherings. Three baby carriages were wedged between tables and chairs. A little one was crawling around on the floor with a bun in his hand, another was screeching in his high chair.

She stood there for a few minutes but none of the customers showed any signs of imminent departure – definitely not the mothers. Lindell sighed and left.

She slowly walked past the flower shop and the kiosk

on the corner and then walked east on Ringgatan, with a vague feeling that things were not as they should be. It wasn't just Berglund who was out of sorts, that much was clear. Beatrice was unusually cranky and Sammy Nilsson was unrecognisable. Even Ottosson was unusually listless. Perhaps it was the approaching Christmas holiday that was making people so down.

She came to a sudden stop outside Konsum. There had been something that hadn't felt right to her during the whole investigation of the severed foot. She had perceived her uncertainty like an irritating static in the background and Marksson had expressed similar thoughts. The way the whole thing had unfolded appeared obvious, even if a frustrating number of threads hung loose. What was it that rubbed?

She turned around in order to try to understand what it was on Ringgatan that had triggered this sudden impulse of unease and incompleteness. But she saw nothing out of the ordinary. A couple of teenagers who laughingly teased each other. The back of an older woman with a grocery bag. She closed her eyes and tried to grab hold of the fleeting feeling again. She had experienced this before, that creeping feeling of apprehension mixed with excitement, which could sometimes feel nightmarish with panic lurking, when realisation about a missed opportunity that would never come again grew stronger. Perhaps it was something at Savoy that had set this off ? She stared back in the direction of the café and replayed the scene: the mothers and children, a couple of older men in the corner whom she had seen countless times at that exact table, and a couple of school kids drinking sodas. The rest of the customers were shadows.

Was it the bun the child had been chewing? Frisk worked at a bakery. Was it a smell? Was it about drinking coffee? At her first visit to Bultudden she had had coffee with Torsten Andersson. Had he made some comment then that had not appeared strange at the time but that now unconsciously had awakened her anxiety? Or perhaps it was Marksson who had said something as they sat in Frisk's kitchen?

Lindell drew a breath and resumed her walk, now at a considerably calmer tempo. In her thoughts she followed the road to Bultudden and finally arrived at Lisen Morell's, but there was nothing along the Avenue that spoke to her.

She picked up her phone and called Bosse Marksson.

'I think there's something wrong,' she said at once.

'What do you mean wrong?' Marksson sounded tired.

'Something wrong in the investigation. With our thinking. We've missed something.'

Her colleague said nothing. And what should he say, Lindell thought.

'I mean, you know that feeling you get sometimes.'

Marksson grunted. She recalled his concerns when they were out in Bultudden. He had also questioned the series of events without being able to point to something concrete that strengthened the sense that they were wrong, but eventually they had laid down their weapons before the indisputable facts: the traces of Patima in Frisk's house, the traces of blood on the chainsaw, and finally the connection in Sorsele.

'We have to meet,' Lindell went on. 'Can I come out tomorrow?'

'First thing in the morning, in that case. I'm going to spend the afternoon in Öregrund.'

'I'll be there at half past eight.'

314

THIRTY-EIGHT

'I want to confess to a murder.'

The policeman lifted his gaze from the paper where he had just written the day's date and Sven-Arne Persson's name, but said nothing.

'It happened many years ago.'

'Go on,' Sammy Nilsson said after a long pause.

'I killed a man in the autumn of 1993. He was called Nils Dufva. It happened in Kungsgärdet. Then I travelled to India and remained there. That's all. How long have you worked in Uppsala?'

'Almost twenty years,' Sammy Nilsson said.

'Then you must remember Dufva.'

Sammy nodded. He remembered it very well, the affair with the wheelchair-bound old man who had been clubbed to death, even though he was on street patrol at the time and did not have any direct involvement in the investigation. It was Berglund's case, he knew that much. Berglund's unsolved mystery. It struck him that he should immediately get in touch with him. He would certainly be pleased, if not overjoyed.

'Can you tell me what happened? You understand of course that I am recording our discussion.'

Persson nodded.

'Were you already acquainted with Dufva?'

'No, I can't say that I was.'

'You just walked in and struck down an old man completely unknown to you in his own home?'

'Not exactly unknown to me.'

'Were you intoxicated?'

'No, completely sober.'

Sammy Nilsson sat without saying anything. The tape deck rolled on.

'Could I have a sandwich or something? I haven't eaten in a long time.'

Sammy Nilsson immediately called Allan Fredriksson and asked him to order a thermos of coffee and a couple of sandwiches, and then join him for the session.

He glanced at Persson.

'It's regarding the Dufva murder,' he added.

Persson suddenly stood up and walked over to the window. Nilsson hung up and observed him. He did not look like a killer.

'Food is on its way,' he said, 'but we can start chatting a bit, if you'd like to have a seat.'

'Of course,' Persson said, and returned to his chair.

'How did you get yourself to India?'

'I flew.'

Sammy Nilsson smiled.

'I had arranged to get a new passport. Bertil Grönlund, if you remember him, assisted me. I can say that now because I know he's beyond any punishment now.'

Bertil Grönlund, often called 'Gävle-Berra', had been a regular with the Uppsala police for many years, mostly because of his predilection for forging cheques. No violent sort, just a notorious scoundrel, not particularly successful. He was put away for a year now and then, came out and was soon caught again, something he took even-handedly. Sammy Nilsson himself had arrested him once in the early nineties, and recalled a thin, middle-aged man, timid in his manner and never reluctant to admit to what he had been accused of.

'I didn't know he was dead,' Nilsson said distractedly. 'How did you know him?'

'I was his parole mentor.'

Sammy Nilsson chuckled and shook his head. Persson sensed that he thought the story was sounding more and more fanciful.

'Did you have any connection to India?'

'No, none, but it was as good a place as any. I liked it.'

'And why have you returned now?'

'I wanted to get this over with.'

'Nils Dufva?'

Persson nodded. At that moment the door opened. Allan Fredriksson put a tray down on the table, stretched out his hand, and introduced himself.

'Wonderful,' Persson said. 'I mean, I'm glad I'm dealing with experienced officers and not a pair of newbies.'

'Let's dig in,' Fredriksson said, and poured out the coffee from a stainless steel thermos. The initials *AF* were written in large letters on the cap.

'Sven-Arne Persson here has just confessed to a murder,' Sammy Nilsson explained to his colleague, and managed to make it sound very mundane. 'Do you want to tell him, Sven-Arne?'

'One thing,' Allan Fredriksson said. 'Before we start, I have to ask if you are Sven-Arne Persson the county commissioner?'

317

'One and the same.'

'I thought I recognised you. But you didn't have a beard back then, did you?'

The former county commissioner helped himself to a ham sandwich, took a large bite out of it, and chewed thoroughly before answering.

'I was another person back then. Without a beard.'

'You are the county commissioner who disappeared?'

Sammy Nilsson stared in amazement at Persson.

'Should we get this over with?' Persson asked.

Nilsson nodded. 'You told me that you killed Nils Dufva.'

'I beat him over the head with some crutches.'

'Crutches? Were there some in the house?' Sammy Nilsson asked.

He couldn't remember any details of the murder, other than that Nils Dufva was handicapped.

'No, they were in the car and I brought them in. They were my uncle's. I wanted to have something to defend myself with, in case of trouble.'

'What kind of car were you driving?'

'A dark blue Saab.'

'Was your uncle with you?' Fredriksson broke in.

'No.'

Sammy Nilsson decided to bullshit a little.

'According to witnesses, there were two men who arrived in a car and parked outside Dufva's house.'

Persson took a new bite and glanced briefly at Fredriksson.

'He waited in the car,' he said finally. 'He had trouble walking.'

'Were you expecting trouble?' Sammy Nilsson asked.

'I can't really remember. But why else would I have brought the crutches?'

He washed down the sandwich with a sip of coffee.

'That's better.' Persson smiled.

'Did you know Dufva well?' Nilsson asked.

'No, not really.'

'Then why on earth did you kill him?' Fredriksson exclaimed.

'He was a war criminal,' Persson said calmly.

'You'll have to explain that.'

'Most of all I'd like to rest for a while,' Sven-Arne Persson said. He had consumed a cheese sandwich and finished his coffee in quick succession. 'Would that be all right? I don't want to be impolite but I am actually completely wiped out. A bit dizzy and shaky, actually. We can talk more later. You must have some little room where I can stretch out for a bit. Then I'll be ready, and we can go through the whole thing.'

'That's all right,' Sammy Nilsson said after a brief moment of hesitation, and formally concluded the session. He turned off the tape recorder.

After Fredriksson had shown Sven-Arne Persson to the jail, he returned to Nilsson's office.

'The things we hear,' he said, and sat down in the chair that the county commissioner had just vacated. 'What should we think?'

'Either he's a crazy cuckoo or else he is extremely clear on what he wants,' Sammy Nilsson said.

'He's no cuckoo.'

'He may have gone crazy in India,' Sammy Nilsson said.

319

'He may have gone there for spiritual reasons. I'm thinking of a guru or yogi or something along those lines.'

'Hard to believe,' Fredriksson said, and helped himself to a sandwich.

'We should get in touch with Berglund. After all, it's his "cold case".'

'I'll call him at the hospital.'

'Can you do that? I'd appreciate it. We'll let the county commissioner sleep for an hour or two. I don't know what you thought about breaking it off but he really did look wiped out. I'll get the case files out in the meantime. Ask Lindell to come in so we can brief her too.'

Ann Lindell shook her head when Sammy Nilsson had finished his summation.

'This is more than unlikely,' she said. 'I met with his uncle just the other day.'

Nilsson and Fredriksson stared at her, perplexed.

'Do you know that his wife was run over on Luthagsleden a couple of weeks ago and is currently lying in a coma?'

'Now you'll have to tell us what is going on. Is it Berglund?'

Lindell nodded and then told them the whole story.

'How does all this hang together?' Allan Fredriksson said.

'The answer is currently sleeping,' Nilsson said.

'Was it his wife's accident that unleashed this whole thing, that he returned to Uppsala after twelve years to relieve his conscience? What role does the uncle play? Is he the connection between Dufva and Persson? What does "war criminal" mean in this context?'

Allan Fredriksson lined up the obvious questions.

'The answer is sleeping,' Nilsson repeated with a smile.

'He does have crutches,' Lindell said suddenly. 'The uncle, I mean. I saw them in his room at Ramund.'

Allan Fredriksson shook his head.

After a brief discussion, they decided that Nilsson and Fredriksson would take on Sven-Arne Persson.

'We'll give him another hour before we question him,' Nilsson said. 'Then he can sleep on it again tonight and we'll see if he sticks to his story tomorrow. After that we question the uncle. And at that point maybe you can help out, having met the guy?'

'I have to get out to Östhammar first thing tomorrow morning,' Lindell said. 'But I could do it in the afternoon.'

She told them about Sune Stolt's report from Thailand. In light of the county commissioner's unexpected confession, the success in identifying the Thai woman appeared less extraordinary, and her colleagues did not look particularly impressed. Their thoughts were completely absorbed in Sven-Arne Persson and the murder of Nils Dufva.

'Have you called Berglund?' she asked.

'He'll come in tomorrow,' Allan Fredriksson said.

'How did he take it?'

'He talked mostly about the motive. He got hung up on that thing about "war criminal." He claimed that you had tipped him off about Dufva being a Nazi.'

'Me?' Sammy Nilsson exclaimed, and looked perplexed.

'There was some book you had shown Berglund.'

'That's right. Damn. Now I remember. It was a catalogue of Swedish Nazis and Dufva was in some kind of register.'

'Nazis,' Lindell said, and recalled Ante Persson's bookshelf. 'If he was a Nazi then Ante Persson is very likely a Communist.'

'And Sven-Arne is a socialist,' Allan Fredriksson said.

'Now all we have to do is come up with someone from the Folkpartiet and we'll have a complete set.' Nilsson grinned.

'I have to go pick up Erik,' Lindell said, getting up. 'Good luck.'

Sven-Arne Persson woke up with a start, sat up in the camp bed dazed, and did not immediately recall where he was. He had dreamt of Lester and planting trees at Lal Bagh. He rubbed his eyes.

Then came the terror. He stared at the greyish, windowless walls, the attached sink and toilet, then lifted the blankets aside, and lowered his legs over the edge of the bed. The cell was several square metres. The solid door was fitted with a peephole.

He lay back down and curled his legs up into his body.

He was lying in this position when he heard a key turn and the door open. He shut his eyes. This is when I die, he thought. He imagined that they would crowd into the cell, strike him with bamboo sticks without saying a word, and thereafter drag him out into the courtyard in order to continue the beating. He knew it was an absurd thought – he was no longer in India – but he still steeled himself for the first blows.

'It's time,' he heard a voice say, and he opened his eyes.

Sammy Nilsson was standing in the doorway. He was smiling.

'Did you sleep well?'

Sven-Arne nodded, stood up, picked the blanket up off the floor, and started to fold it. Nilsson waited.

'Yes, I have slept,' Sven-Arne said. 'And I . . .'

He did not complete the sentence. He arranged the blanket

at the foot end of the camp bed with great care before looking up at the policeman.

'Should we talk a little more?'

Sammy Nilsson nodded.

The session took two hours. It started with questions about India. Persson realised it was employed as a way to put him at ease and he spoke eagerly about the botanical garden and life in Bangalore. But soon the policemen started in on what had happened that autumn day in 1993. Again and again they made Persson go through the sequence of events. He answered Nilsson and Fredriksson's questions vaguely and in monosyllables. They kept asking for clarification.

'How did you enter the house?'

'The door was unlocked.'

'If you did not know him from before, how did you know where he lived?'

'It was in the phone book.'

'How was it furnished?'

'I can't remember.'

'Nothing at all?'

'Nothing. Well, maybe a little. There was some darkish furniture, a table, some sort of bureau . . . I tripped on a rug, I think . . . it was windy that day and I remember that there was some kind of tree outside the window that . . . well, you know, it was moving. The fact is that I don't remember very much. Everything went so quickly.'

Sammy Nilsson stared searchingly at him.

'You want us to believe that a respected politician walks in on an unknown old man and brutally kills him,' he said finally.

During the entire session Sven-Arne Persson had been sitting leant over the table, taking a sip of coffee from time to time, even after it had grown cold, and rarely met Nilsson's gaze, but now he lifted his head and looked him straight in the eye.

'That man—' he started, but stopped at once before continuing with a considerably sharper tone in his voice as if the former politician had awakened for a moment. 'He was a miserable excuse of a human being and I regret nothing. Yes, one thing. I should have gone straight to the police, twelve years ago.'

'But you left,' Fredriksson observed.

'I left.'

'Why?'

That simple question was followed by a couple of minutes of silence. The interrogators had learnt not to hurry Sven-Arne.

'I guess I was too much of a coward,' he said finally. 'I didn't have the guts. I thought of Elsa, my wife, how much shame she would endure. Not that things were so well between us, but she was still my wife. I thought of the party. I was a leading figure and it would have hurt the movement. I thought of myself, how I wouldn't be able to stand being locked up.'

'And now Elsa is in a coma at the Akademiska Hospital, so now it doesn't matter anymore. Is that what you mean? Did you hear about the accident before you returned home?'

Sven-Arne nodded.

'And that got you to come back?'

'Yes.'

'But you haven't made any attempts to see her?'

'No.'

'Do you even want to see her?'

'No. It is over between us. It ended many years ago.'

'Has your fear of prison left you?'

'I'm older,' Sven-Arne said simply, 'there isn't much left. I can take it. Can I have some more coffee?'

Allan Fredriksson stood up and left the room. Sammy Nilsson pressed the pause button of the tape recorder.

Sven-Arne Persson drew a deep breath and closed his eyes. He had lied. He was in fact afraid of being locked up. When he left Ante he had visualised a scenario in which his incarceration consisted of weeding, tending flower beds, and raking leaves in a country setting. He knew this was wishful thinking. A murderer was not likely given such privileges.

Of course he wanted to see Elsa, but for one reason only: in order to ask for forgiveness. Not for Dufva or because he had left her and fled the country. No, he wanted to ask her forgiveness that they had married in the first place, that he had talked her into sharing her life with him.

The party? Deep inside he had never believed in it. He had realised that when he was in India.

Thoughts of Elsa returned. He knew she was the sore point. That was why he had returned. And now he was betraying her again. He did not even want to visit her sickbed. He would always feel guilty for it. He could take a prison sentence of eight, ten years, if with some anxiety, but the knowledge that he had time and again betrayed the person he had lived with was something he would never be free of.

He had influenced many people's lives by his engagement in politics, but then in a more impersonal way. Now that it was about his wife it was different. He knew, and had known all this time, that he had treated her badly. He had known it but had never done anything about it. Instead he had allowed it to continue, and slowly but surely ground her down. It was his fault.

Allan Fredriksson's return with a new thermos of coffee interrupted his thoughts. Persson realised how much he had missed Swedish coffee in India.

'I've lied a bit,' Sven-Arne Persson said. 'About the motive. You know that Nils Dufva was a Nazi. He fought on the Eastern front and in Finland and was even in Berlin at the end of the war. One of the last enthusiasts. Then he came home and almost immediately got a job in the Swedish department of defence. What do you say about that?'

'What should we say?' Sammy Nilsson said.

'He was too valuable and he could be of use,' Persson said.

'In what way was he valuable?'

'He was both an anti-Communist and he was capable. His private register of radicals was one of the most exhaustive in the country. He was, in a word, useful. He fit in the cold war. You know what happened after 1945?'

'Tell me,' Fredriksson said.

'The war continued,' Sven-Arne said. 'I don't know how you think in political matters and frankly I don't really care, I don't ask that anyone should understand. Not today. But Sweden would have looked different if . . .'

He did not complete the sentence. It didn't matter. It was too late to try to convince someone now. He sighed heavily and reached for the coffee.

'But it was a Social Democratic government after the war,' Allan Fredriksson said. 'I mean . . .'

'That doesn't change anything,' Persson said, and for the first time during the questioning he raised his voice.

'You are, or at least were, a Social Democrat. It must have been painful when you discovered that someone like Dufva, who you claim is a Nazi, came back from Berlin and was immediately accepted.'

'It took a couple of years before he got his defence job, but it makes no difference,' Persson said. 'And it was secret. But of course, it is not exactly flattering that it was a Social Democratic government, but I have felt a great deal of pain during my time as a politician.'

'So your motive was political? Dufva's political preferences,' Fredriksson went on, 'gave you the right to club him down like an animal?'

'You could put it that way,' Persson said.

'That's how the prosecutor will put it,' Fredriksson said.

Sven-Arne Persson shrugged.

'How did you know all this, I mean about his activities during and after the war?'

'I came across some papers.'

'What kind of papers?' Sammy Nilsson went on.

'That doesn't matter. And in any case they have been destroyed now. But I can tell you that there were those who didn't like it. Not everyone was an IB agent.'

'What is IB?' Sammy Nilsson asked.

'You are apparently too young to know about it,' Persson said. 'You'll have to read up on it. But IB was a half-military communications organisation that was basically run by the Social Democratic party. The mission was to map everything leftist and oppositional within the union movement. There were moles in every county and in every large workplace, even within the National Radio. What IB was doing was pure opinion documentation and spying, and they even committed burglaries and threats of crime. It was enough to be an opponent of the Swedish nuclear industry or to cast a wrong vote in the yearly union election or subscribe to the wrong newspaper to have your name end up in their registers. Dufva cooperated with the IB.'

'And you found out about this because you had an elevated position among the Social Democrats?'

'Yes, but I don't think that was intentional. It was an old acquaintance who worked at the Televerket communications company who bragged about his secret work once when he was drunk. When IB was later uncovered by some journalists, they ended up in prison. A backward world. And their work continued after the revelation, except in another form.'

Persson turned to Allan Fredriksson and sighed again.

'Isn't that enough? You know that I killed him. What more do you have to know?'

'The fact is I'm having trouble getting this to add up,' Sammy Nilsson said. 'But sure, we can continue tomorrow. We're going to see a lot of each other over the next little while.'

'I have a final question,' Allan Fredriksson said. 'What did you tell your uncle?'

'What?'

'He must have heard or read about the murder. You had both been there. Didn't he put two and two together?'

'He was an old man,' Persson said.

'And by that you mean that he either didn't follow what was going on, or that he was too old to care?'

'Maybe both.'

'Maybe he sympathised with your deed?'

'Deed,' Persson repeated.

'Do you regret what you did?'

'That was a second question,' Persson said.

He tried to smile at Allan Fredriksson, but the monumental fatigue that had crept over him during the course of the interrogation turned the smile into a grimace. Why can't they just leave me alone, he thought.

THIRTY-NINE

Yet another clear night with a moon climbing over the horizon. He was standing out in the garden and followed with his gaze an aeroplane on its way east. Its lights twinkled like stars. He tried to visualise the passengers in their seats and the flight attendants hurrying in the aisles, but only managed brief disconnected images.

He took a couple of steps, the small stones crunching under his feet. The sound echoed in the night and he veered from the path up onto the lawn, past the flagpole and the thicket of shrubby cinquefoil.

It was completely calm. The cold had come creeping slowly. The temperature had been sinking one degree per hour and it was set to be the coldest night of the season so far.

Darkness enveloped him more deeply the farther he went from the house. He looked back but kept walking. He knew the way and did not have to think about where to put his feet. After a while his eyes grew accustomed to the details, the old, half-fallen stone wall, the many stems of the rowanberry tree with its ghostlike blackened fruits, the tarp draped like a shroud over the lumber he had ordered to build a garage. Everything loomed out of the darkness. He walked without thinking of anything except the connections that each object that appeared before him told. Everything was connected, had a story, talked to him about a time gone by. It was like a museum of memories.

This is your place on the earth, he thought suddenly. These four thousand square metres of land is the area that decides your life. Limits. He looked back up at the sky. The plane was gone and was by now a good portion of the way out over the Sea of Åland.

He walked aimlessly but nonetheless reached the sea, where the breakers were slowly rolling in. He felt kinship with the water, how it stiffened in the creeping cold. Winter was inexorably here. There was something – he had always thought this – something sorrowful about the sea as it was engulfed by frigidity and darkness. A faint, repeated splash revealed a stone caressed by a glacial hand. The sea was death. Or was it perhaps the opposite, that the sea was life? He was confused by his ambivalent thoughts. He came from a line of fishermen and perhaps his confusion was an inheritance from those that had gone before? He did not know much about his ancestors more than that they had won their livelihood from the sea but also that several of them had died in boats that had foundered or under ice that had given way.

The endless sea and the limited plot of land, a cottage, between them a swathe of forest, a wetland with alder and the heavy scent of scrubby plants with pale flowers and leathery leaves. Once he had seen his life so clearly, it was from above, in a sport plane. Several years ago an old classmate had taken him on a flight over the coast and they had surveyed the archipelago outside Östhammar at a couple of hundred metres' height. From that perspective the house and surroundings on Bultudden had appeared unnaturally beautiful, like a dreamscape. He had had trouble getting his head around the fact that he actually lived down there.

The dark form of the fishing cottage could be glimpsed some hundred metres away. He set his sights on the gleam of the moonlight in its windows and followed the twisty path along the edge of the water. Suddenly one of the windows lit up, a warm yellow tongue that licked the rock out toward the sea. He stopped short and curled up instinctively, crouching behind a thicket of sea buckthorn, before he was drawn to the light like a moth lurching about in the dark.

He wanted to warm himself. Nothing more. He wanted to be toasty and snug like before. The Magpie would warm him, he was sure of it. She was as fragile as he was, a female outsider who lived by the sea, who had freely found her way to the point in her hunt for images, and he had started to understand her longing.

Slowly he neared the cottage until he stood next to the wall. Her figure formed a fluttering silhouette on the rock. If he was given the opportunity to explain that he was a good man, they would become friends. Her rejecting stance would be replaced by warmth.

He did not wish her ill. She would understand.

FORTY

What was it that made some nights so unpleasant? Even though she had not drunk any wine, which was otherwise one of the usual culprits in poor sleep and nightmares, she had still woken up several times during the night. A couple of times she had got up and looked in on Erik but she had found him snoozing peacefully. It wasn't Erik who had woken her with a night-time whimper.

That was something else. She sensed what it might be but pushed the thoughts away. The night before, after she had put Erik down for the night and picked up all the toys, watered the flowers, and done everything that is required to keep a home in somewhat reasonable shape, she had taken a long and warm shower. Under the jets of water she shaved, first her legs and armpits, finally her bikini line. Painfully conscious of her actions, she had allowed the razor to continue its work until she was completely smooth. Afterward she had studied herself in the mirror, even taken out her handheld mirror and studied her naked genitals, and blushed a deep red when she turned her face to the wall mirror. Never had she been so naked.

Her fingertips against her skin, then the whole hand in a powerful grip, as if she was being caressed by an aroused man, the agonising pleasure when she pretended, when she dreamt for a brief moment. The most hurtful aspect was not the absence of a man but the feeling of not being seen. She was beautiful. Her body, in spite of her middle age and a child, was beautiful. She wanted to be desired, loved and caressed of course, but above all desired. No one saw her, shaved or not, no one stroked her with their eyes.

All this she had paid for. The night had been an anguish. Now she got up, ashamed, not over her body or her yearning but her inability to do anything about it. Hidden deeply under an ever more organised home life – for she had definitely become better at all this that constituted everyday life, the home and Erik, all this bustling about, plant watering, tidying up, and caretaking – was the suspicion that she would never again experience the closeness of a man.

She cracked the door to Erik's room. He was still sleeping and would continue to do so for another half hour. She loved him, it went without saying that he stood at the centre of her concerns, but wasn't there more to life than that? He gave her an incredible amount, but what then? In a few years he would be a teenager, all too soon a young man, and then he would disappear more and more from her sphere. Would she continue to tend her home and go to a work filled with violence and human suffering? Was a well-raised son and the prospect of grandchildren all?

She was starting to believe that if there was going to be a change she would have to do something more radical. It was not enough to shave herself and prance around in front of the mirror, reflecting her own anxiety. She chuckled suddenly as she visualised herself desperately vacuuming or interrogating suspected murderers, while her sex cried out for hands and a pulsating member. She would give everything for a hot breath against her throat.

But what to do? Something radical? Should she quit? What were the alternatives? Start to go out? What she had seen of the city nightlife, the dance clubs, had not tempted her. The chances of scoring a one-night stand were pretty good, but after that?

The feeling of being alone and unloved was more and more replaced, as she got breakfast ready, by anger. It was an anger directed inward. Would she let herself be knocked down, even affected in her dreams by her shortcomings and lack of initiative? Wasn't it just a matter of grabbing the bull by the horns, of starting to live? And what was wrong with only one night of pleasure? Perhaps in all actuality that was the solution. If a man turned up who could become more than a temporary connection then it would have to develop of its own accord.

She paused with her hand on the refrigerator handle, saw herself at Svenssons or Flustret. How would she behave? She couldn't go there alone. I don't have anything to wear, was her next thought. Mentally she scoured her wardrobe.

'I'll buy myself a dildo instead,' she muttered.

She had heard someone on the radio talk about a multifunctional magically vibrating thing called 'the butterfly.' Apparently it provided miraculous pleasure.

She had to force herself to open the refrigerator and get out the yogurt. Being horny slowed her down.

When Erik ran off to the Hedgehog room and had steered his course straight to a teepee in the middle of the room, Ann talked for a while with a newly hired preschool teacher, Lotten, who told her that they were currently working with the theme of housing. Right now they were doing tents, then they would move on to yurts, and after Christmas hopefully igloos.

Ann praised their creativity and hard work, perhaps a bit too forcefully, because the woman looked almost embarrassed and dismissed the approbation.

'I'm envious,' Ann went on, but aware that she was not being completely honest, 'when I see how you work. It seems so . . . inspiring. My job is just about misery.'

Lotten looked closely at her.

'You're a cop, aren't you?'

Ann nodded and saw Erik come crawling out of the tent, turn his head, and flash her a quick smile before he ducked back in again.

'I read about the county commissioner this morning. What a strange story.'

'Do you have the paper here?'

'Yes, I think it's lying around here somewhere.'

They went to the staff room. The newspaper was on the table and Lindell immediately saw the headline: *Missing Politician a Killer?*

Lotten left her and Lindell quickly read through the story, which filled a whole page. One article went through the backstory, how Sven-Arne Persson had disappeared from Uppsala in the autumn of 1993 and what speculations it had triggered.

Now he had returned and freely given himself up to the police and confessed to the killing of Nils Dufva, the so-called wheelchair murder of the same year.

Lindell left the preschool, jumped in her car, and called Ottosson.

'Who's been talking?'

'I don't know,' Ottosson said mournfully.

'We agreed not to let this out and the next thing we know we get wartime headlines. What is this?'

'Fredriksson and Sammy haven't said squat to any reporter, I'm sure of that. They're just as mad.'

'I'll put money on the fact that it's that bitch at the front desk,' Lindell said. 'Or Riis.'

'We don't know,' Ottosson repeated.

Lindell made a violent manoeuvre with the car and nipped in front of the queue at the red light on Vaksalagatan. She wished she had strobe lights on the car.

'And we are not likely to find out,' he added. 'Are you on your way out to the coast?'

'I'm going to meet Marksson at half past eight. I'm already late.'

'How are you doing?'

With Ottosson you could never be certain what he meant by a particular question but she assumed he was referring to the case.

'I think there's something we've overlooked,' she said, but did not attempt to elaborate this further, mostly because she herself did not understand it.

They agreed to meet in the afternoon. Lindell turned off the telephone and thereby Ottosson and the whole unit. She thought about her conversation with Lotten. Was she envious? Was the nursery school – or something equally undramatic – a realistic alternative to police work?

She chuckled.

'Fuck,' she said out loud.

She was on her way to a man on the coast. But it was the wrong man.

FORTY-ONE

The interrogation of Sven-Arne Persson was resumed at half past eight in the morning. Sammy Nilsson thought he looked decidedly more alert than the day before. Persson praised the breakfast but complained that his stomach was acting up.

When the coffee was on the table, Sammy Nilsson turned on the tape recorder, recorded the session details, and thereafter looked at Persson as if he expected him to automatically resume his narration.

'Have you thought about—'

'Yes, I have been thinking,' Persson immediately interrupted, 'I have been thinking as hard as I can. There's nothing for me to add. Now I just want peace and quiet, that is the only thing I want.'

Peace and quiet, Sammy Nilsson thought, and felt a sudden spurt of irritation toward the man on the other side of the table. He kills a defenceless old man and then demands peace and quiet.

'How were you feeling that autumn twelve years ago?' Allan Fredriksson asked.

'Fine,' Persson said quietly, but corrected himself at once. 'No, that is, I was intensely uncomfortable. I had it up to here with politics. All the bitches.'

'Bitches?'

'Yes, haven't you noticed that the old biddies have taken over? All these well-spoken ladies in their trouser suits but without substance, without sense, only air. And there are men who are old biddies too. It may in fact be the case that there are more men than women in this category.'

Allan Fredriksson could not help smiling. Sven-Arne Persson was showing a human side for the first time. Up to this point he had appeared almost completely unfeeling, despite his politeness. Now a little humour was emerging. Fredriksson knew it was good and continued along this path.

'You're talking about your political opponents?'

'And my friends,' Persson said. 'The talkers are distributed everywhere. That is no party-specific characteristic.'

'And would you call yourself an old biddy?'

Persson looked up, bewildered.

'You were a man in the midst of a career. How did you reach your position? Through empty chatter, as you call it, or were you unique?'

'Not unique, perhaps unusual, but I was on my way to becoming a biddy. But we can forget all that now. This isn't a political seminar. I went to India to get away from all this loose talk.'

'So you didn't leave because you had committed a murder?'

'For both those reasons.'

'Were you afraid of being found out?'

'No, not really. You didn't seem to be getting anywhere in the investigation. I had some contacts and kept myself abreast of your progress. Don't take it personally. It was a difficult case, I know.'

'Your flight must have been painstakingly planned. You

had arranged for a false passport, put away large sums of money, and even prepared a disguise so that you could leave City Hall without being recognised.'

'It amused me.'

'To plan this?'

Persson nodded.

'Do you know how you seem to me?' Sammy Nilsson broke in. He had been listening to this dialogue without speaking. 'You seem like a cold, calculating guy, who wants to pose as a defender of the weak, the only honest politician, but in reality he is a remorseless killer who disappears after his deed for his own amusement, not only fleeing from justice and civic responsibilities, but even from his own family.'

'I had a wife, not a family.'

'In short,' Sammy Nilsson said, ignoring Persson's comment, 'you're a bastard who hides behind pseudo-arguments about "old biddies". You leave your wife and your friends to their worries and complete ignorance and you even seem to like it.'

'That is probably an accurate description,' Persson answered. 'I'm not going to argue against your image of me.'

'So the question is why you return all these years later. You do not seem particularly remorseful.'

'I got tired of India. I imagined spending my last remaining years in an institution.'

'Bullshit,' Sammy Nilsson said.

Fredriksson coughed and leant forward, as if he wanted to push his colleague aside.

'If we come back to a thread from yesterday,' he said, and smiled at Persson, 'your uncle Ante. First you told us that you were alone in Kungsgärdet but you later changed your story to say he was waiting in the car. Do you hold firm to this?'

'Yes, he stayed in the car. I took one of his crutches, so he couldn't leave the car.'

'Why did he even come along?'

'We were out for a ride. That was something we did sometimes, went on small excursions.'

'Small excursions,' Fredriksson repeated. 'Did he know where this one was headed? Who you were going to see?'

'No. I said I was running an errand.'

'Why did you choose an excursion?'

'What do you mean?'

'If you had been planning to murder Nils Dufva, wouldn't it have been better to go there alone?'

'Maybe I didn't want to kill him.'

'The crutches.'

'I brought them for self-defence. I was led to believe that Dufva was a violent man.'

'Bound to a wheelchair?'

'What can one know?'

'Can you precisely describe your exchange of words when you were face-to-face with him?'

'We didn't say much.'

'Did he recognise you?'

'I think so.'

'And what did he say?'

'I guess he wondered what I was doing walking into his house. I can't remember exactly. It was a number of years ago. And there was such a racket in his place I couldn't hear properly.'

'What kind of racket?'

'The old man had both his television and radio turned on, and on the highest setting. As I said, it was an infernal racket.'

'You didn't turn off the appliances?'

'No, why would I have done so?'

'You weren't there to talk?'

Sven-Arne did not reply. Fredriksson made a notation in his notebook.

'And what did you say when he wondered why you had walked into his house?' he said after a brief, somewhat ominous pause.

'I asked him if he was Nils Dufva.'

'You did not recognise him from before?'

'I wanted to be sure.'

'You wanted to be sure that you were going to kill the right man?'

Persson did not answer, and to all extents and purposes that was where the session ended. Sven-Arne Persson was unwilling to say anything else. He skirted their attempts to clarify what had happened that fateful autumn day of 1993 and above all why he became a killer. He became bantering in his tone and thereafter more brief in his answers, only to finally lapse into silence. He was escorted back to his cell.

Sven-Arne Persson was in no way pleased with his performance, but he did not know how he could have approached it in any other way. He regretted his outburst over his political colleagues. It was meaningless to waste energy on such things.

He knew that the policemen were dissatisfied, and

he had registered Nilsson's obvious irritation, not to say exasperation. The other one, Fredriksson, appeared to take the whole thing more calmly. Perhaps they were playing two different roles in order to get him to talk. Not that he really cared; it did not change anything.

Despite the stomach pains that had come and gone all night, he felt in fine form. The most freeing thing was that he did not need to make any weighty decisions. He existed in a pleasant vacuum. His cell was small and spartan but he was accustomed to modest surroundings from his time in India. So all in all he found it congenial. The only thing he missed was books, but he had been promised a couple of novels. Newspapers he did not want. He was indifferent to television. He vegetated, but somewhere in his consciousness there was a question about how long this situation would last, and above all how he would stand it. Perhaps he would wake up one morning and feel prison for what it was: a cage.

But right now he felt no great concern. He lay down on the camp bed, closed his eyes, and fell asleep after several minutes.

FORTY-TWO

'This is a good book,' Bosse Marksson said, holding up a slender volume.

'Oh?' Lindell said, perplexed over this start to the conversation. 'What is it about?'

She was late. She had pulled up in front of the little police station in Östhammar at exactly a quarter to nine. Angelina was at the reception desk. Lindell had talked to her before, about travel. There was a globe on the counter and when Lindell complained about stress Angelina had spun it and urged Lindell to stop it with her finger. She had landed in South America. In Paraguay.

'Go there,' Angelina said. 'I'm sure it will be relaxing.'

And this morning as she had hurried into the police station, Angelina had simply pointed to the globe and grinned.

'It's about a man who takes the train north in order to attend the funeral of an elderly relative.'

'Sounds fascinating,' Lindell said.

'Listen to this,' Marksson said, and opened the book. '"Someone who doesn't love us is in the process of changing our land",' he read in an authoritative voice.

He lowered the text and looked at Lindell, whose gaze was fixed on a framed photograph on the window sill. It showed a woman, whom Lindell assumed was Marksson's wife.

'That sounds about right,' Lindell said, suddenly unsure as to what was expected of her.

Marksson had talked about books before. She had understood that he was a bookworm and perhaps also something of an amateur philosopher. For her part, she did not read much. Perhaps a dozen books a year.

Marksson read the sentence again, now without looking at it.

'And the bit before it isn't bad either: "If I am going to participate in bringing change to my country I want to do so because someone I love will later be able to live here."'

He shut the book.

'But you aren't here for a reading. I'm returning this to the library today, that's why I brought it in. It's a Stig Claesson, one of my favourites.'

'I thought it sounded good,' Lindell said.

'Someone is changing this land – we see that, don't we?'

Lindell nodded. She wanted to say something insightful, building on this, but the stressful drive and her thoughts, miserable and ranting, had made her slow.

'Someone who doesn't love us.'

'The National Police Committee,' Lindell said, and Marksson looked at her with an expression that was difficult to interpret.

'You seem tired.'

'I'm wiped out,' she said. 'I mean, it's not that bad, but you know how—'

'Something *is* wrong,' Marksson interrupted.

Lindell drew a deep breath and sat up in her chair.

'I don't know what it is,' she picked up, 'but something in this story doesn't sit well with me. Maybe it's the picture of Tobias Frisk. You knew him and probably know better, but for me he doesn't seem like a murderer. I know it is a silly objection, killers can be a million different ways, but this thought didn't just come out of nowhere. This uncertainty doesn't come from my impression of Frisk, whom I know so little about, but it has come from the outside. Do you know what I'm getting at? I mean . . .'

Lindell leant over the desk and caught the hint of a smile that swiftly came and went in Marksson's face.

'There is something out there that I have seen or heard, something that has led me to the conviction that Frisk is not a killer. He is no longer self-evident.'

Marksson nodded.

'Go on,' he said.

'A visual impression,' Lindell said, and told him about her experience on Ringgatan after she had left Café Savoy. How she had a sudden thought and stopped in her tracks.

'At a café? Frisk was a baker – could that be the connection?'

'That was what I was thinking, but you are the one who has been to his workplace. I've only talked to Ahlén on the phone. I know from previous experience that it is often images that I respond to. I can read for hours and talk to a bunch of people without anything being set off in my mind, but then I catch sight of a single detail – it can look completely insignificant and ordinary from the outside but it makes everything become clear for me.'

They discussed what it could have been at the café. Lindell re-created the picture of the busy eatery, even pulled over a sheet of paper and started to sketch it out to jog her memory.

'Coffee, children, retirees, Christmas cakes . . .' Marksson rattled off. 'There's no space and perhaps stale air . . . there's the sound of children crying, mothers, pushchairs . . . a couple of teenagers . . . a child that doesn't want to take its coat off . . . maybe Christmas decorations on the table . . .'

'Hold it!'

Lindell held her hand up in a theatrical gesture but lowered it after a couple of seconds.

'No,' she said.

She knew she had been close, but the image that had flickered in front of her was only exposed in pieces, and quickly faded away.

'That's okay,' Marksson said after a brief pause, 'I'm sure it'll come back. We'll have to start somewhere else. If Frisk wasn't the killer, why would he commit suicide?'

'Shame,' Lindell said. 'He knew that I was on my way and he wasn't a particularly good liar. He knew he was partially responsible for Patima's death since he had brought her to Bultudden, and he knew he would not be able to bluff.'

'Too complicated,' Marksson said. 'It's one thing to import a woman from Asia and quite another to kill her. A lot of men would—'

'I know, but maybe Frisk agonised over it. He may also have known something about how and why she died.'

Marksson stared at her.

'Implicated, and yet not,' he said finally.

'Shame,' Lindell repeated.

'But then all men would be taking their own lives.'

'He was an unhappy man,' Lindell said. 'My investigations in the area brought everything to a head for him.'

'A skilled baker, a fly fisherman. The Frisk I knew was a pretty considerate man.'

'The considerate murderer,' Lindell mused.

'We won't get much farther now,' Marksson said, confirming her own conclusion.

'Is that your wife?' Lindell asked, and pointed to the photograph in the window.

'Yes, that is Inga-Marie. It was taken a couple of years ago. We were at Lofoten.'

'Was it fun?'

Marksson looked at her and smiled.

'What you are really asking is this: Are you happy?'

'Maybe,' Lindell said, returning his smile. 'Am I so easy to read?'

'You are an open book,' Marksson said. 'I think these visits to Roslagen have caused a bit of inner turmoil for you, haven't they?'

'Maybe,' Lindell repeated.

The tension between them broke when Marksson stood up from his chair.

'Should we go for a spin?'

Lindell sensed what he meant by 'spin.' Drive around on the gravel roads outside Östhammar, and Marksson would talk about his youth, point out various houses and tell her about the people who lived there. After a while they would end up at Bultudden.

'Is there anything in particular?'

'No,' Marksson said, but she heard something else in his tone. She did not know what was going on in his head but had no intention of asking. She realised he was as much a searcher as she was, but as opposed to her, he did not air his doubts.

Just as the last time things had heated up, when they had been outside Lasse Malm's shed, he left. He grabbed the car keys on his desk and walked out of the room.

'Let's scram,' she heard him say from the corridor, and when she found her way to the reception area, he was already standing next to his car.

'Men,' Angelina said, reading Lindell's expression.

That's right, Lindell thought. Wouldn't be so bad.

Once they were at Bultudden, Marksson stepped out at Torsten Andersson's house. They had caught a glimpse of him at the kitchen window. Lindell took over the wheel and continued down the Avenue.

Marksson had not asked what Lindell was planning to do on the point, but she thought he had an inkling. They were going to keep in touch by mobile phone.

Lisen Morell's car was parked up between a clump of bushes and a couple of enormously tall pine trees, just like last time. Lindell could not tell if it had even been moved since then. She looked around.

It was absolutely calm, the sea a polished surface. The low clouds appeared to press down on the bay, a stillness where not a single breeze could be detected, the tall pine tree trunks and between them the dark, oily water as a backdrop, creating a spooky feeling. Not a single movement. A static landscape. There was nothing charming about the scene. This is also the archipelago, she thought. As still as death.

'Hello,' Lindell called out, mainly to break the silence.

She took out her mobile phone and punched in Marksson's number but did not hit the call button.

She walked over to the fishing cottage, listening at the door, but heard nothing. She knocked, then repeated her knock after a couple of seconds. Her hand on the phone was sweaty. Not a sound. A new knock that sounded almost obscene in the intense stillness.

She had stood outside a single woman's door once before, knocking. She had not received an answer that time either. The woman they were trying to reach had been strangled to death.

She pushed down on the door handle, which more closely resembled an old-fashioned iron rod than a handle, with her elbow. The door opened with a faintly mournful sound.

'Hello? Is anyone home?' she called out, even though it appeared unlikely.

Suddenly the sun broke out and beamed a ray of light into the cottage through the window that faced the sea. Lindell ended up standing on the spot. There was a painting on the left wall. It was a watercolour and she recognised the subject, the outermost point on Bultudden.

She took a couple of steps into the room and thereby gained an overview of the space, including the sleeping alcove to the right. The bed was unmade, the blanket turned to one side so that it formed a triangle, and the pillows were rumpled. Lisen Morell had got out of bed. Lindell exhaled. She had subconsciously feared that Lisen would be lying on the bed, strangled to death.

Lindell left the house, pushed the door shut behind her, and heard the lock click. Then she rounded the corner and walked all the way around the building. Next to the bench that she and Lisen had sat on there was a bottle of wine of a brand that she knew well.

The clouds had drawn their veils again. The surface of the water was ruffled by a faint breeze. An old dock lay pulled up on the shore and a bit higher there was a boat with a green tarp over it. The ends of the rope that held the tarp in place were well knotted around nails fastened into the lumber that functioned as underlay. She resisted the temptation of loosening the knots to peek into the boat.

Lisen was somewhere close by, that much was clear. The car was in its place and the cottage was unlocked. But was she alive or dead?

Suddenly Lindell heard a crack and jumped around, crouching as she did so as if she were expecting a blow. Instinctively she also pressed the button on her mobile phone.

'What do you want?'

Lisen Morell's voice was loaded with so much explosive tension that Lindell could not bring herself to reply. She waved vaguely and heard a voice from her phone at the same time. She held it to her ear.

'No, everything's fine. I just happened to knock the phone.'

She looked at Lisen, who was standing a couple of metres away. How had she managed to get so close without making any sound?

'No, no, I've just bumped into Lisen. I'll talk to you later.'

Lindell turned it off. 'Sorry,' she said. 'Did I startle you?'

'Seems more like I was the one who startled you. But

what are you doing here? Are you the one who was sneaking around here last night?'

Lindell shook her head. 'What do you mean?'

'There was someone here last night. I've been walking around taking a look to see if I could find any clues.'

'Clues?'

'Yes, clues. To be perfectly honest, you look trashed.'

'I was a bit startled,' Lindell admitted. 'And I have actually been a little worried. In my line of work that often happens. Can we go inside?'

Lisen nodded and started walking toward the cottage. Then she stopped short and turned around.

'Do you have any reason to be worried about me? I mean, was that why you came?'

'No, no,' Lindell assured her. 'I just wanted to talk to you a little.'

When they had sat down at the old drop-leaf table with a cup of coffee in front of them she asked Lisen to tell her what she had heard or seen the night before.

'There was something out there. I was awake, it was about half past twelve. Sometimes I have trouble falling asleep and then I get up. I've read that it's better to do that, that you shouldn't stay tossing and turning in bed. In bed you should only sleep.'

And make love, Lindell thought.

'Yes, I do that too,' she said dishonestly.

'I pottered around a little. Do you see that watercolour? I framed it last night. Then I heard sounds. It sounded as though someone was sneaking around outside. First there were a couple of steps, then absolute silence, then more steps.'

Lisen Morell picked up her cup but did not drink. Lindell could tell she was reliving the events of the night.

'I may have imagined it, but it was so strong. It was as if the house was vibrating. It sounds silly and I don't mean it literally but you know when you feel something so strongly it translates into something physical.'

Lisen put down her cup, still without having drunk anything. Lindell saw her hand shake and recalled Lisen's words when she had been talking about her mezzotints: the hand that trembles.

'I know it sounds crazy, but I am extremely physical, or rather, it is one and the same. Mind and body. Both are required to be able to paint. And last night I knew – my whole body knew there was someone outside. Someone who did not wish me well.'

'Did you find anything?'

'No. I didn't think I would. A stalker doesn't leave a note.'

'Any idea who it might have been?'

Lisen didn't answer.

'Can't you go to your flat in town?'

'I'm going to spend Christmas here. I can't stand being in town – all the people who run around and think they are partaking in Christmas spirit because they have shopped until they dropped.'

'Have you ever noticed anyone trespassing here before?'

'Maybe,' Lisen sighed. 'This is a strange area, full of lonely souls. We are so far away from everything, exposed in some way, and when I say that I'm not referring to the weather. We should stick together, but everyone stays holed up in their own little cottage. Take Torsten Andersson, for example, the one I rent this place from. You've met him, haven't you? So lonely, so isolated, he practically screams out his despair but does nothing about it, just talks about the past and blames everything that is new. It is as if being on the periphery has hurt him, twisted everything good and made him into someone else. He is a good person, but that is hidden under all the bluster.'

'Was Tobias Frisk the same?'

Lisen shook her head and finally took a sip of coffee. Lindell was strangely disturbed by the fact that she had drained her cup while Lisen's was basically untouched.

'No, he was different. More hesitant, searching. He didn't rant and rave in the same way, he seemed more to be apologising for his existence. And yet he could not conceal his longing.'

'His smell gave him away.'

Lisen flashed a brief smile.

'What was he looking for?'

'What all of us look for. Someone to love, a connection, to feel part of something. I am an artist, and that is the loneliest work in the world. No colleagues, no one to fill in, no coffee breaks on the job. Everything depends on me. You do your thing and hope it means something to someone else.'

Lindell glanced at the painting that stood leant up against the wall.

'Is that one for sale?'

'What does it mean to you?'

'The sea,' Lindell said. 'The shore.'

She didn't want to add anything else, afraid of becoming too personal and vulnerable. Lisen was someone who had earlier seen through her, caught the scent not only of Dove and jasmine but of loneliness. If Lisen was so perceptive, she probably picked up on other things too.

'You can have it,' Lisen said.

Lindell protested but Lisen maintained that the watercolour painting was a gift. She did not want to sell it. If Lindell wanted it, she would have to accept it as a Christmas gift.

'Thank you,' Lindell said. 'It is the most beautiful—'

Lisen silenced her with her hand. Their eyes met. Lindell knew she had a budding friend in Lisen, if only she could nurture the relationship. She lowered her gaze, checked her watch, and knew she ought to call Marksson and pick him up.

'The other ones, Sunesson and Malm. How are they?'

'Lasse Malm has been by a couple of times. He wanted to impress me a little, puff himself up. And he is undeniably powerful. Thomas likes to brag but is basically a nice guy. A little prim. I think he would have trouble letting anyone get too close.'

Lindell recalled Sunesson's neat and tidy home, verging on pedantry.

'They're going to end up like Torsten, so the future of Bultudden is secure,' Lisen said with a smile.

'What will you do if your mysterious visitor comes back?'

'Take out my pepper spray,' Lisen answered.

'I think you should call.'

'Who?'

'Me, or better yet Bosse Marksson. Or 911.'

'You believe me? That I heard someone, I mean.'

'Why wouldn't I believe you?'

'But who would it be? If Tobias wasn't dead I would guess it was him. He was interested in me.'

Lisen stood up.

'I'll wrap up the painting,' she said.

'Do you mind if I take a walk around in the meantime?'

'Of course, you're probably a better police dog than I am.'

The sea was still glossy. A few solitary, fluttering snowflakes strengthened the feeling of isolation that reigned. Lindell walked along the water, convinced that any nightly visitor would have kept to the shoreline. It was not completely self-evident, but walking through the dark and thorny forest appeared more difficult.

She saw nothing out of the ordinary, no trace of any human except for an aluminum can bobbing in a clump of reeds. Had Lisen scared herself for nothing? The fact that she could hear footsteps through the logs of the cottage walls meant she either had unusually good hearing or a lively imagination. Lisen's talk of mind and body had not impressed Lindell.

After a couple of minutes she turned and walked back to the house. Lisen stood in the doorway watching her. Lindell shook her head.

'Here you go, a present from Bultudden,' Lisen said, and held out the wrapped painting.

'Thank you!'

They stood there for a second without speaking.

'Call me if you notice anything out of the ordinary,' Lindell said finally.

'In that case I'll be calling every day,' Lisen said, and fired off the smile that made her entire face light up. Lindell understood that the neighbouring men were interested in being warmed by such a smile, if not her art.

'See you later,' Lindell said, but was not convinced by her own words.

Bosse Marksson was waiting by the mailboxes outside Torsten Andersson's house. Lindell pulled over and her colleague jumped in. He didn't say anything about the fact that Lindell's visit with Lisen had taken a long time.

'So what did our friend Torsten have to say?'

'Not much. Mostly we just chitchatted about old times. He knows everyone.'

'But is friends with no one,' Lindell said.

Marksson looked at her. 'Is that Lisen's analysis?'

Lindell nodded.

'She may be right,' Marksson conceded. 'What else did she say?'

Lindell described Lisen's night-time experience.

'And it wasn't all in her mind?'

'To be honest, I'm not sure, but it feels right somehow. There is some kind of force field over this area, can't you feel it? From Andersson's house to Lisen's cottage: a slab of land jutting out into the sea with four – now three – bachelors, three old couples, and a lonely artist.'

'Force field?'

'I don't know how else to explain it. Maybe it's just my own mind-ghosts but I feel a kind of bubbling energy under the surface. But it is a form of anger that will never be released, at least not constructively. It is a rage that turns inward.'

'I see,' Marksson said.

'I'm trying to understand,' Lindell said, 'and I know I'm going on and on. It's a lot of feeling and not so much knowing. It also feels tragic. If this sliver of Sweden can't be happy then who can? Do you understand? Everything becomes so clear out here. In the city we're concealed by all the people, we hide and are hidden. Here there is no place to hide.'

'What points to them being unhappy?'

Lindell glanced at Marksson.

'I know you think I'm talking nonsense, but, as I said, I think the whole area feels sad and repressed.'

'It is another life, but the people out here are supposedly unhappier than—'

'That's not what I mean! Lisen said something about Christmas, about the stress and crazed shopping. She is going to celebrate it out here. It can seem lonely but the loneliness in town is just as great. Only out here it appears more clearly. Visualise this: A lone woman lights the fourth candle of advent, then eats herring and ham all by herself. That sounds so pathetic. But how many forlorn characters aren't there in Uppsala?'

'You would know more about that,' Marksson said.

'Okay, we'll drop my mind-ghosts. We have an investigation that leaves more questions than answers. What do we do about that?'

'I was thinking about the seal-shooting rifle, the one that Frisk put to his head. Where did it come from? Torsten mumbled something but I never did get it straightened out.'

'What did he say?' Lindell asked.

'That he had seen a lot of those rifles in the past.'

'But not that one? You've shown it to him, haven't you?'

'I think he recognised it, but didn't want to say anything.'

'Maybe he just wanted to confuse us.'

'That would be typical of him, I admit. But all the same I got the feeling he's sitting on something.'

'That would mean the rifle belonged to someone else.

Because if it had been Frisk's weapon, Torsten should have been able to say so. Don't you think? Even if he likes toying with the police.'

'Torsten muttered something about everyone knowing that Frisk had never owned a weapon, never had one. He said something about "what business would a person who doesn't hunt have with a gun?"'

'Inheritance. The gun is old.'

'I asked my dad. He's sure that Frisk's father didn't hunt either.'

Lindell digested this information. It was clear that Marksson had put a lot of thought into it.

'You could play a little fast and loose,' she said after a couple of kilometres. 'Go to Sunesson and tell him we have information indicating it is his rifle. Then do the same with Malm. Just to see how they react. Stir the pot.'

'Risky,' Marksson said, but did not elaborate.

'Does it matter?'

'What do you mean?'

'I don't know,' Lindell answered.

The snowfall was getting heavier, and shortly before they reached Östhammar they encountered a snowplough.

'A white Christmas,' Lindell said.

'A merry Christmas,' Marksson said, and smiled his widest smile.

They parted outside the police station. Marksson was going to walk to the library and drop off some books before having lunch. Lindell declined to accompany him. She felt a need to be alone for a while and had also arranged to meet with Ottosson in the early afternoon.

On top of this, she was dieting, but this was not something she admitted even to herself. I'm not hungry, she told herself. I can stop on the way and buy some fruit.

She felt that they were walking around in circles. The reason for it was dissatisfaction over how the case was developing, or rather because it had ground to a complete halt. They had a confirmation from Sorsele that Tobias Frisk had been seen with a Thai woman and that she had accompanied him when he checked out of the campsite. Their colleague in the area had promised to try to check with the agents who imported the foreign labour to see if they had further information on record regarding their berry-picking recruits.

Stolt in Thailand had collected a saliva sample from the sister in Krabi and sent it to Sweden. In a week or two they would see if there was a match with the dead woman's DNA. Every person's DNA is unique but between close relatives there were always similarities to support an identification.

Everything was falling into place, and yet not. Lindell wanted a motive. She wanted a body. She wanted to understand why Frisk had shot his brains out, and she wanted to know more about where the seal-shooting rifle had come from. Many wants, but the chances of satisfying them were marginal. The question about the suicide weapon was the only one where they could hope for a reasonable explanation.

She had lunch – a banana, an apple and a bottle of water – in the car at a petrol station in Gimo while she thought about the person who had been sneaking around outside Lisen Morell's cottage. Lindell believed her, wanted to believe her, despite Lisen's talk of feelings and spirit that was at times more than a little wacky. If she was correct in her assertion of a prowler, who could it have been? It could of course be someone from Lisen's earlier life, perhaps a rejected suitor returning to spy on her, but it was more probable that it was one of Bultudden's inhabitants creeping around in the dark. And if that was the case, why? Was there a tangible threat to Lisen? Was there some connection to Patima and Tobias Frisk's suicide, and in that case what did it consist of? Did Lisen have some significance that she may not have been aware of herself?

Lindell went through the candidates in the area and three names emerged as the most likely: Torsten Andersson, Thomas B. Sunesson, and Lasse Malm. In that trio there was also – Lindell was convinced of it – a concealed knowledge about Frisk's life during the past year that could help explain what had happened.

She stepped out of the car, walked over to a rubbish bin, and threw out the remains of her lunch. The tabloid headlines outside the petrol station screamed out news of a soap opera star who had had an affair with a married man, who in turn apparently had alcohol problems and a pregnant wife. The headlines of *Upsala Nya* were more discreet but dramatic nonetheless, with the sensational news of the county commissioner's return.

'Bultudden,' she said aloud, trying to imagine a reality show about the inhabitants of the Avenue.

Who is sleeping with whom? Who hates whom? Who is cheating his neighbour? Who is bluffing me and Marksson?

A crow came hopping over the concrete. It had a piece of paper in its beak. A mail crow, Lindell thought. Have you got a letter? She imagined the eagle, a little heavy and clumsy but also majestic, far above Bultudden. In its claws it held a foot. It was dripping blood over the waters of the bay.

A berry picker, she thought, and an image of the chainsaws on Såma's shop wall welled up. She shivered and felt pain radiating out from her midsection. The crow hopped closer, flapped its wings, then lifted off, careening in the wind and finally disappearing behind a car wash.

FORTY-THREE

'He is a psychological riddle,' Ottosson said, and Lindell could not help but smile. 'Come on now, don't laugh at me. A politician. A man at the height of his career who commits the contemptible murder of a defenceless old man, returns after twelve years, and then seems proud of his actions. No remorse whatsoever.'

'We've seen it before,' Lindell remarked.

'But not in this way. Admit that he is a remarkably atypical murderer.'

'He has a remarkably atypical uncle as well. I told you about him before. Talk about an unbelievable character.'

'Beatrice has interrogated him,' Ottosson said.

'Bea? What did he say?'

'Ante Persson was dumbfounded when she said that Sven-Arne had confessed to the killing of Dufva. She could hardly get a word out of him after that. He just stammered. Beatrice assessed him as senile.'

'Completely wrong! He's sharper than most of us.'

Lindell talked about the contents of Ante Persson's bookcase, how he appeared to plough through books in any number of languages and had not shown any signs of decrepitude, except that his legs seemed weak.

'Has he also been in politics?'

'If so, it would have been to the far left,' Lindell said.

'Morgansson went along and took the old man's prints. As you know, we have a handprint from a piece of furniture at Dufva's.'

'And it didn't match the county commissioner's?'

Ottosson shook his head. 'Dufva did not have a large circle of acquaintances. That is to say, he did not have one at all. Jenny Holgersson – the relative who card for him – could not recall a single visitor from outside the family.'

'So you think Ante Persson came along inside the house?'

'We'll see. Allan thinks so. Why would the two of them go there in the car?'

'A murder on the fly.'

'That is what Sven-Arne is claiming, but I don't believe him.'

'And what do you base this on?'

'Thirty-eight years of police work,' Ottosson said, grinning.

Allan Fredriksson popped his head in the door, which was somewhat ajar. He nodded at Lindell.

'The fingerprints in Dufva's house belong to Ante Persson. Left thumb and pointer finger on well-polished oak. There's no doubt about it. The old man was there.'

'Well, I'll be darned!' Ottosson exclaimed. 'Have you talked to Sven-Arne?'

'He's sleeping again. The guy can apparently nod off at any time. Sammy and I thought we would wait for him to wake on his own. We think it's best. But we have to interrogate Ante Persson again and hear what he has to say.'

'I'll come along,' Lindell said impulsively. 'I've met him before. Can't you and I handle it, Allan?'

Fredriksson glanced at Ottosson, who nodded his consent after a second or so.

It was a different Ante Persson who greeted Lindell this time. The power and confidence were gone. What remained was an old man with trembling hands and a gaze that expressed confusion and helplessness.

'The police are back,' he stated.

Ante Persson was sitting in bed. He was wearing a pair of wrinkled trousers and a cardigan that was more or less clean. He had slippers on his feet. One hand was resting on his thigh, the other was pulling bits of wool out of the front of the cardigan.

'Hello, Ante,' Lindell said. 'You remember me from the other day. This is my colleague, Allan Fredriksson.'

Ante lifted his head and looked at her, and something of his old edge gleamed in his eyes. Lindell realised she had spoken too loudly.

'We have some things to talk about,' she went on, and wondered if she should proceed with some small talk. She decided to get straight to the point. 'As you know, your nephew has confessed to the murder of one Nils Dufva. Now we are wondering if you can shed any light on that day, in the autumn of 1993. We have some new information.'

Ante Persson's face did not reflect that he had heard or understood a word of what she had said. His hand continued to pull wool threads out of the jumper and roll them into tiny balls.

'We think you were there,' Allan Fredriksson said.

'What do you mean?'

'That you were in the house when Dufva was killed.'

'I have no idea what Sven-Arne is up to,' Ante Persson said. 'He must have got a bit messed up when he was in India.'

'Were you there?'

'Nils Dufva is dead and buried,' Ante said. 'And that's just as well.'

'Please answer the question.'

Ante breathed audibly. 'Sven-Arne is a peaceful man.'

'Your fingerprints were in the house,' Lindell said, and sat down next to him. 'Were you present at the time of the murder? Had you been there before?'

Ante shook his head. Wrong tack, Lindell thought. Two questions in one breath. She started over.

'Did you know Nils Dufva?'

She put her hand on his left arm. Ante turned his head and stared her in the eyes. Am I going to get this old, she wondered. His cheeks were covered in red dots. A couple of grey hairs stuck out of his chin. He was breathing heavily, his breath sickly sweet and not altogether pleasant.

'Dufva was a Nazi, a full-blooded Nazi. He is dead, and now I think you should leave.'

'Not until you have answered my questions.'

'You can read all about it in my memoirs.'

'You're writing your memoirs?' Fredriksson broke in.

Lindell shot him a look.

'You are a socialist, and he was a Nazi. That much is clear,' Lindell resumed. 'That means you could hardly have been the best of friends. But did you meet him in a political context?'

'I had never seen his face,' Ante said.

'What do you mean?'

'I don't want to think about it, can't you understand that? There's so much else I need to work through. I am old, too old. I am one of the last. What do you know about poverty? Squat!'

That's good, Lindell thought, and gestured to Fredriksson to let Ante talk.

'You go around and catch small-time thieves but the real perpetrators go free. How many have died? My best memories and friends died before my eyes. They collapsed. So what do I care about Nils Dufva? Not a damn thing. There is a line connecting this place' – he lifted his hand and pointed to a pale-framed wall-hung photo of a red cottage – 'and where I am sitting now. The times are different but still the same. It has been crooked at times, but I've always had that line. It has been like a war. The whole time. I was born in a war. Why would I tarnish my last days by thinking about a Nazi?'

He fell silent.

'So, you witnessed your nephew kill Nils Dufva but you don't want to talk about it?'

Ante Persson smacked his lips.

'Could be,' he said.

'As you know, we have to try to understand what happened,' Lindell said pleadingly.

The old man held up his hands, palms facing Lindell, warding her off. She could not help but stare at the stumps on his left hand.

'I have seen the war,' Ante said, 'and that was no playground. Why should I care about Dufva? Dufva, or

367

"Dove", is a hell of a name for a guy like that. He wasn't the least like a dove. Quite the opposite. He loved to wage war and cause pain. He was a vulture.'

'How do you mean?'

'That he got a position in the military was perfectly logical. My tax dollars gave birth to that scumbag, can you understand that? I helped to pay for it! It makes me furious to think about.'

Where does all this hatred come from, Lindell wondered. She glanced at Fredriksson, who had a neutral expression. They exchanged a look and Fredriksson nodded almost imperceptibly.

'I need to see Sven-Arne,' Ante Persson burst out, and drew the walker over as if he was planning to leave immediately.

'What do you want to say to him?'

'That he is an idiot! I don't understand why he ran off to the police. He should have stayed in India, but he must have gone a bit crazy there. Make sure I get to see him.'

'We will have to see,' Lindell said. 'There is another question that I find perplexing.'

Ante Persson chuckled, a dry sound that surprised her.

'Perplexing,' he said with a snort.

'Elsa Persson,' she resumed. 'Why did she get run over? I assume that she had visited you, and from what I understand she became completely incoherent, not to say distraught, after talking with you. Why? What did you say to her?'

'She's never liked me,' Ante Persson said. 'She always gets upset when we meet.'

'She didn't know anything about Sven-Arne being in India,' Lindell stated rather than asked. 'But you were always aware of how and when he disappeared. How did she take it?'

368

'Elsa looked down on Sven-Arne. I'll bet she was relieved to get rid of him, but she never said anything about that. No, the schoolteacher had quite a poker face, didn't she? She never cared about him before, so why would she care when he left? She didn't give a shit about anything. Money and status were all that mattered. She thought I was a loony.'

'Were you a threat?'

'Why would I be a threat?'

'You are close to your nephew and shared secrets with him.'

Ante fired off a new humourless laugh.

'When can I see Sven-Arne?'

'We have to talk to him first,' Lindell said.

'Doesn't he want to?'

'I don't know anything about that. But if you want to see him you will have to cooperate a little. You were in the house when Nils Dufva died and now I want to know what happened. You will not help Sven-Arne by keeping quiet. We know you were there.'

'How do you know?'

'Your fingerprints were in the house. You knew Dufva. You were there. We want a story.'

Ante Persson stared at her.

'How is Sven-Arne?'

'He seems relieved,' Fredriksson said. 'And tired.'

'What did you do during the war?' Ante asked.

'I wasn't born then,' Fredriksson said, and smiled.

Ante Persson scrutinised him.

'Oh,' he said, and appeared to lose interest in Fredriksson. He turned back to Lindell. 'Please arrange for me to speak with him. That is the most important thing.'

Lindell did not comment on this request and waited, but received no further elaboration. Ante Persson refused to speak. It was as if all his strength had drained away. His hands rested limply on the handlebar of the walker and he hung his head.

'Would you like to rest for a bit?' Lindell asked after a minute of silence.

Ante Persson looked sideways at her. There was nothing of his anger or resistance left, only a pair of deeply mournful old eyes that regarded Lindell for a few seconds before his head sank back against his chest.

Lindell looked at Fredriksson, who stood up and walked over to the old man.

'Shouldn't you lie down for a while?' he suggested, and put his hand on Persson's shoulder.

Ante Persson did not reply. Lindell indicated with her head that she thought they should leave.

'We'll talk to the staff,' she said when they were outside in the hallway. 'They can look in on him. We won't get anything else out of him right now.'

'What do you think?'

'I'm not sure,' Lindell said absentmindedly. She had caught sight of a woman down the hall whom she assumed was a member of the staff. 'I'll talk to her. We can't just leave him like this.'

She walked over to the woman, whose name according to her name tag was Anneli Hietanen. As soon as Lindell mentioned Ante's name she started to smile.

'Oh, Ante. Yes, he's something else. He gets a little tired sometimes but in general he's more alert than everyone else put together.'

'I think it would be a good idea for you to look in on him,' Lindell said. 'And keep an eye on him for a while.'

'Are you a relative? I haven't seen you here before.'

'I'm a police officer.'

Anneli's smile extinguished immediately.

'Has anything happened?'

'No,' Lindell said after a moment's hesitation. 'We were just questioning Ante about . . . It's regarding one of his relatives.'

'I see,' Anneli said. 'Is it the girl in India?'

'Who are you thinking of?'

'Ante sometimes gets letters from India. I joke about him having a girlfriend there, a geisha or something.'

'Geisha?'

'Whatever they call it.'

'Do you know if he's kept the letters?'

'I think so, actually I know he does. He puts them in a box in the bookcase. That box is so makeshift. But why are you asking? Has anything happened to her? Is Ante sad? Why didn't you say anything?'

The woman left Lindell and walked to Ante's room with swift steps, knocked on the door, opened it, and disappeared inside.

Lindell rejoined Fredriksson, who was already waiting by the lift. She told him about the letters from India.

'That would be something to read,' Fredriksson said.

'We'll have to bring it up with the district attorney.'

Lindell checked her watch and thought about calling Fritzén, but dismissed the idea. Sammy Nilsson and Fredriksson could handle that. Lindell had the feeling that she should not get too tangled up in the case, because mentally she was still out in Bultudden. On top of that she wanted to get away to the day care and pick up Erik a little earlier. She had been inconsistent of late and now she wanted an extra hour or so with him.

'Let's go,' she said.

Fredriksson leant against the wall of the lift and closed his eyes.

'Geishas,' she said. 'Aren't they Japanese?'

He opened his eyes.

'Sometimes,' he said, and looked at her in that way that made him the colleague she so dearly valued, 'it's enough to make me despair. There's such a struggle inside us. Ante Persson is over ninety and deserves a little peace. Did you hear him say: "It's been a war this whole time. I was born in a war."'

'I think he got to be ninety because of those struggles inside him,' Lindell said.

'He's still caught in a war. Didn't you see his suffering?'

'Sure, but he's still alive, maybe more than I am,' Lindell said.

The lift came to a halt with a little jolt. Fredriksson smiled at her.

'You're something else,' he said simply, and pushed the lift door open. Lindell accompanied her somewhat hunchbacked colleague out into a December day where the snow was falling over Eriksdal's courtyards and rooftops.

FORTY-FOUR

The footprints in the newly fallen snow illustrated the slow progression of a thoughtful man. He turned around once and studied his own tracks. It made him think of hare prints, but hares don't turn around, he thought. Their trajectories are erratic, they throw themselves this way and that. I walk straight ahead. I have always done so.

Once he reached the boulder and the birch tree with the split trunks occasioned by its great age, he paused a second time. The snow whirled in the wind and he loosened the straps of his hat and lowered the ear-flaps. He looked around: a sparse forest with patches of lichen and brush. It was so reassuring and familiar – nonetheless an unease tingled inside him. It was in exactly this area that he had once intended to subdivide a couple of lots. He tried to imagine a development with two or three houses and was glad he had changed his mind at the last minute.

I made the right decision in the end, he concluded, and felt satisfied for the first time that morning. He walked on. To walk oneself warm, he thought. To walk straight but look to the side. I'll harvest the timber this winter, he decided, and the thought gave him a moment's respite. He had actually made the decision earlier, last winter, but confirming it felt good.

He would have to buy a new chainsaw. The old one was no longer usable.

The wind whipped him from the north. He walked himself warm. The sides of the hat flapped but he did not bother to tie the strings under his chin. He would tie his hat after Christmas. Then he would start felling. He longed for the weight of the helmet, the safety headphones cupped over his ears, and the stiffness of the safety clothing against his thighs.

He stopped a third time. Now he was close by and could not opt out of his decision by thinking of woodcutting. It irritated him that he couldn't drop the thought. And the most painful thing was that he knew what caused this inability to give a damn about the whole situation. Maybe because he had seen her. It had been during blueberry season and she had turned up like an exotic animal, so slender and elfin that she occasionally disappeared between the trees. He had followed her at a distance, sometimes coming close, and he discovered she was quick. She worked with straight legs, which he found pleasing. Crouching down or going down on one's knees just wasted time.

Her behind was small and boyish, without a womanly definition to the hip bones, but nonetheless enticing. Occasionally she looked around as if anxious. Then he crouched down. How long had he followed her? An hour? Two? She had appeared inexhaustible.

After that, she also appeared when sleep came over him. Recently – when he had understood who she was, or rather had been – she appeared to him more frequently. He could not defend himself.

He could not drop the whole thing and that bothered

him. He walked straight. Tracks in the snow on the street. Wind coming from the north. The trees sighing. A pine cone that dropped suddenly. The sound of breakers at a distance. He had soon reached Kalle and Margit's. He couldn't walk by without stopping in.

He walked in without knocking. There was a large pot in the hallway. He felt it – still warm. He lifted the lid and saw some kind of stew, glimpses of carrots and onion.

'Hello there!' Kalle called from his seat at the kitchen table.

Torsten Andersson pulled off his boots and hung his coat on a hook. He knew that was how Margit wanted it.

'Well now,' Kalle said.

'How are things?'

'As well as I deserve,' Kalle said cheerfully.

Torsten sat down.

'Coffee?'

'Maybe one cup.'

'Margit!'

'I can get it,' Torsten said, picking out a cup and filling it from the pot.

'It's an hour old,' Kalle said. 'But poison is as poison does.'

'I've been meaning to ask you,' Torsten said, after tasting the coffee, 'has Marksson been by with that rifle? I mean that one that Frisk shot himself with. He came by my house with it.'

Kalle looked out the window and appeared to deliberate over his answer.

'Yes, he came by,' he said finally. 'An old relic. It's been a long time since I've seen anything like it.'

'But you recognised it?'

Kalle looked at his neighbour.

'I think I need a little more,' he said, and got up from his chair.

'How is the hip?'

'The butcher tells me it's going to be fine, but the devil only knows.'

He refilled his cup and took his seat. He was breathing heavily.

'Yes, I believe I've seen that gun before.'

'What did you tell him?'

'Probably the same as you,' Kalle said, grinning.

Torsten nodded. He had suspected as much.

'And what do you think?'

'What should I think?' Kalle said, and drank a little of his coffee. 'This *is* poison,' he exclaimed. 'I'll tell Margit to put on a new pot.'

'It's good enough for me,' Torsten said. 'Where is she?'

'Pottering around upstairs.'

'What do you think of the whole thing? I mean, that Frisk—'

'No, I thought the same thing. He was no one to . . . It's mysterious.'

'Have you talked to—'

'No, I didn't want to get involved,' Kalle said. 'It's bad enough as it is.'

'I know. Who would have thought this would happen. I saw her.'

'Who?'

'Her. The one who . . . disappeared,' Torsten said.

'You saw her? Where?'

'In the woods.'

'What did she look like?'

'Little, thin.'

Kalle nodded as if this confirmed his own idea.

'And then she disappeared,' he said with a sigh.

'What do you think happened?'

'I don't know. But the fact that Frisk had her hidden away seems pretty clear. Maybe she wanted to leave. It's hard to say in these cases. I mean, with women.'

Torsten finished the last of the coffee. It felt better now that he had told someone he had seen her, but now he should move on. He was also grateful to have spoken with only Kalle. Margit would have urged him to go to the police.

He thanked Kalle for the coffee and brought his cup to the sink.

'I'll see you later,' he said, and Kalle raised his hand.

Malm was at home; he knew as much because his car had gone by about an hour earlier. Torsten didn't know how he would take it. They knew each other well, but had not had much contact the past few years. Torsten and Lasse Malm's father had been childhood friends and after his suicide, Torsten had often walked over in the evenings to talk to Lasse. Everyone in Bultudden had done what they could to support him. Margit had invited him for dinner many nights and Kalle had taken him out to sea. For a while it was as if the suicide had brought the area inhabitants closer to each other.

Malm's pickup stood parked outside the front door. There was a large shrink-wrapped package in the back. Lasse Malm stepped out on his front porch as Torsten walked up to the house.

'Your timing couldn't be better,' he said, and gestured to the car.

'Is it a fridge?'

'A wardrobe,' Malm said.

'You can carry that yourself,' Torsten said, and smiled.

Malm laughed and punched Torsten on the shoulder.

'How's things?'

Torsten muttered something and turned back to the pickup. He didn't want to ask, but had to. Now or never. He was no coward, but it felt disloyal to bring up the subject of weapons with Malm. Torsten knew that he had detested firearms of all kinds since the day he had found his father on the second floor.

'There's one thing,' Torsten said, and turned to Malm. 'Something I've been thinking about. I have to ask, even though it doesn't feel quite right.'

'Yes?'

'The seal-shooting rifle,' Torsten said. 'How did Frisk get hold of it?'

Lasse Malm stared at him before he turned his gaze to the side. Torsten tried again.

'I have to—'

'You don't have to do fuck!'

Take it easy, Torsten thought.

'Marksson came by and asked me if I recognised it and I said no. I did it for your sake. I would never—'

Lasse Malm raised an arm to stop the flood of words. His face was dark and there was a flicker of something in his small eyes that could be taken for hatred.

'I knew the talk would start up sooner or later.'

'No one is talking,' Torsten said, and made sure not to

raise his voice. 'No one along the Avenue is talking. No one has said anything to the cops. I just wanted to know. This is between you and me.'

Lasse Malm lowered the tailgate and started to pull on the wardrobe box. Torsten laid a hand on his arm.

'We can do this together,' he said. 'Just calm down. I'll jump up on the bed.'

'I don't need any help. You can go to hell!'

'Lasse,' Torsten pleaded. 'The two of us have to stick together, you know that. I just want some clarity.'

Malm shrugged himself out of his grasp but made no attempt to unload the car on his own. He stood staring out over the yard.

'I sold it to Frisk,' he said finally. 'Sold? I more or less gave it to him. He gave me a couple of nets. I didn't want to see that damn gun, not after . . . How the fuck could I know he would shoot himself twenty years later. How could I! It's not my fault.'

'No one is saying it's your fault,' Torsten said. 'Only Frisk is responsible and everyone out here knows it. No one is blaming you for what happened.'

He felt a wave of gratitude. That explained it.

'Let's finish this,' he said, and climbed up on the back wheel, swung a leg over the side, and climbed up onto the cargo area. 'Now I know, end of story.'

Lasse Malm was motionless for a moment longer, then grabbed the package and pulled it forward so that only the very edge rested on the tailgate.

'You can get down,' he said. 'It's not so heavy.'

FORTY-FIVE

On the 11th of December, Sammy Nilsson and Allan
Fredriksson completed an interrogation session with Ante
Persson, this time with a tape recorder and video camera.
They had decided to hold it at the nursing home. There
was no point in transporting the ninety-one-year-old to the
police station. It would tire him out unnecessarily and the
foreign environment would perhaps diminish his urge to
talk.

It turned out not to matter in the end, because Ante Persson
chose not to say much more than what he had already told
Lindell and Fredriksson.

That same day they were issued a warrant to claim the
letters that Ante – according to Anneli Hietanen – had
received from India. Earlier in the morning Allan Fredriksson
had been able to confirm the existence of a wooden box in
the bookcase.

Ottosson and the DA had not hesitated, despite the
privacy issue of reading personal letters. The letters might be
able to shed some light on the strange murder case.

Fredriksson and Sammy Nilsson were given the thankless
task of returning to Ramund. They didn't like it, and it did
not help matters when Ante Persson threatened to throw
them out. The old man had risen from his chair – this time

seemingly without any problems – and taken a swing at Fredriksson.

Sammy Nilsson had forced his arm back to his side, more or less pressed Ante Persson back into his chair, and laid the official paperwork on the table.

'This is something we have to do,' he said.

'Fucking Fascists! You haven't changed one bit since the war.'

Fredriksson walked over to the bookcase. He let his gaze flit across the spines of the books as he gently withdrew the box, jammed between two maroon volumes. Lindell had been right: Ante Persson's library was impressive.

'We'll return these once we have read them, it's as simple as that,' Sammy Nilsson said in an attempt to calm Ante, who appeared to have drained his strength in the initial attack and now sat limply leant across the table.

'Here is your receipt,' Sammy Nilsson said.

The old man gave him a look, filled with disgust and helplessness, but made no attempt to take the piece of paper, so Nilsson laid it on the table.

Back at the police station, they sat down in Sammy Nilsson's office. Fredriksson fetched the coffee, while Nilsson took out the first letter in the pack and started to read. When Fredriksson returned, he pushed it across the table and kept reading. Ottosson turned up after half an hour, wondering how things were going, but only received grunts in reply so he left them in peace.

They looked up from time to time but did not comment on what they read. Their initial discomfort was replaced by a burgeoning excitement. Sven-Arne's stories from India

381

were amusing and written in an engaging style, completely free of the politician's dry and factual prose. They gave the policemen a good sense of his life in Bangalore. Straightforward descriptions of his work at the botanical garden became increasingly elaborate and detailed each year, and were mingled with glimpses of street life and news of neighbours and colleagues.

It was clear that over the years – there were one hundred letters in all, sent over twelve years – Sven-Arne had put a great deal of effort into giving his uncle entertaining reading and not simply dutiful greetings.

There was not a single musing over life in Uppsala, not a sentence touching on family, questions of everyday life, the weather in Sweden, or county politics. Both of the police officers assumed that Ante had talked about life in Sven-Arne's former home town in his letters, but if this was the case it had not resulted in any comments or other reactions in Sven-Arne's letters.

At one point Fredriksson looked up, put down the latest missive, and shot his colleague a look. Sammy Nilsson nodded but said nothing, resuming his task.

It was a letter dated 28th December, 1999. Perhaps it was the approaching turn of the millenium or something else that gave him a need to sum up his life, that caused him to comment for the first time on what had happened at Kungsgärdet in 1993.

When Fredriksson had put down the final letter, he removed his glasses and rubbed his eyes.

'What a mess,' he said, and sighed heavily.

'But why?'

'I don't understand squat. There was no reason for

Sven-Arne to even mention it. We had nothing on them, back then or now, and then he lumbers in after twelve years and starts to talk.'

'And full of lies on top of it,' Sammy Nilsson said. 'It's the weirdest thing I've seen.'

The reading had taken one and a half hours. Both of them felt as though they had read a novel.

'You could publish these as a book,' Sammy Nilsson exclaimed.

'And what a book it would be. The letters were touching.'

Fredriksson felt conflicting feelings – on the one hand the kick he had received from the sensational information surrounding Nils Dufva's death, in part a feeling that he had walked in on something of a highly private nature. They had peeked into a person's most private thoughts, presented in confidence with the assumption that they were only shared with one person's eyes, not read by outsiders. Now these letters – at least parts of them – were part of official documents.

'What do we do?'

'We'll have to bring in the old man, I suppose.'

'First we talk with Sven-Arne,' Sammy Nilsson said.

'He may resist.'

'You mean Ante?'

Fredriksson nodded.

'This time we're only going to talk to Ottosson, Lindell, and Fritte. We have to be completely sure of this before the papers get wind of it.'

They gathered up the letters and were careful to arrange them chronologically. Sammy Nilsson had marked the most

383

memorable letters with yellow Post-its. They trotted in to Ottosson's office.

It was as if he had been waiting for them, because when they walked in he was sitting passively, his arms crossed. There were two chairs in front of his desk and he executed an exaggerated flourish with his hand. They sat down.

'So we have something to chew on,' Sammy Nilsson started, and held the packet of letters aloft like a prize catch.

'I could tell from the look of you,' Ottosson said, and his whole face cracked into a smile. 'You looked like two monks leaning over a photo album from the time of Jesus.'

Allan Fredriksson briefly gave an account of what they had found in the letters. Ottosson's expression did not betray what he thought of their discovery, and when Fredriksson was done he opened a desk drawer and pulled out a file folder. It looked ancient, archive-brown in colour, with reinforced corners and two linen ribbons tied in a neat bow. It gave Fredriksson a flashback to his time as a clerk in the A6 in Jönköping. The name of his battalion chief was Anner, a man whose incompetence was legend, and he used to wave officiously with incredibly important folders of a similar appearance that contained very little of real value. Fredriksson shivered as he recalled that hateful time.

'This is the second piece of the puzzle,' Ottosson said, and both investigators sensed that their boss had been waiting for this opportunity.

'What is that?' Sammy Nilsson asked, and leant forward.

He knew he had to appear genuinely curious and concerned in order for Ottosson to go through with his performance with the dignity that he clearly felt the folder deserved.

'This is a file on Nils Dufva.'

'I see,' Fredriksson said. 'And what . . .'

'The motive was clearly political,' Ottosson said. 'Dufva's murder was inexplicable, or at least confounding, in 1993, but what we didn't know then is here. There are threads that lead back in time. The motive. With your letters the picture is now complete. The mystery is solved.'

Oh, be done with it, Nilsson thought. Enough already with the speech-making.

'Where did the file come from?' he asked.

'The military,' Fredriksson said immediately.

Ottosson laid the file on the desk and looked at Fredriksson over the top of his glasses.

'Could be,' he said. 'But we can't use it. The file is on loan and God help you if you make the slightest mention of it.'

In order to underscore the gravity of his warning he quickly stood up, leant across the desk, and fixed his eyes on Nilsson, who at first looked astonished, and then started to smile, and then on Fredriksson, who made an effort not to burst into laughter.

'All right chief,' Nilsson said, and made a sloppy salute.

He was pleased with the fact that the investigation had taken a large jump forward. He was pleased with his grinning colleague. He was pleased with his at times spectacular boss who was now attempting to appear intimidating but who was very well aware of the fact that he was failing.

'Okay, guys,' Ottosson said, and changed to a double-edged smile, 'let's set the wheels in motion and nail a ninety-one-year-old who about three hundred years ago killed an old Nazi with his crutches. We'll be heroes, the people will praise us, and telegrams and flower bouquets will overwhelm the station. Ante Persson will be put away for life. Justice will prevail. Hallelujah!'

FORTY-SIX

'Fire!'

She was clearly shaken.

'What do you mean?'

'Go out on the porch, and you'll smell it,' Doris Utman told her neighbour.

Thomas B. Sunesson left his seat on the couch in front of the television – the evening news program had just started – grabbed his cordless phone, slipped on his clogs, and cracked the front door.

The darkness was impenetrable even though the thin snow cover reflected the lights on the garage and created a ghostlike, matte glow over the garden.

'I can't smell any kind of building burning,' he said, 'but someone must have a fire going in their fireplace.'

'The wind is coming from the south. I'm thinking about her down that way.'

He understood that Doris was referring to Lisen Morell.

'Have you called Lasse?'

'He doesn't answer. And he never makes fires in the fireplace.'

Thomas knew this as well. Malm's chimney had been on the verge of collapse for a long time. Lisen Morell had no fireplace, and the wind really was blowing from the south.

'Ulla and Magnus are in Gimo, I know that much. They are visiting Ulla's sister.'

He smiled to himself. As usual, Doris Utman was fully informed.

'And I can't leave Oskar. He's doing poorly again. Otherwise I would go and have a look.'

During the autumn Oskar Utman had grown worse and Doris used a pump to extract the mucus her husband lacked the strength to cough up.

'Doris, I'll go out and take a look around,' Sunesson said. 'I'll give you a call back later.'

He didn't like it. Not only would he miss the evening news, he had to go out in the cold. He had looked forward to a relaxing, cozy time on the couch after having been in full swing all afternoon and evening. He had put up the new shower head and done the last of the caulking in the bathroom and after that vacuumed and mopped the entire lower level.

It would in all likelihood be the coldest night of the season thus far. He walked a short distance along the Avenue and realised he should have pulled on a jumper under his jacket.

Suddenly he felt the smell of smoke, stopped, and sniffed the air. Doris was right. He walked on a bit longer, then turned around to get the car.

A tall figure loomed behind the high flames that leapt up from the bonfire in the middle of the garden, and cast an enormous shadow against the house. He's not right in the head, Thomas thought, making a fire at this time of night!

He turned in and parked behind the pickup, but before he got out he called Doris to calm her fears.

Lasse Malm's smile looked diabolical in the light of the fire.

'Got any hot dogs?' he said in a loud voice, as if to make himself heard above the crackling.

He looked excited. He had a rake in his hand.

'Doris called,' Thomas said. 'She was scared of the smoke smell. Thought the Magpie had turned to arson.'

'Feels good to get rid of this old shit,' Lasse Malm said.

'It's a bit windy.'

'It's not too bad. And there's a lot of snow besides.'

They stood silent, watching the fire and the sparks that flew around in the darkness.

'What are you burning? Is it your kitchen cabinets?'

'No, I'm clearing out the upstairs. I haven't lifted a finger in years.'

Everyone in Bultudden knew that Lasse Malm rarely went upstairs and above all never into the room where his father had shot himself.

'Must feel good to get rid of it,' Thomas agreed, and immediately felt more sympathetically inclined.

The initial outrage over having to go out into the night and then discover that Lasse was burning rubbish late at night and causing Doris to worry had subsided. He took one step closer to the fire and stretched out his hands to the warmth.

'Have you seen her lately?'

'Who do you mean?' Lasse Malm asked.

'The Magpie.'

'It's been a while.'

'She's always driving back and forth, but it's been calm for a while,' Thomas said while he backed up a step. The heat caused his cheeks to turn red. 'Maybe there's something wrong with her car again.'

Lasse pushed some scrap closer to the flames with the rake.

'Does she have a guy?' he asked suddenly. 'I mean, have you seen anyone?'

'Naw.' Thomas grinned. 'I don't think she puts out.'

'She doesn't? Do you mean . . .'

'Not that she's a lesbian, I don't think that. But she seems a bit strange all around. But she's good-looking.'

'You think? Maybe a little skinny?'

'I like it,' Thomas said. 'She's pretty appetising, don't you agree?'

Lasse Malm gave him a sideways glance.

'I wouldn't have anything against rolling around in that fishing cottage, that's for sure,' Thomas went on. 'It'd be nice with a bit of pussy close by.'

'Then go down there,' Lasse said. 'Can you watch the fire for a bit, I just realised I have a bit of stuff in the shed as well.'

He passed over the rake and disappeared like a phantom around the side of the house. Thomas leant against the handle. The flames were no longer as high. The smell was somewhat acrid and Thomas guessed Lasse had been burning a wide variety of items.

Lasse came back dragging a pair of rubbish sacks, and without a second thought, heaved them up on an old pallet that had almost burnt down. The plastic started to curl up almost immediately, the bags burst and revealed old rags and packaging materials. A rag burst into flames, perhaps soaked in a kind of paint thinner. A bottle that had contained oil rolled down, but Thomas sent it back into the fire with a well-directed kick.

Lasse left again and returned with another couple of bags that he threw onto the blaze, which had now received a new lease on life.

'That's better,' he said. 'A little less shit.'

'I've been thinking about this deal with the Magpie,' Thomas said.

'I can take that,' Lasse said, and held out his hand for the rake.

'She may have a man in the background after all.'

'Why do you say that?'

'She can't sell a lot of paintings, can she? What does she live off of ?'

Lasse masterfully raked together some bits of wood, plastic, and other things.

'You think some guy is sponsoring her?' he asked.

'Sponsoring would be a fancy word for it,' Thomas said, and chuckled.

'I don't care,' Lasse said. 'She doesn't bother me any.'

He bent down and picked up a piece of cloth, looked at it for a moment, then tossed it into the fire.

'Oh, come on now, admit that you—'

'Cut it out! If you want to fuck her then drive down there and ask her. Okay?'

A bag started sliding to one side. Lasse caught it with the rake and shifted it back.

'Well now. How is Christmas looking?' Thomas changed the topic.

Lasse shook his head, but didn't answer.

'I'm going up to Fagervik myself.'

Lasse did not ask him what he was going to do there.

'I called Doris to reassure her,' Thomas said out of the blue.

'That's great,' Lasse said, without enthusiasm.

'Have you seen any more of that cop?'

'No, have they been talking to you? I thought they had wrapped it up?'

'That female one from Uppsala . . . I'm wondering if she and Marksson have something together. Why else would she be turning up all the time? Since we know that Frisk killed that girl. Did you ever meet her?'

'No,' Lasse said.

'I wonder how Frisk got hold of her.'

They stopped speaking and stared into the blaze.

'It was unsettling, that affair with the chainsaw. They took yours too, I noticed.'

'They were here poking around,' Lasse said. 'Can you move over a little?'

Lasse resumed his raking. Suddenly the handle snapped in two.

'Damn it!'

'You're too strong.' Thomas smirked.

Lasse Malm tossed the rake aside and stood with his back turned to Thomas before he strode away out of sight.

Something in the bonfire started to spit and an orange flame spurted out. Thomas listened into the darkness by the corner of the house where Lasse had disappeared.

A couple of minutes went by. At first Thomas thought Lasse had gone to fetch another rake but he did not show himself.

The bonfire collapsed further and did not throw off as much heat as before. Thomas peered at the house. Had Lasse gone inside without saying anything?

Finally, after another minute or so, Thomas walked back to the car, turned on the engine, waited a while, then backed out onto the street and drove south.

FORTY-SEVEN

It was twenty to ten when Ann Lindell thought of it. She had
spent the evening putting away toys and clothes, filled two
grocery bags with newspapers that had been lying around
all over the flat, then put them by the front door. She had
vacuumed, and dusted window sills, and done several loads
of laundry. She had been thinking about Ante Persson all
night, his desperate helplessness and anguish as he was
escorted to the police station, brought two flights up in the
lift, and placed in an interrogation room. She had leant over
the frail body in the wheelchair and put an arm around his
shoulders. Fredriksson and Sammy Nilsson had waited in
the background, ready to start the interrogation but aware
of the fact that the old man had to be reassured first.

There was no joy in this. Solving the murder of Nils Dufva
had spread a kind of gloom that was only strengthened when
he was brought in.

Ante Persson had mumbled something about 'everything
goes around.' What had surprised her was the fear in his eyes.
They had all assumed he would be bewildered and perhaps
tired, but they had been unprepared for the apparent terror
he experienced.

Lindell had left the station before the interrogation began
and knew nothing of how it had gone. Had Ante been

allowed to stay or had he been sent back to Ramund? The latter was more likely. At least that was Ottosson's opinion, who maintained that the old man had no possibility of fleeing, especially since they could easily post a guard outside his door.

It was when she was finishing the laundry that the penny dropped for her, when the feeling of unease that had grown so strong outside Café Savoy received its explanation. She had just emptied the dryer and sorted the clothes into two neat piles – one for Erik and one for herself – when the thought of how appealing it would be with a third pile flew through her head. At that moment the memory came back to her with a start and it felt as though she had received a strong electric shock.

She dropped her task at hand and went to the kitchen to check the time.

'It's not too late,' she muttered.

The familiar agitation caused her to – anxiously and without any motivation – walk up to the window and study the thermometer, as if the temperature could explain or determine how she should act.

Then came doubt, and while the clock kept ticking indefatigably she grew more and more irresolute. At last, shortly after ten o'clock, she walked up to the telephone.

He picked up immediately and with an alert voice, which reassured her. He may have gone to bed, but had not fallen asleep.

'It's me,' she said. 'I've realised what it was that was bothering me. I'm sorry I'm calling so late but I have to talk to someone.'

'That's fine, we're night owls,' Bosse Marksson said.

'Do you remember when we visited Lasse Malm? I was going to return the chainsaw and we put it back in the shed behind the house.'

'Yes?'

'There were a couple of rubbish sacks there. One had fallen over. Remember?'

Marksson made a noise of assent.

'A discarded piece of clothing had fallen out and just as we were going to go, I tossed it back into the bag.'

Lindell paused and unconsciously moved her free hand in a gesture similar to the one she had performed in the shed.

'Now I know what it was,' she resumed. 'Or I think I do. When I was at the Savoy there was a one-year-old sitting on the floor, wearing a pink undershirt. She had spilt something on her chest and it looked pretty soiled.'

'I see, a pink undershirt,' Marksson said, to prod Lindell's memory.

'The same colour I saw in the rubbish sack. The clothing rag I tossed back had the same colour.'

'Yes?'

'Do you get it?'

'No, to be honest, I don't.'

'It was a pink tank top that fell out of the bag.'

Marksson digested this information.

'Do you mean . . .'

'What was Malm doing with a pink tank top? He's as large as a house. You said he hadn't had a girlfriend in ages.'

'It was several years ago,' Marksson confirmed. 'Do you think it was the Thai girl's tank top? But there is no connection between the two of them.'

'No, not as far as we know.'

'It's a bit far-fetched,' Marksson said, after having thought about it for a while.

'I know, but who would have thought that your pal would find a foot on the beach?'

'That's not a flawless comparison,' Marksson said, and she heard from his voice that he was smiling.

'Can you go out there tomorrow and check it out?'

Marksson had known Lasse Malm since childhood and she knew he was hesitating.

'I'll go myself,' she said when he didn't answer. 'I can probably find some reason to poke around in his shed – tell him I've received information that Frisk may have hidden things at his place.'

'Hold your horses, I'm thinking.'

'I'll head out there tomorrow,' she said. 'I'll call you.'

They finished the call. It was already twenty to eleven. Lindell broke one of her rules about not drinking wine during the week by going out into the kitchen, opening a bottle of Portuguese wine, and pouring herself a glass.

But before she tasted it she undressed, took a quick shower, wrapped herself in her robe, and sat down on the couch in the living room.

'Cheers,' she said, raising the glass at the television, and taking a sip.

FORTY-EIGHT

She heard the sound of a car and felt more angry at the disturbance than afraid. She had been sketching for several hours. She had returned to the subject again and again, used many pieces of paper, and slowly the idea had started to take shape.

The sound of the engine stopped. She walked over to the window that faced the dirt road but saw nothing but the darkness between the pine trees.

There was a small dirt road between the Avenue and the cottage. If one continued past this road, it was only a hundred metres to the turnaround at Bultudden's end. People occasionally drove down that way and turned around but never this late at night.

She stared out into the December night. Fear came creeping. The card Ann Lindell had given her was pinned to the noticeboard. Her mobile phone lay on the bed. A new look out of the window after she had turned out the light yielded nothing. The darkness and silence were impenetrable.

The knock came out of nowhere. She twirled around and fixed her eyes on the door before running over to the bed, grabbing her phone, and pressing the number keys for 911.

'Who is it?' she yelled.

'It's only me.'

She stared at the door. The voice sounded familiar but her terror prevented her from immediately identifying it. She pressed the dial button on her phone. Her hands shook. One ring sounded, then another, then a voice could be heard. A woman's voice. At that moment the door opened.

'Hello,' said Thomas B. Sunesson.

He stepped into the house and immediately closed the door behind him.

'It's cold,' he said, smiling. 'I don't want to let out the heat.'

The voice in the telephone yelled a 'hello'.

'Did I scare you?'

Lisen Morell shook her head.

'Are you talking on the phone?'

A new shake.

'I just wanted to let you know that Lasse is burning rubbish, in case you were wondering about the smell of fire.'

At last she managed to answer the increasingly agitated voice on the other end.

'I dialled the wrong number,' she said, and ended the call.

'How are you? You look terrible. I didn't mean to frighten you.'

'But you did!'

'I just wanted to . . .'

'I know what you want! You come sneaking around my house.'

'What are you talking about?'

'You can leave now.'

'Calm down,' Sunesson said.

Lisen Morell lifted one hand to stop him.

'Leave,' she said, 'or I'll call the police.'

He looked perplexed.

'What do you mean I come sneaking around? I knocked, didn't I?'

He explained how Doris Utman had called him and how he had gone out to check up on the burning smell.

'She thought there might have been a fire at your place.'

'There's nothing burning here,' Lisen Morell said.

'Okay, then I know.'

He glanced at the table, then bent over and snatched a piece of paper from the floor.

'This looks good,' he said.

'It's a sketch, nothing else. But you are bothering me. I'd like you to leave now.'

He gazed at her, dropping the page so that it wafted down to the floor.

'You're not exactly a diplomat. I came here out of a sense of concern. That's what we do out here. We look after each other.'

'I've noticed,' she said with an acidity that made him pull a face.

'To be honest, I don't think it's good for you to live here all alone.'

'And who has asked you for your honesty? You live alone too.'

'Did you ever talk to Frisk? Did he come down here?'

'Sometimes.'

'Did you meet his Thai girl?'

Lisen shook her head. She suddenly discovered that all

fear and anger had run out of her. She imagined it was the smell of smoke that had calmed her.

'What do you think happened?'

'I don't know,' Lisen Morell said.

'You said that someone's been sneaking around. When was the last time?'

'Just the other night. I heard footsteps and sounds.'

Sunesson walked over to the window facing the sea and stared into the darkness. She watched the back of his neck where the hairs were standing on end. It was as if he felt her gaze, and he pulled one hand over his shoulder.

'Who do you think it was?'

He turned around and looked at her. She shrugged.

'Have you talked with anyone about the fact that someone's been sneaking around? I mean the police.'

'I mentioned it to Ann Lindell. You've met her, haven't you?'

'Sure, she borrowed my chainsaw,' he said.

He walked up to the front door, put his hand on the handle, then turned around and looked at her with a serious expression.

'You should keep your eyes and ears open,' he said. 'If anything comes up, you should give me a call right away.'

Before she had time to answer, he had opened the door and left.

After a minute she heard the sound of his car. Why had he parked out by the turnaround, she wondered as she walked up to the door and fastened the bolt.

Lisen Morell curled up under the blankets. Her limbs were stiff and cold, her back ached. That's how it was when she stayed up working too long. She had always had difficulties with proportions. She exaggerated, worked too much, dipped again and again until fatigue caused her hands to shake. The evening often morphed into night before she finally put away her pencil, charcoal, and brush. Now her body was punishing her for it.

She looked out in the dim light of the cottage where the white papers spread on the floor bore witness to her last session. In this chaos of attempts there was perhaps a single expression actually worth something, that carried forward and that could perhaps, after additional hours, days, or weeks of work, result in a painting that passed muster.

Lisen Morell was poised on a razor-sharp edge, teetering between total collapse, both physical and artistic, and brilliance.

She could not help but smile when she thought about her neighbour's unexpected visit. Was his talk of smoke simply an excuse to make contact? Was he the one who had been sneaking around outside? Sunesson was harmless. He would never become threatening. She decided to invite him in for coffee one of these days. Not that she was interested in him, but to show him what she was working on. Maybe it would be the start of better contact with her neighbours.

She fell asleep late but woke up almost immediately. She sat up in bed, confused. The clock on the nightstand said 2:14 a.m.

It was absolutely quiet. Not even the wind or the sound of the waves could be heard. Nonetheless there was something that had awakened her. She carefully turned the blankets aside, pulled her robe over, and pressed it to her body. A scraping sound somewhere outside the cottage made her gasp. She held her breath and listened. She pressed the robe even harder to her chest, where her heart was racing.

The digital numbers on the clock showed 2:15. She breathed out through her mouth and barely managed to inhale.

She knew she should search out her mobile phone from the mess on the table, but could not manage to make herself get up. She shivered with cold and fear. Paralysed with terror, she saw a severed foot walk across the floor, touch her papers and leave sooty, bloody prints on her sketches, only to disappear from view. A slender and lost foot, a woman's foot. Lisen had the impression it was searching for its body.

'I don't want to,' Lisen mumbled, as she carefully pulled on her robe. It occurred to her that perhaps it was a bird that had struck the windowpane. That happened a couple of times every year, but what birds were flying around in the December night?

She stood on trembling legs and took a couple of steps out into the room. The window to the bay was black. Suddenly there came a gust of wind so strong the cottage flinched and the sea answered with a muted thunder as it mercilessly struck the shore and the worn expanses of rock.

She walked over to the window. Someone out there wishes me ill, she thought. What have I done? Let me be in peace!

Then she glimpsed a movement outside the window. It looked like the shadow of a body, hastily fluttering past. Lisen quickly pulled herself aside and pressed up against the wall. She felt a trickle of warm urine run down her legs.

FORTY-NINE

The Uppland region's first real storm of the season came in already during the night with an intense snowfall and strong northerly winds, causing the police to close many of the roads in the areas around Tierp and Älvkarleby. The E4 motorway was open for traffic but for all practical purposes unpassable, with the result that a number of cars drove off the road. A tractor-trailer had slid off the road by Björlinge Church and the trailer blocked one lane.

It was Allan Fredriksson's first winter as a country inhabitant and at nine o'clock when he finally managed to take himself the twenty kilometres into town, he was in a terrible mood. He had ample time to regret his move during the challenging trip.

'It'll be better in a couple of months.' Sammy Nilsson tried to cheer him up, not without a certain glee.

That summer Allan Fredriksson had been lyrical about his new life in the country and had bored his listeners with descriptions of birdsong. In the autumn he talked about the crisp days and fantastic autumn colours. Now he was made to eat his words at the morning meetings.

'But shovelling snow is good for the body,' Beatrice said.

Allan Fredriksson gave her a crushing look. Ann Lindell glanced at Beatrice and was on the verge of saying something about keeping to her own fighting weight, but left it at a smile. She herself had left an enthusiastic Erik at day care and then slip-slided her way through a paralysed city and at one point had almost run over an older man who had stepped out into traffic, blinded by the snow.

Ottosson loved the silence in the excitable and almost anarchic atmosphere created by the winter storm.

He began by telling them of the letters they had found at Ante Persson's. From his place at the far end of the table, Riis started to laugh.

'What's that all about?' Ottosson asked.

'Nothing,' Riis assured him, and fought to regain a normal expression.

Ann Lindell looked at her colleague, who seemed increasingly to be losing his footing. Was he simply amused that a 'Red' was going to be tried for murder?

'We'll bring the old man in and hear what he has to say,' Sammy Nilsson said, 'but what puzzles me most is Sven-Arne Persson. Why did he admit to a murder that he in his own letters implied his uncle had committed?'

'He only implies?' Beatrice asked.

'More than implies, but maybe not says full out,' Allan Fredriksson said. 'But I think the two of them were in it together, that both Sven-Arne and Ante were in the house when Dufva died. Sven-Arne said something that strengthened his own version. He claims not to remember much about what Dufva's place looked like or what happened, but he did remember that both the radio and television were on. I checked with Berglund – he was the one who was on duty that night, and the first to arrive on the scene – and he said that both the radio and television

403

were on. At the highest volume. Just as Sven-Arne told us.'

'What do the letters say?' Riis asked.

Fredriksson pulled over his notepad and read a couple of extracts.

'"I understand, and yet I don't. What had Dufva done to you?" That's in a letter from the end of 1999. In another, sent a couple of weeks later: "How many Dufvas are there, anyway? He was only a thug – there must be others. Should all of them be killed?" And later in the same letter: "What are we capable of ? I think about this a great deal. Here in India people die of hunger or take their own lives in desperation. What would we say if they left their slums and villages and slaughtered their oppressors and usurers as if they were dumb animals? Would I applaud such an act? To be honest, I don't know. Who am I to judge? I have never been one for violence, you know that. Your struggle has never been mine, even if we have stood on the same side. In a way I am envious of your conviction, but I shiver when I think of what happened to Dufva."' Fredriksson stopped and looked up. The assembled police officers digested Sven-Arne's words.

'I doubt we'll get much out of the old man,' Beatrice said, breaking the silence. 'He seems more than a little confused. When I—'

'You're wrong,' Lindell said. 'He's clearer in the head than the two of us combined.'

'Speak for yourself,' Beatrice said, and smiled.

Bitch, Lindell thought, but did not continue the exchange. Instead she stared pointedly down into her notes. She had not told anyone that she was planning to drive out to the coast again, and while the others were discussing Ante and Sven-Arne Persson, her thoughts were on Bultudden. Ever since the morning she had been wondering if she was wrong. The brief visual impression in Lasse Malm's shed, and the half-automatic gesture of reaching down for the rag to toss it into the rubbish bag – was that invented in hindsight by her imagination?

Was it really a pink tank top? She had been thinking so intensely that her doubts were slowly changing her memory. She knew she had to make the trip to the coast, but considering the weather she was not sure how that was supposed to work. Setting out on these roads would be hopeless. Could she call Marksson and ask him to drive out to the point alone? But given that the personnel number of the Östhammar police was so low, and that storms of this kind tended to hit the coast harder than the inland regions, he probably had his hands full. She decided to wait on a final decision until lunchtime. Maybe the snow would stop.

Lindell heard Fredriksson mention Berglund's name again and she looked up. He was in the middle of a summation of the murder investigation from 1993. Ann Lindell suddenly felt drained, and sighed. It struck her how bored she was. Why am I sitting here? She recalled Erik's joy as they had walked through the snow to the car. He had been ecstatic at the snowfall and she was sure he was tumbling around the day care playground with the other children at this moment.

I want to tumble around too, she muttered. Ola Haver shot her an inquisitive look. I want to tumble around, she mimed. He shook his head and smiled.

I want to fuck, she thought. Is that the same as tumbling around? The lack of a man's closeness, a man to tumble around with, hurt. She looked around and an antagonistic feeling grew inside her. She saw Fredriksson's mouth move, but did not register a word of what he said. She watched Sammy Nilsson, Riis, Beatrice, and the others around the table. Everything so well-ordered, so disciplined, and so damn boring. How many cups of coffee had they drunk? How many words had been wasted in this room?

Holiday, was her next thought. A long holiday. Sun. No snow. Sun. Heat on my body. Fredriksson kept churning on. Ottosson smiled encouragingly. Fredriksson went on.

There isn't much to talk about, she thought bitterly, and when Fredriksson finally stopped, she said it aloud.

'Book the old man, that's all there is to it,' she said, unable to conceal her irritation.

Ottosson looked at her, astonished, but continued speculating what had happened on his own. It was as if he – for unknown reasons – wanted to extend the meeting, but the concentration among the assembled police officers was gone. Sammy Nilsson had pushed the chair from the table, stretched out his legs, and was staring unseeing into the ceiling. Ola Haver was doodling on a piece of paper and smiling in a silly way as if even he was able to think of more pleasant things than murder.

After another ten minutes of discussion, they concluded the session. Everyone left in a hurry. Lindell lingered, as she usually did. Ottosson and she had a habit of exchanging a couple of words on their own.

'I've been thinking about Östhammar,' she said. 'I've thought of something. Or think I have, at any rate.'

Ottosson nodded absently while he gathered up his notes.

'If the weather improves, I'll head out there this afternoon. Is that all right?'

'Of course,' Ottosson said. 'You should do that. Is it anything in particular?'

'Just a thought,' Lindell said.

Ottosson looked up.

'You don't believe that baker story, do you?' he observed.

'I don't know.'

'How are you? You seem a little tired.'

'I just want to tumble around a little,' she said, and left the room.

The snow stopped falling mid-morning and at eleven o'clock a pale sun shone over Uppsala. Ann Lindell called Bosse Marksson. The weather had stabilised even at the coast. About fifty centimetres of snow had fallen during the night and morning but no significant traffic issues or accidents had been reported. Lindell decided to drive out to the coast.

They arranged to meet at two o'clock at the police station in Östhammar. If things were still calm at that point, Marksson would come with her.

FIFTY

All morning Fredriksson and Sammy Nilsson had sat across the table from a sullen Ante Persson. The old man had not protested when they fetched him from Ramund. In fact he had been unexpectedly cooperative. He had put a great deal of care into how he should dress and had finally settled on a pair of grey trousers, a knitted cardigan, and a sport coat over that. One of the nursing home staff members, who had looked at Allan Fredriksson and Sammy Nilsson with ill-disguised contempt, had helped him dress while the two police officers waited outside.

He appeared in the corridor, a smile on his lips, pushing the walker in front of him and refusing any offers of assistance.

Later, when they had transported Ante Persson to the police station and installed themselves in an interrogation chamber, his mood had changed completely. Ante was visibly distressed and gave brief, curt answers to the policemen's questions.

His nephew's letters, that touched on the events in Kungsgärdet in 1993, he did not so much as comment on other than calling it a 'family matter.' He insisted on speaking with Sven-Arne.

After a break, after Ante complained of being hungry – he wanted oatmeal and sandwiches with egg and roe spread – the session was resumed and Allan Fredriksson again turned to the political angle.

'You have many times claimed that Nils Dufva was a war criminal. Could you elaborate on that a little?'

'It is simple,' Ante Persson said. 'He was a registered Nazi. And you let him be! You even gave him a job.'

'We're not discussing his employment. A war criminal – what do you mean by that?'

'I feel as though I'm going through it all again,' Ante said, and gestured with one hand. 'I've seen this all before, and I am not afraid.'

Sammy Nilsson noted that Ante had spilt some oatmeal on a lapel.

'Nor should you be,' he said. 'We are simply trying to establish the truth and surely that can't hurt? You say you have fought for justice and I can respect that, but we also work for justice.'

'What do you know about dreams?' the old man went on, as if he had not heard the policeman's comment. 'I will go to my grave soon enough and I know there's nothing on the other side. It just ends. Now the final analysis must be made and surely my voice should carry as much weight as any other? I remember too much, and sometimes I wish I had developed hardened arteries and become forgetful, just to get some peace. Why should I trust you? I don't want to have anything to do with you. You have pursued me and my comrades in all ages. Yes, I killed a Fascist but that was a matter between me and him and my friends. He deserved it. You believe in justice, you say, and what is more just than sending someone like him into the darkness? He was a man of darkness, and I caught up with him. He thought everyone had forgotten, but I don't forget. I caught up with him.'

'What had he done?' Allan Fredriksson asked after a moment's silence.

'That is between him and me,' Ante said, tired.

'How did you do it?'

'It's not important,' Ante answered. 'Completely irrelevant. He is dead, that is what matters. And now I am going to die. Sven-Arne had nothing to do with this. He is a bewildered coward.'

'It isn't cowardly to confess to a murder you didn't commit,' Fredriksson objected.

Ante smiled.

'Maybe that is the definition of cowardice,' he said.

'Did he help you?'

Ante shook his head.

'Sven-Arne was never inside the house. How many times do you want me to repeat it? But now I want to go home. I am tired. Or else you'll have to lock me up and throw away the key.'

After a consultation with the DA, Ottosson allowed Ante Persson to return to Ramund. It was an unusual decision but they assessed the risk of his escape to be minimal since he had the artificial leg, and they also hoped he would remain more alert in his familiar surroundings.

Ante Persson was formally charged with the murder of Nils Dufva, then he was taken home.

Although an old crime appeared to have been solved, Ottosson was not satisfied. He wanted to understand. He wanted facts about how, when, and why. The only question that had been answered was 'when.'

'I don't understand this,' he said for a second time to Sammy Nilsson, who had returned from Ramund and reported that Ante Persson had been returned to his home and that he had immediately laid down on his bed to rest. On the night table next to the bed there had been a Christmas

410

arrangement of hyacinths and a red tulip, a singular greeting from one of the staff members at the nursing home.

'A murderer who gets flowers,' said Beatrice, who had just joined them.

'I want the two of you to go see Dufva's relatives in Kungsgärdet. The woman still lives there. Inform her of what has happened. I don't want her to hear it through the news media. Beatrice – did you reach her?'

'No, but I talked to her husband. She is apparently sick. He preferred that we leave her alone.'

'Does she have the flu?'

'No, she seemed . . . Her husband said something about her having worked too hard, being burnt out, you know.'

Sammy Nilsson shook his head.

'Let's go down there,' he said. 'I'm curious to see what it looks like, I mean the crime scene.'

The small streets of Kungsgärdet were impressively thoroughly ploughed, but apparently the snow crews had had problems with where to put all the snow that had fallen, for at every street corner there were gigantic mounds. All of the cars parked on the street were covered in snow and also sealed behind snowy dykes. On Arosgatan there was an elderly man who was desperately trying to uncover his Volvo.

As Sammy Nilsson and Beatrice passed, he shrugged helplessly. Nilsson slowed down and considered stopping to help him, but drove on.

'I hope the snow stays for Christmas,' Beatrice said.

I hope winter ends tomorrow, Sammy Nilsson thought.

'It lights up everything,' Beatrice went on, 'and it's more fun for the kids.'

411

'One more platitude and you'll have to head back,' Sammy Nilsson said grimly.

Beatrice turned her head and looked at him. 'Everyone's so fucking gloomy around here.'

'Everyone?'

'Yes, everyone. It seems like the whole station—'

'It is winter, you know that,' Sammy Nilsson said in a more conciliatory tone. 'We're not built for this.'

'That's a load of crap,' Beatrice replied.

They sat quietly until they reached the house that Dufva had lived in and that Jenny Holgersson and her husband had subsequently taken over.

'Take it easy, now,' Beatrice said. 'Think about the fact that she is burnt out.'

Sammy Nilsson wasn't sure if she was being ironic or not, and said nothing.

Niklas Öhman opened the front door before they had even reached the steps.

'I saw you coming. I didn't want you to ring the doorbell. Jenny is sleeping.'

The first thing Sammy Nilsson registered was the exhaustion. Niklas Öhman looked like he had been awake several nights in a row, which he immediately confirmed.

'You will have to excuse me, I haven't been able to get much sleep lately, but come on in. We can sit in the kitchen.'

The air in the hall smelt stale. A faint scent of thinner or perhaps floor polish could not mask the fact that the house felt unfresh. Sammy Nilsson leant forward and peeked into the living room. So that was where it had happened.

They removed their coats in silence and then followed their host into the kitchen.

'Please have a seat. Would you like some coffee?'

'No, thank you, we're fine,' Beatrice said.

Niklas Öhman sank down on his chair.

'I don't understand,' he said. 'It's as if the bad time has returned, and I don't get it.'

'Which bad time?'

'The one after the murder. Jenny took it very hard. She felt guilty because she had not looked in on Dufva that evening. If she had done so, perhaps it wouldn't have happened.'

'Were they close?'

'"Close" is a bit strong,' Niklas Öhman said, 'but she was the one who found the guy.'

'And now the old thoughts have returned,' Sammy Nilsson observed. 'She isn't burnt out at all, is she?'

Öhman didn't reply, but made a face and inclined his head, as good an answer as any.

'We have a new confession,' Beatrice said.

'New? What do you mean?'

'Sven-Arne Persson's uncle has confessed to the murder of Nils Dufva.'

Niklas Öhman stared, confounded, at Beatrice and then at Sammy Nilsson, as if for an assurance that his colleague wasn't being serious.

'We wanted you to know before it reached the media. As you can understand, this is candy for them. You will most likely have visitors.'

'What kind of visitors?'

'Reporters,' Sammy Nilsson said.

Niklas Öhman drew a deep breath and glanced through the doorway to the hall.

'We have already had a visitor,' he said.

'Who was it?'

Öhman told them about Sven-Arne Persson's unexpected intrusion.

'He seemed a bit crazy. He was wearing sandals and looked completely worn out. He attacked Jenny when she came home, but I threw him out.'

'Attacked? What do you mean?'

'He started talking to her.'

'That was a mild attack,' Beatrice said with a smile.

'Jenny isn't well!' Niklas Öhman said emphatically. 'This whole episode is making her suffer.'

'Why do you say that about me?'

The three people sitting at the kitchen table flinched. In the dimly lit hall they could see the outline of a person. Öhman quickly rose and went out. The police officers heard him whisper something, and then a woman's protests.

'Are you Jenny?' Beatrice asked.

The woman detached herself from Öhman and gingerly stepped into the kitchen, blinking in the strong light and stretching out her hand to steady herself against the door frame.

'I have already told you all I know,' she said flatly.

Beatrice explained the purpose of their visit. Jenny listened without moving a muscle. Her blotchy face, with its poorly healed acne scars, was as if carved in stone. Only her tongue moved nervously across her lips. Her hair was combed back and gathered in a marginally clean ponytail. She was barefoot, wearing an oversized jumper and wrinkled sweatpants, and had a noticeable smell of body odour.

In the old case files Beatrice had seen a photo of Jenny Holgersson from twelve years before. A young and pretty woman with serious eyes who gazed into the camera with an almost defiant look. Now she had been transformed into a wreck.

Öhman laid a hand on her shoulder but she immediately shook herself loose with irritation.

'They're lying,' she said with a raspy voice, coughing, and shot Beatrice a look that made her want to reach out for the young woman.

'It's okay,' Öhman pleaded. 'It's over now.'

'It will never be over!' Jenny Holgersson screamed.

'Who is lying?' Sammy Nilsson asked.

'Everyone,' Jenny Holgersson muttered.

'Will you sit down?'

'Jenny has to rest,' Öhman said.

'Can't she speak for herself?' Beatrice asked sharply.

'It will only get worse,' Öhman said.

'It can't get any worse,' Jenny said, almost inaudibly.

Niklas Öhman took hold of her arm and she allowed herself to be led out of the kitchen. Niklas stared back at the two police officers before he disappeared into the inner recesses of the house.

Beatrice and Nilsson exchanged looks. He shook his head.

'What do you think?' Beatrice whispered.

'She needs care,' Sammy said.

'"Everyone is lying,"' Beatrice said. 'That's a good way to put it.'

'Who is "everyone"?'

Beatrice shrugged her shoulders as if implying that 'everyone' simply meant all concerned.

FIFTY-ONE

On the way to Östhammar, Lindell counted eight cars that had careened off the roads, cars that lay in ditches and, in a couple of cases, a fair way out into the surrounding terrain. The snowstorm had claimed its victims.

She drove with unusual care, even though the roads were now decent, in order to have time to think. A long line of cars built up behind her. Shortly before Alunda, half a dozen of them managed to overtake her, and just as many blew past on the straight before Gimo.

The mobile phone rang as she passed Börstil Church. Unknown caller. She considered ignoring it, but after the fifth ring her curiosity won out.

'Hello, this is Thomas Sunesson. You may remember—'

'Hello, I know who you are,' Lindell said, and felt a surge of excitement. 'What's on your mind?'

'I have been thinking about . . . something.'

'Yes?'

'It's about Frisk. Or rather . . . his chainsaw.'

Lindell pulled in to a bus stop. A German shepherd in the adjacent lot came bounding over. It stood up on its hind legs, its front paws on the fence, and barked frenetically. The dog's sharp teeth and red mouth reminded Lindell of what had happened in Bultudden.

416

'What do you mean? I can't hear you very clearly.'

'When you . . . my chainsaw . . . one . . . in your . . . Lasse . . . but . . . always had a Jonsered.'

'Jonsered,' Lindell repeated.

The dog stopped barking.

'Hello! What are you saying?'

'. . . I . . . bought one . . . but that would . . . And then when . . . something . . . here,' Sunesson continued.

'We have a bad connection, you're breaking up,' Lindell answered. 'I can hardly hear what you're saying. But I'm on my way over. Are you home?'

'Yes . . . but . . .'

The call was completely dropped. Lindell stared at the dog. An older man came walking out from the house and Lindell saw him call something out. The dog immediately left the fence and ran over to the man, who bent down and patted it on the head. Its tail was wagging. The man straightened up, said something to the dog, and together they went around the side of the house.

What had Sunesson said? That Frisk usually used a Jonsered. But in Frisk's shed they had found a Stihl with remnants of blood and skin. That didn't necessarily mean anything, but there had been something in Sunesson's voice that convinced her otherwise. He had apparently been thinking about this and now she recalled his faintly bewildered expression when she and Marksson came by to return his chainsaw. She had not been able to interpret his confusion correctly at the time, and had taken it more as a general expression of bafflement that arose among those in close proximity to a deadly crime. Lindell had seen this countless times in family members, neighbours, and witnesses, this amazement mixed with incredulity, sometimes

417

accompanied by anger. What seemed obvious and self-evident and important in hindsight did not always emerge at once. Now the mill in Sunesson's head had finished working.

Lindell pulled out of the parking spot. On the other side of the road, Börstil Church gleamed with a portly farmer smugness, nestled in snow and decorated for the approaching Christmas holiday. A Christmas tree had been erected in front of the church gate. The star at the top was askew and threatening to fall off.

Lindell saw that the time was already a quarter to two and she pressed on the accelerator to reach the Östhammar police station in time.

Bo Marksson looked markedly worn out. He was sitting in the break room with a cup of coffee.

'There is no justice,' he said. 'The snow is just pummelling this damn country. And people never learn! They get pissed off when Public Works can't get rid of all the snow fast enough, then go slip-sliding around in summer shoes and driving like idiots.'

Lindell was sick of all the talk about the weather and chose not to comment on his outburst. Instead she told him about Sunesson's call.

'I see,' Marksson said, without much enthusiasm. 'He wanted to discuss chainsaws with you.'

'It was something about a Jonsered.'

'Should we head out there?'

'If you have the energy,' Lindell said. 'Otherwise I'll go on my own.'

'I'll go,' Marksson said, and got up with some effort. 'It'll give me an opportunity to check the status of the roads.'

'You worked last night?'

Marksson nodded.

'I was called in at four o'clock.'

'Then you should get some sleep.'

'I can sleep when I die.'

They drove in silence. Marksson closed his eyes and looked like he had nodded off, thus eliminating the opportunity to observe the passability of the region's roads.

'I forgot to tell you,' he said suddenly, and opened his eyes. 'The emergency call centre received a phone call. It came from a woman who claimed she had dialled the wrong number. They routinely check up on such calls and it turned out it was from a mobile phone belonging to Lisen Morell.'

'What? When was this?'

'Last night.'

'And you're telling me now?'

'I forgot.'

He turned his head and looked at her. Lindell nodded.

'I called her to check in. She said she had got scared at night and was embarrassed about making the call. There was no danger.'

Lindell did not say anything until they reached the turn-off to Bultudden.

'Let's drive out to Lisen first,' she said.

The landscape resembled a postcard with the snowy spruces and the slender, curvy road that had been meticulously ploughed. Lindell had learnt that Torsten Andersson took care of this road. Smoke curled out of a few chimneys but there was no sign of any people. A flock of bullfinches were perched in a Rowan tree outside the Utmans' house.

Lindell turned in to the small road leading to Lisen Morell's house but did not turn off the engine once she reached it.

'I'll check it out, if you like,' Marksson said. 'If all you want to do is look in and make sure everything is all right.'

'I'll go,' Lindell said.

The chilly sea air made her shiver. A pale sun was shining from the mainland side. She took a couple of steps and looked back. Marksson had already fished out his mobile phone and was dialling a number.

Lisen Morell was sitting at the table, a steaming cup of tea in front of her. She smiled a mournful smile. Next to her was a suitcase and pair of cardboard boxes.

'I'm moving,' she said. 'Bultudden is no good.'

'For good?'

'I don't know. I can't handle it right now. Would you like a cup?'

Lindell shook her head.

'You're giving up,' she observed.

Lisen shrugged.

'I thought you were going to paint here all winter.'

Lindell was strangely affected by Lisen Morell's capitulation.

'I have to have peace in order to be able to paint.'

'Are you frightened? I heard you called 911.'

'How do you know that?'

'Marksson told me. Sometimes women make an emergency call but then are forced to hang up.'

'Men,' Lisen said.

'Men,' Lindell said.

'Yes, okay, I'm scared. I even peed my pants.'

'When are you going?'

'As soon as I've finished my tea. I packed last night and was going to leave first thing this morning but then the snow came.'

'Can I call you in Uppsala?'

Lisen nodded. 'What are you doing out here?'

'We are going to check a couple of things.'

'There are things happening out here you don't know about,' Lisen said.

'Have you had some new visitors?'

Lisen told her about Sunesson's visit the night before and how she had later heard someone sneaking around the house.

'Do you think his talk about smoke was an excuse to come by, and that he returned later on?'

Lisen nodded and walked over to the window facing the sea.

'I saw her,' she said suddenly, turning around and looking at Lindell.

'The Thai girl?' Lindell asked, although she already knew the answer.

'In the forest.'

'And you're telling me this now?'

Lindell couldn't repress her fury. She banged her fist on the table.

'I didn't remember it at first. I was a bit sad at the time . . . in the forest. I was having a bleak phase for me . . . it was . . .'

'A bleak phase!' Lindell exclaimed. 'The woman was murdered and hacked to pieces with a chainsaw and you were having a bleak phase. Unbelievable!'

'It wasn't—'

'Was she alone?'

Lisen turned back to the window.

'Yes,' she said finally, but Lindell no longer believed her.

'Who was with her? It's high time you talked!'

'Torsten,' Lisen whispered.

'Torsten Andersson?'

'Yes, but he wasn't picking berries with her. He was sort of following her.'

Lindell tried to make Lisen become more precise about where and when she had seen the two of them in the forest, but Lisen claimed she couldn't remember. That period of time was hazy.

Ann Lindell left the little cottage in a helpless fury, in part because of what Lisen had told her, in part because Bultudden seemed more and more like a play, an outpost in Sweden, populated by individuals who were appearing on stage in roles that did not fit them. Perhaps the older couples were an exception, but hardly Torsten Andersson, the bachelors, and Lisen Morell.

Marksson was talking on the phone but ended the call when Lindell got back in the car.

She backed out onto the Avenue and drove slowly back north as she told him about Lisen Morell.

'Damn,' Marksson said. 'Torsten . . .'

'This place is sick,' Lindell said.

'Why didn't she say anything before?'

'Torsten is her landlord, I think that was why,' Lindell said. 'She was afraid of losing the cottage. And how she talked before,' Lindell spat.

'Is it so bad?'

'It's completely screwed up!'

'I think you are taking this too hard,' Marksson said.

'I was thinking about what you said, in that book you read, about someone who doesn't like us is changing this land. I think that's right. I'm becoming more and more disillusioned every day. Can't you feel how we are slowly gliding away from everything we value and take for granted? Slowly but surely it is getting thinned out. Only a shell will remain. The surface is there but the content is gone. Soon we won't be able to trust anyone.'

'We mostly see the unpleasantness,' Marksson said. 'But there are actually happy, normal people.'

This irritated Lindell. She knew that police work seldom touched on the sunny side of life, but where was this growing sadness and helplessness coming from?

'We're heading to Sunesson next,' she said, 'and then to that damn fish-man.' She stepped on the accelerator and felt the tyres slipping in the curves but did not slow down.

'I don't know if it means anything,' Thomas B. Sunesson said.

Lindell had heard this phrase so many times before that she could not manage her usual reply – that the most insignificant detail sometimes turned out to be important. She merely waved it away.

Marksson and Lindell were sitting at the table while Sunesson paced around his kitchen. Sunesson assured them that he was not the one who had been sneaking around Lisen Morell's cottage. Lindell believed him and asked him to tell her about the chainsaws instead.

'Are you sure that it was Lasse Malm's chainsaw you had in the back?' he asked.

'Yes, absolutely sure,' Lindell said.

Sunesson shook his head.

'He has always had a Stihl,' he said. 'Always, as long as I can remember.'

'Did he make a change?' Marksson asked.

'To an older Jonsered? I have trouble believing that. Why would he do that?'

A couple of hours later, Lindell and Marksson would know the answer.

FIFTY-TWO

At the end of September 1938, peace in Europe was assured. Neville Chamberlain waved his Munich treaty about. Adolf Hitler pronounced himself a friend of peace. He had admittedly gained a piece of Czechoslovakia but had no further imperialistic ambitions.

The news of 'peace in our time' reached Ante Persson by way of a Polish dentist who had just extracted one of his teeth. It was a frigid October evening. Ante could still recall shivering and spitting blood and listening to how the Pole, very disillusioned, described how the powerhouses of England and France had once again sold out their people.

Neither one of them was surprised. They had fought in Spain for a long time. They belonged to the veterans. Now they were imprisoned and awaiting certain death.

The Pole was a Communist, born in Cracow, and an amateur astronomer. He would entertain Ante and the others with stories about Copernicus and Giordano Bruno. His dental practice had been raided by Polish anti-Semites in 1935 and he had been a fugitive ever since. He came to Spain and Barcelona in the summer of 1937, and immediately enlisted in the defence of the Republic.

He was again employed as a dentist, this time in the field. He made no distinction between Communists, socialists, Catalan nationalists, or anarchists and even pulled out the aching wisdom teeth of imprisoned Falangists.

Now he was talking about Europe and his own country. The evening was growing even colder. Star after shooting star streaked the sky. In a way Ante was happy. He was among friends.

The Pole spoke remarkable German and Ante did not understand everything, but he picked up the fact that Munich was the start of a fire. Spain would soon fall into the hands of the Fascists, everyone knew that; the war was lost and now more and more countries and people would fall victim to the terror.

Ante's left hand ached. He was afraid his whole hand would get infected. The soiled bandages around his finger stumps gave no protection. The repeated abuse drained his strength. In a way it didn't matter. They were all going to die.

His entire body was beaten raw. That evening a week ago when he lost his fingers, he had fainted several times. The torturers had urinated on him. He still felt he stank. There were new questions the entire time. New blows. In the half darkness and through the pain that was like a red gauze over his eyes, Ante had discerned a man who had walked very close, leant over, and grinned in his face. Exhausted, Ante had tried to spit at him, to reach the face with a gob of phlegm, but he was too dehydrated, too weak, to succeed.

He received a blow that landed under the eye. In the haze, Ante had seen the man pick up a pair of pliers and hold it up in front of him.

'Now you're going to lose everything that sticks out,' the torturer had whispered in Swedish. 'We'll start with the fingers on your left hand.'

Ante Persson awoke with a scream. Tanya, the new girl, was standing in the doorway of his room.

'Were you dreaming?' she asked.

He pulled himself up into a half-sitting position. He was sweating. Tanya walked over to his bed and put her hand on his chest. Ante Persson fumbled for her hand, clasped it in his own, and closed his eyes.

'My friend,' he mumbled.

'The police are here,' she said.

Once again an image of the pliers swam before his eyes. The pain made him wince and he squeezed her hand harder.

'That's good,' he said. 'Nothing lasts forever.'

The door was pushed open and the policemen from yesterday came in. Sammy Nilsson approached the bed.

'Were you taking a morning nap?'

Persson did not reply.

'You were supposed to wait outside,' Tanya said.

'That's how they are,' Persson said. 'They just walk in.'

He turned his head and gazed at the certificate that designated him an honorary Spanish citizen.

'What do you want?'

'Could you leave us for a while?' The policeman turned to Tanya.

'I'm going to help Ante dress,' she said defiantly. 'You can wait in the hallway.'

'Ante can stay in bed if he likes,' the policeman said with a smile. 'He won't have to come with us.'

'You can go,' Persson said. 'I'll talk to the Gestapo for a while.'

The assistant gave Sammy Nilsson an angry look and left the room. Nilsson pulled a chair over to the bed and sat down. The other policeman was standing at the window, looking out.

'How did you get to know Nils Dufva?'

Persson didn't answer.

'We think you met in Spain. Is that correct?'

Persson shook his head.

'Why are you lying?'

'I have told you what you needed to know.'

'A couple of hours ago, one of Nils Dufva's relatives contacted us. She came down to the station. Her name is Jenny Holgersson and she lives in Dufva's house, which she inherited.'

'What does this have to do with me?'

'She has another story. That it was neither you nor Sven-Arne who killed Dufva. That is what I believe.'

Ante closed his eyes.

'It was Jenny's husband,' Nilsson said.

Ante Persson looked up and their eyes met.

'According to Jenny, he crushed Dufva's skull with the base of a lamp. The motive was that the old man was about to change his will. Jenny Holgersson would no longer receive a cent. Jenny Holgersson was present, but it was Niklas Öhman who—'

'Shut up,' Persson spat.

'You got there too late,' Sammy Nilsson said.

FIFTY-THREE

The bonfire from the day before was still smoking. A couple of pieces of lumber, ravaged by the flames, were sticking out of the ashes. A sooty piece of cloth blew away.

Bosse Marksson picked up a pitchfork, rummaged in the pile, and uncovered a couple of blackened tins.

Lindell studied Lasse Malm's house and was once again amazed at how dilapidated it was. There was no charm, only decay.

They had noticed that Malm's car was gone, that he had left during the time that they had visited Lisen Morell. The house was locked up and the plastic bags they had seen earlier in the shed were gone. They searched in vain for the chainsaw.

'A couple of steps behind,' Lindell observed.

Bosse Marksson turned his head to look at her.

'When I was a little boy, there was a man out here called Tin Nicholas. He got the name from some character in a children's television program. He was a little slow in the head, but completely harmless. He used to go around on a moped, knocking on people's doors and asking for scrap to sell. He never bought anything and people knew it, but everyone would invite him in for coffee and talk for a while. He would bring a little gossip from place to place and sometimes he ran an errand like buying snuff for some old man or something. He was careful to give back the exact change and never wanted anything extra for his trouble.'

Marksson fell silent. Lindell waited for a continuation. She felt completely calm. The last pieces of the Bultudden puzzle would soon fall into place, she knew that.

'Then he died,' Marksson said. 'It was in the early 1970s. He had no family to speak of, but there were probably a couple of hundred people at his funeral.'

'What made you think of him?'

'My dad attended the funeral and he said that it was unusually elaborate. During the refreshments afterward, several people made speeches. Strange. Torsten Andersson's father paid for everything, gravestone, priest, and all the cakes. No one really understood why, but no one seemed to question it either.'

Marksson tossed the pitchfork back on the ground, turned around, stared at the edge of the forest, and then started walking back to the car.

Lindell followed.

'It wasn't Frisk, was it?'

Marksson stopped and turned around. He shook his head.

'Let's go to Torsten's,' he said.

Torsten Andersson had hung an advent star in his kitchen window. He shouted 'Come in!' when Marksson knocked on the door. He was sitting in the kitchen. His hands were folded and resting on the table.

'I've got a fire going,' he said, and looked at Lindell, who nodded and tried to manage a smile.

She walked up to the wood stove and warmed her hands. The sooty stove reminded her of the cottage outside Omberg where her grandparents had lived the last years of their life. They had died one week apart when Lindell was fourteen. She immediately realised where her fondness for wood stoves and crackling fires had come from.

'How are things, Torsten?' Marksson asked.

Lindell turned around. Torsten made a face, looking down at the table as if he wasn't sure what to say.

'We stopped in at Lasse Malm's,' Marksson continued, 'but he wasn't home.'

'He's probably in Östhammar,' Torsten said in an indifferent voice.

'Bultudden has been well ploughed.'

'It's just the usual,' Torsten said.

'Do you remember Tin Nicholas?'

Torsten chuckled. 'Of course I remember him.'

'He had a red moped, a Puch,' Marksson said. 'There was an old Puch in Malm's shed, that must have been why I started thinking about Nicholas.'

'Malm's father had a Puch,' Torsten said.

'You remember that, do you?' Marksson said.

Torsten glanced at him quickly, and smiled without warmth, before he rose, walked over to the counter, and poured himself a glass of water.

'Why didn't you say anything about the seal rifle?'

Torsten drank greedily, put the glass down sharply, and then returned to his seat at the table.

'I know nothing about that,' Torsten said.

The fire crackled.

'You know everything about Bultudden,' Marksson said.

431

'If a pine cone falls, you know about it before it lands.'

'We no longer believe it was Frisk who killed Patima,' Lindell said.

'Then who was it?'

'Why don't you tell us?' Lindell said encouragingly.

Torsten mopped his forehead.

'I think I'm getting sick,' he said.

'When we met that first time you said something about murderers being treated too well,' Lindell went on. 'You compared it to dogs who were crazy or mean. Do you remember?'

Torsten looked steadily at her but said nothing.

'We know you saw Patima. Why didn't you say anything about that? Did you kill her? Maybe it was an accident. You got scared and decided to get rid of the body.'

'That's not what happened,' Torsten Andersson said in a hoarse voice.

'Then what did happen? Did you get excited? Did you get horny again last night and sneak around Lisen Morell's cottage? Did Patima make you want more?'

Marksson coughed and Lindell shot him a quick look but kept going.

'You forced yourself on her and she started to scream, isn't that right? Resisted. You got scared, maybe even angry.'

'That's not what happened,' Torsten Andersson repeated. 'I saw her, that's true, but I never touched her. She was a skinny little thing. I only followed her for a while. She never saw me.'

'You wanted to know where she lived?' Marksson said.

'I knew where,' Torsten said. 'She lived with Frisk for a long time. But she wasn't headed that way.'

Lindell leant across the table and fixed her gaze on him.

'Then where was she headed? Did you invite her home to taste a little lamb?'

'She was headed to Lasse Malm's house,' Torsten Andersson said so quietly that Lindell could barely hear him.

'Did you see her go in?'

Torsten nodded.

'The rifle was his, wasn't it?' Marksson asked.

Another nod.

'It was Gunnar's rifle, Lasse's dad.'

'You think that Malm . . .'

'I think he's gone down to the dock,' Torsten said finally. 'You know Axel Johansson's old place. The shed is still there. He goes down there sometimes. He's got his dinghy stored down there.'

Marksson nodded.

'Lasse came by a little while ago,' Torsten said. 'He was on his way somewhere but changed his mind. "I'll go down to the dock instead," he said. I wanted him to stay for a while but he insisted and was—'

'Has the road been ploughed?'

'No, not really. I only went down part of the way, maybe fifty metres.'

'Why?'

'Dad always did,' Torsten said. 'He was related to Axel.'

'But Axel has been gone for decades.'

'I do it anyway. An old habit. It's nice to pretend a little, get away from the Avenue. I have feeling of . . . well, you know.'

Marksson smiled.

'I know,' he said. 'One thought gives way to another. Everything is old and familiar, but still new each time. Axel was a remarkable man.'

'He walked his own way,' Torsten said. 'Do you know he once sailed in Australia?'

'I saw a photo of him once in a book,' Marksson said. 'It was about Åland grain shipping.'

'He wasn't old back then.'

'That's how it was. His dad . . .'

'Oh, he was something!'

Lindell wanted to move on, but couldn't bring herself to interrupt. She had been listening to the conversation with ambivalence. In part she was ashamed of her own aggressiveness, in part she was moved by their spare exchange, where so much was said without words. She had experienced this before, the rarefied use of language and phrasing between two people in tune with each other and their environment. She knew that even in this apparently trivial exchange, significant information could be extracted.

'Well, we really should get going,' Marksson said. 'I'll see you later.'

'Malm was unhappy. Really unhappy,' Torsten said. 'Lasse is not really a bad person.'

'No, I don't suppose he is,' Marksson said.

He sighed heavily and lingered in silence for a moment before he stood up, nodded at Lindell – whom he had not looked at until then – and left the kitchen.

'Thanks for the fish,' she said, and followed her colleague.

Torsten dismissed it with a wave.

* * *

434

As usual, Marksson had rushed ahead and was waiting by the car.

'It's Malm, isn't it?' Lindell said. 'He got nervous when he knew we were going to talk to Frisk, and set the whole thing up like a suicide. He swapped the chainsaws, putting his Stihl in Frisk's shed and taking the Jonsered instead.'

'Looks that way,' Marksson said. 'But I wasn't sure.'

'But now you are?'

'Torsten knows something that we don't. He has seen or heard something. Maybe we'll never know what it is, or it will eventually emerge, but he has been thinking about it, and now he is sure. I saw it in him.'

They got into the car, backed down Torsten's driveway, and drove south again. It occurred to Lindell that they were probably dealing with a murderer.

'Shouldn't we call in what we're doing? He may be armed.'

'I don't think we need to worry,' Marksson said. 'But we can let them know what's going on.'

He picked up his mobile phone and called the station in Östhammar. He told them what had happened and that they were on their way to collect Lars Malm for questioning.

'No, we don't need any assistance. I'll call you later.'

He turned off the phone and at the same moment waved his hand at a ploughed side street. Lindell had barely registered it before. She turned, and drove some twenty metres down a road with big pine trees on either side before making a sharp swing. Lasse Malm's pickup was parked by the piled snow on the right.

They got out. Marksson walked over to the car and felt the hood.

'Still warm,' he said.

Lindell loosened the tarp over the back. There was a chainsaw underneath. A Jonsered.

Footprints led straight to the sea, which could be glimpsed between the trees. Marksson took out his gun from its holster under his arm.

The shed was some fifty metres away. Lindell took large steps through the snow in Malm's footsteps. Marksson suddenly stopped. A breeze swept over the water and stirred the yellow-brown reeds at the edge of the shore. Marksson turned and looked searchingly at her.

We stand out too much, Lindell thought. She saw an image of Frisk's bloody head in front of her eyes.

Marksson went on. Suddenly he turned to the left and Lindell knew he wanted to check the door to the shed. It was open.

'Lasse,' Marksson yelled. 'It's me. Bosse. Can we talk? I've just been to Torsten's.'

The only answer was the faint rustling of the reeds.

'Stay here,' Marksson said.

He walked on slowly. Lindell deliberated if she should follow. Marksson reached the door. He hesitated for a moment, pressed against the wall of the shed, before he peeked in. Lindell took a couple of steps closer. Marksson straightened his back and stood still a couple of seconds. He drew a couple of deep breaths and then waved her over.

Lasse Malm hung in a noose that he had fastened to a hook in the ceiling. A wooden box lay at his feet. The rope had cut deeply into his neck. His mouth was open as if he had screamed at the moment of death. The tongue was blue, the eyes closed.

Marksson straightened the box, stood on it, and was immediately able to determine that Lasse Malm was the third case of death in Bultudden in recent months.

Lindell forced herself to look at the dead man's hands. His nails were dirty and the hands black with soot. She recalled the first time she had seen them. Then they had seemed so powerful. Now his body appeared diminished. It struck her that he appeared more human in death.

'He was going to get rid of the chainsaw, but changed his mind and got rid of himself instead,' she said.

'I wonder what Torsten said to him,' Marksson said.

He left the boat shed, went and stood on the granite outside, and stared out at the sea. Lindell looked at his wide back and saw his chest heave in deep inhalations. Then he turned back. Lindell was standing in the doorway.

'Patima left Frisk and went from the frying pan into the fire,' he said. 'Poor girl.'

FIFTY-FOUR

'There won't be any charges,' Sven-Arne Persson said.

Ante lay outstretched on the bed, staring up at the ceiling. Sven-Arne was unsure if Ante had heard what he said, but went on anyway.

'They only have the girl's version. The guy denies everything.'

Ante turned his head and looked at his nephew but didn't say anything.

'It would be strange if he did, of course,' he said. 'He's kept his mouth shut for twelve years, so why would he start talking now? And who knows what really happened? She seems a bit off, to put it mildly.'

'You've met her?'

'I went there,' Sven-Arne said.

'Why?'

'I wanted to see the house.'

Ante snorted.

'"See the house,"' he echoed. 'Why on earth? And then you went and turned yourself in?'

Ante braced himself with his hands and managed to drag himself up into a seated position.

'The police say they have nothing. I talked with the prosecutor this morning. I know him from before. He said the same thing.'

'Why?'

'What do you mean, "why"?'

'Why did you confess?'

'I didn't want you to have any trouble,' Sven-Arne said.

'No, I didn't even get that,' Ante said. 'That man was a pig and lived off of our money, like a civil servant.'

'But why did you want to see him dead? Wouldn't it have been better to reveal his past and let him bear the public humiliation?'

Sven-Arne stared at Ante. He didn't answer. It had always been that way: Ante made himself inaccessible and left so many questions unanswered when it suited him. Sven-Arne had a desire to attack. Ante had closed his eyes to oppression as long as it was done in the name of the working classes, made light when human rights were violated as long as it was for the right cause. But why take up the old worn arguments? He knew his uncle too well and had been through it all so many times. Ante's belief in justice was in large part his own. He had chosen the step-by-step reformer's path and found political work a bottomless marsh. He had participated in the game, been underhanded and careless with the truth, and seen his party lose its health and its original mission. As a county politician he had swallowed and swallowed until his disgust stuck in his throat. He had stepped off the track. Chosen to flee. Now he was sitting in front of an old man who had fought his whole life and who had even been prepared to offer his life to resist Nazism.

'Let's drop it,' Sven-Arne said.

Ante opened his eyes. Sven-Arne saw that he was touched. It occurred to him that he had never seen him cry.

'There's one thing,' Ante said. 'I'm going to die soon. I'm

439

living on borrowed time, as they say, and I have lived an eventful life, but there is one thing that has pained me for seventy years.'

'And that is?' Sven-Arne prompted after a long pause, waiting for the continuation.

'Do you remember the Brush?'

'The Bulgarian who blew himself up?'

'He was a giant.'

Sven-Arne nodded. He had understood as much. The Brush had always popped up in Ante's stories. The miner was the very image of courage and principled action.

'He died a miserable death,' Ante said.

Now he was crying openly. Tears searched their way down the wrinkled cheeks and the wiry whiskers on his chin. Sven-Arne nodded, but could not manage to say anything.

'I betrayed him,' Ante sobbed.

'What are you talking about? You couldn't help—'

'I gave them his name! The story about blowing himself up was pure fabrication. I created that story to be able to live. I made it true.'

Sven-Arne leant over and put his hand on Ante's knee.

'What happened?'

Ante held up his left hand.

'This is what Nils Dufva did! He made me terrified. I didn't want to die. Not then. That man took everything from me, my honour and peace. I could not resist him. There were others who did, but I gave way.

'Every time I used my shovel, every time I worked a load on a construction site, every time I put on my shirt, every single minute of the day I am reminded of my betrayal. You carry your hand with you. It can't be stuffed into a drawer.

You see, two fingers is what the Brush was worth.'

Ante stared at his own hand as if it was an unfamiliar and frightening figure.

'By a coincidence I discovered that Dufva lived in this town. It was many years ago and I should have looked him up right away and sunk the knife in his Fascist heart. But I didn't have the guts. And then it was too late. I didn't even manage that much, and now I'm going to die.'

FIFTY-FIVE

Bultudden was embedded in snow. The bay between the mainland and the point had started to ice over.

Thomas B. Sunesson had helped Doris Utman put up lights in the rowan tree in front of her house.

'It looks pretty,' Lindell said. 'Like a winter fairyland.'

'Oh, I don't know,' Doris had said, but Lindell could tell she was pleased at her words.

Doris had waved at Lindell as she drove by on her way to Lisen Morell and Lindell had pulled over. They had talked about what had happened. Doris was the person in Bultudden that Lindell found the easiest to talk to. She felt that Doris had nothing to hide and thereby nothing to defend.

'Don't judge Torsten too harshly,' Doris had said. 'He was very fond of the boys, above all Lasse Malm. He liked them because they stayed out here.'

Lindell had stopped at Torsten Andersson's house to tell him the results of the forensic investigation of Malm's house. There had been many traces of Patima. In a closet on the second floor they had also located a grease-stained cloth that the technicians could determine the old seal rifle had been wrapped in.

Torsten was full of regret. Lindell knew he was accusing

himself of not having acted in time. He had known about Patima's existence since the day she had moved in with Tobias Frisk and also about her departure. According to Torsten, Frisk had tried to convince her to stay but she had left his house after a quarrel one night in May and had wandered around in the forest only to meet Lasse Malm the following morning as he was leaving for work. He had let Patima stay in his house and promised to help her get a return ticket back to Thailand.

'But he fell in love at once and then he didn't want to let her go. It went completely wrong, but I am convinced that Lasse had no intention to kill her.' That was how Torsten summarised the chain of events.

It didn't matter to Lindell one way or another what his intentions had been. He had killed Patima and violated her body.

That Malm thereafter had shot Tobias Frisk and arranged it as a suicide was something that Torsten Andersson steadfastly refused to believe. But Lindell was completely convinced of it.

'I should get going,' Lindell said.

Doris stretched out her hand.

'Give my regards to Lisen,' she said. 'Will she stay over the winter?'

'It seems like it,' Lindell said. 'She's planning to paint.'

'That's good,' Doris said. 'Now that two houses are empty we need all the people we can get here in Bultudden.'

Lindell left Doris and went back to the car. She knew it was probably the last time she would be driving on the Avenue. She couldn't help wondering what would happen to Bultudden over the next few years.

There was nothing romantic about the area any longer. Putting up lights didn't help. Bultudden would always be connected in her mind with Pranee Kaew Patima's tragic fate.

'Loneliness,' Lindell murmured, and backed out of Utman's driveway.

If you enjoyed *The Hand that Trembles*, you can meet
Ann Lindell again in *The Princess of Burundi* . . .

To discover more gripping crime fiction and to
place an order visit our website at
www.allisonandbusby.com
or call us on
020 7580 1080

THE PRINCESS OF BURUNDI

Winner of the Swedish Crime Academy Award for Best Crime Novel, The Princess of Burundi *is a thrilling work by author Kjell Eriksson, a fast-rising international sensation.*

Libro, Sweden. A mutilated body is found lying in the snow. Husband, father and reformed troublemaker John Jonsson leaves behind a devastated family and friends to struggle on without him. Who would want him tortured and murdered? His body is not the only sinister discovery. Inspector Ann Lindell cuts short her maternity leave to join homicide detective Ola Haver to work the case. Determined to catch this savage killer, Lindell is drawn into a twisted game of cat and mouse which terrorises an entire town.

'Stunning . . . haunting . . . can chill you to the bone'
Marilyn Stasio, *New York Times*